Struggle of Memory

Joan Dugdale was, among many things, a radio producer for ABC Religious Broadcasts before being seconded to 3ZZ, the ABC's community access radio station set up by the Whitlam government in 1974. When it was disbanded in 1977, she published *Radio Power*, a history of the station, and then became a farmer in Western Victoria. She now works full-time as a writer of fiction.

Her first novel, *Struggle of Memory* was shortlisted for the NSW Society of Women Authors' biennial Marjorie Barnard Literary Award and won the Foundation for Australian Literary Studies award for Best Australian Book of the Year in 1991.

Don Gallagher's judge's statement described the novel as "rooted in history but brought brilliantly alive by Joan Dugdale's imaginative insight into the human heart ... It throbs with a rare passion for justice, but it also excites compassion for the creatures who walk its pages."

Her second novel, *The Gripping Beast* (1993), looks at our Anglo-Norse heritage and explores intriguing questions of genetic memory and cultural identity.

JOAN DUGDALE

Struggle of Memory

University of Queensland Press

First published 1991 by University of Queensland Press
Box 42, St Lucia, Queensland 4067 Australia
Reprinted 1993

© Joan Dugdale 1991

This book is copyright. Apart from any fair dealing
for the purposes of private study, research, criticism
or review, as permitted under the Copyright Act, no
part may be reproduced by any process without written
permission. Enquiries should be made to the publisher.

Typeset by University of Queensland Press
Printed and bound in Australia by McPherson's Printing Group, Victoria

Cataloguing in Publication Data
National Library of Australia

Dugdale, Joan.
  Struggle of Memory.

  1. World War, 1914-18 — Deportations from
  Australia — Fiction. I. Title.

A823.3

ISBN 0 7022 2591 6

For Lisette

"... the struggle of [people] against power is the struggle of memory against forgetting."

Milan Kundera
The Book of Laughter and Forgetting

"There is being registered in Australian history a chapter which all real Australians will some day heartily wish could be expunged."

> Letter to the Commonwealth Attorney-General from the Naturalised British Subjects Association of Holdsworthy Concentration Camp, August 1918

Contents

PART ONE – OF COLONY AND EMPIRE

1 The Warrum and the Mill   *3*
2 Land of Promise   *17*
3 Contortions   *27*
4 Remorse   *36*
5 Women's Tracks   *46*
6 Let Us Now Praise Famous Men   *53*
7 A Travelling Salesman   *65*
8 Principalities and Powers   *76*

PART TWO – AUSTRALIANS ALL

1 Thou Ring   *91*
2 Mirages   *105*
3 Home   *112*
4 Drought   *122*
5 Husbandry   *133*
6 An Ordinary Life   *147*
7 The Best of All Worlds   *163*

PART THREE – THE GREAT WAR

1 Rumours of War   *183*
2 The National Hope   *194*
3 Faces of Barbarism   *205*
4 Kites   *217*
5 Weeping and Waiting   *229*
6 A Pillar of Salt   *237*

7 The City   *246*
8 Habitations of the Dead   *256*

PART FOUR – THE NOWHERE PEOPLE

1 Homeless   *267*
2 Stateless   *277*
3 Weary Sailors   *292*
4 Occupations   *301*
5 Returning Shadows   *312*
6 A Sign of Peace   *319*

Part One
Of Colony and Empire

1 The Warrum and the Mill

Hens do not scan the sky for birds of prey. They are alert, instead, to moving shadows on the ground and, at that evidence of a hawk, they summon their chickens to shelter.

For the first five days of the new war with Germany, Miriam Gluck refused it any conscious thought. Isobel, her niece and companion, had remarked that they might soon have to do without coffee. Her son, now a partner in the family firm, had said on the telephone that the Government would certainly want to reorganise the transport industry. He clung, always, to the material, the practical, whatever could safely be handled. Her two daughters had telephoned as usual and could not avoid mentioning the war, but none of the children would discuss it. That was the way in her family now; it had been so for thirteen years.

Apart from these few references, and the wireless broadcasts about Hitler's doings in Europe, the war had hardly impinged on Miriam Gluck, or the routines of her retired, almost reclusive life with Isobel.

It was not until last night's news on the wireless that fear had stirred. The reader, in rounded accents and dispassionate tone, had announced the introduction of the National Securities Bill, with its powers to prohibit public meetings, to arrest without warrant and to try the accused in closed courts.

Isobel was away for the night, so Miriam had no-one to tell of the instant of shadow; the sense that history was wheeling around, circling like a bird of prey, to swoop down again on herself and her children. She got up from her chair and made some cocoa to dispel the shadow's chill. But that night she dreamed, a thing she rarely did, and now, this morning, she was possessed by a sense of some unknown task demanding her urgent attention.

She had dreamt that she was dead; buried in a grave of modest but faultless respectability. She could see her children standing silently above her, clad in their mourning. As she tried to rise they each stepped forward on to the earth that covered her and solemnly trampled it down. She beat upon the sides of her coffin but, though they stepped back and reverently bowed, the weight lay still on her chest. She tried to call out but her mouth was full of ashes. The children turned away. She clawed at the earth which now lay between her and their retreating figures.

In the next instant, she was no longer in the grave but above it. A spade was in her hands and she was digging with a ferocity fuelled by anger. It seemed to her, when she woke in the dark of early morning, that though she had been afraid at last night's news, it was not so much a fear of the future as a shrinking from that long buried anger which the shadow of history had disinterred. The unfamiliar sense of something to be done replaced fear now and prevented further sleep. She got up and sat in the kitchen with a cup of tea.

As the dawn light seeped in at the window, memories, images rather, flitted through her mind. Though they were unbidden and disconnected they seemed to placate the urgent demand and so she let them come. Sarah, her sister, is there, saying it is time she went into stays. Miriam smiled at the memory of how she had resisted stays for a whole year after her friends had gone into them. Sarah insists now and, because she is older by eight years, prevails, and takes her to the outfitters in Queen Street to buy them. There is some excitement in that; her secret delight, despite her protests, that Sarah sees she is grown up at seventeen, ready to present a woman's image to the world. On the bed in her room, the box with its tissue paper and string lies empty. Sarah stands, holding the satin and whalebone corset, while Miriam strips to her shift. She turns her back and lifts her arms, offering her body to the garment solemnly, like a virgin martyr. She gazes out of the unshuttered window on to the garden where sheets on the line slap ineffectually at the wind.

"You have been fortunate not to need these sooner," Sarah

remarks, wrapping the stays around her. There is a doubtful note in her voice and she adds, perhaps to console, "I daresay you'll fill out yet." Miriam feels the tapes pull, first to one side and then the other, and feels the bones, whalebone and her own, meet on her flesh like the teeth of a trap. She tenses against the strains and stares, fixed and frowning, into the garden, yellow-green and grey under the winter sun, as Sarah fastens the final bond. She knows with sudden certainty that neither the garden, the beach, nor the bush, none, will ever be the same to her again: the stays mark the end of a way of being in the world.

Miriam Wemyss had small light bones and supple joints, capable, before the stays, of arching backwards into London Bridge. "You're double-jointed," they said, with grudging admiration, "but it's not ladylike." Her mother, Kathleen, said so in her Irish distracted way when she noticed, and her sisters, Carrie and Sarah, said it more forcefully. Her father Josh generally ignored her, and Joshua and Edward, embarrassed, followed their father's example.

Joshua, Sarah, Carrie, Edward, at least two who had died, one of snakebite and one of measles, one who was stillborn and, at the end, Miriam. Miriam had never been certain where the dead ones came but she knew the stillborn one was two years before her and that she, coming last, had worn her mother out.

"Kathleen, Miriam is running wild. She was hanging around at the mill again yesterday. One of these days she'll cause an accident if she doesn't have one herself. You must take her more firmly in hand."

"Sure and she's such a spirited little thing, Josh. She has quite worn me out and I cannot be answerable for her, that's the truth. I wish you would try and find a good governess for her. The school is no use to her at all and the poor child is lonely. Will you not ask Harriet to enquire in Brisbane for us?"

Miriam remembered that discussion between her mother and father because it was the first she had heard of a governess. Excited, she went about her world, examining it for all its information to share with a governess and all the questions it raised which a governess would be able to answer. But weeks passed and no governess came. Desperation etched every facet of her life so that now, over half a century later, that time of waiting was as sharp as a steel engraving in Miriam Gluck's memory.

In a puddle of tea-coloured water, formed in the track that led to the forest by the wheels of the timber jinkers, a mosquito was walking. Tentatively lifting and placing its fragile, angular legs, it picked its way across the surface. The child, Miriam Wemyss, squatting on her haunches to watch the mosquito's progress, wondered if water had a skin. That would explain some things, like the gooseflesh which prickled the lake in a breeze, but it raised others, such as whether water had muscles to cause the swell and ripple which sometimes disturbed the sheet of water beyond her house. She dipped a finger in the puddle and the mosquito faltered. She withdrew and felt the faintest pull and plop, weaker than the suction of a sea anemone closing around her finger, but still sensible. The mosquito had recovered its equilibrium and Miriam could see that the water also pulled at its feet; tiny peaks of water lifting and falling away with each step.

The puddle in the cart track was almost at the limit of her territory. Here the heavily laden timber jinkers, on their journey down from the forest, turned from the track that led past the village; the houses of the married timber workers, the general store and hotel, the schoolhouse and the foreman's house; to her own house at the top of the low-flowering scrub. The bullocks, straining at the turn, plunged instead down through the warrum to the sawmill on the edge of the lake. Miriam was not allowed to go without an adult into the mill or, beyond it, to the barracks where the single men lived. Nor was she allowed to go far in the other direction, along the track which came out on the road to Boreen and then Tewantin or, if you went north, to Pomona and finally Gympie.

Now, imitating the mosquito's walk, she picked her way from ridge to ridge in the rutted track until she was surely out of adult sight. The tall paperbarks closed over the track, their flaky white and charcoal trunks dense on either side. The wind did not penetrate here but it ruffled the canopy and, from time to time, knocked the trunks together making a sad, hollow note which reminded her of blackfellas' corroborees. You could not see the blackfellas, marked with white clay, when they stood still amid these trees, any more than you could distinguish a snake poised among the tree roots which heaved up from the packed earth. But Miriam was never scared in the warrum. It was a sort of no-man's-land between her home and the mill. She was not officially allowed to play here but, provided no-one called her back as she left the village, and provided she did not enter the mill itself, the adults turned a blind eye to her visits through the warrum to the lake shore. Though it was a dark and mysterious place, Miriam felt the warrum's mystery was protective.

The lake, Cootharaba, had lain here once, the foreman told her. Mr Bell did not talk much but he knew such things and would share them. Thousands of years ago it had retreated (Mr Bell did not know why and he never speculated) leaving the peat, as Mother called it, formed in ridges and ditches and pools of tanned water. The track ran along the ridges and where it crossed the ditches the men had put down split logs to keep the jinkers from bogging. The smell of the ditches was intimate, like Mother.

After the lake withdrew, the blacks lived here for a long, long time but they, too, had retreated. Miriam knew that because Doddy had told her. They went when the mill was built and now lived upstream, near their corroboree grounds at Figtree Point, where the Noosa River entered Lake Cootharaba. Now they were the Kabi Kabi – the Nowhere People, Doddy said. But they came daily, along the shore track to work at the mill or to hunt in the warrum, or along the back track to work in the village or, like Doddy, in her mother's house. Miriam was not scared of the blacks, either, although people said they were very fierce. They had captured a white woman once, years ago, before the mill was built. Eliza Fraser had been shipwrecked and washed up on the sand dunes, the distant horizon on the far side of Cootharaba. After a time she was rescued from the Kabi Kabi by a convict and taken back to her own people. Miriam sometimes wondered if she wanted to be rescued.

The noise of the mill barely penetrated the warrum. The harsh screaming and snarling of the great saw and thwomp-

thwomp of the pistons were blotted up by the paperbarks, and only thin, diffuse capillaries of sound seeped between the trunks. As she drew nearer the mill, the paperbarks thinned, their ranks broken by kululu, the fine, delicate cypress which gave the district its name, Cooloola. Miriam thought the fruit doves said "kululu, kululu" and that the blacks had learnt their language from the birds. Pink-flowered hibiscus was here and Gympie stinger with its rosy fruit and nettled leaves. Casuarinas trailed their needles on the coarse, shelly sand which covered the peat here and the din of her father's mill was no longer muted.

Fresh salt wind from the lake blew in Miriam's face as the track broke into open ground. A huge quandong fig stood at the land's edge, its buttresses slapped by wavelets blown up by the breeze. The spray caught her pinafore. To the left, as lofty as the fig and the paperbarks behind her, was the shed of the mill. Miriam knew no other building as large, except in Brisbane. Its lakeside face was open, exposing the cavernous space which housed the stationary engine and the great saw. Between Miriam and the mill stood the winch, its steel cables running into the water where, between piles driven into the lake bed, the logs of cedar, beech and Kauri pine were corralled. These logs had been nosed down river from the forests by steamboat. Others, stacked in pyramids beside the mill, were brought in by bullock-teams from the nearer forests beyond the warrum and the heathland. All would be sliced by the saw and piled on to the barges which, harnessed to the long wharf, were bucking now on the wind-driven lake.

At the far side of the shed the boilers which drove the steam engine spewed out their smoke and steam, warning of the death they could deal. In the year before Miriam was born a boiler had exploded, killing five mill-hands. Pa had had to instal new boilers with modern gauges and safety valves. It had set him back, he said. But it was not just the boilers: everything about the work was dangerous, Miriam knew. A man could be crushed between the logs on the water or felled along with a tree. He could be smitten by an axe or torn apart by the great saw. She was afraid of the mill and fascinated by it. Though her father had beaten her for going where she was forbidden, the whine of the mill crawled like tentacles through the warrum, drawing her towards its open maw.

Now she went to the mill gate and stood there, searching again for Flash Sam. Loggers, timber-fellers and sawyers came and went from her father's employ, living for a while in the men's camp behind the mill and then humping their blueys and moving on. But Flash Sam had remained except for occasional absences — sprees, Pa called them.

Flash Sam's name, his sprees and his wonderful muscles had made him splendid to Miriam. She was not supposed to have much to do with the men who worked the mill. They were said to be a rough lot and the bullockies, especially, used language to their teams she had been beaten for repeating. But they waved and called out to her from the top of the log piles or alongside the bullock teams that strained on the turn to the mill. Because she was lonely, Miriam was warmed by these exchanges and hung around the mill and the camp as often as she dared, in the hope of a game of knuckle-bones or marbles or a bit of a yarn with the men.

By the yard gate stood stone water troughs fed by a hand pump. Here bullocks and men could drink and here, one hot afternoon when the mill had shut down for the day, Miriam had surprised Flash Sam. He had doused himself with water from the pump and, with arms held up and out, he was flexing his muscles. He turned and, seeing her enraptured face, grinned his gleaming smile above his shaggy beard. Without a word he put his muscles through a scintillating performance. He turned his head first one way and then the other; he bent each knee in turn, arched his diaphragm and thrust out his chest to allow each set of muscles full play. Droplets of water slid off his skin as the muscles beneath rose and fell, twisted and rippled; possessed, it seemed, of a life independent of Flash Sam who admired them down his nose as disinterestedly as Miriam did. Then he dropped his arms, bowed, picked up his hat and his singlet and sauntered sinuously towards the men's camp. Since that day Miriam had often stood at the mill gate to watch Flash Sam work. If he saw her there his gestures became more flamboyant, his gait more swaggering, but he never repeated what she called his muscle dance.

Miriam Gluck's mind veered from the pain stirred by the memory of Flash Sam's beautiful body.

Miriam's mother had no more babies, dead or alive, after Miriam. She had hard work managing her large household, her vegetable garden and hens, her house cows and dairy, and to Miriam she seemed old and fretful. But when her grandchild Isobel came, Carrie's baby, Miriam's mother stopped being worn out.

Isobel's birth, when Miriam was nine, came close on the appointment of Miriam's governess. Miss Spender arrived, with her trunk and her parasol, in the jingle which Pa had driven to Gympie to meet the train. Mother showed her the room she would share with Sarah, the bed which had been Carrie's, and then introduced her to Miriam, leaving them together on the verandah while she made tea. "Such a pretty home you have, Miriam," Miss Spender exclaimed. "Soon you must show me all your favourite places and games." Miriam was dismissed when the women sat down together, sipping from the best cups.

Miriam yearned for Miss Spender, could hardly wait for her to finish her tea and chat with Mother. The awful days at the little school next to the butcher shop were over. Yet she had wanted to go to school for all the years before she was six. Edward was still there then and she envied him the things he learnt. Though he told her all about them, the knowledge seemed secondhand and she wanted to hear, direct from Mr Anselm, about numbers and letters and geography. But Mr Anselm went back to Brisbane in the same year that Edward was sent as a weekly boarder to a school for older boys in Gympie. A new teacher greeted her when, in the year of her sixth birthday, she had at last been allowed to go to school.

The teacher's name was Mr Ford and he rubbed his long, thin hands together and seemed to bow over them when her mother took her to the steps of the schoolhouse. His body was knobbly and permanently bent over so that, when he wished to look straight ahead, he craned his neck. He offered her mother so many assurances of his care that Miriam felt doubtful even before her mother left. Then he grasped her by the shoulders and propelled her before him into the classroom.

"Now, boys and girls, most of you already know Miss Miriam Wemyss. She has come to join us in our work and we must take special care of her. I think she must sit here," and he pointed to a desk in the front row, already occupied by Cec Philpotts, the dairyman's son. He made the whole school move back a row, isolating her from the children of her father's employees. There she sat, immediately under his eye, for the three years she endured his tutelage. When her mother tentatively suggested (she seemed awed by teachers) that Miriam might be happier if she were allowed to mix more with the other children, Mr Ford was quite emphatic that it would not do at all. "Children", he said, "must learn their proper place at school, Mrs Wemyss. We must fit them for their life in the world, must we not?" And her mother had no answer to that.

Now Miriam sat under the edge of the verandah at the side of the house, listening to the women talk and silently begging them to hurry with their tea so that she could begin to ask Miss Spender all the questions she had not asked Mr Ford.

"Miriam seems shy, Mrs Wemyss."

"No, not shy so much as reserved, I would say. But she's certainly quiet and I thank God for it. Carrie now, Carrie talked all the time. And Joshua was a shouter, no less. I could not have managed if she'd been one of those for I was quite worn out when she came along. But, thankfully, she was a quiet little thing. She's a mind of her own, just the same, and I'm kept anxious all the time over her. It's no place, the bush, to be bringing up a little girl, particularly when her father's away such a deal and her sisters are grown up and one of them gone. Carrie and Sarah have turned out well, God be praised, but I was stronger then and Mr Wemyss was not so often in Brisbane. And so I'm depending on you, Miss Spender, to give her the benefit of your education and upbringing. As Mr Wemyss has told you, I shall be away from home for a few weeks soon because my daughter's time is near. Carrie, that is. Sarah will manage the house and she's a capable girl, to be sure, so you've only to care for Miriam."

Miss Spender was pale gold and pink. Her dresses were gauzy and her boots were small and soft. Miriam thought her inaccessibly pretty, like the best china in Mother's glass-fronted cupboard, and she hung upon her at first, sure that her ethereal quality promised enlightenment.

"It's a relief to me, Miss Spender, to see that Miriam has taken so to you," said Kathleen, as she packed her grip for the thirty-mile journey to Gympie. "I may go to Carrie with a less anxious heart."

But, in the weeks of her mother's absence, Miriam discovered that Miss Spender's mind was as vapid as her body. Eager and lonely, she had taken the governess first through the mysterious warrum and down to the muddy verge of the lake where the mangroves grew. Here were crabs and shrimps and worms and insects of such size and variety that Miss Spender would surely be interested to see.

"Take your boots off, Miss Spender. You can't see from there." Mud oozing up, almost black between the toes, was part of the experience.

She took her to see the carcass of the steer the men had slaughtered. Its remains, after the butchering, had been thrown out behind the mill for the dogs. Its skull was almost stripped of flesh now and you could see how the horns grew out of the bone and how big the spaces were where the eyes had been. In the men's camp, by the door of the stores hut, there was a barrel where the steer's hide was soaking, preparing to be fleshed for tanning. Miriam showed Miss Spender the hide, hoiking it out of the barrel on a stick and disturbing the blowflies and the fatty scum which had gathered on the surface of the brine. Miss Spender recoiled violently, flapping her hand before her face. One of the timber-fellers, recovering from an accident, began to play a harmonica as he sat on the verandah of the sleeping quarters. Miriam dropped the slimy hide back into the barrel and moved towards the music. "No, Miriam!" Miss Spender gasped. "I'm sure it cannot be right for us to go in there."

So Miriam took her to the mill where the giant-toothed saw

blade would soon begin its work. They watched the men winching a log from the water on to the saw platform. Flash Sam was not among them. Miriam explained as best she could how the engine worked. She did not tell Miss Spender what her mother said of the saw: "A banshee, it is, a harbinger of death, screaming outside our homes!" Nor that it had caused several deaths among the mill-hands. Miriam had herself seen one body torn by the saw but she would never think of that, not even now. She continued to go to the mill as though it had never happened.

Whenever she was allowed to visit it, usually under the protection of Mr Bell, she sat in the huge pile of sharp, resin-scented sawdust and watched the men, torsos gleaming with sweat, nostrils rimmed and hair powdered with the fine dust, as they hauled the logs into position and drew off the sawn flitches, stacking them on the barges. She always sat quite still (she was sure of that), never waving or calling out, so as not to distract the men. The stationary engine which drove the complicated system of pistons and belts and, finally, the savage saw itself, was a source of wonder to Miriam. Though Mr Bell had explained how it worked, he had not dispelled its magic. But Miss Spender would not sit on the hill of sawdust and stood tensely, her hands pressed over her ears and her face screwed up against the noise, refusing all that Miriam offered.

Miriam sighed. She had not talked much to Miss Spender, believing that the interest of all these places was self-evident. But there were questions she had wanted to ask her, questions stored up ever since she'd been told someone was coming to teach her.

" Does water have skin, Miss Spender?"

"No, Miriam, only living things have skins and water isn't a living thing, now is it?"

Miriam was not sure but was dissuaded from advancing her own arguments by the governess's tone. She asked instead whether the gentle-eyed milking cow who licked your face would go to heaven.

"Why, no, Miriam, how could she? Only people with souls go to heaven and we know a cow has no soul, don't we?"

"Do blackfellas have souls, Miss Spender?" she asked, getting as close as she could to an unformed question.

"Natives, dear. We don't say blackfellas. Yes, the native people do have souls. But they must be redeemed souls, you know, before they can enter Our Father's Kingdom."

Miriam knew that she had not asked the right questions, but she needed someone to understand what she wanted to know before she could manage to get them right. Miss Spender would not squat by the puddles to see the mosquitoes walking; she would not come close to the cow and be licked, and it had been clear to Miriam, from the moment Miss Spender first met Doddy, that she could not take the governess to visit Doddy's home. Miss Spender had been reluctant to accept the tea and scones Doddy had served on the first day and only her good manners persuaded her to do as Kathleen did, although she spoke her thanks in a tight voice, almost as though she were frightened. Later, Miss Spender had firmly suggested that now she herself was available to Miriam, there would be no further need to play with Doddy's daughter. So, while Miss Spender remained, Bess stopped coming to the house with her mother.

In a last bid to engage Miss Spender, Miriam begged Mr Bell to take them to the forest with him on the dray. Mr Bell was a Scot with a strong sense of responsibility for the mill. Miriam liked him and would pester him with questions whenever she had the chance. Mr Bell was both busy and taciturn so, although comforted by his presence and his "Aye, ye may well be right" or "Nay, lassie, I canna say", she only learned from him what he certainly knew and that was largely to do with trees and the mill. He was glad to share that knowledge and to take them with him to the forest. Miriam was not often allowed to go, even if Pa or Joshua were there; she would be in the way or might get hurt, they said. So this was an occasion of excitement, though Miss Spender was doubtful, and was only persuaded to go because Miriam said Mr Bell had arranged it and would be put out if they declined.

The forest was an awesome place – like a cathedral, Mother said. Miriam had never seen a cathedral but knew reverence in the presence of the great trees. This morning, since it had rained heavily during the night, they could hear above the dray's creaking the noise of water. Water cascaded down gullies and splashed into pools, flinging fine rainbowed mist over the tree ferns and emerald rocks. Water like glass beads rolled from the leaves of pendant vines and fell sonorously into still brown ponds. Water gurgled in runnels between the horses' feet and mud splattered Miss Spender's dress.

The forest was dark and steamy on either side of the track. Intermittent shafts of light, penetrating the canopy, caught the fleeting colour of birds, the textures of grass-tree and fern, the hard cross-hatched barks of the bloodwoods and ironbarks, the glowing ivories of gums. Vines wreathed trunks with glimmering flowers. Miriam held her breath with the pleasure; Miss Spender exclaimed with every jolt of the dray. Soon they heard axeblows, the sound muffled by the thick, damp vegetation. Too soon they rounded a curve in the track and entered the cleared space, the enormous scar in the forest where the men were working.

This was the base camp and, from it, tracks like tunnels radiated into the forest. It was an area large enough for the bullock teams to turn and for the great trees felled in the forest to be trimmed and loaded on the drays. Here the timber jinker stood, its bullocks lying in the shade, and, above the scar, the sky's intensity emphasised the soaring height of encircling trees. A felled cedar lay across a saw-pit where two men, one below and one above, were lopping its branches with a two-handed saw. Frenzied birds hovered and darted above their heads, searching for their homes in the ruin. Some distance away, at the further end of the scar, where the ground inclined and the exposed trees took on the appearance of a cliff-face, a beech would soon fall. Two loggers were operating a crosscut-saw and the tree's crown shook with its vibrations. Shrieks of alarmed birds punctured the rhythmic noise.

Mr Bell drew the horses to a halt and jumped down. He held up his hand to Miss Spender who gingerly alighted on to the torn and littered ground. Miriam leapt and ran, calling over her shoulder, "Look, Miss Spender, here's a stump with rings you can count!"

Miss Spender picked her way across the open space, holding her skirts, and looked down at the stump, a yard wide, where Miriam's fingers were inching, counting. "Ah, Botany," she breathed. "Do you know that each ring represents a year, Miriam?" But Miriam did know and had finished counting. "One hundred and four!" she shouted and ran off.

"Come and look at the vines, Miss Spender. You can swing on some of them!" She pushed into the undergrowth, reaching up and hauling on intertwined ropes of vine, some as thick as a logger's wrist. Miss Spender followed her to the edge of the clearing where she stood uncertainly, peering after Miriam. Finding a vine which curved down at the right height to swing on, Miriam turned back to call the governess. Against the light of the clearing, Miss Spender was a hatted silhouette, but into a pool of sunshine behind her a snake slithered and stationed itself in coils.

"Come here, Miss Spender," Miriam made her voice sound as commanding as she could, suppressing alarm.

"No, Miriam, I can see the vine from here. It's a very fine specimen but I think you should come out of there now." She turned to go back to the stump, saw the snake, emitted a tiny scream and fainted. Miriam ran. She grabbed Miss Spender under the arms and dragged her backwards, yelling above the noise of the saws for Mr Bell.

The snake was dispatched quickly enough and Miss Spender, her dress stained green down the back, was laid on the dray to recover. But the expedition was over and Miriam's hope of understanding writhed and died.

2 Land of Promise

Over breakfast, about three weeks after Mother had gone to Gympie, Pa broke his usual porridge silence. "If the weather holds, we'll be taking a load downstream tomorrow. Would you like to see that, Miss Spender?"

Miss Spender looked puzzled and, since Pa seldom volunteered to take his girl-children anywhere, Miriam interrupted before doubts could be expressed. "We go on our boat and have a picnic on Munna Island. Say yes, Miss Spender, it's enormous fun!"

In the candlelight next morning Miss Spender's face looked cold and pinched and her expression did not warm during the dark walk through the warrum to the mill. The lake was a still silver and the wharf timbers slippery-black with dew under the pewter sky. Miss Spender shivered audibly but Miriam refused to notice. The men had fixed the tow ropes and the boat's engine was stoked and ready to leave. Pa, who was there already, had stowed the picnic basket and now helped Miss Spender down from the wharf. Sarah and Miriam followed unaided.

Miriam stood in the bow watching the lake part before them. The water, folding back, was green under its glossy skin. Behind them the barge slid silently, its wake lapping at the shore. At this hour, and despite the chugging engine, the silence was thick and oily. Voices, from boat to barge, from bow to cabin, cut it as the boat cut through the water. Then the sun rose and the heavy silken texture of the morning dissipated. Miss Spender emerged from the cabin warmth to stand at the rail with Sarah and watch the lake slip by.

After Lake Cootharaba, the river returned to itself for a

while. Confined between steep banks of forest, kookaburra laughter was deafening. Cooroibah, Little Water, opened beyond, ice-green and rose. "Are you quite safe there, Miriam?" called Miss Spender. Miriam merely waved.

It was not until they turned out of Cooroibah Lake, where the banks of the Noosa were scarred with clearings, farms and houses between clots of tea-tree, that Miss Spender became at all animated. "There's a pleasant house" and "How tranquil it does seem here," she exclaimed. Sarah told her the names of the landholders as the boat passed. Tewantin came into view around the next bend, a clutch of wharves, sheds, hotels and cottages huddled together on the brink of the lagoon.

"Civilisation," cried the governess.

"Oh hardly, Miss Spender," answered Sarah who, though she dreamt of London, did not appreciate the extent of Miss Spender's deprivation.

Pa, at the wheel, seemed to take offence. "The mill was there first, in any case," he said. "The niggers called this place Tewantin because it means Place of Dead Logs. So, you see?" Civilisation depended on pioneering enterprise and not the other way about. It was a dictum Miriam understood, but she doubted that Miss Spender saw the point.

On the northern shore of the river, opposite Tewantin, stood the wharves and sheds of the timber depot. Joshua Wemyss and Sons, Timber Merchants, said the large painted sign above the sheds. Moored at the far end of the wharf, her white paintwork dazzling bright in the morning sun, was the paddle-steamer *Culgoa*. In a difficult exercise of navigation (the channel to the sea changed according to the shifting sand) the *Culgoa* would take the timber across the bar and down the coast to Brisbane. Pa drew the boat in so that the barge came alongside the wharf and the men made it fast with ropes. When Pa had tied the boat to the barge he sprang across the timber to the wharf. Miriam, familiar with the routine, knew that they were expected to wait until he had seen the wharfingers and the captain of the *Culgoa*. He would be perhaps half an hour. Miss Spender evidently hoped to go ashore in Tewantin and her frustration was obvious.

Sarah explained that Pa would take them ashore, if they needed to go, either when he came back or after lunch.

"There are needs and needs," said Miss Spender, sourly.

Pa returned and shouted some orders to a group of blacks labouring on the wharf. "You get along there now! Double quick time! I come back two hours; these fellas all finish!" He held up two fingers of his left hand and pointed to the barge with his right. Then he jumped down and loosed the hawser with a flourish. Miriam knew that he was showing off.

The sandbar was ahead of them now, shimmering gold in silver-blue. It was among the most beautiful things Miriam knew, like Mother's opal brooch on its gold bar. To the right, at the edge of the royal blue channel that led to the sea, was Munna Island, little more than a thicket of casuarinas and tea-tree, perhaps a quarter of a mile across, and ringed by gold. Pa brought the boat up to the jetty built for picnickers and tied it up. Miriam did not wait to disembark but stripped off her pinafore and jumped over the side.

Sarah or Pa must have explained that this behaviour was usual because, though Miss Spender's face was tight when Miriam ran up the sand and flung herself down by the picnic cloth, she made no remark. But after lunch, when Miriam stripped off her wet bloomers and left them to dry while she swam again, Miss Spender gasped and averted her face. Miriam understood that neither Miss Spender nor Sarah could do as she did and was dimly apprehensive of a time when the world must close in on her too. But Sarah took off her boots and stockings, hitched up her skirt and petticoat and paddled in the shallows, kicking water in Miriam's face whenever she surfaced. If Sarah's skirts were bedraggled on the homeward trip, who would notice or care? Miss Spender thought differently and reclined on the sand under her parasol. Pa, sitting beside her, pointed out landmarks and explained the hazards of the bar. Because he had devised this method of transport for his timber; because he thought himself the first cause of Tewantin and its chief upholder; because he was the biggest employer and the richest man in the whole Cooloola district, Josh Wemyss was proud and willing to talk of it, even to a woman. Miss Spender's periwinkle eyes widened. She laughed prettily and seemed impressed.

Pa offered to take them all to the hotel in Tewantin so they could refresh themselves before the journey home. He handed Miss Spender up from the launch and manoeuvred her by her elbow between the drays and spring carts on the road. Miss Spender bathed her face and resettled her hat in the ladies' room. Miriam went to talk to the publican's wife and to her sulphur-crested cockatoo in a cage by the back door. Sarah, who wanted to visit the haberdashery and collect the mail from the post office, invited Miss Spender to go with her but Miss Spender was overcome with heat, her face burnt pink despite hat and parasol, and chose to remain in the ladies' lounge. Pa offered to get her a glass of something to revive her. When Miriam returned, however, Miss Spender's face seemed redder than before and her temper not the least improved. Pa had joined the captain of the *Culgoa* in the bar.

"She's a prissy little bitch and of no use whatever!" Miriam heard Pa tell Mother when she returned from Gympie.

Kathleen came home bringing Carrie and Isobel with her. They were to stay for a few weeks while Carrie got used to the baby. Miriam saw immediately that her mother was no longer worn out at all. She laughed and played with Isobel and sang Irish songs to her. Miriam heard her get up in the night to soothe the baby and again early in the morning to make Carrie a cup of tea; despite the extra work, she seemed young again.

But during this time of activity and heat (it was November), Miss Spender's education and upbringing got the better of her. Kathleen, so absorbed by the baby, expected the governess to share her interest, and some of the chores too, if Miss Spender lingered on the verandah where Isobel was being tended. Since babies were not to her taste, Miss Spender was forced to withdraw to the other side of the house where there was less shade and no breeze from the lake. Here she would recline in a cane chaise, a book in her hand and notes in her lap, pretending to prepare Miriam's lessons. Miriam knew it was a pretence because what lessons there had been had stopped.

*

Miriam Gluck, sitting at her dawn-filled window, a cup of cold tea before her, was surprised out of her reverie. All these vibrant memories had sprung from bones: whalebones, her own bones, crushed and constricted by the stays; the bones which had been forgiving when she came to bear her children, spreading themselves easily at their supple joints to allow safe passage. But the memory of Miss Spender, the stored-up questions to ask and interests to share, had provoked another constriction in Miriam Gluck's chest, as though an unbreached sorrow swelled again there. The tight, wary half-smile of the disappointed child afflicted her face. It was an expression she had seen on the faces of her own children when she had turned them away because of her burden of preoccupation. And her coldness; that had to be recognised. There had been a sealing down of affection somewhere.

Still, the children – Else, Eric and Caroline – had not been left entirely to their own devices. Isobel had played with them, taught them, sung to them. She had been vivacious then, like her grandmother who had got over being worn out when Isobel was born. Watching Isobel play with the children, Miriam had been reminded of her own mother, sitting on the verandah with Carrie and the baby while Miriam watched from a distance. Isobel was getting on now, but was still spry. Affection had been denied her too, in the end, though never by Kathleen.

Miriam Gluck had not wished to be reminded of her own mother, then or now. She had held Kathleen and her memory at bay and the tangle of love, hurt, and disdain she felt for her had never been unravelled. But as she had grown older herself, she thought it strange that, despite her father's absences from her childhood and his disregard, it was he and not her mother who had completely dominated her mind: his opinions, his achievements and his values. Though she knew the elements of Kathleen's story, she had never entered it with imagination or sympathy and had denied its power to shape and colour her own. It was as though her mother's story was a minor theme suppressed by the strident brass of her father's work.

Of her father's story she knew at least the major events because they were public facts, important to the society in which she had grown up. The flour mill on the south bank of the Brisbane River bore witness to the success of her grandfather, Matthew Wemyss, who, after the death of his wife in 1850, had come from Bradford in England with his two sons, James and Joshua. The timber mill and its thriving village of workers on the banks of Lake Cootharaba, a hundred miles to the north of Brisbane, was her father Joshua's initiative. The transport business, of wheat to the mill, wool and sugar to the wharves, of secondary produce all through the colony of Queensland, had been begun by James and joined by Joshua's timber from Lake Cootharaba to Brisbane. When Matthew Wemyss died the brothers inherited wealth and importance. On the strength of it, Josh Wemyss had become mayor of South Brisbane and was later appointed by the Governor to the upper house in the Queensland Parliament. All this Miriam had absorbed as she grew up; it became part of the context in which her father loomed large. But of the world beyond this seemingly complete society she knew nothing and so had nothing by which to measure and judge it, or her father.

Miss Spender had tried to teach her History. After the failed expeditions into the Cootharaba mill and its dangerous excitements, Miss Spender had said, drawing her into the shade of the verandah, "Now Miriam, you have shown me your home. I must show you something of mine." She opened an atlas and pointed out where they were now, in Australia. Then she traced the route across the sea by which she had come from England, pink, on the map, like Australia but so very small that Miriam wondered how anyone fitted there.

"Yes," agreed Miss Spender, "it is small, though one does not feel it so when one lives there. But it is very, very old. Australia, though it is big, is very young: only ninety-five years old. Not very much older than your grandfather!" She arched her eyebrows and raised her hands from the map in an artificial expression of amazement. "Shall I tell you how this very old England began? A long, long time ago, before our Lord Jesus was born, there was a city called Rome. Here it is on the map."

And so Miriam learned how the Romans, though pagan, had

been the Great Civilisers, builders of roads and drains, monuments and empire. They brought this fruit of civilisation to England and in it was a tiny seed, Christianity. The pagan empire of Rome fell but Britain, inheritor of all that was fine in it, proved a fertile ground for the seed of Christianity to flourish, and so an even greater nation than Rome grew there, full of wise, good and compassionate men. These men, Miss Spender explained, resolved to take the story of our Lord Jesus to every corner of the earth. She pointed to the places on the map where they journeyed and settled. They were all coloured pink.

"You see, God has called these men, just as he called Moses in the Old Testament, to go to new Lands of Promise and build God's Kingdom in them." Her finger came to rest on Australia. " So that is why your grandfather, and many good and great men like him, came to Queensland. And it is why we are here now. We must help to build a great nation here and bring the message of our Lord Jesus to the poor natives. Isn't that a wonderful story?"

Miss Spender's use of Miriam's grandfather as an historical reference point sprang from the fact that she was distantly related to Matthew Wemyss and had arrived in Australia with a letter of introduction to him. She had spent a short time in his house in Brisbane before being engaged by his son to bring learning and refinement to Miriam. She had been impressed by the old man's importance, the respect with which he was regarded in the colony, and had therefore believed she was getting a good position when she was hired by his son. The colonial town of Brisbane and its society was rough enough when compared to Home, but the disparity between Brisbane and the primitive settlement at Cootharaba was beyond belief. Nor was the son, in her opinion, of the same stature as his father. The child she was expected to teach was little better than a poor savage herself and seemed almost as unacquainted with Our Lord Jesus. By fostering Miriam's pride in her grandfather, Miss Spender hoped to encourage her to emulate his values. In fact, as the child Miriam dimly perceived, the governess's simple history was not far wide of Matthew Wemyss's view of the world.

Grandfather Wemyss's house in South Brisbane smelled different from her own and was much darker, screened along its verandahs with thick vines. The furniture was heavy and seemed to grow out of the polished wooden floors on which it stood. Only the dining chairs ever were moved. Grandfather Wemyss had a housekeeper who polished the furniture, and polish was part of the smell of the house. A long-case clock ticked in Grandfather's silences.

"How long is it since you last visited me, Miriam?"

"Pa says it is almost a year, Grandfather."

"And have you been a good lass, the while?"

"I don't know, Grandfather."

"Have you minded what I told you?"

"Yes, Grandfather."

"Let us see, then. Who were you named for?"

"The sister of Moses."

"And who was Moses?"

"A great man who led the Chosen People out of . . . Egyp' into the Promised Land."

"Who told Moses to take his people to the Promised Land, then?"

"God did, Grandfather."

"And when the people got to the Promised Land what did they find there?"

"Milk and honey, Grandfather. But they didn't just sit under the trees and eat it; they had to fight for the land with the natives and then they had to work hard for God's blessing!"

"Good lass! You have minded me. Now, who was God's Son?"

Once she had thought it was Moses but now she knew the right answer was Jesus.

"And why did God send Him down to earth?"

"Because the people were wicked and didn't obey the laws God gave to Moses."

"And so what did Jesus do?"

"He died for . . . what we done wrong, on the cross so we can go to Heaven when we die."

"Aye, for our trespasses. And he rose again from the dead,

three days after he died so we would know, without a doubt, that it was so. Will you remember that for next time, lass?"

"Yes, Grandfather," she said positively, thinking the examination at an end.

But Grandfather Wemyss had a new question and his eyes looked sly under his bushy white eyebrows. "And do you know who Mary was, child?"

Miriam was glad she knew the answer. "God's mother, Grandfather."

"No, Miriam! God has no mother! That is a blasphemy, a sin against God's name. Mary was the woman who gave birth to Jesus, that's all. Never say that again, mind!"

"No, Grandfather."

"Promise me, child. Never!"

"I promise, Grandfather. I'm sorry."

"Run away now to the kitchen and ask Mrs Benson for your tea."

While she was in the kitchen she heard Grandfather's voice raised in discussion with Pa and when they got home again, two days later, she heard Pa's voice raised to her mother in their bedroom. "If you must talk that sort of nonsense to the niggers, for God's sake don't let the child hear you. And don't let her see you mumbling over those beads!" From her mother came only snuffling noises.

So Miss Spender's history had authenticity. She knew about the Promised Land and about Grandfather, and if England was not Egypt nor Grandfather Moses, still there was a close correlation. Miriam had difficulty placing Our Lord Jesus since he was only God's Son, just as Pa was Grandfather's son and lacked his authority. It seemed Our Lord Jesus was especially good for poor natives, though. Mary, on the other hand, was only a woman and to say anything else was blasphemy (which Miriam understood to be terribly wrong) and nonsense for niggers.

Miriam Gluck remembered that particular visit to Matthew Wemyss because of the sudden and frightening anger he had displayed, directed, she felt, not at her but at something much older and stronger; something that was represented, strangely, by her mother. Yet Kathleen Wemyss was afraid of her father-in-law and rarely visited Brisbane. When she did, she spent much of her time in the kitchen with Mrs Benson and she called Miriam's grandfather "Mr Wemyss", almost as if she were the maid. Which she was, of course, but that only came out later, after Pa had died.

Miss Spender's history lesson had attached itself to Miriam's memory of that visit to Grandfather Wemyss as though they had happened on the same day, which they could not have done. There must have been weeks, perhaps months, between the two events and yet they had fused in her recollection. Now, oddly, the fusion lit her mother's story and melted Miriam's disdain for Kathleen Wemyss. The spreading pink under Miss Spender's finger on the map seemed, in Miriam's memory, to have crushing weight and force: an aggressive colour under whose progress mountains and rivers were rolled out and the great trees of the forest were brought down. Matthew Wemyss was characterised, in his own mind and Miss Spender's, as an instrument of that inexorable progress. He had crushed Kathleen in its name, just as others of its agents had pulled down Miriam Gluck. But it was too soon to think of that. And Kathleen's story was her own, not to be poached for her daughter's excuses.

3 Contortions

Kathleen Wemyss's religion had the same status in the family as her husband's marital infidelities: both were known and neither was directly spoken of. Occasionally it was necessary to make an oblique reference to one or the other, in the way people will refer to their relatives' socially embarrassing physical handicaps. But between Kathleen and Josh there had been a compact which he had broken, and thereafter she returned to her own way. It was not until after her husband's death in 1916 that Kathleen explained the compact to Miriam or spoke of what it had cost her. She might not have done it then had she not become ill and, fearing her own death, sent for Miriam and the local priest. Kathleen had been alone in the house at the time as Edward, who still lived at home, was at work and the housekeeper had gone out. Miriam came across town by train to be with her.

"Ask Father Corcoran to come," her mother had said. Miriam waited in the garden for the priest to arrive and returned there after taking him to her mother's room. She wanted as little as possible to do with this faintly disgusting ritual. But when he had gone the confession Kathleen had begun could not be stopped.

Kathleen Wemyss, or Hanaford as she was, had renounced her faith in order to marry the second son of the Quaker miller, Matthew Wemyss. Or rather, Matthew Wemyss, in a ferment of righteous anger, had insisted that this young Irish maid who worked in his house give up the practice of her religion as a condition of her marriage to his son. She had not, she told Miriam, chased after young Josh. It was unthinkable she should defy her faith by seeking out a non-Catholic for her husband. She had been content in her work as servant to the three men which had given her a sense of identity and purpose in the midst of the new colony's strangeness and excitement. She had come to Queensland with her brother and sister-in-law as a result of a recruiting drive by Bishop Quinn among the good Catholic men and women of Ireland. She knew that the bishop had encouraged young women immigrants especially, because the colony was short of marriageable women and the Catholic men were falling into immorality as a consequence. So in 1862 she had come, prepared for hard work, sacrifice and marriage to a Catholic.

Josh had been timid and furtive in his advances to her (he did not have marriage in mind) and she had resisted him. She looked for another place but employers, she found, were unwilling to take on a servant without a reference from the previous employer and she could not tell Matthew Wemyss why she wanted to leave. Because she was entirely alone in Brisbane (her brother and his wife having gone north to work in a new settlement near Rockhampton) and because she was only seventeen, she fell in love with Josh.

"Marrying your Pa was a mortal sin and bedding with him, unwed, was a mortal sin. One mortal sin is as good as another; they're both death to the soul. But I would not bed with him and so he asked me to be his wife. He wanted to go off to the bush and start on his own business of the timber milling and he needed me, Miriam. So, God forgive me, I accepted him. Oh, Mr Wemyss was angry. I could not blame him. My own father would have been angry had he known, but I'd stopped writing to them, I was so ashamed. They would think I was dead. And I was! Dead to God; dead in my immortal soul.

"Mr Wemyss would have none of me. I was a Papist, I was Irish and I was a maid in his house. He said he would have none of Josh, either, if he married me, and Josh would be cut off from his inheritance. But though he was a hard man he was just, according to his lights, and Josh had worked in the business for the twelve years, since they came out. So then, after a few days of dreadful arguments and me keeping in my little room – I was so afraid of them – he said Josh could marry me if I would give up my faith. It was a terrible thing to ask. Terrible! But, you see, if I married Josh I would be in mortal sin already. I knew that, even if they didn't. And Josh said there'd be no priest or church in the bush, in any case. So I agreed.

"But the worst of it, Miriam, the very worst was that I could not teach you children anything about God or His Blessed Son or His Holy Mother nor about the saints and angels. Nothing! I loved your Pa and all of you children and I loved the bush, Miriam; loved it all with an awful ache in my heart because it was a helpless love, do you see? Father says it's only the love that has kept my soul alive to be reconciled with God and I'm surely grateful for that. But what about you and Otto and your Pa and all the world I loved? That's not reconciled now, is it? Holy Mary, Mother of God!" And she wept afresh.

It was a sad dry story, so Miriam thought. Like a dead leaf blown from a living tree, it was of no account to continuing life. She did not perceive Kathleen's need for absolution from her daughter. She washed her mother's face and tended her until the housekeeper returned, but all the time she wrestled in her mind with her own living story and its meaning for her life and for her children. Kathleen Wemyss's story blew away like a dead leaf before that wind.

On this sixth morning of war, Miriam Gluck, in her safe dark flat and her safe dreary routine, thought about her mother's dead story. She knew that she did so because the other, her own story, which she had thought dead as well, had been resurrected by this new war; had cast off its respectable interment and was angrily demanding to be heard. But she could only approach it obliquely, needing to find first its proper context, its antecedents. She did not know if she was doing this to stave it off or to give it strength, but her memory could not be directly goaded to it and insisted on its own path, probing the pain of Kathleen's renunciation.

Faith did not, even now, seem significant to Miriam Gluck. Catholic, Anglican, Presbyterian, Reformed, Lutheran: they were all like stays; they supported an acceptable social image while exercising a suffocating constraint on one's way of being in the world. Miriam regularly attended Evensong at the Anglican Cathedral where she was both recognised and anonymous. It would not have caused her particular pain to renounce that. Her mother's faith, unpractised and untended all those years, had still been deeply rooted, mysterious to Miriam, seeming heavy with superstition and ritual.

Holy Mary, Mother of God! Kathleen said it in moments of deep distress or horror. When the timber-feller had been brought to her, dying of the wound the saw had given him, his torso hideously riven, she had cried it aloud, it seemed to Miriam, almost in anger. It was an aspiration, her mother said: it came out with her breath; the involuntary articulation of a hope as vital to life as breathing. For Miriam it was the answer to Grandfather's question, found to placate his urgent catechising, to win his goodwill. It was the wrong answer, a blasphemy. A woman cannot bear God but only, and at best, mortal sons. It was swept away on the angry pink tide of his certainties.

And it was Matthew Wemyss with whom Kathleen had had to contend, because the father's faith had not taken with his son. Josh Wemyss made no claim to speak with the authority of God or of Holy Writ but relied instead on a secondhand word to justify him. But he had needed a wife and an independent enterprise to initiate his manhood, and he had needed his father's blessing and legacy to ensure continuity for his sons. For these essentials he had traded his wife's faith, which was only foolishness for niggers. He did not know that he had also traded his own authority.

So now Miriam Gluck understood what she had not seen before: that her mother had renounced her way of being in the world. Her faith was neither a comfort nor a constraint, but her own way of creating, nurturing and binding her world — of reconciling it, as she said.

In the same transaction she had lost her respect for the husband she loved and looked instead to her sons. Kathleen Wemyss had worshipped her sons. Joshua, her first-born and named for his father, was eleven years older than Miriam and, by the time Miriam was old enough to notice him, he was accompanying his father with an exaggerated length of stride or calling in his adolescent voice from the top of the timber jinker, the tallies of logs brought in from the forest. Conversations about the affairs of the mill were conducted between the two Joshuas at the family dinner table as though no-one else were there. Kathleen intruded into these discussions from time to time.

"But Josh, dear," she would say, touching his arm, "remember when we talked of this before, we felt it was not economical"; or, "Josh, we must think of the safety of the men." But hers was a voice from the past when she had been her husband's confidante and partner. Now, increasingly, he ignored her or brushed aside her suggestions with impatience.

Edward, too, put in his oar, as his father said. "Why don't we build a railway line from here to Gympie and join up with the freight train there?" he once suggested. Joshua brayingly ridiculed his young brother's idea but he had an eye on his father and soon hiccoughed into silence when, for the first time, Pa did not mock Edward. Though Edward's idea was not practical, Pa adopted a modified form of it and installed tramlines to transport the logs from the nearer forest to the mill. Edward's was a voice of the future, increasingly heeded.

Kathleen in time accepted that her day was done as partner in the business and began to defer to her sons, watching them with pride, almost reverence, as they asserted their ideas and tested their power. But sometimes when her gaze rested on her husband it was wistful, as though she would call him back to the days when they had established the mill together and laboured side by side. And sometimes, if he noticed, Josh would humour her. "Come on, Kath, old girl! The boy's right, you see, and one day it will be his responsibility to decide." So Kathleen was encouraged to see young Joshua and Edward as the fulfilment of her hopes and the justification for her labour and sacrifice. Miriam observed and knew that to be loved and revered she should be like Joshua or Edward.

Edward was closest, only six years older than Miriam, and his care of the new baby sister when she came was legendary in the family. He was too young to amuse his older brother, and his older sisters were so close in age that they were sufficient for themselves in the games they played. Of the two boys, Edward was fonder of their mother, but he was undemanding in his affections and she paid more attention to Joshua, who was not.

Because Kathleen was exhausted from childbearing after Miriam, Edward became her helper and Miriam's minder. Miriam's earliest memory involved Edward. She had fallen over in the shallow water at the edge of the lake and remembered a mouthful of black mud and mud in her hair, on her arms and smock. The choking sensation and the taste of the mud were still vividly evoked by the memory, but more striking was Edward's distress. He ran into the mud and dragged her up the little bank, weeping for her safety and in anticipation of their mother's fright.

"Don't cry, Miriam, please don't cry! Mother will hear you and she will be upset. There's a good girl. You're safe now, so don't cry!"

He had brought her to the water tank behind the stables and helped her out of her smock. He had washed her clean of the mud and rinsed her clothes under the tap, spreading them over a bush to dry. Miriam remembered sitting on the ground watching her toes with detached interest as Edward, with his wet handkerchief, removed the last of the mud from between them.

Miriam had felt confident of Edward, secure in his company. When he rode into Tewantin once a week for the mail, Miriam remembered being obscurely aware of the world's fragility, as though she must tiptoe through the day until he brought substance back to it. Miriam would sit on the steps of the verandah and wait till she heard the horse. Then she would run inside calling, "It's teatime, Mother! Edward's home!" And Edward, at that time, saw nothing incongruous in explaining his lessons to her while he helped to dress her doll or build a card house on the mat outside the kitchen door.

But there had been a growing tension around the tea-table which made it difficult to eat. One evening (she must have been about five and Edward, therefore, eleven) Miriam had been unable to swallow the slimy-textured prunes and rice in her bowl and sat stirring it all into a brown-streaked slurry. Pa had been called away by one of the men and when he had gone Edward began to coax her, playing the one-for-me one-for-Mother game. Suddenly Pa entered, slamming the door behind him.

"Edward, is it not your job to tend and stable the horse of an evening?"

"Yes, Pa." Edward put the spoon down and looked at his father.

"Did you rub her down today?"

"Yes, Pa."

"Well, that horse is now down on her knees, sweating and feverish, and if you had not been so anxious to rush in here and play girls' games with that child and hang on to your mother's apron, you would have noticed. Be quiet, Kath: I blame you! You've encouraged him to be a milksop. Look at him! He's snivelling now, the useless tripehound!" Pa's face was contorted into the ugliest expression Miriam had ever seen and, frightened, she began to wail.

"And shut that brat up!" Pa shouted as he turned and went back to the stables.

Kathleen got up and cupped her hand round Miriam's chin to quieten her. To Edward she said, "Son, be strong now. Go and help your father." Edward cleared Miriam's bowl from the table and went out.

After he had gone Kathleen addressed her daughters and there was sharpness in her tone, as though they were in some way to blame for the situation. "Carrie, Sarah. I want you two girls to take more responsibility for Miriam from now on. It's only right that you should, after all, and then Edward will be freer to help your Pa." The girls had been playing Tinker, Tailor, Soldier, Sailor with their prune stones and they stared down at their plates, making no response. "Do you hear me, now?" their mother demanded.

"Yes, Mother," they chanted together. Their eyes slid sideways under their lowered fringes and they collapsed on each other, snorting and giggling.

At that time Carrie was fourteen, Sarah a year younger. They had always shared games, clothes and secrets and now the mysteries of pubescence wrapped them together in an invisible membrane. In obedience to their mother they took over the buttoning of Miriam's clothes and boots, washing her face before meals and giving her her bath. Occasionally they would read to her or take her with them for a walk but they were unable to include her in their bond and they did not love her as Edward had done.

Edward. The memory of him, as he had been to her in those days, hurt Miriam. He had continued, sometimes, to read to her or play marbles or jacks but never, after that, card houses or dolls and never when Pa or Joshua was near. He became silent, sullen perhaps, but he tagged on to Pa and Joshua as they inspected logs and supervised loading and unloading, for the journey across the lake and over the sandbar to the sea. He seemed as distant from Miriam as the pale sandbar itself, drifting like a mirage on the horizon. When Pa and Joshua were near he was brusque with her, pushing her off into the enveloping loneliness.

It was then he began to put his oar in at table. At first he was ignored or mocked but he persisted until that day came when Pa answered him, taking up his idea and shaping it to suit. Pa's acceptance made his separation from Miriam complete. He grew as loud and swaggering as Joshua, but seemed joyless. Only with Kathleen was he still tender and he remained so; faithful to her in her old age and widowhood, though then he was seldom sober. He would not abandon his mother but Miriam had become a living rebuke to him. At times of insecurity in his manhood, he needed to reject her afresh.

Only once had she called up their shared childhood and pleaded with him, because of it, to help her in her troubles; to help Otto. It had since seemed to Miriam that his heavy drinking dated from that year, or at least became obvious from then, and she had watched his decline with a hardness of heart which had not dissolved since his death. She had watched his features, once sensitive and fine, become bloated with the defensive liquor. In death they looked slack and unprotected.

Only now, seeing again in memory the writhing of his unformed boy's hands, their large knuckles locking together, changing from red to white to red again, clenched and unclenched under Pa's scorn; only now did the nub of bitterness crack open and spill out in anger against Pa. Too late for Edward, too late for Pa, this rage against her father's weakness. For that was how she suddenly saw it: a bitter weakness which contorted all that was gentle into its own image.

And she saw herself then, a child of nine, performing backward somersaults on the patch of rough grass beyond her mother's garden, showing her bloomers and twisting her body in a grotesque courting display. The men, preoccupied with the world beyond the distant sandbar, noticed her rarely and with embarrassment. The women, trapped on the verandah by the baby's golden aura, called to her but had no power to draw her in.

"Miriam, love, you're behaving like a hobbledehoy! Don't, please! Now then, Carrie, I've made Isobel cry with my shouting. Where's Miss Spender?" But it was Sunday and Miss Spender had gone to sit by the lake. "Go and talk to the child, Carrie, if you please. It's beyond me to make a lady of her!"

It was attention, of a sort, when Mother noticed and Carrie scolded her, yet she might have had more by paying court to the baby, joining the intimate feminine circle on the verandah. These contortions were a demand for the love which was due only to sons. Miriam knew that it was by physical prowess and deliberate distance from the cloying ties of women and children that masculinity was proved. She studied Joshua as Edward had done and spurned the example of her sisters.

4 Remorse

One day, when Miriam came home from visiting Doddy's camp, Miss Spender, her trunk and her few books, had disappeared. "Miss Spender has returned to Brisbane. I'm sure I don't know what we shall do with you, Miriam," said her mother.

Miriam was not sorry Miss Spender had gone and could not account for the hollow feeling in her chest. She could read, but there were few books at home, and she could write but did not know she had anything to say. Her mind was full of questions which she could not formulate because there was no-one to answer them. Since Edward had withdrawn from her she had felt only one affinity, and that was with Doddy's people. Pa referred to them as "niggers", Joshua and Edward called them "Abos". Mother spoke of "the natives", always in a parenthesis of sighs. Doddy herself said "us blackfellas" and "them whitefellas", so that was how Miriam called them.

Doddy came most mornings to help Mother. If it was washing day, Doddy would rub the linen on the wooden washboard or bash it with the copper stick as it bubbled over the fire in the wash-house. She and mother would take turns at the mangle, feeding the linen through the rollers or straining at the handle. Mother said Doddy did not understand about starch so Mother herself made up the bluish mixture and separated the clothing into batches for Doddy to dip. Together they hung it on the line which was propped across the yard on forked gum saplings. On baking days Doddy thumped the dough and when it had risen in basins before the kitchen fire she thumped it again and divided it into lumps, to prove the second time. She was allowed to take a loaf back to her camp in the afternoon. She turned the handle of the churn when Mother made butter and dug in the vegetable garden. On days when the wind from the lake blew the dust away from the house, she swept the rugs with a millet broom on the verandah.

Doddy said very little, but sometimes, while rhythmically turning or thumping, sweeping or hoeing, she sang. Mother often stopped what she was doing to listen to the alternate droning and keening sounds that Doddy made as she worked. "I love to hear her sing," Mother once explained. "It reminds me of the songs the fishermen used to sing at home. They led a poor, harsh life too, and they sang like that. It reminds me of gulls crying out against the wild sea."

Mother said Doddy's name was really Dorothy but Doddy could not say that. Miriam thought it strange to have a name you could not say. (But then she herself had never managed the tight vowel in Glück".) Later, when she visited Doddy's home, she heard the other women call her by a name Miriam could not catch. It was long and full of cooing sounds which seemed to spill over one another. Doddy looked very old because her face was deeply lined and her hair was almost white, but she had a daughter a bit bigger than Miriam called Bess, or sometimes Bess-Bess, but those were not her names either.

Bess came with Doddy some mornings from their camp on the lake, a mile or more to the north of the mill. When she was very small she hid behind her mother while Doddy worked, peering with one dark eye at Miriam who peered back from behind Kathleen. Sometimes the little girls were each given a piece of dough to play with and they would sit on the verandah or at the kitchen table and mould the dough into stories. But neither understood what the other chanted and the stories never mingled. In time they broke free of their mothers and played in the dust below the verandah. They drew their stories then, and built tracks and fortifications which were unsatisfactory in the dry earth. The mud by the lake was better, when they ventured so far, and here Bess was happiest. She would point and exclaim at minnows or crabs or worms and Miriam knew Bess was trying to teach her. Bess had a little woven grass bag tied around her middle and sometimes put into it the creatures she drew out of the mud. Miriam understood that these were good to eat and so took some home to Mother, who threw them to the hens. They made short work of worms and crabs but were not interested in the waterlily roots, which were left to rot on the scratched earth of the fowlyard.

Gradually the little girls wove a light web of language between them but Miriam, remembering, did not think anything important depended on it. What they shared was a transitory freedom in the shallows of the lake, among the mangroves at its fringe or the casuarinas, native figs and tea-tree thickets of its margin. Here they played Hide and Seek, but Bess could walk in the bush without a leaf stirring and she laughed at Miriam's noise. She could climb a tall tree like a lizard and disappear, brown against the bark. In the lake they were more equal because Miriam could swim (Edward had taught her) and they splashed and dived, stalking one another underwater and bursting to the surface in explosions of laughter. The laughter sprang not from wit or even amusement but from pure pleasure. She had shared it with Edward and then with Bess but never, since, with anyone else. Her own children might have provoked it but by then she had become grave and could only watch, amused, as Isobel or Otto romped with them.

Miriam could no longer remember the occasion of her first visit to Doddy's camp. Had she been older at the time, the difference between Doddy's way of living and her own might have been remarkable enough to stay in her memory. As it was, she remembered only her secretiveness about the visits. She must have known from the beginning that her parents would not have approved.

Mother sewed dresses for Doddy – payment, along with flour, tea, bread and tobacco, for her work. Miriam remembered her shock when she first saw Doddy strip off her dress when she came home and fling it into the back of her humpy. She had seen Doddy naked before at her camp so it was not that; it was the relief of taking it off, so evident in Doddy's gesture, that shocked.

Miriam did not know how many people lived at Doddy's camp. There seemed to be more women than men. Doddy's husband was called Charlie, though not by Doddy, and he wore a half-moon of pewter on his breast, tied around his neck by a cord. He was the only man in the camp with such a decoration and Miriam understood this made him important. If Pa wanted to talk to the niggers he summoned Charlie. Charlie was old, with white hair and beard. He sat, when in the camp, in front of his humpy and stared into the distance, chewing meditatively on gum from the trees. Beside him lay his hunting weapons, a bundle of spears and boomerangs loosely tied together. His wives sat in a circle nearby and ground seeds, skinned game, wove grass baskets or threaded bright berries on string made from their own hair. They seemed always busy though they never bustled in the way Miriam's mother did and they gossiped or sang as they worked.

The children worked, too, but they made games of the tasks. They dived for lily roots, collected the berries their mothers were stringing, dug for mangrove worms or grubs in the bark of trees. Bess was the oldest of the girl children and she sometimes joined the women. Miriam would then sit with her for a little while, hearing the gossip, basking in the circle of acceptance. They would give her something to do and show her how to thread the berries or roll the hair against her thigh to make a rope of it. Sometimes, she knew, the talk was about her or about Doddy's work in Mother's house. Then the woman sitting nearest would gently stroke her arm with a fluid hand. Their hands fascinated Miriam. They were so nimble and soft, the nails startlingly pink against the black skin. When they laughed, hands would fly to mouths, covering the flash of white teeth, fluttering there till the laughter had passed. Doddy would sometimes interpret for Miriam.

"Me wash'm, wash'm, wash'm," this accompanied by strenuous rubbings at an imaginary washboard. "All fall down in dirt. Me wash'm, wash'm all *agin*!" The group was overtaken by another spasm of merriment at this retelling of Doddy's plight and Miriam understood that it was the pointlessness of it all that made them laugh. She joined in because she was at an age when much adult preoccupation seemed irksomely pointless. It was delicious freedom to see it as funny. Later her laughter would seem like a betrayal of standards.

Once, remembering Miss Spender's history lesson, Miriam asked Doddy if she knew about the Lord Jesus. Doddy was silent and serious for a moment, then she crawled into her humpy and returned with a picture, brightly coloured, of Jesus with the children. Long blond hair fell around his face and his beard was blond. He held out pale hands to the children at his knees and his eyes were sad. Most of the children were also blond, their blue eyes lifted in childish wonder to his face. The artist had included one dark child on the sidelines of the scene and Doddy's pink fingernail indicated this one.

"Him love us," she said. "Him no like whitefella kill us blackfellas."

She looked to the other women for confirmation, repeating what she had said in her own language. A murmur rippled through the group and the picture was taken from her and passed around. One woman began a keening song which the others took up and they wept and tore at their hair as they sang. The women were so transfigured by their mourning that Miriam could no longer look at them. She crawled backwards out of the circle and ran home, feeling for the first time the keen edge of her difference from them. They were oblivious of her going.

Miriam knew that whitefellas killed blackfellas; she had heard Pa speak of it when other men asked him the extent of the native problem at the lake. In an offhand way Pa would explain that the previous owner of the timber lease had been driven off it by marauding niggers who had stolen his stores and killed two timber-fellers in the forest.

"The native troopers went through these parts after that and put the fear of God into the niggers," Pa would say. "There weren't too many left when I took over. They regrouped, of course. Persistent beggars. We had a bit of trouble a couple of years later but as soon as I saw what was brewing I shot a couple of young bucks and they've behaved themselves pretty much since. Old Charlie rattles his miserable bundle of spears occasionally to emphasise his displeasure, but I'd say they're finished hereabouts."

It had all seemed so much a matter of course, and so little to do with herself, that Miriam had not thought of it as exceptional, in the way that the timber-feller's body, ripped apart by the great saw, had been. Only now, since she had seen that riven body, only now, in the desperate song of the women, did she recognise the horror. The incident made no difference in the attitude of the women to Miriam when next she went with Doddy and Bess to the camp. But Miriam felt a barrier growing. She loved Doddy but had learnt that whites brought death to blacks. She had loved Flash Sam's beautiful body and knew that love had fed it to the saw. For black or white, love carried only the gift of death and Miriam would armour herself against it.

When the timber-feller had died, his wife had run to the verandah of their house, summoned from the loggers' camp by one of the men. When she saw her husband's body she became hysterical and flung herself at Pa, screaming and tearing at him with her nails. Though Mother tried to comfort her she had to be restrained by the men from harming Mother as well. Miriam understood from the scene that the woman believed Mother and Pa were responsible for the man's death.

Afterwards Pa said, "Bloody fool had only himself to blame. Shouldn't have been anywhere near the damn saw at the time. Now I'm supposed to make good with a month's wages for that woman!"

"Just the same," her mother returned, "you can't turn the poor thing away with nothing and there's no work for her here, feeling as she does!"

There was an argument between them which ended with Pa calling the bereaved woman a grasping whore and Mother a snivelling fool. Miriam was afraid of her father's contempt and she saw that to pity or to be pitiable was to invite it. But she knew that Flash Sam had not been careless with the saw at the time.

It was early in the morning and the men were setting up the mill for the day. There was no log on the bench but they had stoked the stationary engine and were running the monstrous blade. Miriam, escaping notice because Mr Bell was not at the mill, had run into the yard and made the top of the pile of sawdust in three bounds. She could see Flash Sam standing by the whizzing belt. It went so fast she could not really see it, even though it was thick leather and wide as her arm from wrist to elbow. She slid on her bottom down the side of the hill nearest the saw. It was great fun even though the sharp dust prickled. She ran round the heap and up again to the top shouting, "Hey! Flash Sam! Look at me!"

Flash Sam turned, startled. He stumbled and fell on to the belt. The great saw spat blood.

No-one but Flash Sam knew Miriam was there and no-one but Miriam knew how much she loved Flash Sam. By the time the leading hand had thrown the clutch lever Miriam was out of the mill yard, waiting to see Flash Sam get up. By the time they had him on their shoulders at the house, Miriam was on the verandah waiting for Mother to come and mend Flash Sam. And then the woman came, screaming and tearing at Pa. Miriam watched and listened. It was not until she overheard Pa and Mother arguing that she began to scream in her bed on the verandah outside their room. She remembered the screaming now and the medicine they gave her which made the world recede to a pinpoint of pulsing red. When she woke up she had forgotten.

Bess still came to play, and Miriam still went home with them sometimes, joining in the work of gathering and making, laughter and gossip. But she knew, when she saw her hands beside those of the women, that she was a whitefella. And now she knew, as well, the power of remorse to overwhelm the self.

Perhaps she had wanted someone to stop her visits, because she remembered being more careless about concealing them, though she never actually mentioned that she went to the camp. Perhaps her mother already knew and turned a blind eye, knowing that Miriam was lonely and that Doddy would take care of her. Pa certainly did not know but he never noticed Miriam now unless she was in the way.

One Sunday, however, when the mill was idle and the family was resting after the midday meal, Miriam went to see Doddy and Bess. The men were absent from the camp and the women were all in the lake, bathing, fishing or diving for roots. They were pleased to see her and waved to her to join them. It was a hot afternoon and the water was cool and brown under the overhanging trees. The women splashed and laughed so much that all fishing was pretence, but suddenly one of them, standing waist deep further out from the shore than the rest, called in a sharp whisper and held up her hand. Miriam thought she must have seen a fish she wanted but she was staring inshore and her eyes were frightened. Miriam and Bess were together near Doddy who suddenly grabbed them and pulled them down, under the water. She must have issued a warning which Miriam could not grasp because Miriam had no time to breathe in before she went under and she thrashed around, choking, until she could get free of Doddy's grip. When she surfaced most of the women were invisible but, lurching drunkenly in the mud at the edge of the lake, were two of Pa's timber-fellers, each struggling with a woman. Miriam dived again, holding her breath, and now she could see Doddy, dim in the mud-clouded water, clutching Bess with one hand and a mangrove root for anchor with the other.

After a little, Doddy eased her face to the surface, allowing her eyes to rise out of the water, like a crocodile's. Miriam had seen it done and knew her head would be tilted back and she would be looking along her nose. Then Doddy pulled at them both, gently. They, too, poked their faces out of the water, and then their ears. Miriam could hear the cries of the women and the oaths of the men, the branches breaking under their stumbling feet as they forced their way along the narrow track that ran around the lake to the mill and the men's camp. Miriam ran from the water to find her clothes.

"Doddy, I'll go and get Pa!" She panted as they struggled up the bank towards her.

"Old man boss, him know already! Him know!" Doddy was arguing with her but she would not wait to hear.

She ran as fast as she could along the path that, cutting through the bush, bypassed the mill and led to Mr Bell's house and her own.

"Pa, come quickly!" she called at her parents' door. "The men are taking the lady blackfellas! Hurry, please Pa, quick! The timber-fellers are . . ." The door burst open and Pa stood there in his underwear, his face ominous.

"What's the matter with you? You're all wet! Where have you been?"

"At Doddy's camp and the men came, two of them . . ."

"You were at the niggers' camp? Kathleen, get dressed! You, Miriam, wait on the verandah!"

Miriam sat on the verandah steps, knowing that Doddy had been right. She knew, too, what the men had been after because she had once seen a logger heaving above a black woman in the bush by the lake. She remembered his stark, white buttocks and the expressionless face of the woman as she stared up into the trees. She did not know then that he had taken the woman by force from the camp but now she saw that that was the way of things.

Pa beat her with his leather razor strop. He did not do it often, and he never hurt her very badly – though she had seen him thrash Edward – but this time she cried a great deal and for a long time. Mother gave her the medicine to calm her and when she woke on Monday afternoon Doddy had already gone home from work. Miriam never went to the camp again. She would not have gone even if Pa had not forbidden it and Mother had not pleaded. Mother explained that the women did not know any different and the men generally gave them some whisky or a trinket afterwards. Miriam did not want to ask Doddy if that was so.

Bess still came sometimes with Doddy but only when Pa was in Brisbane. Now she helped Doddy with the housework and seldom played with Miriam by the lake. Miriam would polish brass with her at the kitchen table or help her beat the rugs over the verandah rail and it was as though they had gone back to their first days, now years ago, when their stories ran side by side and never mingled.

One day Doddy said, as they were leaving, "Bess getting ready for husband. Him come for'm few day soon." Bess briefly stroked Miriam's arm and then they went home.

Miriam never saw Bess again. Doddy stayed away from work for a time and when the wind was in the north Miriam heard singing from the camp. She would not visit them but felt the pain of exclusion. When Doddy came back she said Bess's husband had come with members of his clan from the hills and had married Bess, taking her away with him after a week of celebrations.

5   Women's Tracks

Kathleen had an easy sisterly relationship with her two bossy elder daughters and Carrie's marriage at seventeen (to a land surveyor named Brian Warrington, from Gympie) opened out the map of womanhood for all three to study. If Sarah, because she was more ambitious than Carrie, was mildly scornful of her sister's rather plodding husband, she was none the less awed by the hurdle of marriage which Carrie had successfully negotiated. And Kathleen, whose married life had begun as early but in much greater privation, was pleased to rehearse and compare her experience. Miriam was not included in these conversations and did not want to appear interested, but womanhood, for which it seemed she was inescapably destined, appeared uncharted to her. And since the wedding itself had introduced her to unimagined adult vagary, piquing her curiosity about the grown-up world in general, she was drawn to eavesdrop.

Because Quakers did not have formal religious services, Kathleen's marriage to Joshua had been celebrated by the Presbyterian minister in Brisbane, that being the sparsest ceremony Matthew Wemyss could discover. For Carrie, although her husband was a Presbyterian, Josh Wemyss decreed something richer, more in keeping with the family's position. Carrie was married in the Church of England in Gympie. Grandfather Wemyss attended but remained seated throughout, head bowed in entirely silent prayer. This solitary act of resistance provoked nervousness in his son and admiration in Miriam who was bewildered by the unexplained need to kneel or stand at various times. Her mother wept in a way that puzzled Miriam and embarrassed Sarah, whose own tears merely bespangled her smiles.

When the ceremony was over, the wedding party repaired to the best hotel in Gympie for the breakfast but, in deference to Grandfather Wemyss, no alcohol was served. Miriam noticed that many of the men, including her father and elder brother, slipped out to the bar. Edward stood at the connecting door biting his nails. Afterwards Carrie and her new husband, accompanied by Grandfather Wemyss and the guests from Brisbane, departed on the train. Her Uncle James, so dashing earlier, now appeared disordered and had to be helped aboard by his elegant wife, Harriet. When all the guests had gone, Edward drove the jingle the thirty miles home, Pa and Joshua lolling on their horses at the rear.

They next saw Carrie when Mother, Sarah and Miriam visited her house in the busy, rather ramshackle mining town. The land surveyor's office with its gilt sign fronted directly on to Mary Street, Gympie's main thoroughfare, and the house stood at a right angle behind it. The little space between house and street was taken up with a narrow verandah and a tiny yard. The women, heavy-hatted for the occasion, took tea together in the parlour. Soon Miriam was encouraged to go into the yard and watch the colourful commerce of the street. She sat, instead, on the verandah steps from where, through the open window, she heard the women fall to their conversation.

"Ah, my dear," her mother sighed with the pleasure of beginning, "don't you think it wonderful that whereas I set out in a dray from Brisbane on my wedding day, you should ride to Brisbane on yours on a train, and in such style? So much has changed since my day, thank the good Lord."

"I'm sure it must have been much harder for you, Mother." Carrie sounded unwilling to surrender quite all the hardship to Kathleen but her mother was determined that the lot of her daughters had improved.

"To be sure! Just think now. I spent my wedding night in an evil smelling posting house along the way while you were set down so quickly at a fashionable hotel." She sighed again at the thought of so much progress. Carrie was not to be led so quickly into talk of wedding nights but Sarah was eager and prompted, "Was your wedding night very dreadful, Mother?"

"It was a terrible place, that inn. Filthy and dark, with drunken men laughing and brawling half the night. Your Pa was so worried about our stores, all stacked on the dray, that he had to sleep under it. I lay wakeful all night on a greasy mattress in a hole — sure, t'was no less! — off the common room."

"Heavens! I should have been scared out of my wits!" Carrie conceded.

"I should have been furious with my husband if he did that to me!" exclaimed Sarah.

"I was frightened and I cried a great deal, I confess. But I could not have been furious with your Pa, Sarah. He was all I had in the world and my future depended on him. And it was a hard life for him, too, remember. The colony was very rough for most folk then and women had to share the hardship with their men. You'll all be spared that, I'm glad to say, though there'll be trials enough ahead, I daresay."

There was a solemn silence as the women considered the future and then Kathleen laughed, "But it was not all so dreadful, to be honest! Next night we camped out under the stars and oh! that was a different thing. Can you imagine, girls, I'd never really seen the bush before and now here I was, sleeping by a waterfall in the forest with a little fire your Pa had made. That was a lovely place and I'll never forget it. Your Pa was so pleased to be out on his own at last. He capered like a child and dived into the pool, laughing like a jackass. I'd never seen him like that before and I stopped being quite so frightened then." Her voice was tender. There was a small silence and a slight rustle of clothing.

"Brian enjoyed Brisbane, I'm sure," Carrie sounded rather starched. "We went to the theatre, you know, to see a company from Home. It was very entertaining: singing and dancing and a gentleman reciting poetry. The ladies in Brisbane are very grand, Mother. But I wore my blue sateen and Brian said I was the equal of any of them."

"I think I shall marry a very rich man and go Home to London for my wedding tour," said Sarah decidedly.

"Where you will meet him I can't think!" Carrie was defensive.

"Oh, Brian will meet lots of rich and important men in his work and you will introduce them all to me so I may make my choice of them!" Carrie, mollified, laughed with the others. "Now, Mother, you must come and look at my fine kitchen. You should persuade Pa to buy you a stove like mine; it's ever so much easier to manage than yours".

The women withdrew from Miriam's hearing and so she swung on the yard gate, watching the miners and tradespeople in the street. Swarthy men in bright shirts, their trousers tied round with thongs below the knee, called out in languages she did not understand: Italian, perhaps, or Polish; she had heard Pa speak of them. Their voices, like vivid streamers, were tossed across the street to one another. They strode over the muddy potholes and boarded pavements with an assertiveness as though they would encompass the whole world. A Chinese man scurried past, bearing heavy baskets. His sandalled feet, barely leaving the ground between his tiny hurried steps, made furtive scuffling sounds. Miriam watched carefully but could not imitate his walk, although she held out her arms and pretended to be laden. She had been forbidden to go into the street and could not follow him or leap across the puddles to penetrate the mysteries of the store opposite. Soon, Pa came in the jingle to take them home.

It was another three years before Sarah married and in that time Isobel was born, Miss Spender came and went, Bess married, and Pa began negotiations for the sale of the mill.

After Bess left, there followed a jumble of time threaded together in Miriam's memory only by a sense of things winding down. Pa was away a great deal and Mother seemed to be waiting for an end. She did not begin any new work and delayed mending or replacing furniture, curtains, crockery. It was suggested once that Miriam might go to Gympie to school and stay with Carrie; she could help her with Isobel, since there was another baby on the way. Nothing came of it. Miriam neither wanted to go nor resisted the idea and it was allowed to shrivel. Instead Miriam drifted, helping Mother or Doddy in a desultory sort of way, or sitting by the lake, idly picking up shells or stripping leaves to their skeletons without conscious thought — the lack of an apparent future robbing her of the present. Sarah's wedding did nothing to clarify the grey suspension of Miriam's life.

Sarah had met Alfred Borden while staying for a few weeks with Uncle James and Aunt Harriet in Brisbane. He was an accountant whose practice included the book-keeping for Wemyss and Sons. Certainly he was richer than Brian Warrington but seemed no more colourful to Miriam. Though he came to visit the family at the mill, Miriam could not really remember his presence in that landscape. When she tried to visualise him there she found herself remembering her brother Joshua, who had taken charge of Alfred, showing him around.

Joshua, better than usually dressed for the occasion, was tall, thin and sallow of complexion, his well-moulded mouth pulled downwards in an habitual expression of responsibility. Before he spoke he would flick his tongue across his lips as though preparing them to deliver his calculated remarks. For, though his laugh was still harsh, Joshua was no longer loud and garrulous: he was silent and watchful. His eyes darted about in a stealthy, rather predatory way and Miriam thought, even then, that he resembled an eel. She had never loved Joshua but she continued to look to him as though he would one day signal a direction she could follow.

Pa had not been there for Alfred's visit; was hardly ever there in those two last years. Grandfather Wemyss had retired into muttering old age and Pa and Uncle James now ran Wemyss and Sons. But James, according to Pa, was inclined to high living and increasingly trusted his business responsibilities to his son, Oswald. So Pa spent most of his time in Brisbane, leaving Joshua in charge of the timber mill with Edward as his lieutenant. When he came home, though, Pa countermanded Joshua's decisions whenever it suited him; Joshua did not argue but seemed to wait and to watch.

Miriam's impressions of Alfred Borden dated from her visits to Brisbane, where the marriage was to take place. She remembered an affable man, given to the kind of fatuity which children treat with disdain. He had a large high-bridged nose and a short soft moustache which moved in two independent sections when he spoke or laughed. She discovered, by staring at him, that the moustache masked a scar on his upper lip. He had also a nervous tic which made him blink at the end of his sentences so that he always seemed surprised by his own silliness. Miriam did not dislike him but was puzzled that Sarah seemed to think him clever and handsome.

To her mother's relief, Aunt Harriet had taken charge of the wedding arrangements, but still it was necessary for her to go down to Brisbane from time to time. Miriam went with her twice to be fitted for a gown for her role as Sarah's attendant. But the preparations were a blur in Miriam's memory and the wedding itself passed her like a pageant, leaving her with an even more desolate sense of her own aimlessness. It was Bess's wedding, not Sarah's, which had marked the end of Miriam's childhood. Now she stood on the margin of a new land, without a map or compass.

Alfred had not taken Sarah to London for their wedding tour. He had no imagination and the idea of London held no romantic attraction for him. "Home" was an institution, revered in his philosophy, not a place of pilgrimage. His opinion and his devotion to work had proved unexpectedly stubborn, so that the couple went instead for a month to Toowoomba, to a smart guesthouse. When they returned to their new house in Brisbane, Sarah set about furnishing and fashioning a life in society.

Some time after the wedding (how long Miriam could not remember), Pa announced he had found a buyer for the timber mill and was looking for a house for them in Brisbane. It was time, he said, for Kathleen to have an easier life.

Mother did not demur, but later said wistfully to Miriam, "It will be better for you in Brisbane, lovie. You shall have some schooling and there will be outings and parties and young gentlemen for you to meet. Life will begin for you there."

Of the children, only Joshua seized his opportunity in the move to Brisbane. Everyone had expected him to join the family business there but, when Pa mentioned positions for both his sons, Joshua announced that he would like to get some independent business experience. It might be useful to Wemyss and Sons later, he said, careful not to offend Pa, if he were to learn something about finance and investment. Perhaps Pa was pleased not to have his elder son barking at his heels, especially since he had not long ago persuaded his own father into retirement. He agreed to look for a place for Joshua with the Queensland National Bank in which he was a shareholder.

It was ironic, Miriam thought, that it should have been Edward who continued with Wemyss and Sons. After Pa had driven her and Edward apart they had continued to share an adulation of Joshua, watching him from their different perspectives and straining to emulate him. Edward had succeeded where she could not, and had been inducted into the circle where Joshua shone. But when Joshua stepped aside, claiming his own authority and choosing his own direction, Edward could not follow. He had no impetus of his own. It was as though Joshua took Edward's power with him. Edward had received the mantle of son-in-the-firm and had no choice but to continue to work under his father, losing ground constantly to his more daring cousin, Oswald. Even on the day of Joshua's decision to leave his father's employ, Edward had blanched, as though he feared the role he was inheriting. Miriam saw it and admired Joshua, but for Edward she felt a creeping contempt.

The listless days quickened now, with packing and preparation for the move. Pa took Mother to Brisbane to see the house he had bought; when she came back she seemed resigned and spent the last week going about patting or stroking things, murmuring under her breath. Miriam also took farewells of special places and stood for a long time on the heap of sawdust, staring at the great saw. But she felt as though she had in some way already left Cootharaba and could never return. Only when Doddy came to say goodbye did Miriam clutch, for an instant, at the present.

6 Let Us Now Praise Famous Men

The morning had established itself while Miriam Gluck sat at her kitchen table and now the sounds of commerce on the river intruded on the past. Her sciatica was sharp as she got up. Sitting aggravated it, whereas walking, she believed, was beneficial. She went to a window which overlooked the river and the Botanic Gardens on its farther shore. Beyond the massed greens of the Gardens, the slates and pink stone of the city shone in the sunlight. Below and to her left, the factories and wharves flanking Stanley Street stretched out to the Victoria Bridge and beyond. Among them, three-quarters of a mile's walk away, at most, but much closer as the crow flies, was the flour mill her family had built, its squat silos and brick chimney just visible amid the clutter of sheds and warehouses.

She would walk now. Not far, probably: just around the block and down to the river, where grass and trees reclaimed the bank. She seldom walked further than that these days and it was years since she had visited Wemyss and Sons. But today she felt unbound. Isobel would be away until evening and there was no-one to remind her she had had no breakfast, to insist she should be home for an early lunch, or to urge an umbrella against the sun. She attributed her sense of freedom to Isobel's absence.

She had not liked Brisbane when they first moved there. Although it was further south, the atmosphere seemed stifling. The afternoon breezes which had ruffled Lake Cootharaba, rattling the jalousies and lifting the curtains in their house, did not often reach so far into the Brisbane Valley. The river was close to their new house but it was usually a sluggish creature, its skin often slicked with oil. Flooding, it tossed dead animals in its brown rage: carcasses of cows, horses, dogs and sheep in frenzied imitation of life. The parks and gardens of the city were demure and she remembered longing for a patch of wilderness to hide herself.

The house her father had bought still stood at the top of the hill, behind the flats in which she had lived these past two years, and she usually passed its formal gardens on her daily walks. It was built of brick, and Miriam had always thought it a stiff place. With its two storeys, it was much larger than their house at the lake, but was not as relaxed or open and she missed the wide verandahs of the earlier home. This one had porches, a terrace at the downstairs doors, and rarely used balconies above; from their height one could see the river, the city and the flour mill — and she supposed that was why Pa had bought it. Certainly its height and commanding view had been some compensation to Miriam for the constraint and displacement that the house, and the move into Brisbane society, had imposed. And perhaps that was why, two years ago, she had chosen the same location to live: fifty-two years on, she had again needed air and a vantage point.

She was just thirteen when they moved from Lake Cootharaba and her mother said it was high time she had some smoothing out. Sarah was harsher: Miriam heard her say she needed making over. But the teas, luncheons and evening parties to introduce them to Brisbane society had a curious effect on Miriam. She felt at once painfully obvious and yet invisible. She was awkward and gauche, she knew, lacking conversation and animation. The faces of people who tried to engage her took on a patient, rather pitying expression and soon looked over her shoulder for a reason to move on. She was glad when they did. Her own tentative reality fled from her and the diffident, graceless creature substituting for it embarrassed her. Her mother, too, was uncomfortable. Miriam watched her hide behind a camouflage of chatter which, because she could not share it, irritated her. Only Sarah seemed at ease. Brisbane, marriage, a smart house and a circle of well-placed friends gave her poise. She bossed her mother into buying suitable clothes and furniture and, since her father now expected his wife to entertain colleagues at home, her mother depended on Sarah's advice.

For Miriam, Sarah proposed Miss Habgood's School for Young Ladies. The schoolhouse had long since become a nursing home and Miriam could not remember much about her time there. Miss Habgood was the sister of an archdeacon. She had come from England with her brother, kept house for him until his death, and saw the polishing of raw colonial girls as a continuation of his missionary vision. She complimented Miriam on her reading and writing, skills which four of the six young women enrolled with Miriam barely possessed. Most, however, were better endowed with the equally important gifts of deportment, etiquette, music, dancing and drawing. Miriam applied herself to these arts for survival's sake and, though she never shone at the piano or learnt to draw, she developed, in three years, what Miss Habgood called dignity.

The shooting pain of sciatica halted Miriam in front of her old home. She leant on her stick and looked across the valley which had encompassed so much of her youth. In the distance was the South Brisbane Town Hall where, ten years after moving here, Pa had been invested as Mayor. Before her, the hill fell steeply away to Miss Habgood's schoolhouse at the bottom. Miriam sighed, remembering the ease with which she had run up and down it as a girl.

Resting, Miriam watched a young woman pushing a cream cane perambulator up the hill towards her, imagining what the woman saw as she approached: an elderly lady dressed in a grey silk blouse, long black jacket and skirt to just above her ankles, good lisle stockings and sensible low-heeled black-laced shoes, three loops of jet beads, black brimmed hat with veil, grey suede gloves with jet-embroidered decoration, stick, straight back, stiff smile, stiff inclination of the head in acknowledgment of her "Good morning". Yet, she thought, if this woman should ask, "Are you quite well?" because she sees me resting here on my stick, I should like to say, "No. I am in pain and not just from sciatica." But, though the urge to break silence was strong, she did not know what she wanted from the stranger. The young woman raised her eyes briefly in passing but did not speak. Miriam, shaking off the fantasy, resumed her walk.

She had made a friend at school. Hetty Percival had lived on the opposite hill, in a house with big grounds. Her brother, Frank, owned a bicycle which he kept in the garden shed and, with skirts bundled up to prevent them catching in the spokes, Hetty and Miriam loved to take turns riding it along the garden paths until Frank caught them. "Hey, girls!" he would say in a high, aggrieved voice, and whoever was riding at the time would fall off, giggling, into the arms of the other. Indoors, they read popular romances aloud, hooting with derision at the swooning heroines. But Hetty was small, pretty and accomplished at parties and she succumbed to romance at eighteen.

They had remained friends after Hetty married; it was the war which put enmity between them, causing Hetty to renounce their friendship in patriotism's name. After Hetty's husband was killed, healthy vigorous childless Hetty had gone into a decline. Perhaps, if Miriam had visited her then, something might have been re-established between them, since they were both husbandless again. But Miriam had been deeply hurt and would not risk another rebuff. And yet they had been very close as schoolgirls, close enough for Miriam, after swearing Hetty to eternal silence, to confide the knowledge of her father's women.

It was Sarah who had told Kathleen about her husband's philandering, a year or so after they came to Brisbane, but she implied that Aunt Harriet had prompted her. "You ought to know," she said. "We feel it isn't right you should go on in ignorance." She was standing by the fireplace and speaking loudly, as though to shore up her right to speak at all. Kathleen was seated and did not move or turn her head when Miriam, unexpected, came in.

Sarah attempted to change the subject but Kathleen said, "And did you think I could still be in ignorance, after all these years? Did you think I needed you to tell me, you foolish girl? There's no cause for you to hush me because of Miriam. Like as not she knows already and if she doesn't she might as well, since it seems to have been a talking point elsewhere. Your father," she turned her head now, "has for some years been bedding the whores of Brisbane." Sarah gasped at Kathleen's crudeness but her mother ignored her and continued to speak to Miriam. "Your sister and Harriet are alarmed because now he has taken up with a woman on a regular basis. Socially, it seems, that is more shocking. It is not so shocking to me," she turned again to Sarah, "whatever you and Harriet may think. The hurt to me was done long ago." She got up. "I'll be glad if you'll not talk of it to me again." And she went out of the room. Sarah was confused and embarrassed before Miriam's obvious shock, and soon left. Kathleen did not advert to the matter again but, from then on, she began attending Mass again, though while her husband lived she would be denied Communion. To Miriam she seemed suddenly stronger and less pliant, though her outward relationship with Josh remained unchanged.

There had been some cruelty, Miriam thought, in Sarah's revelation. Her own status as worldly daughter was enhanced in the telling, at the expense of Kathleen's private grief. Moreover, Miriam was not sure that Sarah absolutely disapproved of their father's behaviour; it seemed to go naturally with his importance, and that was a thing Sarah valued. Kathleen must know so that she would make the right social responses and not awkward, ignorant ones at which others might snigger. Miriam wanted reassurance that the thing was awful in itself, not merely a public embarrassment, and so she told Hetty. It was the sort of secret she had to tell someone and Hetty, she knew, would thrill with the same horror she felt.

"Oh, my dear! How dreadful! Your poor mother, how can she live with such a thing?" Hetty had shed real tears, and Kathleen afterwards took on heroic proportions for her. Miriam was gratified by Hetty's reaction but did not know whether to admire her mother or to pity her.

Kathleen's equanimity had coped with all the hardship of being a pioneer at Lake Cootharaba. She had borne her children alone or with the help of crude midwifery and had been nurse and teacher to children, blacks and timber-fellers. She had endured with dignity the humiliation and pain of her husband's unfaithfulness. But when Josh announced that he was to be the mayor of South Brisbane she had wept before all the family because of her inadequacy to be the mayoress. Josh was impatient with her. It had not occurred to him that anything more would be demanded of her in the role, so far had she slipped from the forefront of his life.

On the day of his investiture, in 1896, Kathleen had had to sit with Josh on the platform, surrounded by dignitaries and their wives. The Town Hall was hot under the new electric lights and Kathleen's face was red.

"She should never have worn that colour," Sarah murmured. "It heightens her complexion." But Kathleen had worn lettuce-green silk because the shade had suited the auburn tints of her youth. Now she looked hot and uncomfortable, unsure of where to fix her gaze, while a beefy man of some importance made a speech about her husband.

Josh, his legs crossed and body turned sideways to the speaker, stared modestly at the polished toe of his boot while a small, gratified smile flickered on his lips.

The speaker began by describing the lofty and civilising values of Matthew Wemyss, a pioneer of South Brisbane industry, who had died a year or so before: ". . . called out of England by the challenge of the Reverend Mr Dunmore Lang to build a great nation in this new land. . . unstinted service to the young colony of Queensland. . . laboured with his sons to build the flour mill and transport business. . . not only provided the bread of this city, but brought that golden harvest to the tables of our kinsmen at Home in England."

"Do you think they are going to make Grandfather Wemyss Mayor?" Miriam whispered to Sarah. But Sarah was basking in importance and frowned, moving her head closer to her husband. Miriam glanced at her uncle, James, across the aisle, who caught her eye and winked.

The speaker came at last to Josh Wemyss who, "after working for twelve long years with his father and brother, branched out on his own, as a young man of spirit must, and bought a timber lease . . . braved the terrible odds ranged against the pioneer — floods, fire, isolation from his own kind and the dreadful depredations of the natives — to win from the land the cedar for which Queensland is so justly famous." Then he painted a picture of the sacrifice Josh had made in leaving his rural retreat (the terrible odds suddenly transformed, Miriam thought, into bucolic bliss) to spend more and more time in the family business and in the service of the Council (to say nothing of the arms of the city's prostitutes). The citation descended abruptly to improved drains, and the electric lighting which Josh had persuaded the Council to introduce (he had put money into Barton and White, producers of the electricity). "This, ladies and gentlemen, is our new mayor, Joshua Wemyss: a true Britisher and a true Queenslander; a man of great energy and dedication in the service of progress; a fine example to our young men and a worthy leader of our community." The men in the audience stood to applaud; the women, smiling indulgently, patted their gloves together.

Her father, Miriam knew, had worked hard to achieve recognition for himself, perhaps to outstrip his own formidable father; but she doubted he ever had any noble ideal of service to the community. It seemed ironic to her that, even in this moment of honour, it was the ideals and faith of Matthew Wemyss which were being celebrated. Energy and determination were common to both men and each had profited, socially and financially, from his work. Perhaps, in the early days of the colony, notions of a civilising, christianising mission, of harvesting souls as well as profit, of creating a new and better world, had been necessary to induce men and women to come and to work. Now, in the space of a generation, the inducements of personal wealth and power had proved sufficient. But they had still to be decently clad in the trappings of idealism, much as the physical evidence of Kathleen's labour, her rough hands and thickened body, had to be disguised under the lettuce-green silk of leisure.

At the reception afterwards, James came to talk to Miriam, capturing a tray of champagne from a waiter on the way. "Your face betrayed an unseemly levity during the proceedings, I thought," he remarked and raised his glass, "To Matthew Wemyss and all he has bequeathed to us." Miriam smiled. His cynicism was refreshing, like honesty. "Harriet and I were saying just now that you are looking distinctly peaky – lovely, of course, but peaky. We think it's time you came to spend a few weeks with us again. Next month, when the weather is cooler. What do you say?" Miriam accepted gratefully.

Harriet and James entertained prodigiously in the cooler months of the year and Miriam was usually invited to stay with them for a while. Miriam had no illusions about her welcome. James was fond of her, perhaps because he had no daughters of his own, and she was useful to Harriet in the preparations, and in making up a dinner party or a table for bridge. Single men abounded in Brisbane society but respectable single women to make up their numbers were hard to come by. In return for her help and presence, Miriam had the benefit of some pleasant company. She was not lively and had very little conversation; no-one expected that of her any longer. But she enjoyed watching the other guests and silently comparing their experience of the world with her own. She did not expect much more, though Harriet and James obviously believed they would one day turn up a husband for her. "No young woman can remain unmarried for long in this town," James would say cheerfully.

Harriet and James had four sons. The youngest, Guy, was a year older than Miriam, and the only one still at home. Miriam thought Guy, at twenty-four, was probably very much as James was at twenty-four. He was handsome and energetic, sought after by young women at dances, and automatically gallant with Miriam whom he otherwise ignored. Neither he nor his father had anything of the calculating ambition that her father and Joshua had inherited, though Guy would marry well, as his father had done.

Harriet was the daughter of a "true merino", a grazier of the Darling Downs, now dead, whose wealth had added to the comfort James and his family enjoyed. James felt no need to assert himself in Wemyss and Sons but was content to let Josh rule there. Oswald, his eldest son, would one day take his place, because he had his father's imagination combined with the shrewd business sense of Matthew Wemyss. The other sons, Henry and Piers, had gone into sugar and mining, respectively. Guy felt no urgent need of occupation and was "looking about him". Harriet was sure that some future father-in-law would provide a niche for her favourite child. In the meantime, his energies were absorbed by horses, cricket and society.

Miriam found Guy's punctilious charm towards herself depressing. It had in it elements of pity, she thought, and it emphasised her spinsterly role in his family. James was less offensive in his frank concern for her matrimonial prospects, and Harriet's contract with her was businesslike. Only Guy drove her to contemplate her future, or her image in the mirror, with near despair.

Though she was not in any sense pretty, Miriam knew it was not her looks which were at fault. She was comparatively tall and finely built – willowy, Carrie had once said. Her hands, feet and ankles were shapely, and her neck long. She had level, well defined eyebrows and her eyelids were heavy, with straight lashes which drooped slightly over grey, direct eyes, modifying what might have been a challenging gaze. Her nose was too large but was well moulded and her nostrils were soft, indicating sensitivity. She had a long upper lip and her mouth ran exactly parallel to her eyebrows. It was sharply drawn, inclined to be firm or tight. She did not smile readily, even in those days, and her narrow teeth were rarely exposed. She had inherited Kathleen's pale skin and auburn tints, but had so far been spared the broken veins and dark blotches the sun had wrought on her mother. Her whole face was rather narrow and her cheekbones were high, often touched with round, bright patches of colour like those on a Russian doll. They gave her an appearance of repressed intensity, even of passion, which was at variance with her general reserve.

Miriam had watched many less pretty girls capture the attention of men, and knew it was a matter of technique, of deliberate coquetry and cultivated animation. They laid themselves out for admiration and, in return, they offered rapt attention to the men who, however fleetingly, responded to their attractions. Miriam saw them as beggars, pleading for notice, love and the guarantee of a future. At first she felt physically unable to be like them, prevented by her lack of schooling in the social arts. But even as she was being initiated into the rituals of courtship, she held back from what increasingly seemed a demeaning role, pitiable and therefore contemptible. Her natural reserve began to appear as an assumption of superiority, but it protected against pity or contempt.

Miriam would not beg for the attention of men and she would not behave as if she had no future other than marriage. Guy's charitable courtesies implied disbelief in any satisfactory alternative and filled her with self-doubt. Being immured to an interminable old age with her mother and father, and probably Edward, was hard to contemplate. She could not expect to be a welcome extra at dinner parties past a certain age and she had no real occupation of her own. She scorned charitable works because she detested charity towards herself and, since she had no need of an income, she was not inclined to look for employment. In any case, there was nothing she was equipped to do besides shepherding young children, for whom she had no particular liking, or accompanying old ladies, and she had one of those at home. She knew of women who had set up enterprises of their own – shops, schools, even hotels – but her father would never agree to that. It was not suitable to his social position for his daughter to go into business. Miriam knew, besides, that by nature she was a passive observer rather than an active participant in the affairs of the world.

Miriam had walked down the hill and was now outside the house which had been Miss Habgood's school. Its gardens had been curtailed by a widening and straightening of the road. It, and the surrounding district, had come down in the world since Miriam's days there and the school was now a nursing home for geriatric patients. On the grass verge outside was a bus-stop and a seat. Miriam sat down, stretching her painful leg out before her. Most of the verandah of her old school had been enclosed with weatherboards and casement windows. At the top of the steps, a section had been left open and men in flannel pyjamas and plaid dressing-gowns were waiting in cane chairs for visitors, or death. She thought, I am fortunate to have a home of my own to wait in and a less impersonal nurse to keep me company, but I am really no different from these men. She wondered whether any of them desperately wanted to come down the steps to the bus seat and seize her arm, insisting that she, that someone, hear his story before he died. They would come and get him if he did, she thought, and I would pull my arm from his grasp, fearing he was mad. I would get up hastily, making excuses, and leave him here, talking to himself — as I am doing now.

There had been only one occasion, before Otto, when Miriam's reserve had been breached by a man. She was eighteen, the age when everyone expected her to make an effort to be attractive and secure a husband. Perhaps because of the sense, like electrical activity in the atmosphere, of everyone waiting expectantly for her to make her play, she had allowed a young British naval officer to release her. He was related in some way to Admiral Lord Wemyss, of the aristocratic branch of the family from which the Society of Friends had separated her forebears. He was visiting Brisbane with his ship and someone, she had forgotten whom, had invited him to a dance which she was attending. They had been introduced particularly, because of the relationship, and they had had an immediate topic of conversation.

He danced with her while they talked, but his dancing was so sublime she lost track of what they were saying. Her feet bore no weight, which was all caught up in his arm. She had no need to think of the steps; he had them without thought and swept her effortlessly through them. Dancing with him was a transcendence she had never experienced. Her whole being was suffused with delight and no longer knew its boundaries. When he left her to dance with his hostess she remained suspended in bliss until he should return. When she saw their hostess introducing him to another woman with whom, she could see, he felt obliged to dance, her elation was unperturbed. But at supper time he had still not come back to her. She could see his head inclined towards another woman as though she were the only one in the room, just as Miriam, when he danced with her, had felt herself to be. He returned for the last dance of the evening and devoted the same exclusive attention to her, but by then her joy had seeped away, leaving her boundaries rigid again and only emptiness within.

Her grief over him was so acute that Miriam sealed herself up against any similar experience. Sarah, who had been with her at the dance, said in the carriage which afterwards took them to their homes, "My goodness, Miriam, you are withdrawn. I do believe that young officer has quite won you."

It was a conventionally teasing ploy to provoke laughter or weeping according to the strength of the charge, but Miriam, her voice frosted with warning, said, "Sarah, you risk becoming vulgar," and so protected herself from any comfort as well.

That was her only experience of young love's gratuitous power to transfigure the self. When she met Otto, five years later, there had been, in her older self and in the emotion he aroused, an element of control, of intent, which was entirely absent from that youthful experience.

Miriam could recall the young naval officer's face quite clearly this morning. She knew that she had a much more detailed memory of Otto but it would not come. All morning, she had vainly striven for the sound of his voice or the smell of his hair at their last parting. Now, sitting on the bus seat outside the place where she had been schooled to womanhood, she suddenly felt she need only turn round to see him walking down the hill towards her, his panama hat tipped a little back on his head and a flower in his lapel. Her heart trembled so violently that, for a moment, she feared an attack.

"I will go and sit by the river where it will be cooler," she said aloud and, without turning, she took up her stick and walked away from him. But Otto had entered and would not be denied.

7 A Travelling Salesman

The wooden bench she sat on snagged the voile of her dress. The river ran, low and brown, at the lip of the grassy space under the native fig. Spring airs eddied about her, bearing the scent of jasmine. Her face was averted from him but she could smell him, too, on the breeze; a rich, leathery smell of sweat and pomade. Her body, stiff and upright on the edge of the bench, trembled. He did not touch her but said, "Miriam?" and not, "Miss Wemyss."

"Yes, Otto." She turned her head. He was not kneeling in the exaggerated way she had feared but sat sideways on the bench, one knee bent so that the cloth of his trousers strained against his thigh. His face was shining because he had recognised assent in her voice, but his lips were white with the effort of control.

"Will you be my wife?"

"Yes, Otto." She knew her answer well, having considered the question carefully for some months. She had thought the energy which drove him was like her father's; she likened his urbanity to that of her uncle James and she recognised in his gentleness and sensitivity the qualities she had loved in her brother Edward. Because of these similarities, and his maturity and prosperity, she thought him an appropriate choice. Only dimly did she perceive the attraction of his difference, his foreignness, as a German and an outsider to their society. But she saw that his energy was not devoted solely to business; it burned in his eyes and flowed through his every gesture. His urbanity was not cynical worldliness but charm, studied and cultivated as a woman's, such as she had never seen among the men of the colony. His sensitivity had not been corrupted to weakness and he had no shame in it. Now his eyes, so intensely blue, were flooded with tears of relief and joy which he had no need to hide.

"It was *because* you were an outsider that I loved you," said Miriam Gluck. The dead air pressed down on her, laden with the rotting smell of the river. "You were not pitiable, then. You stood against their notions of acceptability and, for a while, you triumphed."

"I love you, Miriam," Otto said. She simply smiled, because to say, "I love you, too," seemed trite. He took her hand and they sat by the river in silence.

The river was as slow and brown now as it had been forty-two springs ago. Whether in flood or drought, passive or turbulent, through change of course and passage of time, Miriam thought, it remains the same river. She felt a warmth of kinship towards it. Whether I am Miriam Wemyss or Miriam Gluck; wife, widow or mother; Britisher, Australian or alien; lover or repudiator of niggers and Huns, I, too, must answer to the one identity.

Miriam first met Otto Gluck in the early autumn of 1898, at a dinner party given by James and Harriet. It was not the first time James had invited a man whom he thought she might take to, but in Otto, from the moment he entered the room, she sensed a possibility — not of love, but a kind of recognition. She spoke very little to him during the evening but she listened and watched.

"Have you had the opportunity of seeing very much of our countryside here in Queensland, Herr Gluck?" Harriet asked him.

"Oh please, Mrs Wemyss, you must not give me a German title. I am simply Otto Gluck but, if I must have an honorific, let it be plain English 'Mister'". His speech was correct and without a marked accent; only his inflection was foreign. "But, to answer you, indeed I have been fortunate in seeing a great deal of this wonderful land. I came to Australia eleven years ago, you see, though I have spent some time since then in New Zealand."

"And does your work allow you to travel?" Miriam was surprised that Harriet knew so little about him and wondered if, this time, it was Otto and not she who had been invited to make up the numbers.

"It does not allow, it insists! I am a sort of travelling salesman," he replied gaily, disconcerting the snobbish Harriet. "Actually, I import medical and veterinary supplies from England, from Europe and from the United States of America so, you see, I must travel to buy overseas and also I must travel in Australia to establish my markets."

"Your sales are not restricted to Queensland, then?" Harriet was quizzing him quite unashamedly but he seemed not to mind.

"Most, certainly, are made in Queensland but increasingly we have orders from farther afield and I must supply them if I can. The demand from New South Wales has grown so much that, the day after tomorrow, I am off to Sydney for a month to examine the possibility of establishing a branch office there." A month seemed suddenly long to Miriam.

At dinner she was seated across the table from Otto who was flanked by two matrons. They vied for his attention throughout dinner. Guy, on her left, was preoccupied by a beautiful young woman whose father, on Miriam's right, was in close conversation with Harriet. Miriam, having no-one to talk to, was glad simply to watch Otto. He was handsome, she thought, and she judged him to be about thirty, though he had a boy's frank enthusiasm and might have been younger. He was a little above her own height, not tall for a man, with small, expressive hands. His hair was dark, almost black, and cut close to a round head. His upper lip was concealed by a thick, curled and waxed moustache. A faint hint of blue-black lay under the skin of his cheek but his complexion was otherwise pale. His forehead was high, his eyebrows long and fine, and his brilliant blue eyes were well spaced. Physically, he seemed better defined than the other men present and she thought him compact and well-made.

At the end of the evening when Otto made his farewells Miriam wished him a good trip to Sydney.

"Thank you, Miss Wemyss, I shall enjoy it, I'm sure. It is a wonderful city to visit, don't you think?"

"I believe so, Mr Gluck, but I have never been there and must rely on the word of others."

"So! When I return I shall add my description to your store." She looked briefly into his eyes and felt that he meant it.

When all the guests had gone, James said, "What did you think of our friend Herr Gluck, Miriam? Entertaining chap, isn't he?"

"Very charming, I should have said," Miriam replied.

"Entertaining and charming, both," said Harriet, "but he is a German, James, and I do wonder. . ." she glanced meaningly at Miriam.

"Rubbish, my dear. If you knew him as I do you would see that Herr Gluck is more English than the English."

Otto sent her a note from Sydney: *As I dash about this beautiful city I am making notes for the travelogue I promised you. May I call and give it on my return? I shall be home on 25th of May.* And he gave the address of his office at the Courier Building in Queen Street. Miriam replied that she would be glad to receive him at her home for morning tea on the 27th.

Curious to see the establishment he ran, she delivered the note herself, a few days before he was due to return. Miriam had hoped to be able to walk past a showroom window, leaving the note in a letter box. She was disappointed to find that, though there was a letter box labelled Otto Gluck & Co Ltd, Medical & Veterinary Suppliers, in the foyer, the offices themselves were on the second floor. To personally deliver the note to an employee would signal particular interest; to leave it in the letter box was to deny her curiosity. She hesitated in the foyer. How seriously interested in this man am I? she asked herself, and decided that her interest must depend, in part, on his substance.

The offices of Otto Gluck & Co Ltd had a small show window on to the landing through which, past a display of X-ray equipment, Miriam could see into the establishment itself. The showroom was long and rather narrow but was lit by windows along one side of its length. Glass counters ran down the middle of the room and at the far end were several half-glassed offices. Miriam could see at least four people who appeared to be employees and three well-dressed customers, two men and a woman, who were inspecting the large and gleaming display of appliances and equipment. There was a letter slot in the door so that Miriam might have left her note and gone without being noticed. Instead, she turned the door handle and went in. A woman of about thirty approached her with the discreet manner of those who fit undergarments.

"I should like to leave this letter for Mr Gluck," Miriam said. Outside, she watched through the window to see in which office the woman would leave the letter. Except that it was in the corner with windows overlooking Queen Street, Otto's appeared to be no grander than the others.

Miriam left the building with an elated sense of her own power. She could not remember another occasion on which she had so clearly chosen for herself or acted so decisively. Since the evening of their meeting she had not discussed Otto with anyone. To do so, she felt, might raise the prospect of a match before she was committed to it in her own mind. It might also aggravate her warm feeling towards him which she was determined to keep at bay, for she would not fall, unwittingly, into a pitiable state of love. Instead she had gone over her memory of him and had not found anything to dislike; she had visited his offices and was pleased with their appearance of well-ordered and prospering activity. She had gone further than she had intended in signalling her interest but as a result she felt stronger, more in command of her life. Now she was ready for what would follow: his visit, his introduction to her mother and the opportunity for her own closer scrutiny.

In retrospect it seemed to Miriam that all this careful calculation and detachment was merely a pathetic defence against the assault she must have known he would make on her senses. He came on foot that Wednesday morning and Miriam saw him from her window, striding up the hill towards the gate, swinging his cane as he went. He wore a straw hat tilted slightly back on his head and an English marigold in the lapel of his blazer. He looked vibrant and entirely self-confident.

"Here I have been, in Sydney," he explained to Kathleen, over tea, "marvelling at its beauty. How fabulous! How wonderful! Now that I am home again in Brisbane on such a bright autumn morning, I wonder to myself what all the fuss is about. Because Brisbane also is wonderful. The truth, Mrs Wemyss, is that we live in a glorious country. But I promised Miss Wemyss that I would make her a travelogue of Sydney to put in her mental library because, she tells me, she has not been there and that, certainly, is a grave misfortune."

Miriam could see that her mother was completely spellbound. He had been yachting: Kathleen's head inclined with him as he demonstrated the way the boat heeled over in the breeze. He had walked in the bush around the harbour: her eyes peered into the distance as he pointed through the trees to the city buildings on the other shore. When he described his visit to the theatre she clasped her hands before her in a characteristic gesture of enthralment. "Oh, Mr Gluck, you have quite made me believe I was there! What powers of expression he has, Miriam."

Miriam agreed. "Did you learn English at school, Mr Gluck?"

"A few words, only." He laughed, "You will not believe me when I tell you that the great Charles Dickens taught me my English?" They willingly disbelieved. "It is true! During my voyage to Australia I had with me a copy of *David Copperfield* and a dictionary so, for all the long weeks at sea, I was a student of Dickens. Of course, I pestered the other English-speakers on board, as well, and they were very kind to correct me, but if my English is good it is Mr Dickens who must have the credit."

He is larger than life, thought Miriam. His voice and his gestures fill the room.

He did not stay a moment longer than was proper and, throughout the visit, Kathleen had been the focus of his charm.

"I'm sure I have never been so entertained, Mr Gluck," she said. "I do hope you will visit us again."

"I should be delighted, Mrs Wemyss."

"Then perhaps you would come to a small party for my birthday next month. On the 28th?" Miriam's voice shook a little.

"I shall come indeed. My own birthday is tomorrow, also the 28th. I had planned to mark it with a solitary dinner and half a bottle of good wine, but now I shall save up my celebration to share it with you."

In the weeks that followed, he sent flowers with his note of thanks and then a photograph of himself and another man on a pier in Sydney. The yacht moored behind them was, he said, "the very one which brought me so perilously near to the sparkling waters of Sydney Harbour!" A week before the birthday party he invited Miriam to picnic with him in the Botanic Gardens, collecting her in a hired trap which he drove with carefree skill at such a speed that she was frightened. When he noticed her white knuckles clutching the rail, he was contrite and slowed to a funereal pace. He seemed to have no half-measure in anything.

He had brought with him a hamper of potted meats, cold chicken, bread rolls, fruit, seedcake and wine, with a cloth which he spread on the grass and a rug for her to sit on. No man of her acquaintance had ever before provisioned a picnic. When he had poured the last of the wine he took from his pocket a parcel wrapped in tissue paper and tied with silver silk cord.

"I am sure, on your birthday, you will receive many grand presents and mine will seem insignificant, so I would like to give this to you now." It was a round silver locket, elaborately engraved with her initials and suspended on a fine chain. Inside, a magnifying lens covered an empty frame.

"Perhaps you will have a photograph you would like to put in it," he suggested.

"I should not like to cut the only one I have," she replied and stood up, feeling she had come too close to a declaration. "Let's feed the swans."

The evening party to celebrate her birthday had originally been planned as a family gathering but, after Miriam invited Otto, Kathleen hastily expanded it to make his inclusion less remarkable. When she saw the locket, Kathleen wondered whether this camouflage had been necessary, but was hesitant in asking whether her daughter had entered into something more than a casual friendship. Miriam cut across her, "I think, if he were to ask to marry me, I should accept him, Mother. But I'd rather you kept that to yourself for the time being."

Carrie and her husband, Brian, had come from Gympie for a few days. James and Harriet, Sarah and Alfred, Joshua and his wife Lucy, came late in the afternoon, and the family shared an early dinner before the other guests arrived. Despite the season, the night was mild and after dinner the men, except James who liked the company of women, went on to the terrace to smoke, leaving open the french doors to the drawing-room. Otto was the first guest to arrive and was shown into the room where the women and James were gathered. Kathleen introduced him first to Carrie as "our new friend, Mr Gluck".

"Miss Wemyss has spoken to me of you, Mrs Warrington," he said, "because I go often to Gympie for my work." Miriam, who was standing near the french windows, heard her brother Joshua say, "Who's the foreigner?"

"No idea," her father replied, "but I suppose we'd better go in and find out." A crawling sensation puckered Miriam's skin.

Otto's manner was more subdued that evening than previously. Kathleen seemed intent on urging him to perform and was, perhaps, disappointed that he did not live up to her introduction of him as the most entertaining of men. Miriam, however, was grateful that, though he continued to charm the women, he did not dominate the room; nor did he attempt to monopolise her own company but circulated among the knots of family and friends, picking up conversations with ease. Her friend, Hetty Percival, now Curthoys, was quick to notice that Miriam watched him with admiration. "What a delightful man Mr Gluck seems to be. Your mother is evidently quite taken with him."

Kathleen was standing beside Otto, rather protectively Miriam thought, as he talked to the two Joshuas, father and son. Miriam could not hear the conversation but saw that her father, who was slightly shorter than Otto, had puffed himself out and was rising and falling on the balls of his feet for emphasis, as he spoke. Young Joshua, taller than either, stood slightly behind his father's shoulder, one hand in his pocket, staring down his nose at Otto with what seemed studied distance.

"Pa and Joshua don't appear to share her enthusiasm," Miriam remarked.

"Oh, men are strange like that," said Hetty, airily. "They need to guard their territory, don't you think?"

Very soon the party separated into two groups: the men congregated together at one end of the room and spilled out on to the terrace, while the women sat around the fireplace where unnecessary embers glowed. James and Otto did not join the other men but remained leaning against the mantelpiece until Joshua called, "James! We need you over here. Come and give us your advice!"

With a show of reluctance, James disengaged himself and the men now disappeared entirely on to the terrace. Their laughter began to grow raucous. If, for a moment, Otto looked wistfully after James, he quickly made himself the centre of the women's attention, regaling them with anecdotes of Paris and Vienna, London and New York. They had never been to such places and were in awe of him. But when he spoke of New Zealand, he allowed them to feel smug, painting a picture of fashions and customs even more parochial than their own. Whether he flattered or teased them, he engaged them absolutely and only the announcement of supper broke his spell.

At supper, he stationed himself next to Miriam and his manner, though not exactly proprietory, claimed the right to be at her side. Her father proposed a toast to her, after which, turning to Otto, she said, "Mr Gluck, I have not forgotten that you are sharing my celebration. Here's to your birthday, as well!" There was a little stir around the table.

"Is it your birthday, too, Mr Gluck?"

"No, no, Mrs Borden! I am an interloper! My birthday was a month ago and I have merely wormed my way into this party for Miss Wemyss on the strength of it! It was a feeble excuse, I'm afraid, but I am so pleased it has worked."

"Oh, Mr Gluck, I would not have taken you for a prevaricator, indeed I would not!" Kathleen was filled with mock outrage. "Your invitation was given before we knew about your birthday and I won't have anyone believe different!"

"Now you have spoiled my story, Ma'am, when I was striving for an effect!"

"And what effect was that, pray?"

"That I would appear the humble supplicant for your blessing which I feel myself to be!" and he looked for a moment directly at Miriam. Kathleen clapped her hands together and laughed with approval.

When the guests began to leave, Hetty and Charles Curthoys offered Otto a lift in their carriage, since their way passed his rooms. Hetty whispered to Miriam, "I'm taking your gentleman friend away with me in a minute. I'll go and say goodnight to your mother." Miriam took advantage of the moment.

"Mrs Curthoys tells me she is about to carry you off. Thank you for coming to my party. I hope you didn't find us too boring a crowd of colonials?"

"I think that I, too, am a colonial, Miss Wemyss, since I have made Queensland my home. But no party of which you are a member could be boring for me, even though the rest were Barbary apes! If you are willing, though, I should like to introduce you to some of my friends, many of whom are ponderous Germans, and then we shall see who is boring!"

Miriam watched him leave with her pretty friend clinging to his arm, following the amiable Charles to the carriage, and felt a pang which was almost jealousy.

Josh had taken Edward and Brian Warrington into his study for a nightcap, leaving Miriam, Carrie and Kathleen to drink tea by the drawing-room fire. Of all her children, Kathleen was most comfortable with Carrie. She most resembled her mother, physically, but had not been compelled by society into smart manners, so that she had about her an openness and ease which was a relief to Kathleen.

"Well, Miriam," Carrie said now, "Mr Gluck was very attentive. Do you plan to marry him?"

Miriam laughed, "He hasn't asked me yet!"

"No sensible girl waits to be asked before she makes up her mind! It wouldn't be fair to the gentleman concerned. It's quite clear to me that he will if you want him to."

"And do you think I should?"

"Since you are now twenty-four, I don't think you can afford to wait forever for the perfect match."

"Now, Carrie!" Kathleen protested. "Surely Mr Gluck is perfect in every way! He has beautiful manners and is so handsome and lively. And James tells me he is very well set up in his own business so that he can afford to marry. What more could Miriam ask?"

"There's no sense in pretending, Mother. He's a German and that will not suit Pa. It won't please the boys or Brian, either, I'm sure."

"Why ever not, Carrie, love? A German is not a heathen or a black!"

"I don't know what it is, Mother, but he is not one of us and I am sure that the men will mind."

"He is different," said Miriam slowly and deliberately, "but since I shall not need anything from Pa, and since I'm old enough to please myself, I don't particularly care if they do mind. Though I should prefer, of course, that they did not."

Carrie reached across and squeezed her hand. "I could see which way the wind was blowing, so I talked to him most particularly. I think him quite wonderful, Miriam, and I hope you will be very happy."

Kathleen dabbed at her eyes with a handkerchief. "I was different, too, being Irish, and Grandfather Wemyss minded. It will not be easy for Mr Gluck if they do mind. But I feel I love him already, Miriam."

8 Principalities and Powers

And the men had minded. Miriam remembered their minding chiefly as an ambient cold contempt, rarely articulated. But the words her father had used to describe Otto pierced her like the murderous whine of the great saw.

On the night of her birthday party, her father sat up late with Edward and Brian. Miriam, lying happily wakeful, heard them leave the study, loud in their goodnights to each other. Next morning, still sleepless, she rose early and went to the balcony. The morning was still dark and the breeze was chill, but she sat wrapped in a rug for an hour, watching the sun light up planes of stone and glass in the town on the other side of the river. She was not so much thinking of Otto as luxuriating in him, feeling the texture of his hand in hers when he said goodnight; the timbre of his voice, lowered in invitation; his burning blue gaze on her face; all felt, rather than consciously remembered.

Then she heard her parents stirring in their bedroom, heard the wardrobe doors and drawers opened and closed as her father dressed, heard her mother's voice greet him sleepily and her father's demand: "Who the devil is that grovelling little foreigner Miriam's taken up with?"

But her ears were deafened to her mother's muffled reply by the anger which shot up in her like flame. Her tongue thrust itself out of her mouth as though she would vomit, and foaming spittle fell from it on to the hands clenched in her lap. Struggling to control her limbs, she stumbled back to her room and buried her face in her pillow, stifling the grunts of rage which seemed torn from her bowels. A shattering pain took her head in its vice. The growing light in the room burnt through her closed lids, searing her brain, but she could not move to shut it out. The sounds of people rising and moving about the house were transmitted through the floorboards in intolerable waves of pain. Finally, her mother came to rouse her and, seeing her condition, brought her some opiate medicine. Then, it seemed the bed began to rock, gradually soothing away the rigidity from her body till the pulsing light in her head was extinguished. When she awoke the devastating anger had burnt low.

In the days that followed Miriam thought it curious that only Edward, who had been gentle and had loved her, made any effort to voice his dislike to her directly. One morning, as she was preparing to go out with Otto, Edward said, "It's a mystery to me, Miriam, why you must go chasing after a foreigner. Aren't there enough marriageable men around without that? . . . if you must get married at all."

She refused the plea in his voice and answered to hurt. "What should I do, Edward? Stay and keep house for you in your old age because *you* do not choose to marry? And Mr Gluck is not a foreigner. He has been in Australia now for eleven years. He contributes his work and his ideas to this country's progress and he speaks a better sort of English than most of the men I know, including yourself!"

Her brother's mouth twisted with disgust but there was stark loneliness in his eyes. Miriam realised that she had answered the question he had not directly put, and his fear was now confirmed. "I shall marry him if I can, Edward," she said quite gently, "and I hope that you'll grow to like him so that you will want to come and visit us, and we might be friends again." But he flinched from her pity and left the room.

Otto had arranged a Sunday lunch at the German Club for her to meet some of his friends, and he collected her after church. The day was very wet and he hurried her down the path under his umbrella to the cab.

"Most of my friends are Lutherans," he explained, "but I worship at the Church of England." Since none of the manifestations of religion held any particular interest for her she did not find this remarkable.

The German Club was a modest building, close to the centre

of town. Otto ushered her into the taproom where several groups of people, most in church-going clothes, were drinking before lunch. Streaming umbrellas stood in the hallstand and the room smelt of wet clothing. Taking her arm, Otto led her towards three men and two women sitting at a low table in the corner. They waved and beamed in welcome, opening their circle to admit them. She could not grasp their names and felt panic. I shall have to resort to Sir and Madam, she thought. But Otto, recognising the difficulty perhaps from his own experience, repeated the names often for her so that gradually they became clear.

The little, wiry man with the dark, thinning hair and piebald moustache said genially, "Dear lady, I shall fetch you some schnapps. In Germany we drink it to keep warm. In Queensland we do not have that excuse but today we may drink it to get dry!" He got up to signal a waiter and spoke to him in German.

Miriam dared not risk his name, which she thought was Mr Schuler but it might have been Schiller, so she smiled rather stiffly in thanks as the glass of clear liquid was put into her hand. The waiter distributed fresh drinks to everyone and Mr Schuler proposed a toast "to our new friend, Miss Vemyss." Miriam sipped and spluttered sharply, causing the fiery liquid to splash on to her dress. Everyone laughed and one of the women, perhaps Mrs Schuler, called for a napkin from the waiter.

"Ah, my dear," she exclaimed, dabbing at Miriam with the cloth, "you are not used to our strong drink! It is always so the first time!" But they all apparently expected her to persist with it. Miriam, feeling humiliated as much by the dabbing Mrs Schuler as the spilled schnapps, put her glass firmly on the table.

The other woman in the group, a Miss Ryko, who lounged indolently in a chair opposite Miriam's, said loudly, "Otto, she does not like it. You must get her something else!"

"You are right, Baiba!" Otto slapped his forehead, "I have been thoughtless!"

"No, please," cried Mr Schuler, leaping to his feet, "it is my fault, I did not even ask, I merely presumed. Forgive me, dear lady, and allow me to order something you would like." It had become farcical and, to everyone's relief, Miriam laughed.

"May I have a glass of sherry please, Mr Schuler."

When it had been ordered their attention wandered from her and she was able to observe them. Baiba Ryko reminded her of a ripe pear. She was a golden-brown colour, lightly freckled, with high cheekbones and wheat-gold hair piled up on her head. Her figure was full and her clothing rather loose and untidy. She sat with her legs crossed at the knee and allowed one much-bangled wrist to hang over the arm of the chair when it was not needed to conduct her rich voice. She was what Sarah would have called "fast", Miriam decided, and was not surprised to hear that she was a singer of some renown. Apparently she was not German at all but Latvian, and Miriam stopped feeling obliged to like her.

The man sitting stiffly in the upright chair beside her was called Kurt von Kotze, so far as she could grasp. He said very little but, though seated, he seemed to bow from the waist when he was spoken to. He appeared colourless in every respect and his expression was solemn. Miss Ryko gave the impression of owning him, occasionally leaning back in her chair to address him or placing her hand briefly on his knee. Yet when she spoke to Otto she conveyed an intimacy with him, too, which Miriam found shocking. While it was common enough for women who knew men well to call them by their Christian names, her repeated use of his seemed calculated to exclude Miriam. She felt the red patches on her cheeks begin to burn and deliberately transferred her attention to the others.

Mr and Mrs Schuler were similar, as people long-married to each other often are. Both were small-boned but if he was wiry she was delicately made. They were obviously older than the others and the white streaks in his moustache were matched by two wings of white at her temples. He chewed on the end of his moustache and Miriam could see by its colour that he would otherwise be chewing a pipestem. His wife followed the exchange of conversation around the group with keen, bright eyes and would break into it with an introductory "Ha!", as though catching it on the bounce. But when she did so her husband would take it as his cue to speak and so they would talk over each other briefly, pause to unscramble themselves and then begin again on the same instant. Miriam was amused to discover that they were called Willi and Lili and that he was the editor of the German language newspaper, *Vorwarts Australien*. She wondered whether they wrote his editorials together in the same fashion.

The seventh member of the group sat on the other side of Otto and so Miriam could not see him clearly until the party had moved into the dining room where he was seated opposite her at the table. His name was Klaus Buchbinder and he was an engineer with the railways. "I make the bridges and the culverts, the viaducts, the embankments – everything!" he explained, holding up his large hands as if to encompass all Queensland. He was a big man with a red-gold complexion and small grey eyes buried in good-humoured lines. About the same age as Otto, he too was unmarried and full of restless energy which made him fidget when he was not directly engaged in the conversation. He and Otto obviously knew one another well.

Otto explained the menu to Miriam and when the waiter came he, as host, ordered the meal. It was the first time she had heard him speak his own tongue and she felt an extraordinary rush of admiration and pride. His mouth, with its deep bow in the upper lip, seemed formed especially for the difficult vowels and his manner of speech was precise and commanding. Perhaps her face expressed her feelings because Klaus remarked, shaking his head lugubriously, "Ah, this Otto! He is a dreadful man; one should not know him! No, really! I will tell you many things about him, Miss Wemyss!"

"Please, Klaus! Spare me!" Otto protested, but he was shouted down by the others.

"No, no, I will tell! So, our friend Otto, five, six years ago, is running around the country – visiting the farmers, visiting the doctors, visiting even the cows and sheeps, perhaps – and he is telling them about his big business, how he imports this thing and that. He can supply anything! And he has only this little tiny office – how you say, where you put the brooms?"

"Cupboard," Otto prompted with delight.

"Cupboard, yes! He has only this little, dark cupboard in Brisbane. And that is all. Nothing! So he must order everything special when he is asked and when the doctor says, 'Where is my operating table? Where is my saw for bones?' you know what he says? 'Oh, there is a wretched shipping strike and I cannot get them from the wharves.'" The party roared with laughter and Otto wiped tears of mirth from his eyes. "But there is worse, Miss Wemyss! Now that he has indeed the big business, what does he do? He goes up and down the country pretending he is a, what-to-say, low−?"

"Humble," Otto supplied with resignation.

"Yes, that he is a humble travelling tinker. This is worse because I will wager he has not told you, Miss Wemyss, that as well as his big business he owns a whole hospital? No? Exactly! How can one ever believe such a man!" He threw himself backwards in his chair with mock disgust.

"And do you own a hospital, Mr Gluck?" Miriam asked, surprised.

"I do, Miss Wemyss. That part of this bounder's story is true, I confess. But it is only a small hospital. I bought it cheaply when it was run-down so that I could furnish it with the very latest equipment. It is a sort of showroom of my wares. Now I think I must sell it, if only to make an honest man of myself!"

"Oh, I must come to Otto's defence," called Baiba Ryko from the other end of the table. "He has done so well for himself, and so quickly, that Klaus is jealous of him. But we all know Otto is as honest as his eyes are blue!"

"Ha! Klaus is a wonderful . . ." "If only I could get him to write his stories. . . " "He should publish. . . " "But he would have to change our names!" said Willi and Lili.

"Take no notice of them!" Klaus leant across the table to Miriam, " Just remember to be careful of him."

The focus of conversation changed then, but it continued to be in English and Miriam became aware that theirs was the only table in the room at which German was not being spoken. She felt a slight sense of affront that the fifty or so people in the room, though they lived in Queensland, should continue to speak in a language which the native-born could not understand.

She simply thought that Otto's party were better educated than the rest and did not appreciate their courtesy to her.

"And so now our friend von Bismarck has finally died, heh?" said Klaus.

"He was no friend to Austria!" and "Ha! He will be long in the purgatorial fires!" said Willi and Lili.

Von Kotze leant forward and said, crisply, "Von Bismarck has taken a rabble of disorderly princedoms and has turned them into a disciplined nation. Before, they were nothing. Now we shall be great."

There was a cry of protest from Willi and Lili, and even Baiba took issue with him. "You Prussians are all alike, Kurt. You only wish to subject us all to your own idea of order."

Otto held up his hand. "I am no friend to Bismarck, but we must be reasonable and see the thing globally. Unification is the direction of the future. For trade and for peace we must bring down the barriers. Here, we are considering federation; perhaps with New Zealand also. It must happen. The same language, the same currency, the same Queen, will all lead to a strong nation here. Why should it not be so in Europe? Bismarck may have been before his time but, for my part, I think it must happen also between Germany and England. We are the same people!"

"What my friend is saying", Klaus leaned across to Miriam, "is that he does not like the tariff barriers for his business!"

"No, Klaus. Although I'm an importer, I am also a protectionist, because I see that we must strengthen the industry in this country for the present. But in Europe this is not so, and also here, between the colonies and with New Zealand, we must build a unity and have no barriers."

"Otto, my friend, you have no regard for culture," Willi, uninterrupted, managed to say.

"He is a meathead!" snapped Lili.

"But, Lili, he loves the music!" interposed Baiba, but von Kotze dismissed the diversion: "Music crosses the barriers without tariff. But what you call culture, my dear Wilhelm, is often just an excuse for more and more fragmentation and weakness."

"*Nein*, Kurt, *nein*! It is the heritage of a people! You cannot take it away in the stroke of a pen and say, 'Now you are no longer Austrians, you must forget all that and be good Germans.' Then you are a robber and the people will fight against you."

"And what for," asked Lili, hard on the heels of her husband, "is this strong nation you speak of, if it is not for war?"

"Peace, please! Peace!" Klaus's voice was loud. "All this I began, so now I say to you brawlers: here we are in the German Club. This is because of our language and our culture and also because it would cost us very much money to have a club for each of the German states."

"And we should have to drink a great deal more if we must meet in each of them every Sunday instead of just one!" Baiba held out her glass to von Kotze to be refilled. The argument subsided into laughter.

After the meal the party returned to the taproom for coffee. They settled into the club chairs as though they meant to stay all afternoon but, when the cups were drained, von Kotze suddenly leapt to his feet. "Now it is time to play skittles!" he proclaimed. It was an order rather than a suggestion and it galvanised the party into immediate activity. They gathered themselves and made ready to go wherever it was that the game of skittles was played. Miriam was astonished at this curious mixture of formality and impulsiveness and, since she had never played skittles, she was disconcerted to be included in their plan. She pleaded fatigue and Otto suggested a short drive instead, before returning her home.

As they left, Baiba said, "You will come back, Otto?"

"Of course. In an hour or so."

The rain had stopped but the wind was still keen and the hansom's windows had to be kept shut. The air inside was damp and close. Otto did not speak as they drove and he seemed depressed. Miriam could not think what to say to him. She was glad to be away from the luncheon party because, though she did not dislike Klaus or Lili and Willi, they had all seemed too familiar to her. They had touched one another constantly and had not thought it intrusive to pat her arm or even her knee from time to time. She supposed there was no harm in it but it had repelled her, making her more formal and reserved in response, and she found it difficult now to relax.

"So, did you find us boring?" Otto said at last.

"Not in the least!" she replied, quite truthfully. They had been so different from her own society that they had fascinated her. "That is to say, except Mr von Kotze, and he said so little one could hardly tell whether he is boring or not."

Otto laughed. "Oh, he is boring, all right! And I told you the truth, you see, since he was the only true German there!"

Miriam did not understand. "But aren't you German, yourself?"

"No, no! I am from the Rhineland, which was taken over by Prussia just before I was born. But I never became a German. In my country one does not become a citizen until the age of eighteen. I was seventeen when I decided to emigrate and so I formally renounced my rights to citizenship then. In return I received my *Demit*, a document which released me from my responsibilities to the Prussia government. One day, perhaps, I will become a citizen of this country."

"And the others?"

"Well, Klaus is from Saarland but now he is a naturalised Queenslander. Lili and Willi are both Austrians and Baiba is from Stettin in the Hanseatic League. So only von Kotze from Prussia is a natural-born German and that is why there was such dispute about Bismarck."

But still she did not comprehend it. She fell silent, thinking that they were all none-the-less foreigners who spoke German, and that the nice distinctions he was making were irrelevant to people like her father and even, really, to herself. Till now, in her mind, he had stood solitary on the fringe of her own society. Today she had seen him at the centre of another society to which she had been the lone outsider. This new perspective had emphasised his foreignness for her and she was full of confused feeling which words would not sort out. The cab swayed and she allowed herself to lean against him a little. The electric charge which thrilled through her arm instantly clarified her mood. She did not doubt that she loved him and, if they married, their bond would dissolve all foreignness between them. Then, when he had a family of his own, he would not need the German Club.

He seemed not to notice the intimacy and had relapsed into gloom. "For you British it is all so simple," he sighed. "You are one people and can clearly see your destiny. That is what makes Britain a great nation. We Germans can only envy and imitate you."

The cab drew up at her gate and he sprang out to help her down. She wished that she could hold him; that he need not go back to his friends.

"Come in and have some tea," she suggested.

"No, I am not good company. I should bore you."

She waved as he drove away but his head was bent and he did not notice.

Inside the house, Harriet and James were having afternoon tea with her parents. Miriam had not known they were to come and, instead of going to her room to rest as she had planned, she joined them. She was conscious of a feeling of relief in the polite distances they maintained, after the closeness of the group at lunch. Her uncle and father were discussing federation while the women listened. They were not expected to take part. Miriam watched her father as he held forth against the idea and she saw him clearly now, as she had not remembered seeing him since her childhood at the mill. His face, as he talked, moved along a series of well-worn lines. The contemptuous curl of his lip and sardonic lift of his right eyebrow were graven into his flesh. From time to time he ran his well-manicured hand over his shock of blue-white hair, but it was not a gesture of worry or distraction. Rather, it underscored his confidence, his vanity, perhaps. He was regarded, she knew, as a good speaker though there was nothing pleasant in his voice, which was generally harsh, ascending to a whine when he was crossed. She supposed his power sprang from his certainty of opinion, because he never admitted to doubt and few, therefore, doubted him.

"If we federate," he was saying, "we'll have the other colonies clinging to our coat-tails. They can only impede Queensland's progress. We will be restricted by namby-pamby southerners — in trade, in immigration, in labour laws — to some sort of lowest common denominator. If we remain independent, we'll shoot ahead. We've the money, the resources, the enterprise, all here. I admit that since the Germans moved into New Guinea the whole country must look to its defence, but even that could be managed by co-operation. Federation will do nothing for us!"

But James, as usual, was not taking the argument entirely seriously. "Come, Josh," he said lightly, "tell the truth. You object because you're in line for a seat in Parliament and you don't want to see your powers passed over to a federal Government!"

Her father smiled. "Well, James, and what of that? Isn't it true that what's good for me, and for men like me, is also good for Queensland?" His smile, though quite broad, operated within the lines of his face and did not transform them. His brother, he knew, would not deny him, because what had been good for Josh had been good for Wemyss and Sons, and that had been good for James.

"We will all cheer you on," James conceded. "Except perhaps Kath," he smiled at her, "who will not like to be a Member's wife and who would rather have her husband to herself." He got up. "We must go home. But Miriam, if you've nothing better to do on Tuesday morning, come for a jaunt with me. I must go and look at some property at Wilston, out on Breakfast Creek, and you look as though you need air."

Tuesday was blustery, a bright, hard-edged day which stripped the distant hills of their usual blue haze and burnished the sky to silver. The land James wished to look at was a leisurely drive from town of about twenty minutes. New railway lines ran beside the road which passed small dairy farms and market gardens. They came to a hamlet and turned from the road at a track just beyond the railway station. It ran through thin bush and low scrub till it reached the water meadows of Breakfast Creek where cows grazed, pastured by some nearby farmer. James got down from the trap and hitched the horse to a tree.

"Peaceful spot, isn't it?" he said and kicked the shaly ground with his toe. "Apart from the creek flats, it's not much good for farming though, I'm told. Government's about to release all this, from the creek to the railway, for sale. The idea would be to buy it and divide it up into small lots for housing."

They walked back up the hill, turning from time to time to admire the view across the meadows and the creek to the town, just visible now on the horizon.

"Will it cost a great deal of money?" Miriam asked.

"More than I'd want to tie up in it. But several people are urging me to go into it with them, your friend Herr Gluck among them." Miriam was startled, as much by the reference to Otto as by the news of his business dealings.

"Why do you refer to him that way?"

"Apologies, my dear. I do it to tease him, usually. He dislikes it so, but he's a a good fellow and takes a joke." Miriam was silent. James sat on a shelf of rock. "Sit down. It's quite clean." He brushed the place beside him with his handkerchief and Miriam sat. "Of course, there would be a good return and fairly quickly since there's a big demand for housing. But I don't know, at my age, that I want to be bothered. Still it seems a good proposition to the younger fellows." He took out his pipe and began to fill it. "He's an enterprising man, Otto. I've had a bit to do with him over the last twelve months and he's impressive. You like him, don't you?"

"Yes." She paused before making the confidence, "But I don't think Pa would have much time for him."

"Oh, Josh is like my father, you know: territorial and dynastic." He puffed and looked at Miriam who raised her eyebrows in puzzlement. "Well, fierce old Quaker though he was, Father was still conscious of the aristocratic blood in his veins. The colony provided him with the chance to establish a new burgeoning for the Wemysses, away from the decadence of the old world. But the model was still the old aristocracy. Leaders and rulers again, instead of the decorative impotence of the old families at home. I must be a throwback, I think." He chuckled and relit his pipe.

"Josh, of course, is not concerned with ideals and visions. But he translated what Father wanted into his own terms: money and power . . . and dynasty, which is the business of keeping your money and power after you're dead, of course. Father maintained a belief in the hereafter where he would not need money or power, but he was delighted when I married Harriet and furious when Josh married Kath. Harriet was the closest thing to a blue blood the colony had to offer; Kath was the furthest away."

"And Pa would object to my marrying Otto because he thinks him beneath us?"

"No, not beneath. He's not, you see. He's as good as Josh at Josh's own game. But he's not one of us, my dear, and must not presume to our right to rule this newfound fiefdom of ours. Even if he *were* one of our tribe it would be better if he were not quite as good as the fief. Look at Brian or Alfred; they're quite satisfactory sons-in-law. They don't challenge your father, do they? Forgive me for saying it, but even within his own firm Josh would rather have Edward than Joshua because Edward is no threat. In my view, that's why dynasties collapse. The old stag doesn't encourage the younger ones to be any good. But I've strayed, haven't I?"

"So it's not just that Otto is a German, but that he is as clever as Pa?"

"Cleverer, probably. He has more imagination than Josh. No, because he is as enterprising. That's the quality your father most prides himself on and Otto has it in abundance."

"What do you advise me to do?"

"Marry him, Miriam! Marry him if you like him and good luck to you both!"

Miriam took his arm as they walked back down the hill to the trap. Her feet skidded on the shifting stones but her head felt light.

"Shall you buy into the land?" she asked.

"No, I think not. I'll let the young blokes have this patch to themselves."

Part Two
Australians All

1 Thou Ring

On the bench by the river Otto had held her hand in silence. Opening her palm, he began to stroke the inside of her fingers and it seemed to her that they sang in response to his touch like the strings of a harp.

"We will have such a good life together, Miriam, I promise you. My business now is good but with you beside me it will leap forward. And we will have a wonderful big house for our children." He caressed her wrist and the tender skin of her forearm with one finger very gently, hardly touching, and softly said, "Will you like to have children, my Miriam?"

She barely heard her own assent. The blood had gone out of her lips, had seemed to drain from her whole upper body leaving it utterly weak, while her belly felt gravid and turbulent with its excess. He put his arm around her shoulders and she had no strength to remain upright but sank against him. His face loomed before her so that she could not focus and she closed her eyes. His cheek grazed hers and then, without warning, he encompassed her whole mouth, wetly, in his own. She could not breathe and struggled against him.

"Oh, my dear girl, I am so sorry!" He got up and walked away.

"You were too sudden, Otto," she said, wiping her mouth while his back was turned.

"I am impetuous! Always. It is my worst failing." He turned to her and bent to catch her downcast eyes. "You will forgive me? Yes?" And he smiled the disarming smile of a child.

"Yes!"

"And shall we marry soon? We must marry very soon, my

own dear girl!" He capered before her in his insistence. She laughed.

"But Otto, first we must have somewhere to live."

"It shall be arranged in a jiffy! Where would you like to live? Until I build the nest for our little ones we shall find a house in town, near to my work so that I can be with you as long as possible every day. And then our friends will come, because it is not far for them, and we will have glorious parties!" Suddenly he stopped and sat again beside her, taking her hand. "But then we will build a beautiful house. On a hill. And there will be a garden for the children to play and for the vegetables to grow. The children and I will pick the peas and you will sit in the shade of a tree and shell them for our dinner." He was spinning a dream. It filled his eyes with distance and, to bring him back, she said, "If it can be arranged I will marry you before Christmas."

Marriage, people said, was a state which one entered; seemingly given and fundamentally unalterable. Miriam knew it varied from relationship to relationship. She saw that it changed women in ways which were beyond their power to resist, but that it had very little obvious effect on men. The internal workings of her parents' marriage were mysterious. Her mother's affection for her father had been open and deep, and even now, despite his betrayal of her, she continued to love him. From time to time Josh responded with a rough affection and then Kathleen seemed pathetically grateful. Between times he treated her with disdain.

The marriages of Carrie and Sarah, though happier than Kathleen's, were also shallower and easier to plumb. Carrie was brisk and bossy with Brian but she was direct in her affections and she looked after her husband as though he were another of her children. He loved her, it was obvious, and submitted to her ministrations with resignation, but if there was a dispute, Brian's wishes held sway. Sarah, on the other hand, was supreme in her marriage but masked her domination in wifely manners. Alfred was a property to be managed, fostered, and she had learnt early that he needed to believe he was master. Now it was her ambitions and desires which he played out.

James was unashamedly docile in his marriage to Harriet but

he preserved an area of his life which was quite outside her control. The arrangement seemed to suit them both. Hetty and Charles Curthoys had an almost boyish relationship. They played tennis, picnicked, swam and rode horses together and their displays of affection were rather like Indian wrestling. Childlessness seemed appropriate to them.

Miriam could not imagine her marriage to Otto fitting any of these patterns but neither could she see the distinctive nature of their relationship. She put this down to Otto's otherness, which she could not penetrate but which offered subtleties denied to colonial experience. She expected that he would set the terms of their marriage and, because he was courteous and considerate, she did not doubt that they would be acceptable to her. As for children, Miriam gave them notional acceptance but was unable to imagine herself as mother. Again, she trusted to Otto since she had seen that he loved the company of children.

Miriam's own experience of children was limited to her nieces and nephews. Carrie had a brood of five. Miriam did not see them very often and only Isobel, whom she had known as a baby, figured very much in her consciousness. They were a brawling, lively clot of creatures who exasperated their mother and generally gave Miriam a headache after not very long with them. Carrie loved them but rarely said so. Sarah, on the other hand, professed to adore children and had two, Harry and Edith, aged eleven and nine, whom Miriam saw frequently. They were well-mannered, well-dressed and unobtrusive. Sarah was pleased with them.

About a week before Otto proposed marriage, Sarah and Alfred had invited Miriam and Otto for afternoon tea at their house at Kangaroo Point. The children were presented and allowed to remain in the room for a few minutes.

"Do you like school?" Otto asked them.

"Yes, Sir," Harry answered promptly, but Edith said, "Sometimes," rather more doubtfully.

"I'll bet you like holidays more!" Otto challenged. The boy nodded, looking furtively at his mother.

"We've got a hoop," Edith volunteered.

"A hoop! Will you show me how to play?"

"I've got a cricket bat," said Harry, encouraged.

"Then I shall definitely join you in the garden after tea!" And as soon as he reasonably could do so, he did.

"You will excuse me, Mrs Borden, if I go and keep my promise to your delightful children?" She was surprised, Miriam saw, but flattered out of any objection.

Alfred went with him to the garden and soon the women could hear yells and squeals of excitement. Sarah, looking indulgent, suggested they go and see the fun and they went out on to the verandah. The hoop was careering along the path, followed by Otto and the two children. Alfred stood watching as though bewildered. The three charged through a shrubbery and disappeared. Alfred joined the women on the verandah.

"Much too vigorous for me," he declared.

Otto emerged from the bushes carrying the hoop. "Time for cricket!"

"Oh no, not yet!" begged Edith.

"Yes! And you shall bat first."

He arranged a pitch for them on the path and bowled gently to the little girl who swung wildly and missed. He stood behind her, positioning her hands on the bat. "Now watch very carefully the ball and you cannot miss." She hit his next delivery and was hugely delighted.

"See! See, Mummy? I hit it!"

Sarah was clearly uncertain of the propriety of this, but excitement had gained an unstoppable momentum. When Harry caught his sister out on the next ball, she was determined to get back to the crease as soon as possible and fielded with intense concentration. Otto encouraged them both. "Run, Harry! Catch it, Edith! Well done! My turn to bat!"

Not until the shadows lengthened on the path did Otto call a halt and by then knees were scraped and clothing stained with grass. The children were over-excited and Sarah was distinctly cross. Realising his misdemeanour, Otto was abject in apology. "Shall I read a story to them, Mrs Borden, so they will become quiet?" he offered, and was dragged away to another room by the children before Sarah had time to reply. Miriam doubted, from the sounds of story-telling echoing down the hall, that much quietude would descend, but she was impressed by Otto's uninhibited enjoyment of the children.

"It seems he is a favourite with them, at any rate," she said.

"I wonder if he will treat his own in that way once he has had them a while," Sarah replied darkly.

Though Miriam had protested that she was twenty-four and did not need her father's permission to marry, Otto insisted on speaking to him.

"I will not ask him, Miriam," he assured her, "but I must confer with him, as man to man, about your future so he will know you are to be well looked after."

"I do wish you wouldn't, Otto," she pleaded, fearing the rebuff her father might give him. But Otto's need for everything to be done properly was strong.

"If I don't speak to him perhaps he will think, because I am a German, that I'm ignorant of my responsibilities," he explained. "And I want to be a good husband to you more than anything else in the world, dearest girl." She conceded because she could not resist the appeal in his eyes and because she trusted his judgment, but she knew that what had been her own decision, carefully considered, was now to become the province of others. He left her at her gate that day, promising to write and make an appointment with her father as soon as possible.

Kathleen heard her news with an anxiety which surprised Miriam. "I think Carrie was right and it will not be to your father's liking," she said. "But I will try to make him see reason."

And in the discussion between them, which this time Miriam deliberately overheard, she said, "The girl is twenty-four, Josh, and this is the first time any man has proposed marriage to her. You surely would not have her remain a spinster for the rest of her days?"

"There are plenty of men who would have had her if she wasn't so perverse. And I'd rather no man did than see her married to that foreign nancy with his absurd manners and his cringing opinions. He's not a man another man can respect, Kathleen!"

"I've heard enough, Joshua!" Kathleen's voice now came

harshly from the lowest reach of her throat. "Mr Gluck is a cultivated man. He would put your rough mates to shame, and that's the truth! And don't be forgetting that it's me who has to entertain them, and will have to put up with more of them if you're to be a Member of Parliament. I warn you that I will not do it, Josh, if you stand in Miriam's way. I will not!" Kathleen had chosen the most effective of her few weapons.

"I shouldn't have thought you were the one to talk about cultivation, as though you were to the manor born. And, may I remind you, it's through me and my rough mates, as you say, that you've all the comforts and society of this colony at the tips of your oh-so-refined fingers. But, you have it your way. Just don't let her come to me when her card-house collapses and this cultivated ladies' man shows his true colours. I'll be damned if I'll rescue her!"

Miriam knew her mother had exposed herself to great hurt in defending Otto. She would have gone to her when her father left, but she thought it better that the hurt should be private and so she let the moment go.

When Otto came, two days later, for his interview with Josh, Miriam waited anxiously in the drawing-room. She could see the study door from where she sat and when Otto emerged alone she caught a glimpse of his face before he became aware of her. His mouth was turned down in disappointment. She ran to him, putting her hands on his shoulders, but he held her away and his face, now, was smiling. "Your father is very glad for us," he said. She knew that he lied and felt a sudden distaste but his expression was fixedly pleased and she put the sensation away. "Let's go and see your mother!" he said gaily and, taking her hand, he ran with her to the garden where Kathleen was planting out seedlings.

Kathleen had spoken the truth when, after only two meetings with Otto, she said that she loved him already. There was immediate warmth between them which never diminished. "He is like a son to me," she would say, but he was not. Though he called her "Little Mother" from the day of their engagement, he was more like a lover to her, courting her affection and attention with flowers, stories, presents, teasing and cajolery. None of the men in her family had ever treated her in that way and it was a balm to her womanhood. Now it was Otto whom she congratulated first, forgetting to take off her muddy gardening gloves and so streaking his neck and collar with dirt.

"We must have a party to celebrate!" she said.

"We haven't time! Miriam has agreed to marry as soon as I can make the arrangements and find a house for us. I intend to be quick! I have been looking for a house already. There is one in New Farm which will be available at the end of the month. You must come and inspect it with us, Little Mother. Come tomorrow!" And so he rushed them along in the flood of his enthusiasm.

Next day, when they arrived at the New Farm house to discover it had been sold, Otto's despair seemed disproportionate.

"There are bound to be others," Kathleen comforted him.

"But I could imagine a home here for us."

"Otto, you promised to show me your hospital and you haven't. Since we are out, we could go now. Mother would like to see it."

The suggestion transformed him. "My dear girl, why did I not think of it! Of course, it's the answer!" He laughed at their amazement. "There's a house at St Julian's! The superintendent's house is unoccupied at present. We will see!" He drove the horse at a cracking pace across town to show them.

St Julian's Hospital was a large sprawling house on the river, just to the north of the Victoria Bridge. Its grounds, and those of the house next to it, were lush and well-kept. "It has served its purpose for me and I was planning to sell it. But now, if you like the house, perhaps we will keep it a little longer," Otto said, as he ushered them into the lobby of the hospital. "We must collect the key from Matron and so first we must look at her wards."

Matron Bloom was summoned to meet them by the taciturn orderly and groundsman at St Julian's who, Otto told them, was also Matron's husband. Matron's own manner was effusive and seemed at odds with her starched apron and cap. They toured the wards with her and visited the operating theatre. Otto was proud of his shining steel equipment, and Matron, of her polished floors and snowy bed-linen. Kathleen marvelled at everything. Miriam had never been in a hospital before and did not know how to judge it, but was proud in Otto's wake. The patients' faces were merely greyish blurs in the speed of their inspection.

At last, Matron surrendered the key of the superintendent's house: "But you know, Mr Gluck, nothing has been done in the residence since Dr Grogan took the position. It must be over three months since Dr Barry left. It will be in a state. I do wish you had advised me you were to visit it."

The house had been tightly closed up and smelt musty but it was perfectly clean. Dust sheets covered the furniture and carpets were rolled in the hall. The previous Superintendent had been sought in England, Otto explained, and furnished accommodation was part of the inducement to migrate. But Otto behaved as though the house, up to now, had been of no account: he had not noticed how pleasant was its view of the river, how secluded it was from the road and the hospital, or how well proportioned were its formal rooms. Suddenly possessed of shyness or modesty, he insisted Miriam and Kathleen should look at the bedrooms and the offices without him. "I'll wait here for your verdict," he said.

In the kitchen, Kathleen urged Miriam to agree. "To be sure, the bedrooms are small, my dear, but it's a lovely position the drawing-room has and this is quite serviceable. Otto is so keen for it to suit you!" She sighed. She had not been consulted in the choice of their Brisbane house.

Miriam returned to Otto alone: the moment of accepting his house was more intimate to her than the moment of his marriage proposal. He, facing her in the white draped drawing-room, took her hands in his own and she felt his joy fluttering in them. When Kathleen came they withdrew their hands and folded them away, as though afraid of their power to transmit, beyond themselves, such extraordinary force.

Now the decision was made, nothing about the house, in Otto's mind, was good enough. "We shall not be here long, I promise you!" he declared as he revisited every room, pursuing its faults. "We will build as soon as possible. In the meantime, we must have these floors polished and this door must be rehung. The plaster in the hall has been damp; I will engage a plasterer tomorrow. Oh, Little Mother, we shall have such fun, Miriam and I! We will make this house as good as new and then we will know what we want particularly and so, when we come to build our own home, we will have the very best of everything! Do you like Turkey carpets, Miriam? I know a fellow who imports them. We must go and see him." He seemed on fire; unquenchable. Miriam loved him.

Of the time that remained until their wedding, Miriam remembered only excitement and pleasure. The undercurrents of her father's scorn, Joshua's dislike and Edward's grief did not impinge on her because the women closed about her and, in any case, love had made her invulnerable to everyone but Otto. She remembered no lover's tiffs and her only pain was in separating from him at each day's end. No period of her life, before or since, had been so unalloyed with anxiety, and few were so difficult to recall. All her senses seemed interlaced in common pleasure. The time was brief and slid like silk through her fingers. Kathleen had arranged a party, a statement of gladness in defiance of Josh: it was a whirl of colour and light in memory. There had been a rowdy celebration at the German Club, twittery afternoon teas, family fuss about clothes and furnishings, ceremony and wedding breakfast: they were a counterpoint, only enhancing the serene melodic line.

Her wedding, on the other hand, was clear, distinguished by contrast of light and shadow. It was not to be grand; neither Otto nor Josh had wanted a society event. The parish church of St Philip was a broad, timber building, dark inside with timbered ceiling and floor, cavernous and cool. It had never afforded her any spiritual insight, but now, on every Sunday morning of their engagement, she sank to her knees hoping for a metaphysical counterpart to the awesome joy of her life. She had no schooling in prayer and found instead only reverie. The priest, bluff and worldly, gave no instruction in the vows when they visited him but said, "Well, well: you are both mature people and I feel sure you will do splendidly together. May God bless you abundantly." Miriam was reminded of Miss Spender and felt cheated.

Kathleen attempted more. She came to Miriam's room on the night before the wedding and sat on the bed. "I never said much to Carrie or Sarah when they were wed but with you I feel a need, Miriam. Perhaps it's because you want more than your sisters. Sometimes I think, when I see you together, that you want to be Otto, not just to marry him. Then again, perhaps you have more to give, too, but I'm not sure you know how to give it." She frowned, searching for words. "You know all you should, I'm confident, about what happens between married people; it's not that I'm concerned for. But your sisters are more straightforward and their husbands could quite plainly see what it was they wanted. And Otto is different, too, as a man. He is kinder and more considerate than most, to be sure, and I know he will treat you well. But men are not the same as us, Miriam, however good they may be. They have needs we cannot enter into. You will have to take the difference into account and learn to give what he needs if you're to be happy always."

Miriam was uncomfortable, believing her mother had nothing to offer, and gave her no encouragement. Kathleen sighed and contented herself with reviewing Miriam's clothes for the morning.

The church was close and Otto had hoped she would walk there, but Josh had rejected this "peasant behaviour" and drove with her in the carriage. The church glared white in the November sun, dazzling her so that she was blinded in its dark interior. Not until she reached the chancel steps could she see Otto at all. Then, as the organist finished playing, he stepped forward into a shaft of light and a moment of absolute quiet was filled with his glowing image. It was all she retained of the service but she thought it enough.

The trees in the garden of their house shaded tables laid with the wedding breakfast and there was room, in the garden, for the guests to maintain their separate identities. Otto's friends were seated at the table furthest from the wedding party. Only Klaus Buchbinder, Otto's best man, and Johann Heussler, the German consul, represented them at the main table. (Kathleen had insisted the consul deserved a seat of honour and Josh had agreed because, though a German, he was a prominent wine-merchant and a Member of the lower house of Parliament). Between those two tables were ranged three of family friends. Hetty Curthoys, Miriam's attendant at the family table, commented, "We must mix them up a bit, as soon as we can."

There were speeches and toasts. Josh talked about prosperity, and the couple's good fortune in living in Queensland where, for the enterprising, that blessing was assured. It sounded like a political speech. Klaus, when it came to his turn, looked uncomfortable in his stiff collar. His face was red and he shuffled some bits of paper as though he did not remember what they were for.

"You will please excuse my English. I am not so good at it as my very clever friend." Then he found his place in the notes, which Miriam suspected Otto had written for him, and began: "My friends, in my language *Glück* means luck. The words are very close, *glück* and 'luck', yes?" He looked at the consul who nodded vigorously in encouragement.

"My friend Otto believes he is lucky by nature," he went on. "He says it was his good fortune to come to these shores and to make a good life here. But never has he dreamed he would be so lucky to meet such a beautiful, lovely lady as this new Mrs Gluck." Here he raised his eyes from the paper. "But, my friends, I can tell you, Mrs Gluck now also is lucky because her husband is a very special man. He is what you English call an adventurer, I think. He loves the life and the new things; he loves the travel and the peoples he meets."

Recovered from his nervousness now, Klaus became expansive and confided in his audience. "I will tell you a story about him. One day, when he was driving in his buggy out in the bush, he suddenly sees a young native lady who is being chased by some bad boys. They had in them the drink and they were not very nice. So my friend hurries up his horse and he drives into their middle and grabs the young lady and pulls her up! woosh, like this, and drives off! So he is not only lucky, this Otto; he is brave like St George, I think: saving the young lady from the beast, yes?"

There was brief applause from the German table but Otto looked embarrassed. Klaus returned to his notes. "In Europe, the British people and the German people are very close; even

Queen Victoria and Kaiser Wilhelm, they are grandmother and grandson. But the Germans and the British, they are still separate peoples. In this new land where we are so lucky to live, we can all become one people — Australian people; like when the man and the woman marry they become one flesh, as was told to us in church this morning? — And this is very good. And so, Otto and Miriam, today is a very happy one for all of us because of this, and we wish you happiness and good luck!"

When the toast was drunk, the consul leant across the table and raised his voice. "Mr Wemyss, Sir! May I congratulate you on a capital wine? I know the vineyard well. Just near Rosemont. A German vintner, as a matter of fact, and excellent Queensland grapes: a very good combination and a happy choice for the occasion!"

Josh raised his glass: "Your health, Sir," he said, but Miriam saw that he drank the wine as though it were lemon juice.

Later he came and drew her aside. "Since you are now, apparently, blest with such good luck, perhaps you won't need this, but it's yours in any case. It's what I did for your sisters." He handed her an envelope and turned away.

"Pa?" she said, and he looked back, his eyebrows raised as though to enquire what more she could want of him. And there was nothing, after all, so she said, "Thank you," and set her face against hurt. She did not look at the cheque but knew it was for £500. When she gave it to Otto she said, "It's from Pa. I have thanked him for us so you need not."

"But I must! It's very generous."

"Then write him a note," she urged. But he would not be spared and, a little later, she saw him before her father, holding the envelope as though he were a mendicant.

When the speeches were done, Hetty seized Klaus by the hand and demanded he introduce her to the German party. Theirs was by far the merriest table, she said, and it was true. Miriam and Otto, Kathleen and Carrie soon gravitated there. Isobel too, chin in her hands, sat listening avidly to the story-telling and laughter; at thirteen, and a country girl, she was enthralled.

"Oh, it is a lovely wedding, Auntie Miriam!" she said. "Aren't these exciting people?"

Miriam smiled at her intensity and thought that Otto's friends, like the child, were unselfconscious, freer of feeling, younger, in some odd way, than the new colonial society which decorated the garden like an ancient stiff tableau.

"There is a piano in the house?" Baiba Ryko was demanding of Hetty who sat next to her; "Then I must sing!" And she rose, pulling von Kotze up with her. "You must show me where it is! Klaus, please tell the people that now I shall sing for the bride." She bowed to Miriam and swept away, with Hetty and von Kotze in her wake.

Klaus, now full of confidence, stood on a chair and clapped his hands for attention. Then he remembered that he did not know how to direct the guests and had to ask Kathleen where the piano was. Kathleen was flustered by the turn of events.

"I should have invited Miss Ryko to sing, shouldn't I?" she whispered to Otto. "She will be offended."

"She will not in the least. She is perfectly used to taking things over!" They none of them expected Kathleen to be offended, however, and she was not, but Miriam caught a glimpse of Sarah's face during Klaus's announcement and it was appalled.

The party trooped into the drawing-room and Klaus hustled Miriam into a chair drawn up to one side of the piano. Otto stood behind her. Von Kotze had taken his seat at the piano and Baiba stood, one hand on the instrument, facing Miriam. All her habitual languor had fallen away; she was majestic, imperious and beautiful, Miriam thought.

"I will sing for you, 'Thou Ring upon my Finger' from *A Woman's Life and Love* by Robert Schumann," she announced and nodded to von Kotze. As he leant to the piano his body remained stiff and controlled but his long white fingers, which Miriam had not noticed before, were lithe on the keys. Then Baiba's voice swelled out in words Miriam did not understand, but with power and depth that her heart recognised. Otto put his hand on her shoulder. She had shed no tears in church but now the music articulated emotions unacknowledged in her world and she wept into its flood. There was silence in the room when Baiba finished and then a disconcerted rustle, peppered with applause. Baiba bowed and bent to kiss Miriam, then Otto. The room emptied quickly of people who had witnessed too much intimacy.

Miriam and Otto were to catch the afternoon steamer north to Sandgate and now they must hurry to meet it. A wave of excitement lifted them above the flotsam of women in the bedroom, the chaos of stockings, hats and flowers, the flurry of good wishes and goodbyes, and, surging, bore them to the open sea.

2 Mirages

Sandgate. It had become a symbol of home in her mind; a metaphor of happiness. When she was landlocked in frozen Germany it had drifted in an aura of summer light on the horizon of memory. Now, by this rank river in the strident heat of noon, its young seabreeze smell wafted through her. She allowed it to transport her, knowing it to be a mirage but glad, in her wasteland, that it could still appear.

She had not been simply happy on her honeymoon but for the first time in her life she had been persuaded that happiness was possible. When the steamer thudded against the Sandgate wharf the conviction seized her heart. As their heels clacked in and out of step on the long pier's silvered timbers, and the guesthouse on the ridge above the strand reached out its evening glow, she felt it swell in her chest, as though to burst through and release a self long captive. When they were shown to their room she tried, in the presence of the maid, for the assurance of a matron, rigid against the trembling joy. When the door was closed she dared not meet her husband's eyes, fumbling instead with bags and wardrobe doors. Otto came and took both her hands in his.

"Let's go and have some tea," he said.

He was kind, she knew, but he had misjudged her. She ought to have said, "No, I am ready now," but did not know the words to use.

After tea, they followed what she supposed were the conventions; he allowing her time to prepare for bed and joining her later, clad in pyjamas and darkness. By then her imminent self had curled up into a tight knot in its furthest recesses and would not be called out.

The pain he caused her was brief, surpassed by sadness that the floodtide which lifted him had left her stranded and alone. Otto's weight, returning, fell in on her. He murmured breathily in her ear and then slowly slid back into the pillows, asleep. She got up and groped her way to the basin where she washed away the blood she could not see. He did not wake when she climbed back into the bed but breathed on, regularly, through his nose. She did not sleep for a long time but woke laughing, because he was tickling her ear. Then, and in the weeks that followed, his lovemaking was like sudden bursts of brilliant spring sunshine to her; frequent, fitful and soon withdrawn. It tantalised her with the hope of summer. Her body, like the ancient bones of the land, yearned for deep and lingering heat to warm it through.

"The Haven" guesthouse was smart, generous and relaxed, seeming to cast up an unobtrusive shelter from the world. The other guests gently encouraged them from their cocoon of self-absorption into card games, table-tennis and singing around the piano. They smiled indulgently when the two retreated to their room or set off for long walks. Miriam gloried in Otto's convivial ease when he sang with the others or darted to the ball in a game. At the same time, lacking it herself, she felt excluded by it and could only watch. Noticing, he would put his arm about her, drawing her in, but all the time talking, laughing, singing with others. Sometimes she felt his concern as pity, implying her inadequacy, and would become stiffer. Then he would look for the chance to spirit her away to their room and beguile her out of herself again. "Darling, precious girl," he would say, "when we are together like this I wonder why should we waste a single moment with others. But, you know, it's because we have the whole of our lives together now and we can do this whenever we want. Isn't that true?" She would nod the head buried beneath his shoulder, knowing that soon he would rejoin the party outside.

Of the other guests, Miriam best liked Maud and Geoffrey Pendle. They were a younger couple, married for over two years, and were revisiting the scene of their honeymoon because

Maud had been ill. She hinted at miscarriages and declined vigorous exercise, though she would bathe with Miriam when the water was calm, at the time and place appointed for ladies. When they sat together under an umbrella on the lawn or in the parlour after dinner, Maud would entertain her with piquant commentaries on their fellow guests.

"What a ridiculous creature that painter woman is with her airs and her loud voice! No wonder her husband is such a dried-up old stick. Do you suppose she hangs him on the back of the door with her dressing-gown at night?"

Because she said such things lightly and was perfectly civil, even friendly to Mrs Baldwin, the painter woman, Miriam did not think her malicious. The painter was hearty and abrupt and Miriam rather liked her but, because Otto was very taken with her, she enjoyed hearing her criticised. Mr Baldwin read Latin and Greek in leather volumes and seemed of no particular account. Miriam thought he did resemble a shabby dressing-gown. Both were English – touring the colonies, as they said, for their general edification.

"Mrs Gluck, you must allow me to draw you!" Mrs Baldwin exclaimed suddenly one evening over coffee. "Such a splendid nose, Baldwin, do you not think? Pride, I believe, with a bridge like that."

Her husband looked up from his book. "Gallic!" he responded. "Where are you from, my dear?"

"Brisbane," Miriam replied, blushing for her worst feature.

"No, no, no! I mean from where, at home, do your people come?"

"My father is from Bradford and my mother from Ireland."

"And whom do you most resemble?"

"My mother, I think."

"Ah well then – Gaelic." He smiled at some hidden joke and returned to his book.

"Take no notice of him, my dear. Most provokin'. But draw you I must. You won't mind?" She had already opened her sketch pad. Miriam could not refuse but was wretchedly uncomfortable under her scrutiny. Mrs Baldwin, however, lost all other interest in her and talked to Otto as she drew.

"Do you know anythin' of phrenology, Mr Gluck? Ah, you should study it. Most illuminatin', especially as to the races, you know. Takin' it into account with what Mr Darwin has told us, one can quite predict what will be the outcome in all the colonies. Except in India, of course. There you might lose your wager. Chin up a little, my dear; don't let it droop. But in Australia, tragic as it is, you can be sure the natives are doomed. Baldwin and I have seen it. I will show you my heads when I've done your wife. I've quite a collection, from several different tribes, and they all tell the same story. One can only hope to make them comfortable I believe and, to be frank, I find a great deal wantin' here in that respect. I'm afraid we shall be puttin' in some very adverse reports on our return, shall we not, Baldwin?"

"Most reprehensible, my dear," he murmured, responding to her tone.

"The British Government would not approve, I'm sure," opined Otto.

"No, indeed, Mr Gluck!" and she snapped the lead in her certainty.

Miriam had never heard of phrenology but felt a burning humiliation that her head had joined those of doomed natives in Mrs Baldwin's collection.

They were fortunate in the weather because, in November, heavy rain was likely. They had only two days of it and spent the time playing cards with the Pendles.

"Manchester is the most tedious business imaginable!" Geoffrey remarked. "My old man's family has been at it for generations and one doesn't easily escape that sort of tradition. When people speak of Fate, I see a bolt of linen! My uncle got out of it, of course. Got himself appointed to the Legislative Council. But he's as big a scallywag as the rest of them."

"Scallywag?" Otto did not know the word.

"Rogue, old man. Those Councillors are a bunch of rogues, all of them on the take!"

"My father-in-law has just been appointed to the Council. Joshua Wemyss, you know."

Geoffrey was mortified: "Oh Lord! Forgive me, Miriam! I

spoke in generalities and exaggerated!" But Miriam had heard her father hint at advantages to be gained from accepting the appointment to the upper house of parliament and she wondered. Otto turned the conversation.

"So, you are not 'scallywag' enough for the upper house. What is it you would prefer to manchester?"

"I'm blest if I know! I shan't have any capital of my own for years, so there's not much use thinking of it, but I'd like to hit on something everyone wants and provide that."

"Ice-cream!" said Maud, throwing down her hand. "That's what I want. It's so excessively hot and steamy in here."

"Maud makes wonderful ice-cream. You won't get it here, I'm afraid." They ordered cold beer instead, but Otto and Geoffrey were taken with the idea of manufacturing ice-cream and played with it for the rest of the afternoon.

Maud and Miriam wandered on to the verandah for air. "I'm probably in the family way again," Maud said. "I can't bear to be cooped up for long when I'm like that. But I don't seem to get very far with it. Not past four months. I've lost three, now." She said it baldly, as though she were talking about her success with African violets.

Miriam was confused. "How awful for you," she said.

"I don't know. I'm not very keen on children, actually. Of course, you know what men are, so it's hard on Geoffrey. I expect you want a family?"

"Yes, we do." She knew, at any rate, that she wanted something to burgeon from their lovemaking, but she put her hand to her narrow waist and wondered about the cost to herself.

The Pendles were to leave next day and Maud and Miriam swam together in the morning. When they returned to the guesthouse, Otto was on the verandah with Mrs Baldwin who was doing a watercolour of the bay. "Come and look, Miriam!" he called. "See how well Mrs Baldwin has got the water. I thought it was simply blue but now I see it has currents clearly visible."

Miriam considered the sea and Mrs Baldwin's painting. "It reminds me of mother's blue damask tablecloth: dull blue and shiny blue, together."

"You have a painter's eye, Mrs Gluck. You should take it up!"

"I cannot draw even a teapot, Mrs Baldwin!"

"The hand can be trained, Mrs Gluck. It is the eye that counts. You must come with me tomorrow. I intend to tramp over the headland to the fishin' village. There are boats there. Very picturesque, boats, and easy to draw. I'll show you how it's done. Baldwin won't come — will you, Baldwin? — so I shall need your husband to carry my easel. We will take a picnic."

"Of course! It will be delightful, won't it, Miriam?" said Otto. Miriam had hoped, with the Pendles gone, that they might spend the day alone; might miss breakfast, perhaps, and lie in bed. Their honeymoon was slipping by.

Next morning she had a slight headache. During their engagement she had had none of the terrible, vice-like attacks which had beset her from time to time since childhood. "It's not bad, so far, Otto, but I think I would be foolish to risk walking in the heat and the glare."

"Is there anything I can do for you? Anything that would ease it; some ice from the kitchen, perhaps?"

"No, nothing. I think I shall stay in bed, if you don't mind." She hoped he would stay with her but would not ask.

"Shall I bring you some breakfast, then?" He was already out of bed.

"Just a cup of tea, please."

When he came back from the dining room with the tea he said, "Mrs Baldwin has already ordered the picnic from the cook. I shall have to eat for two of us! I am so sorry you can't come, my dearest, because it's sure to be a very jolly day." He settled his straw hat, jauntily, before the mirror and took up his cane. "I shall make sure we are not late back. Have a good rest, and perhaps a little walk in the garden before it gets too hot?" He glanced out of the window. "There is Mrs Baldwin, now. I must run. Take care, dearest girl!"

He must always run, she thought. His energy and appetite for adventure were so great. She had nothing to fear from the middle-aged Mrs Baldwin and so she did not call her unhappiness jealousy. She knew only that she had tried to hold him and had failed. The headache began to claw at her eyeballs.

He returned with the first breeze from the sea, blowing open the door, gusting his enthusiasm from the end of the bed.

"Look, my darling! I must show you my effort!" He held up a child's painting; a bright boat on a cobalt ocean. "Mrs Baldwin tells me I am a 'natural primitif'. You British are so funny!"

He had not noticed her ghastly face and stopped in amazement as she flung herself off the bed and retched violently into the basin. He caught her in his arms and held her steady as she vomited.

"Dearest, you should have told me you were so ill. You must always tell me. I would not go away if you were ill."

Mrs Baldwin had taken a study of Otto's head as he painted at her easel. His hat was pushed back and his necktie discarded. She had caught on his face an expression of total absorption as he gazed at his subject. He looked as though he were learning about boats and the sea for the first time. Mrs Baldwin had given it to Miriam.

She had it still, somewhere in her belongings: an image of something she had hoped to contain.

3 Home

The steamer trip to Sandgate had been Miriam's first venture on the sea. In her childhood at Lake Cootharaba the sandbar had been her boundary, since the voyage over it was dangerous, the business of grown men. Except between Brisbane, Cootharaba and Gympie, she had never travelled at all and, for her, Australia was a triangle of town, bush and coastal lake. Within that territory, "home" conjured an image of the warrum where the paperbarks, in their ceremonial paint and rich intimate smell, stood silent and protective about her.

Otto had travelled the world. He had a photograph of the parents he had left behind in the village of Grenzhausen when he was only seventeen. His mother was a harsh-looking woman of square, determined jaw and jutting bosom. His father, bearded like a patriarch, had weak eyes behind thick round spectacles. Standing behind his wife's shoulder, he peered at the camera, while she stared resolutely into the distance. "I would not be a German," Otto said. "I wished to be a <u>citizen of the whole world</u>." But he was not, now, a citizen of any country.

Miriam had seen the hunger for "home" in Otto's eyes and knew that, in his imagination, it had a particular texture and light. It was also a peopled place, as she saw from the affection he lavished on Kathleen and the hope he held of children. Because she was determined to create his dream for him she searched her own understanding for its furniture and found it almost barren. She supposed most brides had firm notions of married life and the shell they would build for it. Carrie, for instance, had seemed to know by instinct what was required and leapt to the task; bearing children, cooking, sewing, generating a pulsing energy on which her taciturn, phlegmatic husband fed. Hetty, who had no need to cook and sew, assembled all the elements of a socially suitable marriage and transformed them from slavish routines into supportive structures from which she and Charles launched their vigorous pursuit of living. Of their own marriage Miriam could see only the appurtenances: social position and the appropriate ordering of their house and its functions. These originated, not in her own experience of home, but from the decade of her life in Brisbane. But Otto had married the schooled Brisbane woman and not the unbound child of Lake Cootharaba.

Klaus Buchbinder was the first visitor to their house at St Julian's. He came on the morning of their third day there. Miriam was in the small parlour at the back of the house, sewing on her machine. She wore an old gown and her hair was roughly screwed into a knot. She was in a rush to finish some cushion-covers so that their drawing-room, at least, might be ready for entertaining.

"Miriam! Klaus is come; Klaus is here!" Otto threw open the door and stood aside. Klaus, framed in the doorway, held up his hands as though in wonder. "Ah, my friend," he said, "now you are at home!"

When Miriam reproved Otto later for giving her no warning and allowing her to be seen in such a state, Otto replied, "But darling girl, Klaus is my dearest friend and he would like to see you as I do: the precious heart of my life, beating at its very centre!" And it was at times when she was busiest about the house that Otto was most loving, most inclined to ruffle her clothing, to clasp her from behind and passionately kiss the back of her neck.

Christmas was almost upon them when they returned to Brisbane so that, besides the work of settling into their house, there was a flurry of social engagements. Foremost among them for Otto was a party he had arranged for her to meet his staff and the landlady of his former rooms. She had never heard of people giving parties at home for their staff and was puzzled.

"They are like family to me," he explained. "They have been loyal and devoted to the business, some of them almost from the beginning. Miss Smallwood, for instance, was my first employee."

"But Otto, you pay them for that, surely?"

"Yes, and I have always paid them as well as I could. But there were times when they were not paid as well as they deserved, because I could not afford it, and yet they have stood by me. And Miss Hunt, my landlady — she is the niece of an English writer; you will like to meet her — she kept me on when I was very ill and could not pay the rent." Miriam had never imagined Otto poor or ill. The thought was disturbing and did nothing to enhance her pleasure in meeting the people who had known him in those circumstances.

It was to be an informal garden party, though the food Otto ordered was lavish. As they dressed for it, Otto insisted she wear a cotton rather than a silk gown. "We don't need to impress these people. My book-keeper knows every penny I earn and the others, because they are clever, will have a very good notion." Miriam complied but pointed out to him, as the guests began to arrive, that Miss Hunt was wearing her finery. "Ah, but she has a position to maintain," said Otto, as though they did not. Despite it, Miss Hunt was nervous and excessively polite. Miriam noticed that her cerise taffeta was painstakingly patched above one elbow and at the hem.

"Well, Mr Gluck, I had hoped to get a traveller," Miss Hunt said, in answer to Otto's question. "You know how particularly fond I am of travellers. Such interesting tales they have to tell. But I fear our travellers these days prefer the modern hotels. So I have had a little difficulty in replacing you. Not that you could ever really be replaced, dear friend! But yes, I think I have found someone suitable: a Mr Bertle or Bartle — I can't quite read his writing — who was recommended to me by a cousin at Home. He is at present lodging in Melbourne but he hopes to be with me shortly after Christmas. I confess to being just a tiny bit lonely without you but I shall start 1899 in much better spirits, I do assure you. And it is worth a great deal to see you so happily set up here with your charming wife!" She held Miriam's hands between her own and looked up into her face with what seemed like genuine pleasure.

Jack Dakers, Otto's manager, came with his wife, and Miss Smallwood with her sister, Mrs Brown, who had worked for Otto until her marriage. "And how's the little fellow?" Otto asked her.

"Just the same, Mr Gluck. He never improves. But he does like the engine you sent him for his birthday." She had an idiot, Otto explained, by the worthless Brown who afterwards deserted her, leaving her dependent on Miss Smallwood.

Matron Bloom, with her husband, swept in with a most proprietary air and there were several more, including Peter Forward, the book-keeper, and "young Master Tim", the office boy, whose trousers were too short above his large shiny boots. When all the introductions were made, Otto took his coat off and the men followed his example; the party became very relaxed. Everyone professed delight at meeting Miriam and most drew her into some conversation about Otto's virtues. She felt they laid claim to knowing him better than she did and his pleasure in them was plain. Longing to possess him utterly, to throw a net around him and draw him back from them, she accused herself of snobbery. I'm becoming as bad as Sarah, she thought, and did her best to be gracious to them. But she did not expect that they would invite her to return their visits and when Miss Hunt, the first to leave, extended this courtesy she was surprised into agreeing. To Miss Smallwood and Mrs Dakers she merely smiled her thanks.

"Of course we must visit them," Otto said later. "They are good people and kind. But also, here it is said that Jack is as good as his master. My Jack Dakers has shares in his brother's goldmine. Next week they may strike it rich and Jack might set up in business – perhaps a business like mine; he knows it thoroughly. Isn't it better that he should be loyal to me so that he will not take away my livelihood? Or perhaps he will join up with a union of workers and persuade Peter also to join. Then they may demand wages I cannot give them and so put me out of business. If I have already given them as much as I can, and if I've shown friendship and loyalty to them, then they will not do this. The British call it enlightened self-interest. To me, that is right."

Miriam did not resist his philosophy. She thought that he had spoken more truly, however, when he had said "they are like family to me" and that was the root of her discontent.

On Christmas Eve they were late in arriving at the German Club and most of their party were already seated at a table well forward in the hall. On the stage was a huge Christmas tree, aglitter with candles. The hall's pillars were festooned with coloured ribbons and regional emblems. Waiters in traditional costumes hurried about with trays of beer and schnapps and an orchestra played a waltz. No-one was yet dancing but many people were milling about between the tables, greeting friends. Otto introduced her to a couple who had come to Brisbane for the festivities from west of Toowoomba. Gaspar Bielefeld and his wife, Marthe, were seed merchants.

"Business is ver bed. Furst we hev der ticks plague end der strikes end now we are heving der drought so bed der farmers cannot afford der seeds. Also they cennot plant der seeds, der ground is so hard, end der seeds will not grow, anyhow, because dere is no rain. But still we are comm to enjoy ourselves because we must hev always der hope!" Mr Bielefeld spoke cheerfully. When Miriam caught Lili Schuler's eye and went to join her at the table, the conversation went on in German. Soon there was a knot of people around Otto and Mr Bielefeld and it was some time before Otto came to the table.

"Welcome, my dear Miriam!" called Lili. "You are looking so well! It is the sea air has made you to shine, eh?" and she winked roguishly. "Ha! I have made you to blush. You Englishers are so sensitive! Here is another one you must meet." She turned to the woman sitting next to her. "Jane Rohl, Miriam Gluck. Jane's husband, Heinrich, knew your grandfather, Miriam. Where is he? Ha! He is talking politics with Willi. Never mind, you must talk to Jane because she also speaks no German and everywhere it will be German here tonight! I think I shall have to give you both lessons."

"Heinrich forbids me to learn German and he won't speak it to the children, either," said Jane with a plaintive shrug.

"Then he is naughty! Such a shame to lose a language to the children. And yet he keeps it himself?"

"He says he can't think in English. But we are Australian and must not speak German."

Lili was indignant. "Surely Australians may speak another language! I am Austrian but also I speak French and Polish, as well as English. How is there to be any culture in this country?" She was shrieking like a parrot now. "Why does your husband come here tonight if he is so against Germans?"

The man talking to Willi heard her and turned. "Not against Germans, Lili," he called good-humouredly. "They are very fine in Germany. But in Australia we must have Australians or how will my children know where they belong? Just the same, I admit that at home we know how to celebrate Christmas! There we have something to teach these Queenslanders!" He lifted his beer glass to her.

"This is rot what you are saying, Heinrich. There are many things a man may belong to which cross the national frontiers. Language, religions, political movements."

Otto came up at that moment and slapped his forehead in mock horror. "Have I just come from speaking to the farmers about the terrible state of the country to find my wife in league with the Socialists?"

Willi and Lili, together, replied, "We were speaking of the German language..." "The labour movement is not itself Socialism!" But it was Willi Otto was after and he walked round the table to join him.

"You do not tell me your last editorial was not Socialist? Come, Willi! You speak of collectivism and equal sharing of wealth. Where is leadership to come from and where the wealth to share? What of your own paper? The money of the wealthy Germans here has financed it. It will go out of business and then what will happen to the culture you are always going on about? And again, if the newspapers are nationalised, is the government to own a German newspaper? It will all go out of the window!"

He poured himself a glass of beer from the jug on the table. Lili, in her eagerness to answer him, sprang up from her place and ran round the table where she knelt on the floor next to her husband. Heinrich Rohl gave up his chair to her and came to sit with his wife. Miriam could see Lili's face, dark and animated, as she leant into the argument, and she wondered how any woman could become so impassioned about such things. But the music had begun again and she could not follow their discussion because they were now speaking in German.

"I was fortunate to know your grandfather, Mrs Gluck," Heinrich was saying. "I am an agent for wheat and wool in Ipswich and he used to buy from me. I think he was the most honest man I ever met. There are not many like him now." The noise and heat, the smell of sweat and beer, the beer itself, had all made Miriam's head swim. She looked at Heinrich's blurred face and saw, for an instant, the pink and angry image of Matthew Wemyss.

"But would you say he was a kind man, Mr Rohl?" she asked. Her question was drowned in applause and she saw that Baiba Ryko had come on to the stage. A bracket of carols and sentimental songs began and, softly, people around the hall joined in. When at last Baiba came to *"O Tannenbaum"* everyone stood up and sang at the tops of their voices. Otto and Willi had their arms around each other and swayed to the music, but then Willi broke into some other words and Otto offered him a playful punch. There was laughter from the group around them.

The music ended and they sat down. Lili darted through the crowd to embrace Baiba and bring her to their table.

Willi said, "The trouble with you, dear Otto, is that you are a good man and a foolish one. You think freedom is in the gift of the ruling classes. Because you are good, you try to give it where you can, and you expect others to give it to you. But you are wrong; freedom cannot be given by good rulers. That is a contradiction. Freedom is the right of every man and every woman. If we would all seize and exercise our right there would be no rulers or bosses at all, good or bad. And you are foolish to think others are so good as you. They do not wish freedom for others, they wish only more and more for themselves. If you do not exercise your rights others will deny that you have them." He stared into his beer and shook his head. But Otto laughed and ruffled his hair.

"And the trouble with you, dearest Willi, is that you are a pessimist and do not believe, even though it is Christmas, that good will triumph!''

"Our Lord", said Willi, "has told us we must be wily as serpents, my heathen friend, as well as gentle as doves!"

Miriam was liverish on Christmas Day and the world seemed drawn in charcoal on buff. They were to eat dinner with Miriam's family at the house her brother Joshua and Lucy had recently finished building, and they went there after Matins, their carriage half-filled with parcels. Otto had supervised their Christmas shopping and had insisted on buying presents even for Carrie, Brian and all the Warrington children, though they would not be there. He seemed as excited as a child and unaffected by the previous night's revelries, despite being quite drunk when they had gone home.

"Mother doesn't much like Christmas," Miriam told him on the way. "It makes her feel lonely."

"She will not feel lonely when we are there!"

"There is no-one to go to Mass with her," she explained dully.

"Miriam, you should have told me! We could have gone with her this morning."

"But we aren't Roman Catholics!"

"They don't prevent others from attending the service?"

"Of course not, but we would not belong and that's what makes Mother feel lonely." The thought seemed to depress Otto's spirits and Miriam was glad because she had a presentiment, borne perhaps of jaundice, that his exuberance in her family might not be tactful.

Kathleen looked tired and rather irritable, Miriam thought, but the day was hot and, because Joshua's wife Lucy was six months pregnant, Kathleen had taken it on herself to supervise the preparations for their Christmas dinner. Miriam wondered why her mother had not preferred to have it at her own house.

"Joshua seemed so anxious to show off his new home. It is a very fine one, don't you think? But, to be sure, it's hard on Lucy, and she's worn out with the move here, and all."

Lucy was a tiny red-haired woman who, even in full health, looked frail and transparent. In her pregnancy, she seemed to totter rather than walk and Miriam could see that her feet, in soft shoes, were very swollen. She was timid and rarely initiated a conversation, but she was very pretty and her face held a look of shy appeal.

"You must be very glad to be here at last," Miriam said, sitting down with her and Sarah on the verandah.

"Oh, I am, Miriam. It has been such a long time in building and the baby getting closer and closer. Joshua has been so busy with his work and there does seem to be a great deal to worry about with a new house." The men were walking about in the garden and Lucy watched Joshua anxiously. "I think they are coming in now. I must go and see that everything is ready for dinner. I mustn't leave it all to your poor mother."

"She is terrified of Joshua, isn't she?" said Sarah when she had gone. "I can't imagine why. He's so quiet and dull, really."

Miriam thought that though Joshua was a closed and secretive person, his silences were not dull but highly charged. They might be frightening to his fragile wife.

Lucy fainted half-way through the meal and was carried to her bed. Miriam almost envied her. The heat was intense and the food too rich. Her father dominated the table with his loud voice, and all the younger men seemed to jostle with each other for importance. Their opinions on prices and investments, their predictions for the economy, the next government, the drought, the threatening rise of Labour, all pushed and shoved in a mental sweat like cattle in a holding pen. Of the women, only Sarah occasionally thrust a view between them and it was trampled down.

The women communicated with one another across the table largely by gestures. Kathleen cajoled Harry and Edith, Sarah's children, together on her left, or talked to Otto, on her right, when he could be abstracted from the ruck. Miriam tried to engage Edward, next to her, but he retreated from conversation into intoxicated petulance. She gave up and sat in silent and growing vexation with them all. Lucy's illness provided them with an excuse to leave early.

"You are out of sorts, Miriam," Otto said in the carriage after several failed attempts to talk to her. "Why is it?"

Society

"Why must you men behave the way you do?" she demanded angrily in reply. "You talked entirely to each other throughout the meal and it was all about business and politics and more about how clever you are. You ignored Mother and Sarah and me and you made Lucy ill."

But she knew, as she attacked him, the seething source of her anger was not that. Otto alone had begun conversations that included the women. Each time he had been snatched back by her father or Joshua, as though they would test his determination to stand apart from them. When they had him, they tore at him, goading with sarcasm and slamming with bombast. Alfred Borden had been called on to back them up, like a cattle-dog to nip at Otto's heels. Otto was a newcomer to the family, at bay in their midst. He did not attack, did not confidently defend. In his bewilderment he smiled at them. Miriam's wounds were full of maggots.

Otto did not answer her charges. He stared out of the carriage window in silence all the way home.

4 Drought

The sharp hope of happiness, thrusting up like a green shoot through bare and shaly ground, had withered. Miriam did not notice it had gone until the morning she found its place smothered with contentment, as milfoil will cover the ground in a dense mat of tiny roots and leaves.

Hetty Curthoys and Maud Pendle were visiting, as they often did, during the week, when their husbands were at work.

"We're going to have a baby in May," Miriam told them.

"Oh, good luck with it! You're past three months? Well, you're probably safe enough now," Maud said.

Hetty, full of generous pleasure, hugged her. "Congratulations, darling! You must be so happy!"

"Otto's thrilled, I'll bet," Maud added.

In the space between the two women, the one who hoped desperately and the one who did not hope for a child, Miriam realised her contentment. Against the background of Otto's soaring joy she saw that it was earthbound.

The first year of their marriage had settled on them like a layer of dust, blurring their distinctions. The piquancy of otherness had dissolved into comforting familiarities, making them sluggish. But awareness of her pregnancy immediately quickened the love and excitement in Otto. Miriam was suddenly mysterious to him as no other woman had been, and newly precious because she carried his future in her womb. "My little Queenslander," he would say, patting her belly. The child was not just his continuity in the world, it was his anchor in the country he had chosen. "Now I am to be the father of a citizen, I must become one myself."

Miriam wryly pointed out that he had felt no urgency to become a Queenslander when he had married one. For a moment he looked abashed and then a thought occurred, "And I will not become a Queenslander now, Miriam! I shall wait until Australia is one country and then I'll become an Australian."

The idea took on symbolic force for him. "After Federation," he told their friends, "my wife, my child and I will all be new citizens of a new country."

Otto's energy found fresh impetus. The home he had promised must be begun and he thought the land he had bought, as an investment with others, might be suitable. They went to look at it, to the place where James had taken her and advised her to marry Otto if she liked him. It had been cleared of its low scrub and roads had been scratched across its rough denuded face. The blocks were large, intended for wealthy buyers, and some ran down to the flats of Breakfast Creek, but money for development had been in short supply and few houses had been built there. Otto had a plan of the lots and pointed out the best of those still for sale. Miriam, protective of her pregnancy, would not scramble about with him but sat in the buggy as he paced the boundaries.

"This one is the best, I think. We could build here at the top, where we would have the view. And there is room at the bottom, where the soil is better, for our vegetable garden."

But it would take time to build. The drought, which had parched the whole of Queensland for nearly eight years, had dried up orders for Otto's veterinary equipment. "We could build immediately — something. But I want us to have the best house possible, Miriam, and that will take more time and more money. Do you mind the waiting?"

"Of course not! I'm content at St Julian's, Otto. And with the hospital so close."

As the baby grew inside her, swelling her body and draining her energy, Miriam began to be afraid. She did not know why and was unable to speak of it to anyone. Otto, in his extreme delight, accentuated the fear. The importance he attached to fathering this child, the difference he made in his treatment of her because of it, conspired with the physical changes to deplete her sense of self. It was like coming to a place one knew and finding all the landmarks changed. There were moments when the fear became panic. Then, though the people around her went on in their usual ways, she did not hear or understand them. It was as though she were in a glass tank which magnified and distorted their gestures, but through which she could make no contact with them. She struggled to fix her attention on external happenings and so keep her reason.

There was an election in November that year and she remembered that, after it, Lili was jubilant: "The first Labour government in the world! Imagine it, in Queensland! Who would have believed . . ."

Willi was gloomy. "It is a country of contradictions," he said. "But it is also a Party of contradictions and nothing will come of it, you will see."

"Who has voted for them?" Otto marvelled. "My farmers will not and nor will my doctors. I know no-one. Apart from you two dangerous radicals, no-one! And, fortunately, you do not count!"

"Otto, you do not know anyone who counts!" said Lili. "You know no mine workers, no cane-cutters, no railway workers; you do not live in reality at all."

"You are forgetting that I know the railway workers, Lili," said Klaus, "and I know that if we do not have the Kanaka and the Chinaman we will not get the railways built because the workers will not work. And what will be the progress then, if the railways are not?"

"Progress!" snorted Willi and Lili together. "Progress for whom?"

Miriam was surprised to find her father not displeased by the election result. The previous government had been led by liberals and Josh Wemyss was a member of Robert Philp's conservative faction which, if Labour fell, was now set to take power. "Labour government, rubbish!" he snorted. "It won't last a week and then Philp will get up."

He and Willi Schuler were right: the new government did fall in the next month and Josh Wemyss rose in importance. The gentle political raillery Otto enjoyed with Willi and Lili developed an acrimonious edge.

Early in the new year, Otto brought a strange man home for dinner; strange because he was older than Otto and had the manner and bearing of one long settled in his opinions and profession, yet he had, in Otto's words, run away from home. Dr Hugo Leclerc was a French Canadian.

"It was, I think, the approaching turn of the century which inspired in me a desire for the new; a need to re-examine my life and its objects. I decided, perhaps on an impulse, that I would begin the twentieth century in a new land. So now I am here and I have thrown myself on the mercy of your husband, Madam, in the belief he may be able to help me make a beginning."

"And perhaps I can. I have been telling Dr Leclerc about the hospital at Marburg, Miriam. It is for sale and it's a good practice. The farmers in the district are not rich; they are mostly German peasants on small holdings and have suffered much over the last ten years. Yet there is very useful work to be done among them and a sufficient income for the right man. The hospital is well equipped; I have supplied it regularly for some years." Otto was excited.

"Alas, Sir, I doubt I would have the money to buy it."

"There also I may be able to help you."

Otto took Dr Leclerc to inspect the hospital during the second week in February. "I wish you were able to come with us, dear girl, but it is much too far and the mail coach from Rosewood is not a comfortable trip." He was to be away for three nights. Miriam was afraid to be alone but said nothing.

The third night of his absence was the hottest of the summer. Miriam lay sleepless, waiting for a breath of air from the river. The windows of her bedroom were open, letting in mosquitoes, but she could not bear the stuffy confines of the net around her bed. The hot darkness pressed in on her, palpable, suffocating, so that she no longer knew the direction of the floor or the ceiling. Then the pains came, tearing and ruthless. She cried out but there was no servant living in the house to hear. The pain subsided leaving her breathless and in a sweat of fear. She could hear her heart fluttering like a terrified bird against the mattress. Cicadas shrilled like banshees in the garden she must now cross for help. The pains came a second time and she dared not wait for the third. It took her twenty minutes to stagger and crawl along the path to the hospital steps. By the time the matron and her husband had lifted her into a bed, the baby had come and had died.

If she screamed, Mother would surely come and would give her the medicine. Dr Grogan came.

"Now now, Mrs Gluck, you must not upset yourself like this. The little lad has gone, could not have lived. But there will be others. You ladies are very resilient, you know, and it often happens this way. There's no sense in grieving; you must conserve your strength. Mr Gluck will be home tomorrow, Matron tells me, and will need you to be strong. I'll give you some morphia to make you sleep and in the morning you'll see it differently."

Departing, he tapped the foot of the bed with his hand, and it seemed the bed began to spin; slowly at first but gathering speed, until she was sucked into a black and screaming maelstrom.

The morning was bleached white as hospital linen. Matron came and went on silent feet and spoke only in whispers. Miriam, voided of all feeling, lay in an antiseptic limbo awaiting the sound and colour of judgment. Mr Bloom went to meet the train from Ipswich. The matron soothed her forehead with a sponge. "Your husband will soon be here, Mrs Gluck."

Then Otto stood alone beside the bed. He had no words of blame nor tears of absolution for her and his face was of the defeated.

"I'm so sorry, Otto," she said.

"Oh Miriam! It's not your fault; it cannot be your fault. He was not ready to come. Perhaps we wanted him too much." And then he wept, kneeling on the floor beside the bed, his face buried in the counterpane. She stroked his head until he stopped.

Otto had her carried home next day but she would not go back to her own bed and lay instead, neither asleep nor awake, on a couch in the drawing-room. Otto tiptoed about her. She wished he would take her up in his arms and chafe some life into her. She wished he would shake her until she broke open so that remorse would spill out. She wanted either anger or love but not the respect due only to the dead.

It was Kathleen who unloosed her grief, folding her in her arms, rocking and crooning, "You did your best, Miriam love, you did your best. It's in God's hands after that. Blame Him if you like; He's big enough and He'll take the credit fast enough, too, when things go different!"

"Did you blame Him, Mother, when you lost yours?"

"Then and many times, dear love, but don't you tell another soul! That's between me and Him." Miriam smiled out of her swollen face but knew she did not have her mother's special relationship with God to call on.

As she grew better, Miriam became capricious. Sometimes she felt an unaccountable elation, as though freed of a great weight. Then she wanted to run on the grass and shout as she has not done since girlhood. At others, she was irritable and snapped at Otto as at a stupid dog. When he protested, always mildly, she would weep copiously. He could not follow her through this maze of emotions. She knew, too, that his own grief was still raw and she was not surprised that he withdrew from her, busying himself with arrangements for Dr Leclerc's purchase of the Marburg hospital.

Hetty came to sit with her in the garden. Her tears welled up, magnifying her pretty eyes. "Oh, what you must be feeling, Miriam!"

Because Hetty was her best friend, Miriam tried to tell her. "I had a kind of presentiment, I think. It was as though I was losing my self. I was very frightened. I can't help wondering, Hetty, if that is why I lost the baby instead."

"Oh, my dear, that's very morbid! I can't imagine it could be anything like that. You mustn't think so!" And she persuaded Miriam to go out for a drive.

Otto must have been worried about her because he brought Dr Leclerc home one afternoon and then absented himself for half an hour at St Julian's: an order for equipment had been delayed.

Dr Leclerc was direct. "You are not recovering as fast as you should, I think. May I be of any help?" He looked into her face as her father had never done and she told him what she had tried to explain to Hetty. Because she saw that he understood, the question came out right.

"Medically," he answered, "it is not possible. There would have been some other, physical cause. Whether there can be a spiritual cause of the physical, who knows? These things are beyond us. But suppose that it is so. You are young and it is natural that you were frightened. We are, all of us, sometimes afraid and turn away from life. We must learn to forgive ourselves because, if we do not, we will never try again. So we do not heal, we do not grow, we do not get better at life. Guilt is a most corrosive emotion, the brother in crime of vengeance. Forgiveness is the best medicine I know."

"But difficult to administer to oneself, Doctor."

"Then you must allow your husband to administer it to you. And perhaps he, also, is in need of forgiveness from you."

Miriam had not seen her husband in that light, any more than she had imagined him ill or poor. Over the next few days, in his averted eyes and long silences, she saw the signs of his need.

Dr Leclerc took over the hospital at Marburg in the autumn. "As soon as I am settled I hope you will both come and visit me," he said, parting from them.

"I'd like that, Dr Hugo. May we go, Otto?"

"Of course! And perhaps we will spend a few days in Toowoomba as well. The mountain air would do Miriam good, wouldn't it, Doctor?"

"I think a little holiday would be beneficial for you both."

When winter came, Otto decided they should take the train to Toowoomba and visit Dr Leclerc on the way home. "You will be stronger then, and better able to cope with the coach from Grantham to Marburg," he said. They left Brisbane in the late afternoon and as the train hurtled through the Lockyer Valley, Miriam could see only the sparks from the engine and the lonely lights of farmsteads, adrift on waves of dark.

Winter in Toowoomba was colder than Miriam had ever imagined. Their guesthouse hung on the mountainside and in the morning the mountains were swathed in mist which dazzled and dissolved as the sun rose . Then the land rolled out below, golden in the winter light. Miriam had not known before the vastness of her country. "It's so very beautiful," she said and felt for Otto's hand. "Thank you for bringing me here."

"It looks beautiful but really it's very dry and sad with drought," and he rested his cheek against her head.

"But it will rain again soon, Otto." She turned her face and kissed his cheek, tasting the salt of a tear.

They walked in the sharp mornings, hand in hand among the rhododendrons and azaleas. At night they sat close, with hot drinks beside log fires. In bed they curled around each other, nurturing between them a bud of tenderness. When, after four days, they descended again to the valley, they agreed the mountain air had done them both good.

At close quarters the valley was brown and the earth cracked by drought. From Grantham, where they left the train, the road wound, rutted and dusty, between low swells of ground and over shallow rifts where no creek ran. Frail cattle grazed the roots of grass. When they stopped at a hamlet along the way for tea, the faces of the people were closed, stubborn against their freshness. Most were Germans and responded only slowly when Otto spoke to them in their own tongue. "Life is very hard for them," Otto apologised. "They have no room for pleasantries."

Marburg, named for a famous town in Germany, was on a hill, the highest for some distance, and the hospital stood on its crown. It was cool there towards evening when they arrived. Dr Leclerc waited in the doorway, holding out his arms to them. He was a short man but there was about him a magnanimity which made him seem large to Miriam. He kissed them both on each cheek and drew them into the warmth of his study. "Soon I will be finished here and then we will go to my house. It's very fine, much too large for an old bachelor."

Over dinner, he said, "You Germans are remarkable people. I have never met such tenacity as these poor farmers have. They cling to their holdings despite everything.

"They are tough, yes," Otto agreed, "but they have little choice, surely. Where else are they to go?"

When Miriam remarked that Dr Leclerc looked tired, he replied, "I have to travel around a great deal. My farmers do not believe in coming to the hospital. I must persuade them that medicine has something to offer them. They rely on folklore and suffer much in consequence. And, of course, I do not speak German. The children learn English in school and so, often, I must rely on a child to translate to its parents what I have to say. That is always a strain and sometimes it's distressing or embarrassing to the family. Perhaps you will help me while you are here, Otto?"

And before they were finished their coffee the doctor was summoned to the hospital. A man had brought his young daughter in from an outlying district and she appeared to be very ill. "Come with me, I may need you," the doctor said.

The man who sat on a bench in the waiting-room seemed carved of knotted wood. He held his hat between his knees and raised only his expressionless eyes when they came in. Otto sat down beside him, putting his hand on his knee. The man neither flinched nor relaxed but he answered Otto's questions. Dr Leclerc went to the child and when he returned Otto said, "He wants to know if he will need the bag he has brought."

"Tell him, no; he will not need it. I will remove her tonsills and she will recover. He may stay here tonight, we will give him a bed. His daughter must stay a few more days."

Miriam asked, "What does he mean? About the bag?"

"They bring a bag for the body on the return journey."

Next day they accompanied Dr Leclerc on his nearer rounds, to families where Otto's translation would be most useful. The roads were rough and though it was winter the sun was hot. Women and children laboured with men on the farms they passed, pruning vines, hoeing rows and carrying water. Their houses stood in barren paddocks, unsheltered except for a few fruit trees – and those were withered by drought. Miriam could remember nothing so harsh from her own childhood, which drought had never touched. Yet, at the farms they visited, women smiled from leathery faces, their bones highlighted by the kerchiefs they wore. They offered food and drink: a glass of homemade beer or spirit, bread, cheese, sausage, pickles. Miriam, conscious of their poverty, was reluctant to eat but the women gestured insistently at the food and Otto said, "You must have something. You will offend them." Grave-faced children watched.

Otto and the doctor examined the patients, and talked and joked sometimes with the families. They inspected a ham which had been cured, a recent batch of cheese and, once, considered the fate of a cow that was down. Miriam, having nothing to do, felt awkward and superfluous. Next morning she said, "If you'll excuse me I won't come with you today." Dr Leclerc directed her to sit in the garden with a book from his small library but she sensed Otto's strong disappointment. As she brooded on it her pleasure in the day soured.

When the men returned in the late afternoon they brought with them a tall thin man in a shabby black suit, whose fair drooping moustache gave him a disconsolate expression.

"Meet Pastor Gerhardt Ullrich," said Dr Leclerc. "We collected him on our last call and he has come home for a sundowner."

"Already you are picking up the local tongue, Dr Hugo!" Pastor Ullrich sank into a chair and stretched out his long legs before him. "Ach, this country!" he sighed.

"You don't like it, Pastor?" Otto asked.

"I dream every night of the green fields at home. Of the church bell ringing out over the valley and the people walking, peaceful and contented, to church; as the cows walk, heavy with milk, to the dairies. Here all is despair and desolation of spirit."

"Here is challenge, surely! A new people in a new land; a future that demands we become more than contented cows waiting to be milked!" Otto was irritated.

"Pastor Gerhardt has hard work here, Otto, to retain hope among the people after so much drought." Dr Leclerc was faintly reproving.

"That is hard, yes!" the pastor responded. "But also I must teach German to the children and English to their parents. And when they cannot speak to each other any more I must try to hold them together in their families and in the Family of God."

"Drink! Drink, Pastor, and cheer up! You know your people better than I, but since I have been here I have discerned among them a great courage and surely a pastor must have at least the courage of his flock?''

"Pastor Ullrich," Miriam interrupted, "I understand the need to teach the parents English, but why do you work so hard to teach the children German?"

"That is an important question, *Frau Glück*, and I have thought about it a great deal. It seems to me that, after the Faith, the language is God's most precious gift to man. It is a living thing, like a great vine with its roots in our deepest history and its tendrils catching at our future. It came before the Faith, of course; and through it, as through the stem of a vine, the Faith is carried from one generation to the next."

"But isn't one language as good as another for that? The faith can be carried as well by English as by German, surely?'' Miriam was surprised by her own insistence.

"Faith, dear lady, incarnates itself in culture. And so English is the best language to carry the culture of the British. But for us Germans, English cannot carry our culture, cannot incarnate our faith in a way proper to us. Our culture is very great; the culture of Luther and Goethe, of Kant and Hegel. It is also the culture of the great masters of music and, though music is a language of its own, it is influenced by the spoken language. You will hear that most particularly if you listen to the cacophanous language and music of the Chinese. We owe the best we have to God and so, in short, our faith must be the best fruit of our language and our culture."

"And what culture is to prevail in this country, where we are such a polyglot crowd?" Dr Leclerc asked.

"Ah Doctor, your beer must have done me good because I see hope there. Something rich and splendid will grow in this land, I am sure, but it will be a product of many grafts and must have the sap from all these strong vines coursing through it."

"A good analogy, Pastor, and a poetic image! I shall remember it."

Otto was placated but Miriam thought it all great nonsense and had no sympathy for a man who drove himself so hard for such stuff.

5 Husbandry

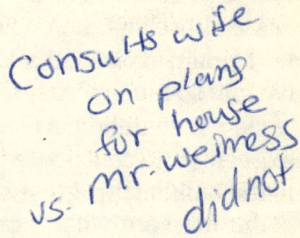
Consults wife on plans for house vs. mr. weiness did not

Miriam did not become pregnant again in the first year of the new century, as Otto had hoped, but the building of their house went ahead, the new focus of Otto's energy and the symbol of his belonging.

"An Englishman's home is his castle and our castle is to be most splendid!" he boasted to Kathleen as he unfolded the plans for her.

"Otto, you're a terrible braggart, to be sure!"

"Not at all, Little Mother. Building a house is a statement of faith in the future. You build a temporary shelter if you have little faith and a fine solid house if you have much. I'm an optimist, that's all."

His optimism led him to plan what, in the end, he could not build. The house that resulted had grand formal rooms, wide shady verandahs and a struggle of small rooms for bedrooms, study, kitchen and offices. It was not so much that he ran out of money, though the continuing shortage of rain and capital in Queensland impeded him, but that he lost enthusiasm for the project.

In the beginning Miriam had tried to regulate his ideas to manageable proportions but soon discovered that his idea of house design had little to do with architectural or practical realities. Rather, he proceeded by imagining a setting; a musical evening on a summer night, perhaps, with guests spilling out from the drawing-room and into the garden, and then incorporated it into his plans. His drawing-room must have the alcove for the piano in just the place he had imagined it. Or it must open on to a conservatory: "But you would like to have a conservatory, Miriam." She had no particular desire for a conservatory but it was as though, having once imagined her sitting amid ferns and orchids, he could no longer conceive of her without one. Miriam conceded and humoured him since his dreaming gave him so much pleasure. He grew disappointed, not because she did not contend his ideas, but because she did not enter into his dreams and contributed none of her own. His interest waned and the building progress slowed.

"I'm not sure what he expects of me," Miriam confided to Hetty.

"I expect he just wants to please you."

"But I am pleased! So long as he's happy, I don't mind whether the house has six conservatories!"

"Oh, Miriam, you must have a clearer idea of what you want than that!"

"I suppose I should. But Otto always has such strong opinions and his ideas run on at such a pace. It's as though he's used up all the ideas before I get to them." Hetty laughed at her but Miriam had never before been encouraged to have ideas or dreams and, under the pressure of Otto's demand for them, she felt her poverty.

In September Otto's dreams were forced by an offer for St Julian's. It was a good offer and he thought it unwise, despite the inconvenience, to refuse. The house was hurriedly finished and they moved, awkwardly, on New Year's Day when all around were celebrating the proclamation of the Commonwealth of Australia. Miriam was sitting in the conservatory surrounded by packing cases, blowing her nose to be rid of dust, when Otto opened the champagne he had promised in celebration of their new home and the new country. Then he took an envelope from his pocket and laid it in her aproned lap. "Open it, dear girl. It's for you."

The deeds of the house were there and they were made out in her name. Staring at the thick, cream documents, she was beset by conflict. Her mind acknowledged a gift of great value and the honour of his trust and esteem. In no marriage she knew was the wife the owner of the family home. But her heart quailed before the responsibility his gift implied. She felt he had laid on her a burden of their future which should properly be his. Otto studied her face and his own fell. "What have I done, dearest? Aren't you pleased to have this house?"

"Yes, of course, Otto. I suppose I'm just surprised; shocked, almost. It's so unexpected and so generous of you. I don't know what . . ." She waved the papers distractedly.

"Not generous, only fair. Your father gave us a generous wedding present and I was determined his money should go into a house for you. And then, Miriam," he was suddenly solemn, "if anything should happen to me, and there are our children to care for, I should want your future to be secure. I'm impulsive, as you know, and something of a gambler with life. But no matter what I may win or lose, this always is yours and no one can take it away from you. Do you understand me?"

She was ashamed of her rejection and kissed him, spilling her champagne down his neck.

Because the new owner of St Julian's had bought the house furnished, it was necessary and agreeable to buy everything new for their Wilston home. Otto revelled in the choosing and buying and forgot, for the time, his intention to become an Australian. His taste in furnishings was lavish. He liked gilded mirrors and Chinese vases, French brocades and Meissen china. The blue and grey stoneware from his family pottery in Grenzhausen was especially important to him. Then they had to have the latest kitchen range and two water closets with septic tanks. Electricity and gas were not connected to the Wilston area so Otto installed an acetylene plant for lighting and, because they were now so much further from town, they also had to have a telephone.

Miriam had never admired her own looks or devoted much time to fashionable clothes. Now, the more Otto decked her house with finery, the plainer she felt. When she caught sight of herself in a mirror, she thought she looked like the maid in her white pleated blouse and navy skirt, the red patches bright on her cheekbones and her hair carelessly caught up. She sometimes stopped to think, as she had never done before, about the other women Otto must have known. She thought of the sensual Baiba Ryko, the intimacy she conveyed when in Otto's company, and she wondered why Otto had chosen to marry someone as reserved and unexciting as herself. She had come to understand that, for him, everything represented something beyond itself and pondered what it was she stood for in his imagination. The question made her uneasy; submissive and defiant by turns.

Otto would not allow her to invite her mother and father until everything in their new house was in place. Then they came in the morning, when the house was to be seen at its best, and Otto conducted them around, pointing out all the advantages. When the tour was over and they sat down to lunch, Miriam asked, "Well, do you like my house? Otto has given it to me, you know."

"He has what?" Her father's head snapped around and Miriam saw, in his expression, one unacknowledged reason why Otto had done so.

"There, Josh! I knew Otto would provide for her! It's a wonderful house, Miriam. And Otto must be the perfect husband."

"Foolery, giving property to women!"

"We shall be having the vote before too long, Josh, and we shouldn't vote for you if you courted us with that sort of speech, should we, Miriam?" Kathleen was gay, buoyed up with vindicated love for Otto.

The garden was Otto's next project. The drought had made fruit and vegetables scarce so he employed a gardener and spent all his own spare time directing the establishment of his vegetable garden and fruit trees. A pump brought water for them from the creek and Otto called Miriam to watch the first brown gush flooding into the channels dug beside the vegetable beds. The smell of the creek came with it, mingling with the warm fragrance of the soil. Miriam, holding Otto's muddy hand, could have watched for hours as it found its way through the maze of channels.

But Otto was never content with the simple pleasure of things — the gardening, too, had to be elevated to a philososphy. Johann Heussler, the consul, had introduced Otto to his friend and fellow parliamentarian, Dr Jean-Baptist Isambert, a man well known for his advocacy of better agricultural training. When he came to dinner with Otto's friends (Miriam always thought of them as "his"), Otto seized on him.

"It's my belief, Doctor, that the problem in this country is too much land!" Dr Isambert raised his eyebrows. "In Europe, we have had to conserve what little there is; to husband it gently and treat it with respect. Here there is the view that there is always more. We are like men surrounded with beautiful women who do not regard any one of them as precious."

"There's merit in what you say." The old man considered it. "But it is not the whole, I think. The methods of Europe are not entirely suitable here. The soils are different — more fragile — and, of course, the seasons are so different, as well. Our old ways have failed but nothing has been done to find appropriate ones. There is a reluctance to spend money on such things as research, experimentation . . ."

"The same with the music," said Baiba Ryko, suddenly animated. "It does not make any money so no money is given to it!"

"It is a country of exploitation, not of husbandry. In that sense, Otto is right." Willi would have led the discussion into politics but Otto was not to be deflected.

"Surely we must not simply sit and complain, however. I intend to conduct my own little experiment here, in my acre of vegetable garden. If I'm successful, I shall publish my results."

His vegetable garden was not only the realisation of a personal dream, a cameo German idyll in which his wife and children were nostalgically set, but it also had to be a contribution to the progress of Australian agriculture; otherwise he could not justify it. Miriam laughed, "I thought you were simply trying to cut down on the household bills, Otto!"

"Your husband, Mrs Gluck, is a dynamo of ideas," Dr Isambert said and Miriam was proud.

For weeks, Otto consulted the library, scribbled notes on the garden's progress and issued a variety of instructions to the gardener. Sometimes he took off his shirt and assisted; often he called Miriam to examine the soil, newly friable with household compost, or to exclaim over the budding of a shoot. The gardener would lean laconically on his spade and watch Otto's exuberant antics. He seemed condescending and Miriam, despite her pleasure in the garden, wished her husband would not lay himself open to ridicule.

When Otto was at work Miriam liked to walk alone down to the creek where mangroves mazed the bank and wild duck made their nests. A small stand of the fine native cypress grew there, familiar from the lakeside of her childhood, and she would sit on a rock beneath them, listening to the lazy hum of insects and the soothing call of fruit doves in the warm autumn afternoons. She felt in herself the possibility of integration, the running together of past and present, and the slow healing of rifts. Though no child was yet conceived, Miriam's contentment thickened.

"May I give the house a name, Otto?" she asked one evening.

"Of course, my darling; it's your own! Have you thought of one?" She was shy about revealing so much and he hardly heard the name she spoke.

"It's the name of the district where I grew up," she explained, and was surprised by the urgency in her voice. "Cooloola", she repeated, strongly now. "It's a native word, the name of those pine trees by the creek."

He was delighted with her. "It's a beautiful name and the trees, too, are beautiful; soft and delicate, like my own dear little wife!"

But the pines had suppleness and strength in their long fine limbs and Miriam knew, as she lay in Otto's arms, that she wanted to be more than a delicate possession to him. It seemed to her that, at Cooloola, she could tap the earth for strength.

Miriam did not think of her house as financial security because she had no apprehension of need. Nor did she see it as a symbol of wealth, so that when Maud Pendle, in her blunt way said, "Look at that carpet! My, you must be wealthy", Miriam was surprised.

"I suppose so," she said, but did not really know. She thought her father was wealthy and knew he was important, which had counted for more in the stern world of her childhood. But if her friends thought Otto wealthy she was proud of that. And certainly the sale of St Julian's had left him with money to play with. He took up with Geoffrey Pendle their old idea of ice-cream manufacture and, this time, they settled to figures. Otto was to lend Geoffrey money at a favourable rate. Geoffrey offered Otto a partnership in the embryonic business but he declined.

Maud saw, in the venture, the opportunity for a telephone. "Geoffrey won't have one because he says the only person to ring us up will be his old man, wanting him to do something. If we have our own business he will have to have a telephone and then I can ring you up, Miriam."

Miriam herself shrank from the instrument, finding it intrusive of her peaceful solitude when Otto was at work. For Otto, though, it was almost an extension of himself, putting out his feelers to clients, colleagues, friends, and when he was away from home, to Miriam.

"I wonder however I managed without it," he said.

"The people at the exchange can listen to everything you say, you know, Otto."

"I know, my darling, but I'm not a keeper of secrets and so that doesn't concern me."

Miriam was surprised that Otto had rejected the opportunity of partnership in Geoffrey Pendle's venture.

"I only want the fun of it, dear girl," he said and she thought him frivolous. "No, it's true! I think it's a good idea and provides something people want in a way no-one else has done. But I dislike partnerships. I like to take my own risks without jeopardising others. And I confess I find other men often lacking in imagination and daring. Does that sound boastful? It's just a difference in style, I suppose, but I am frustrated when I'm obliged to take another's caution into account."

"So you're willing to lend money at low interest just because you like an idea? When you will get no public credit for it? You are a dear, funny thing! I'm sure Pa would be horrified at such wantoness!" But she laughed at the thought of her father's outrage.

Otto thought about it as if for the first time. "Well," he mused, "I like Geoffrey and so, I suppose, I wish him to like me. But you're right; I cannot go round giving money to everyone in the hope that they will like me!" He laughed and then thought again. "Perhaps I have a special sympathy for Geoffrey's position. You see, like him, I come from a long family tradition. Mine is pottery and in Grenzhausen I grew up with kilns and clay just as he has done with bolts of linen. After so many generations, that can seem an unbearable weight on a young man. I felt it and I knew, from boyhood, I could not bear to stay in my village, doing every day, every month, every year of my life what my grandparents and great-grandparents had perfected before me. As soon as I was able, I renounced my heritage in the business, and in my country also, so that I could find my own challenge elsewhere. I've done that and I'm happy, so I am glad to help Geoffrey do the same." As an afterthought he said, wryly, "You must remind me, when I have sons of my own, that they, too, may wish to find their own challenges and not simply inherit mine."

But no child had been conceived to him when, the following summer, he told her he must go to Germany as soon as possible. He had come to her in the kitchen, holding a piece of paper in his hand. "Here is a cable from my sister, Freya. My mother is ill and may not last the winter. She hasn't been strong since my father died five years ago, and that's odd, because it was he who depended on her and not the other way. But now she is failing. You will not mind my going very much, Miriam?"

He telephoned the shipping companies and got a berth to Europe on a ship leaving Sydney in three weeks. He expected to be away at least five months.

Miriam recognised his need to go and did not think she minded but was seized, instead, with anxiety. She knew, when the cable came, that she was not pregnant but, despite the lapse of two barren years since her miscarriage, she became obsessed by the thought that she might conceive before Otto left, and so face her pregnancy alone. She withdrew from him, holding herself aloof in their bed.

"Are you angry with me, Miriam, because I am going away?" She denied anger but was ashamed to explain her anxiety. "Please understand, Miriam: my mother is a hard and demanding woman and I do not love her. But she is my mother; I am her oldest son and she is dying. I feel I must go to her. Don't punish me for that."

She cast herself, weeping, into his arms and he took her tears for forgiveness but, when he made love to her, Miriam felt he took advantage of her weakness.

There was a buoyancy about his preparations for the trip. He committed her into the care of half a dozen different friends: "Look after my dearest girl for me while I am away." But he said it gaily, as though he were embarking on a holiday, and even when he demanded pity for himself because of the cold into which he was going, she knew he was excited to be travelling. Never did he suggest that she might go with him and Miriam would not have wanted it. Only necessity, she thought, would drive one away from home. His exhilaration was mysterious to her.

His German friends gave him messages and gifts for their families and even Kathleen, drawing him aside on the day before he left, gave him a commission.

"I have never been to Rome, Otto," she said in a conspiratorial tone. "I don't expect I ever shall, now. Would you make a pilgrimage for me? And pray for me at the High Altar of St Peter's? I should be so happy if you could do that for me."

At the station Otto was surrounded by well-wishers and, though he kept his arm about her, Miriam felt insignificant among them. She wished she could go with him to Sydney and farewell him, alone, at the dock. When the train had pulled away, Kathleen suggested she go home with her, and Willi and Lili invited her to the German Club, but she preferred to return to "Cooloola" alone. She sat by the creek for most of that day, trying to imagine Otto's progress to a city and a world she had never seen. She sought his face in her memory but it was the face of Mrs Baldwin's painting, filled with distance, that she saw, and not the close tenderness of her husband's farewell.

She had a letter from Otto, posted in Perth.
The Bight crossing was very rough and many of my fellow passengers disappeared below for a day or two. But those of us who remained on deck had some very jolly parties in the saloon and kept our spirits up by singing. Dancing was out of the question while the

ship rolled. Perth is a very beautiful place and I am determined to spend longer here one day.

From Durban he wrote: *South Africa reminds me a bit of Australia and has made me homesick. I am impatient now to be in one place or the other.*

Not until he reached Europe could she tell him of her own sickness in the mornings.

Although she was not left alone while Otto was away, his absence seemed emphasised by the attentions of others. Willi and Lili invited her to dinner at their flat. Though she had never been to their home before, since they usually met at the Club, Otto had told her that Lili was an excellent cook and Miriam, fascinated by their vitality and their belligerent devotion to one another, was curious to see them at home. Lili, she knew, was half Jewish and, according to the doctrines of her own family, that would account for a great deal of perversity. It did not prepare her for the shock she felt, when Lili took off her shoes and stood on a chair to adjust a gas lamp, to see that she wore one red and one purple stocking. Nor did it help her to accommodate to the casual serving of so much food on the table at once; fish, chicken and sausages, fruit and cheese, all brought out of the tiny kitchen without regard to orderly courses. Then Willi signed himself, perfunctorily, with the cross, they raised their glasses in salute to Miriam, and fell upon whatever took their fancy from the dishes before them.

Lili and Willi talked almost continuously to one another: about the newspaper, the exorbitant price of the vegetables they were eating, who should be the next president of the German Club, the importance of some spice in the sausage recipe, the value and morality of importing coloured labour to the cotton and sugar industries; all jumbled together like the papers on their overflowing desks. Occasionally one would break off to ask Miriam's support for a point of view, but she rarely got to the end of a sentence before the other cut in. It was a bewildering experience, though not unpleasant once she realised that nothing at all was expected of her except that she should eat enough. Had Otto been there, she knew, it would have been entirely different; he would contribute to the conversation and make demands on his hosts which would alter the shape of their evening together. Miriam could only observe them. But she was unable to categorise them and did not know whether their extraordinary domestic manners sprang from their foreignness or their class. Otto had told her that Lili's people in Austria were very wealthy, so she supposed foreignness accounted for their peculiarities. After dinner, Willi accompanied Miriam home in a cab while Lili stayed behind to wash up, because they had no maid.

Hetty giggled when Miriam told her about Lili's stockings. "How extraordinary! She looked quite distinguished at the wedding, I thought. But perhaps you can't always tell with foreigners. Oh dear, I am sorry, Otto's a foreigner, too, isn't he? But I don't quite think of him like that and he has such beautiful manners. Most Germans seem so stiff and formal, don't you think? Or else they are very hearty, like Mr Buchbinder. Charles didn't like him one bit, you know, but I thought him very amusing, really, with his speech about St George and the dragon!"

It was strange to see her husband and his friends through Hetty's eyes and Miriam wondered for the first time what class of people Otto came from and whether, now he was at home with them, he was a different man from the one she knew.

Maud and Geoffrey Pendle came to visit Miriam at "Cooloola". Miriam was glad, at first, for their company, but Otto's absence lent a subtle difference to their behaviour. The day was hot but the house caught what air there was and circulated it through the dining room where they sat. "Nice enough now, I grant you," Geoffrey commented, "but very draughty in winter. Still, I suppose Otto doesn't feel the cold like the rest of us. These Europeans think it's summer all year round, compared to their climate!" He laughed and Miriam was vaguely affronted. And he helped himself to port after lunch, saying, "Don't trouble, Miriam. I know where Otto keeps it."

Maud, fingering her glass, remarked, "Otto does have extravagant tastes, doesn't he? Being a German, I suppose. They like a lot of stuff in a house, I've noticed. You'll have to watch you don't get cluttered. But then I don't suppose you'll mind if it's all such good quality as this. That's what counts, after all."

Miriam put this down to envy but felt that her husband was

being studied and commented upon as though he were a rare specimen under glass. And not only that: her friends appeared to assume, when Otto was not with her, that she, too, would see him as other, foreign, and in some way inferior to herself. Their assumptions ruptured her oneness with him, making him seem as distant and inaccessible to her as another species.

Even Miss Hunt, Otto's old landlady, brought herself out from town on the train, carrying a cake and a bottle of homemade cordial. "I have had such a charming letter from Otto and did so want to share it with you," she said. Miriam was touched by her effort but seeing a letter from Otto to someone else accentuated her feeling that he existed, now, in another world which she could not penetrate. She wished, increasingly, for more time to herself in the house she had shared with him. When she was alone at "Cooloola" she sat without reading or thinking, as though sounding some new depth of herself, dwelling on the pregnancy that linked her being with his. Only then did she feel secure in him and confident that their baby would be born.

She had told no-one but Kathleen of the pregnancy and felt guilty that her mother knew before Otto. But when Dr Leclerc telephoned from Marburg she told him, too, because she knew he would understand her sense of pride.

"I have decided not to write and tell Otto until I am past four months and then it will be nearly time for him to come home anyway," she said.

"Then I shall not mention it when I write. But I will be in Brisbane next month and, if I may, I shall come and see how you are."

I miss you, darling girl. Everything here is cold and dreary so I think every morning of the view from our window and of the garden where, in my mind's eye, I see you sitting. But in another letter, written at the end of April: *You cannot imagine how gay everything is here. The spring flowers are thick in the woods and the fields are bright with new grass. I have just come from a visit to Cologne and the city was so lively, with people sitting at the outdoor cafes enjoying the spring sunshine. Everywhere there seemed to be music and the smell of good coffee.*

She wrote then and told him of the baby, although four

months had not passed. He cabled his joy to her. He would return, he said, as soon as he had been to Rome.

Dr Leclerc came in the rain. Miriam could see him struggling up the path from the cab through swirling curtains of water. He was drenched to the skin when he reached the door.

"You have broken the drought, Dr Hugo!"

"Then I should have stayed at home! Please God, they are getting it there."

They stood together at the door, watching the rain bounce back from the hardened earth and form in rivulets to run downhill to the creek. "It will take a lot more than this to make a difference for the poor farmers."

"Come inside. You are wet through and cheerless."

He was a heavier man than Otto but she found some pyjamas and an old dressing-gown for him to put on while his clothes dried. Seeing him clad like that, familiar in her husband's clothes and vulnerable without his own, an old man sitting beside her fire, Miriam felt a rush of love for him which was quite new to her. She brought two cups of cocoa and sat on a low stool at his feet. "I'm very glad you've come," she said.

"Even though I sounded so bad-tempered?"

"You've been very worried, I can see."

"It has been so hard, this summer. The people are reduced to cutting prickly pear and roasting it to take off the spines so the cattle can eat it. And as for me, there is more work than I can manage. There are two good midwives in the district, thank God, but in the hospital I have only three young local girls and no-one to train them. I have no time to do it and who would come to work there with things as they are?"

"Have you advertised?"

"Yes, but with no result so far. I am sorry, Miriam. I did not intend to burden you with my troubles. A doctor of my acquaintance has been kind enough to take over for a few days so I could have a little holiday. I came to see how you are making out." She could hardly hear him, the rain on the roof was so loud.

"Doctor, I'm sure this must be the end of the drought. Why not telephone the hospital and find out if it's raining in Marburg?"

She watched him while he spoke into the mouthpiece on the wall; watched his impatience when he was cut off and, finally, the relief and pleasure which spread across his face. "Since this morning? And it's heavy? Thank God for it!"

"There now!" She poured him a glass of brandy. "Light your pipe, Doctor, and enjoy it. If the drought is really over I'm sure you will find a nurse for your hospital and all your luck will improve." She encouraged him as a daughter might and he, with tears of weariness and relief, patted her hand and drank off his brandy.

"What an old fool I am. Tell me about you and this baby."

For the first time since Otto had left she felt she could conjure him up in the presence of another. Dr Leclerc, she sensed, loved them both; differences of age, gender or origin were to him of no account. And she felt that he loved them separately, but not by contradistinction, freeing her, in some way, to be independent of Otto without renouncing him. She did not know whether it was love or wisdom in him that enabled her to voice such ideas which, otherwise, remained locked inside her, but she remembered Miss Spender as the incarnation of the opposite power. They talked for an hour or more and had their meal on a trolley by the fire. Then they sat in companionable silence, listening to the steady beating of the rain.

6 An Ordinary Life

Miriam's memory baulked now, wanting to leave off there, in 1902; not wanting to disturb the next twelve years. They were a precious relic, a frail fabric which close inspection might cause to crumble away. She was hungry and the day was now uncomfortably hot. Her sciatica demanded movement and she thought she should be sensible; should go home and eat. She stood up, preparing to leave. But her mind was divided. She took off her jacket and walked up and down the riverbank, exercising her painful leg, tentatively probing the nagging ache of the past. A police car went by on the road above her, its bell ringing urgently. Memory bent again to its task as if under a lash.

Undisturbed by hindsight, those years were ordinary. Twelve years of seemingly humdrum family life: occasional shafts of joy riving grey reaches of boredom or fatigue, intermittent flares of anger and pain slashing the rosy cumuli of pleasure and contentment. Most people had whole lives like that. She had only such a short span and it was precious beyond measure. Yet the official version of events belied her memory, insisting that something exotic and poisonous grew unnoticed in that landscape. Ordinary people like herself, whose lives had run side by side with her own, claimed, looking back, to have seen it there.

Otto was not ordinary, he was larger than life and that was why she had loved him. Yet there was some force in marriage itself which demanded plain serviceability of people and which, in its daily ebb and flow, wore away impulsiveness, flamboyance, eccentricity. Miriam felt that she had been its agent, imposing an orderly pattern, subduing the exotic in Otto, eradicating, slowly but persistently, the very qualities she had loved in him.

Perhaps they were never done away with but merely diverted, driven under the surface of their life to emerge elsewhere bearing the fruit of treachery. If she was to deal truthfully with the past she must now acknowledge that possibility. It was an irony, she thought, that though she had never faced it before, the whole of her life for over twenty years had been governed by the unchallenged assumption of its truth.

She had no objective view of Otto; she doubted most women could sufficiently separate their own lives from those of their husbands' to judge them in that way. Confronted with undreamt criminality or perversion, they could only inspect the man and the marriage they knew for indicators of truth or falsity. But then, such accusations, asserted as truth by strangers, cast doubt on all previous certainties and suggested sinister interpretations of the most mundane events. It was difficult for Miriam even to assess whether or not her marriage had been happy, so coloured was it now by the larger events of its context. But, happy or unhappy, she had been conscious almost always of the slack and strain in her hold of Otto and the tensions had reverberated through her being, sometimes threatening disintegration.

When Otto came back from Germany, Miriam knew that they both had changed. She felt stronger and deeper, he seemed more solid and directed. His mother had not died while he was with her but her death was daily expected and that may have gathered and quieted him. Miriam was heavy with their baby and Otto was not tempestuously excited, as last time, but steadily glad. She had feared the assaults of his blustery enthusiasm on the timorous independence she had developed in his absence, and was grateful for this slower, gentler joy. She felt herself unfurling in it, shedding protective layers.

Otto's public face seemed tougher. He no longer wore a bewildered smile under her father's scorn or her brothers' condescension. Instead, where his argument could not prevail, he turned aside their goading with a light remark and then ignored them. In this he was helped by Kathleen. She had organised a family party on his return, ostensibly for Carrie's birthday, but Miriam thought it was also to welcome Otto home. He used the opportunity to distribute the presents he had bought for them all; cigars for the men, scarves and trinkets for the women, carved wooden toys for the children. He left Kathleen's till last, when he had everyone's attention. As he handed her the package, he said, "And the best is for you, Little Mother; blessed by the Holy Father himself!" so that she knew, as she unwrapped the rosary beads, that he had fulfilled her commission to him. It was an act of defiance performed with utmost confidence and grace, Miriam thought. Kathleen's face was marvellous. There was an instant of alarm in it and then she realised what he had done; saw, in this public presentation, her symbolic release from a long purdah. She had no need of words to thank him. She took his hand and held it, tears shining in her eyes, and it was as though the two had taken up positions, back to back, challenging the family to do their worst. For a time the antagonists fell away.

For a while after his return, Otto's spare time had been engaged in preparations for the baby. Though Miriam told him the child must sleep in their room at first, he was keen to decorate a nursery and buy the furniture and fittings he imagined a baby would need. He brought home catalogues, samples of wallpaper and friezes, clippings of fabric for Miriam to choose from, because she was no longer up to going with him to the stores and warehouses. He came home from work as early as he could in the evenings and, though she was too tired for visitors, he was content to stay at home alone with her.

"What shall we call a boy, Miriam? You must decide. Shall it be Joshua, after your father?"

"No, let's call him Hugo, after Dr Leclerc, and Eric after your father."

"My father is dead and won't mind whatever we do, but yours will be offended, surely, if we call him after someone who isn't in the family."

"If we have a boy," Miriam said, gravely, "I would rather he grew up like Dr Hugo than like my father."

Otto was worried by her choice, it did not seem proper to him, but he deferred to her, as he did in everything to do with the coming child. Miriam was entirely happy and wanted nothing more, she thought, than to be the sole source of his happiness and centre of his tender anticipation.

Else Kathleen was born in November, three months after Otto's return. Miriam remembered very little pain from it and the image of Otto predominated, standing at the end of the bed, cradling the tiny bundle of child.

"I don't in the least care that she's not a boy, Miriam!" he exclaimed, responding to her only anxiety. "She is entirely wonderful!"

She remembered how his tears ran down his nose and formed great drops which fell, unchecked, all over Else. Miriam and the midwife had laughed at him.

"I've never seen a father so pleased as to cry before, Mrs Gluck!" the midwife said, approvingly. "They're normally that awkward and embarrassed they can't put the little things down fast enough."

When they were alone together, Otto sat beside the bed and took Miriam's hand. "I could never have imagined such happiness, Miriam. You have brought me all I have hoped for." He always said everything first, leaving her own expressions to limp lamely behind.

"Oh Otto," she said, almost reproachfully, "I feel just the same as you." She held his hand to her cheek and closed her eyes so that the tears of her gratitude and joy slid out and ran over his fingers.

Since Otto's mother had died ten days before the birth, it seemed natural to name the child after the dead woman, and after Miriam's mother as well. Josh Wemyss called her Elsie but there was no point in protesting. Sarah and Hetty were her godmothers and Klaus, who returned from his work in north Queensland for her baptism, was her godfather. At the christening party in the garden at "Cooloola", Miriam and Otto also celebrated their fourth wedding anniversary.

Hetty carried the baby around for everyone to admire. "I'm so jealous, Miriam," she whispered. "I swear I shall steal her!" And Charles hovered behind, looking over his wife's shoulder into Else's puckered face.

Maud Pendle, on the other hand, affected disdain: "Goodness, Hetty, she's dribbled all over your shantung. No, don't give her to me! I'm not cursed with maternal feeling, thank God!" Miriam saw the sharp spasm on Hetty's face with a feeling of shame for her own happiness.

Though Else's birth had not been difficult, the summer was steamy hot and Miriam did not recover her strength. The very light seemed to tax her so that she stayed indoors with the blinds drawn against it. Else was a nervous baby, distressed by sharp noise or sudden changes of light, and Miriam thought it best to keep her at home and tend her in the quiet, half-lit house. Now she was reluctant to let anyone else handle her and Hetty's frequent visits became an embarrassment.

"Let me carry her around the garden, Miriam, now she's awake."

"It does seem to upset her routine if she's over-excited."

"Oh, I shan't over-excite her, I promise. We'll just have a tiny stroll, won't we, Else, my love?"

But Miriam was uneasy and fussed until Else was again asleep in her cradle. In time, Hetty relinquished the tug-of-war and returned to her previous habit of visiting Miriam every alternate fortnight. Miriam frequently cancelled her own monthly visits to Hetty and a faint shadow of mistrust fell over their relationship, which Miriam, in her fatigue and anxiety, was unable completely to dispel.

Otto seemed invigorated by the heat and spurred on by the birth of his child to extremes of activity.

"I wish you weren't so often away, Otto," Miriam complained, longing for a return to the wholeness she had felt with him before Else was born.

"I don't want to be away, dear girl, but now that we have Else I must drum up more business! You have done your part and continue to do it, but I feel I must fashion a future for her. She will want an education and society when she's grown. She'll want to travel and meet interesting people and then she will want to marry well. I must provide for her the means and the setting, don't you think?" Miriam had no argument against him but saw that the child was now the substance of his dreams.

The heavy rains of that summer had revived business confidence and orders for Otto's equipment steadily grew. Miriam had never taken much interest in his business dealings and so remembered very little about them. He travelled a lot in the country and often came home with a new idea: he had seen a mine that was promising and would buy shares; in an expanding town he had bought land that he would subdivide and sell for housing when the time was right. When he came home he wanted her opinions and ideas, as he had done when they planned "Cooloola", and he was disappointed that she, trusting his judgment and preoccupied with Else, merely acquiesced in his decisions.

He was disappointed in Else, too, for a time. At first he had come home early, eager to see her, longing to play with her. "Where is my tiny girl?" he would say, making a distinction between them, and would throw Else into the air or tickle her and pull absurd faces. Else would scream with alarm and Miriam had then to spend hours in the darkened bedroom, settling her to sleep. Otto, though apologetic, did not understand and seemed to expect that, next time, Else would enjoy the rough and tumble of a father's attention. In the meantime, he went out: to the garden to dig or supervise, or to the German Club for a game of skittles or beer with friends. He seemed to be at home very little.

The remaining blocks of land around "Cooloola", which had attracted small interest during the drought, now sold rapidly and well.

"It's been a long time coming to anything but our investment in this land has realised far more than we expected," Otto said. "It has come at the right time, too, because I can't continue to service the New South Wales orders from Brisbane. But I think it's still too soon to revive the idea of a Sydney office; the need is really to the north of the state."

He had bought a shop in Lismore and installed a manager, a man called Dobbs. The enterprise did well, servicing and increasing the number of orders from the southern states, so that within two years of its opening Otto had been forced to think again about opening a branch in Sydney. "It's difficult, though," he had explained, "because it's too far away and too expensive for me to do what I've done in Lismore. I really need a partner for the Sydney end and you know how I dislike partnerships." His problem was solved when Jack Dakers, his Brisbane manager, made money from shares in his brother's mine. Instead of leaving Otto and setting up his own business, Dakers agreed to establish a Sydney company in partnership with Otto. Gluck and Dakers Ltd opened in Angel Place, Sydney, in 1905.

During 1902 the noise of building in the area disturbed Miriam's days and the prospect of closer neighbours did not especially please her. She had grown accustomed to solitude at "Cooloola" and found herself making excuses, principally centred on Else, when Otto suggested they go out together or invite friends home. Yet Else was not a very demanding baby and Miriam kept to a strict routine that allowed her long, untroubled hours with nothing to do but sew or sit idly watching the drays of building materials being hauled along the road. She seldom went down to the creek now because she could not leave Else alone for long and would not take the child out with her for fear of chill, heat rash, mosquito bites, flies, any one of a dozen reasons for not waking Else, not disturbing her routine. She was jealous of the child to whom she had become an adjunct, she realised now, and saw hope only in fastening more tightly to her. She was lonely and only Kathleen challenged her solitude.

"You must get out more and you must take that baby out, too. It's not good for the child to be cooped up in this dark room all the time. And Miriam, it's not good for Otto to have a wife who broods at home and is no company for him."

But, though Miriam knew her mother was right, she felt incapable of the effort needed to throw off her isolation and Otto was too busy and engrossed in his work to insist. Their lovemaking, too, had diminished. Otto now treated her as an invalid. Though she knew she was responsible for that image of herself, and though she sometimes wished she could reach out to him after he had turned on his side to sleep, her inertia was defeating. Kathleen sensed all this, Miriam knew, and she wished she could talk to her about it, but they had never discussed such things and could not broach them now.

Else was slow to crawl, to sit and to talk, and Otto now

showed little interest in her. Only when she was teething and grew fractious did Miriam expect him to take any part in her care. Otto walked up and down the hall with Else for two nights and then hired a young woman to be her nurse. Miriam could no longer remember her name and, in any case, she had not stayed very long: Wilston was too far from town and her friends. But she and her successors had occupied the bed in the nursery and freed Miriam from the chores of motherhood.

"Now, Miriam, you'll be able to come with me to the Club. Our friends have missed you. And perhaps, when Nurse has settled in, we'll go for a little holiday. Dr Hugo would like us to visit him. I spoke to him on the telephone yesterday and he's found a new Matron for the hospital. He'd like you to meet her. He said to tell you you were quite right and all his luck changed when the drought broke!" Otto spoke as one might to a child who needs encouragement.

"But Otto, Else isn't weaned yet. I can't go away from her for more than a few hours!"

"Surely she could soon be weaned, Miriam. She's over a year old." There was a rare edge of irritation in his voice which brought Miriam to tears she could not control. They flowed silently but steadily all morning and finally Otto called in the local doctor who prescribed a tonic for her nerves and a few days of complete rest.

"You are not strong, Mrs Gluck," he said, "and you're exhausting yourself unnecessarily by continuing to feed the baby. She will do quite well now if you wean her. And then you must get out more, Mrs Gluck. You need stimulation if you're not to get depressed."

Miriam knew that Otto and the doctor had colluded but she was relieved by this permission to wean Else. She did so rather abruptly and both she and the child were uncomfortable for a while but she clung to her instructions, resting while the young nurse looked after her daughter. Otto became attentive again and cancelled a trip he had planned to Mt Isa.

"We must invite the Pendles to dinner. It's ages since we saw them. And what about the couple who have moved in over the road? Let's have them, as well."

Miriam wondered if the woman who had moved in across the road was quite respectable. She had seen her only a few times, in the garden or getting into a carriage, and thought she dressed rather flashily. She had several small children whom she called in a loud, cheerful voice from the verandah of the house. Her husband worked in town, a manufacturer of light machinery apparently, and Otto had met him once or twice on the train. They seemed quite well off, he said, and their name was Telfer.

Maud Pendle was querulous and Geoffrey irritable with her when they came to dinner. Geoffrey, Maud complained, was nowadays entirely taken up with his new business, expanded from ice-cream production to a range of confectionery, and she felt neglected and bored. Her face was pinched in peevish lines and, by contrast, Doreen Telfer's large expressive features, though painted, Miriam felt sure, looked innocent and generous. She had a way of laughing off husbands and children as though she could manage quite well with or without them, but she held her husband's hand from time to time during the evening and once, towards the end, Cedric Telfer slid his hand down his wife's back in a way which made Miriam avert her eyes. But she was intrigued by them and, when Doreen suggested that Miriam should bring Else to play with her youngest, Miriam was pleased. After the Telfers had left, Maud wondered aloud whether the district was attracting quite the class of person the Glucks might have expected when they bought into it. Miriam felt ashamed but did not know whether for herself, for Doreen, or for Maud.

Doreen, Miriam discovered, was vulgar. She would talk quite openly about the worms or lice the children contracted and she liked to go to the races with Cedric and boast about her winnings. She often got a little tipsy on those occasions and when she fell pregnant again with her fourth child, she said, laughing, "It was the champagne that did it, you know. Naughty, wasn't I? No self-control. I shall call it Bubbles, whatever it is." And though the baby was christened George he was always Bubbles to his family.

Miriam could not approve of Doreen and was astonished when Otto referred to her as a woman of character. But once, when Otto was away from home and Else got croup, Doreen left her own children in Cedric's care and came to sit with Miriam all night.

Doreen did her own baking and used to run across the road, still in her apron, to bring Miriam hot scones or biscuits. One day she slipped on the gravel and twisted her ankle. The cupcakes she was bringing rolled into the gutter and Doreen uttered language Miriam had only heard from the bullockies at Cootharaba. Miriam had been shocked into uproarious laughter.

"Oh Doreen," she cried between sobs of merriment, "I'm so sorry you've hurt your ankle but you are a tonic!" Doreen laughed too, then, and clutching Miriam's shoulder for support hobbled to "Cooloola" for a cup of tea.

"You know," she said, when Miriam had fetched a cold compress for her, "I've never seen you laugh before?"

Miriam considered it. "I haven't laughed for a while, I suppose. Not since Else was born."

"First babies!" Doreen understood immediately. "It's often like that. They make such a difference to a marriage. You have to build up your life all over again. Cedric and I had some blazing rows after Morley was born." She looked thoughtfully at Miriam. "What you need is a new hat! Seriously! Something quite outrageous to cheer you up! I'll come with you into town as soon as my ankle will hold me up and we'll have a really jolly day. Lunch and everything!"

Though a hat seemed quite irrelevant to the distance which had grown between her and Otto, Miriam went to town with Doreen and they tried on outrageous hats, giggling like schoolgirls. Their outings became regular events and, in time, Miriam came to love Doreen, though she was careful never again to invite her with the Pendles or the Curthoys. The Telfers, too, were sensitive to their difference and never asked the Glucks to the noisy parties which sometimes followed race-meetings.

Else benefited, too, from this new friendship, growing livelier and more articulate from playing with Doreen's youngest child. Seeing her laughing face and animated chatter, Miriam would sometimes catch Else up and kiss her in a way she had never done before. It was with Doreen that Miriam left Else when Otto persuaded her to go with him on another visit to Marburg.

"One more won't make any difference, Miriam," Doreen said, "but you may lend me your nurse for the week, if you like."

It was nearly five years since Miriam had been to Marburg and, though she had seen Dr Leclerc since then, both the place and the man were almost unrecognisable to her. The plains now were so green they hurt her eyes and the farms, then so poor and barren, were flourishing. New barns and houses were being built and gates and fences renewed. Fruit trees and crops were lush in garden and paddock. By contrast, the hospital on the hill looked old and shabby. It was smaller than Miriam remembered, hardly larger than the doctor's house. The linoleum in the lobby was cracked and worn, the paintwork peeled, and two verandah posts seemed askew, giving the whole place the appearance of imminent collapse.

Dr Leclerc, however, was a younger man, full of vigour and enthusiasm. He had lost weight, his clothes were spruce and his beard trimmed. "Come! You must meet my Matron, Mrs Eunice Cummings, who is now also my dear friend," he said. "She has transformed everything!"

Matron Cummings was a little, compact woman, efficient in her movements but charged with energy. She advanced with both hands outstretched in greeting and, by the way Dr Leclerc stood aside and smiled on her as she did so, Miriam knew that she was more to him than an employee and helper in his hospital. She felt a twinge of jealousy and of shock because, though nothing had been spelled out, she and Otto understood that Dr Leclerc had left a wife behind in Canada. As if sensing their hesitation, Dr Leclerc put his arm around Mrs Cummings and said, "Dearest friends, I hope that you and my Matron will learn to love each other. Come and have some tea and we will tell you of all our excitements here."

Because he had laboured beside them through the drought and had not taken money from those who could not afford to pay, Dr Leclerc had won the trust and respect of the local farmers and his fame had spread beyond the immediate district.

"You have no idea the stories I've heard about him since I

came here," Matron told them. "The one thing he did not go short of was food, because the women were so worried about him and so fond of him they would insist on feeding him up! No wonder you were so stout, Hugo. And then as soon as I came he got sick. The first time in four years that he could afford to be, I suppose. But the women thought I had poisoned him and I had a great deal to do to persuade them I hadn't. They insisted on seeing him and there was a constant procession of women to his door. I wouldn't let them stay, he was too ill for visitors, so they just peered round the crack to assure themselves he was being properly treated and then, giving me baleful looks, they crept away. Not until he was up and about again would they trust me to treat them but now . . ."

"Now we are so busy because everyone thinks Matron is a saint. And so do I! But our hospital is bursting open and falling down with work and age. And so, my dear Otto, one – and only one, mind you! – one reason I have wanted to see you and Miriam is to discuss with you the possibility of rebuilding. We have all that land at the back, as you know, and we could build there and pull this place down when it is done so that we would not go out of business in the meantime. I am now in a position to pay off the capital you lent me originally, but I would be glad if you could renew the loan so that I can put the money into the new hospital. We can afford to pay a higher rate of interest on it, now."

"I wouldn't hear of a higher rate, Dr Hugo! You know how delighted I am, always, to be in on a new scheme. Have you drawn up plans yet? Let's have a look at them." Otto fell on the plans as though they were an adventure. The doctor and his matron sat at the table with their arms about each other, pointing with their free hands to this aspect and that: big windows, because light and air are so important to the sick; a nursery that opened on to a verandah so the mothers could nurse their babies in the sun or the shade. Miriam thought they were like a young couple planning their first home, but for the fact that their concern was not for themselves. She watched them with envy because they were so loving.

Perhaps Otto, too, was envious. Their room in the doctor's

house had two single beds and when Miriam came in from the bathroom she found Otto standing in his pyjamas between them.

"Where are we to sleep?" he asked, indicating a bed with each hand. She looked away, blushing. "Miriam, it's so long since we have made love together, isn't it?" She nodded and he took her in his arms. "Doctor Hugo was telling me a story just now. One of his patients, an elderly woman, told him recently that he had seen more of her body than her husband had in forty years of marriage. Dr Hugo thought that was very sad. But I thought, 'That's just like Miriam and me! We are sad, too.'" He held her away from him, pushing her dressing-gown back from her shoulders. "Let me look at you now, Miriam," he begged, and bent to lift her nightdress over her head.

She did not resist but trembled with outrage. His motive seemed prurient to her, his action violated a privacy she had always thought sacrosanct. He was demanding from her more than she had to give and she felt belittled by him. If he had wanted a woman of that sort, why had he married her?

She was tense as he made love to her, imagining his conversation with Dr Leclerc. Afterwards, when he lay slack beside her in the narrow space, she demanded, "You didn't say that to Doctor Hugo, did you? About us being sad?"

Otto sighed and got out of bed. "No, Miriam, I did not. I only wanted to say it to you." He blew out the lamp and got into the other bed where he lay sleepless. Miriam could hear his eyelashes blinking on the starched linen. She wanted, now, to talk to him, to confess her own inadequacy and unhappiness.

"Otto? I'm sorry for accusing you of that."

"Never mind, dear girl, it doesn't matter. Go to sleep, now." He turned over and faced the wall. She got out of bed to put on her nightdress and stood for a moment, wondering whether to slip into the bed beside him, but she could not muster the courage. Instead she lay awake, pondering her own incapacity for love.

Miriam shook off that memory. It was not in Otto's marriage that his accusers had claimed to see the adumbration of his crime. She tried, instead, to think of those characteristics in him which might have drawn their suspicion and dislike. She knew that his enthusiasm often seemed like high self-opinion and bombast; and his magnanimity, an affectation of superiority and condescension. On their way home from Marburg, she had taken issue with him over his philanthropy to Dr Leclerc.

"I don't understand why you did that, Otto. Dr Hugo said quite plainly he could afford to pay a higher rate. He doesn't need your charity. It's demeaning — to him and to you!"

"I don't see it that way, Miriam. Dr Hugo is an honest man and my friend. He would have said no to my offer if he really didn't need it or if he felt demeaned by it. And I didn't offer it as charity but so as to be part of the project myself."

"But you would still have been part of the project if you had taken the usual rate of interest."

"Perhaps. But I would feel no particular credit if I were making as much money as I could from it. You see, I know it sounds foolish to you, but I like to think I'm sacrificing a little for something worthwhile."

"Yes, and that demeans Dr Hugo. It puts him in your debt!"

"But I don't do it primarily for Dr Hugo! Think how that little town will benefit from a new hospital. And those people will never know they are in my debt. They will simply be healthier and happier and work harder on their farms! It comes down to this, Miriam: whatever we do to develop Australia must, in the long run, benefit all of us."

Miriam was reminded of her father's remark: "What is good for me, and for men like me, is also good for this country." She saw there was a difference between the two views and her father's irritated her less. Although he was a Member of Parliament, Josh Wemyss was not in the least concerned to influence history. Otto was less modest. The embarrassment he caused Miriam was like that inspired in her by the Salvation Army, praying, singing and preaching on the public street; regardless of how good their message or intentions, she shrank from them, instinctively repelled. Miriam's father and brothers called Otto "the Big Noise" and, though it hurt her to hear them speak so of him, she knew it was justified.

When his business outgrew his rooms, and he moved to a

larger place in Queen Street, Otto had bought a printing press, ostensibly to produce his own advertising brochures. But with every brochure, a message, sometimes a whole tract, was included. He urged efficiency, economy, health, or the importance of protection for Australian manufacturing. In 1905, when he had been in Australia for twenty years, he published a brief autobiography to advertise his probity and enterprise. His vegetable garden formed the basis of a small treatise, with photographs to illustrate the value to health and economy of such a garden for every home and farm. Was it here, in this self-important belief that he could and should influence the shape of the nation, that people saw the poisonous growth? Or was ownership of a printing press in itself nefarious? Joshua had said it left him open to the charge of printing seditious literature.

And then there was the ludicrous charge that he owned a short-wave radio transmitter. Remembering that, Miriam thought suddenly of the Most Modern Electrical Massage Machine advertised in Otto's brochures; Reserved, in a Private Room, Exclusively for the Use of Physicians and Their Patients. Otto employed an assistant trained in its use and Miriam herself had had massage treatment for her rheumatism. She thought of the machine with its valves and its meters, and of the sinister mysteries of the X-ray machine. Was that where they got their radio transmitter from, these ordinary people who went in and out of his rooms, the doctors and their patients who made free use of his services? It was no less ridiculous, surely, than the neighbourly opinion of that absurd quadrangular contraption of wires, strung from a central pole, that Otto invented to dry the washing. Some housewife nearby or some worthy visiting tradesman, perhaps even the handyman who built it, had declared it a short-wave radio antenna. Sensible citizens nodded their solemn agreement. Dear God, it was laughable!

Miriam cast herself down on the bench again, exhausted, and her stick, which she had clutched and waved and banged on the ground as she marched up and down the riverbank, slipped from her hand. There were strands in those twelve ordinary years which were more difficult to explain than the massage machine and the washing line, but Miriam was unable to tease them out from the warp and woof of their common life.

7 The Best Of All Worlds

Their son was born in April 1907 and christened Joshua Eric, but by tacit consent Joshua was a formality and they called him Eric. Otto was ecstatic at his birth. He studied the child daily, examining his tiny feet and hands, measuring his growth, marvelling at his awareness. He carried Else with him on his evening visits to the nursery and together they discussed what the baby might have learned about the world that day. Else reported that he had lain in his carriage under the persimmon tree.

"So he might have seen a birdie, then, or a big buzzing bumblebee?" Otto asked.

"Oh, yes! And a persimmon might have dropped on him and squashed him!"

"No! Mummy would have caught the persimmon and given it to you to eat."

"But Mummy would have been having her sleep."

"Well, Nursie, then."

"No, Nursie would have been talking to Maggie at the gate."

"Then you must have looked after Eric all by yourself, especially for Daddy!"

"Yes, I did! 'Specially for you!"

"And so, my very good girl, you deserve a story."

When the boy was about eight weeks old, Otto discovered that his hair would be red. "Definitely a redhead, Miriam! Eric the Red, aren't you? No? No, Miriam, he says he is not Eric the Red, he is Bluey, he tells me; Bluey Gluck, a real little Australian!"

Miriam never understood why redheads were called Bluey, but Otto had developed a fondness for Australian idiom and their son was Bluey to everyone until the war, when he became Eric again.

With the birth of his Australian son, Otto finally determined to become an Australian himself.

"I have delayed long enough. Perhaps I am a wanderer by temperament but, when I was last in Germany I realised that, if I am anything, I am an Australian. There is something about the scope of this country which changes your view of life. Germany seemed cramped to me, and not just geographically. I planned to be naturalised as soon as I came home but then you were ill after Else, and somehow I never did. Now, with two babies, and one of them a boy, we're a real Australian family!"

He framed the certificate of his naturalisation, signed by the Governor-General, Lord Northcote, and the Prime Minister, Alfred Deakin, and hung it in the hall, where everyone coming into the house could see it. "We must have an enormous party to celebrate, Miriam!"

"Sure and you're a terrible braggart, Otto Gluck!" Miriam imitated Kathleen who could say such things to him. She organised the party to coincide with their ninth wedding anniversary a month or so later and, though Otto would have liked his staff and business acquaintances to be there, she invited only family and friends.

It was James Miriam chiefly remembered from that day. She had not seen him for some time and was struck by his age. Although older than her father, James had always seemed more youthful to her, a freer and a happier man. Now his hands shook when he filled his pipe and his jowls trembled as he drank. The whisky confused his mind quickly, and when he took it on himself to propose a toast to Otto's new status, his thoughts seemed to ramble.

"Otto, my friend, welcome to the fold of British citizenship! A very worthy sheep indeed. As the eldest member of that flock here today, it's up to me, I think, to tell you we're glad to have you among us. 'Entitled to all the rights, powers and privileges, and subject to all the obligations of the natural-born British subject', it says on that certificate. Not given lightly, I'm sure. Not conferred at all on Aborigines, Chinese, Kanaks; not given to riff-raff. Whereas in the past you have slaved for the good of this country, now you are entitled to slave for the Empire. You may even, for all I know, be entitled to fight for it. Perhaps there are other benefits which may accrue to you from being a British subject that I don't know of, but mostly it is the great honour of the thing, the honour of being one of us. I congratulate you, Sir. But there is one benefit I should like to propose which may be of some material use to you. With your permission, I should like to nominate you for membership of the Brisbane Club. I wish I could suggest the Queensland Club, as well, but they wouldn't have you, you know, because you're not a squatter; you're only one of the sheep. If you will hurry up and buy a big sheep-run before I die, I'll propose you, of course. It would be interesting to see how you got on. In the meantime I wish you the best of British luck!"

Everyone was embarrassed and Harriet was clearly angry. James, seeing Otto's bewildered expression, took him by the arm. "I was serious about the Brisbane Club, at least, Otto. It will be good for your business." And, ignoring the rest, he took Otto aside to talk about the procedures for joining.

Miriam overheard her father declaiming angrily, "Disgraceful! Silly old fool. Drunk or senile, one of the two. But he's always bitten the very hand that fed him. Same bloody attitude to Father and the firm. Someone should have stopped him. Why didn't you shut him up, Joshua?" She saw that her father, too, was old and delivered his diatribe sitting down.

Joshua said nothing, but his sallow complexion had darkened. Edward laughed, "Nobody shuts James up when he's really got something to say. You know that, Pa, or you'd have done it yourself. He's always had the intellectual edge, hasn't he? While you, of course, had the gift for money. Who got the better part, I wonder? Bit of a toss-up there, I'd say!" And he laughed again, bitterly.

"What James got was a wealthy wife and the benefits of other people's labour; I suppose that was brains. But thank God mine are not addled!" his father retorted.

Miriam shared some of her father's anger. James had mocked the institution Otto revered, perhaps because he did revere it, and so had mocked Otto, too. The nature of the mockery itself she dismissed as unimportant, the product of James's disordered mind. Otto, at any rate, seemed unperturbed by it. "Don't be angry with him, Miriam," he said. "He may be cynical but he is kinder than most."

As he left, James pinched her chin and said, "You haven't lost your sense of humour, have you? You need that!"

Miriam did not see James alive again. He sponsored Otto's membership of the Brisbane Club but he died of a cerebral haemorrhage the following autumn.

Kathleen was distraught. "He was an honest man, Miriam, and good to me. He lived according to his lights, which may not have been great, but I always respected him as a Christian gentleman and I trust the good Lord to do the same, even though he was not!"

Though Miriam grieved at his death, she was glad he had been spared long senility. It was not until years later that she wondered if he had been senile at all.

Otto was immensely pleased to be a member of the Brisbane Club and made a point of spending time there; dining, playing billiards, reading the interstate and English newspapers. As a result, he often missed the only train home after work and had to hire a hansom. Miriam had expected that he would become less involved with the German Club now but, on the contrary, it was almost as though membership of the one fostered his commitment to the other. Before, his interest in the German Club had been largely social, but now he was elected to its Committee of Management.

Miriam was sure that during this period Otto was the happiest she had known him. His energies were completely absorbed, his mind fully extended. She and the children were the justification for his effort and when he was tired he would often say, "But it's worth it, Miriam. We have such a good life here and the children will have a secure future. In Germany such space, such freedom to be anything they liked would not have been open to them."

When he spoke like that the children he referred to were his children, who could equally have been born to some other woman in Germany, had he stayed, as here, in Australia, to her. Then she felt that, because of the work of her father and grandfather, her own children would always have had such opportunities. The impersonal hypothesis distanced her from him. Similarly, when he reflected aloud, as he often did, on the future of Australia and his own hopes and work for it, she felt that he took too much to himself. The country from which she drew her own identity had not depended on his efforts and guidance. At such times, although she was glad to see him happy and fulfilled, she became possessive of her children and her country and irritated with her husband. Perhaps, if he had been less often away from home she would not have resented his lofty assumptions. As it was, she had a great deal of time to reflect on them and, once or twice, thought wryly of Matthew Wemyss, whose own pioneering claims had not been so very different from Otto's. Then she missed James, the only person she had known who might have understood her conflict of feeling.

Sarah's husband, Alfred Borden, was a member of the Brisbane Club and he took Otto up after James died, introducing him to valuable contacts. Otto said to Miriam, "I like him much better away from your family, I must say. He's really a decent bloke and he took me for a drive in his motor-car. Do you know, it's only the third in Brisbane? I wouldn't have thought Alfred so adventurous, would you? Anyway, it was the most tremendous fun, Miriam, you can't imagine! It's like nothing else on earth. I'm convinced we must have one; it would make travelling so much easier, especially for you and the children. It will take some time to get because I shall have to order it from England. Perhaps I'll order a couple; they're bound to be the coming thing and I'd have no difficulty selling the other one. You know, Miriam, it might be a good agency to have."

The image of Otto, capped and gloved in his new car, Else beside him and the nurse sitting with Eric in the back seat, was like a patch of sunlight in Miriam's memory. Otto was so happy, and Else scared and excited together. Miriam herself was afraid of the noisy speed of the machine but Doreen ran across the road to inspect it with them.

"What fun!" she cried. "Oh, Miriam, don't be a nervous nellie! I'll come with you; I'd love a ride in it!" So Doreen sat in the front seat, cheering Otto on, and Miriam clung to Else and Eric in the back, while Otto drove round and round the block and down to the railway station, sounding the horn and waving at the neighbours who came out on to their verandahs to stare. It was the perfect vehicle for Otto. He delighted in taking all their friends and the neighbourhood children for a spin and he loved the notice it attracted. It was too showy, too noisy and too fast for Miriam and, though she tried, she never really got used to it.

Otto did not pursue the idea of an agency for importing motor-cars. In 1908 he branched, instead, into manufacturing veterinary equipment. "Since I support protection for Australian industry," he told Cedric Telfer as they drank beer together on the front verandah, "I suppose I might as well have an industry of my own to protect! And I'm increasingly impatient with the long delays in getting simple items from overseas."

Cedric agreed to advise him in setting up the plant, but Otto was unable to find in Australia the skilled toolmaker he would need. "I shall have to go to Europe to find someone, Miriam," he said, and began to plan for his trip. Once he had decided on something he could not bear to put it off.

Miriam was apprehensive about her ability to cope in his absence but knew him well enough now not to try to prevent his going. "There's so much here to manage, though, Otto," she ventured, hoping he might see her need of him.

"You won't have to worry, dearest. I'm putting my affairs in Alfred's hands while I'm away. It makes good sense. You can talk freely to him if there's anything you need. And with Doreen handy to keep you company you'll be right as ninepence and you won't miss me one bit! Else will, though, won't you my very good girl? But you must look after Mummy and Bluey for me until I get home. Promise?"

Else was six and a half and there was loneliness in her eyes. Otto left in June and promised to be back for her birthday.

Quiet fell on "Cooloola" then. The car, swathed in protective cloths, was shut away in the shed. Else began to have lessons at the Telfers' house, from a tutor Doreen employed for her own children, because there was no school nearby. Else took Otto's commission very seriously and wrote a list, in her new, clumsy print, of her daily duties. Alfred came regularly and Miriam was pleased to see him. On his own, as Otto said, he was a gentle person and his nervous inanities were fewer, but sometimes he brought Sarah who usually found something to lecture Miriam about.

"Are you quite sure, Miriam, that it's good for Else to spend so much time with those children? They do seem rather wild to me."

"Perhaps," Miriam answered mildly, because she knew better than to antagonise Sarah. "But without them she would be very lonely and it's only until she's old enough to go to school."

"I never understood why Otto chose to live out here. You would have had a better society in a more established suburb."

Without Doreen Telfer, Miriam, too, would have been lonely and she wished she had the courage to defend her home and her friend more stoutly against Sarah.

At the end of March, Hetty and Charles Curthoys had gone to England for six months. Charles had confided that Hetty was overwrought and needed a change. Though her longing for children had become twisted and hardened into bitterness, putting a constraint on their confidences, Miriam missed Hetty greatly. They were more like sisters than friends, she thought, because they had shared the experience of growing up and they understood each other's weaknesses. When Hetty returned, midway through Otto's absence, Miriam was eager to see her.

"You look so well, Hetty! And aren't you fashionable?" she exclaimed, admiringly.

"I am, aren't I? You don't realise how behind the times we are here until you go Home, Miriam. My goodness, it's gay! Do you know, I saw a woman smoking cigarettes? In a most elegant holder. I confess I tried, myself, but of course one couldn't here, it would be too shocking. We went everywhere: often to the theatre and once to the opera. I don't remember the name of it but it was all very grand. For the people we were staying with, cousins of Charles, it wasn't very special at all. They go to balls and supper parties and operas all the time. And their houses are so splendid. We went boating on the Thames, Miriam, and had a picnic on the lawns of a house belonging to friends which ran down to the river. Can you imagine, they had a butler and maids for the picnic! So civilised. The lawns were camomile, as soft as velvet. You'd never get it to grow here. And swans sailed past the bottom of the garden as though they owned it. It was too idyllic! There seemed to be nothing out of place, no weeds, nothing awkward or irregular like we have here. I wish you could see it."

"So do I!" And for a moment she was transported on Hetty's rapture. "But perhaps you will miss it all and be discontented with us now."

"Oh, I shall miss it! But I thought about it a lot on the ship coming back and I don't think I would really want to live there. It's too perfect, do you know what I mean? Everything is so settled and ordered, it's as if there was no room for anything new; no crack for a stray thing to grow. After a while I was longing for something a bit rougher or wilder, just to look at. And then we went to Scotland for a bit and I got quite homesick because the scenery there has an unconquered quality which reminded me of ours. Not that it's at all the same, of course; it was more a spiritual sense than a physical one. But, you know, I'm convinced now that scenery creates different people. That sounds fanciful, doesn't it, but the Scots are quite different from the English and we are quite different from them, too, which I hadn't expected. They are so much more correct. Even the woman with the cigarette was formal in a way we are not. Of course, we're British, as the Scots are, but we aren't English, you know, whatever we might think!"

"Hetty, you are funny! That means people who live in the outback ought to be different from people on the coast!"

"Well, perhaps when they've lived there for hundreds of years they will be!"

"In any case, I'm so glad you didn't want to stay there. I've missed you terribly, especially since Otto's been away."

"I missed you, too, Miriam. It would have been so much more fun if you'd been there to talk to about everything. I had Charles, of course, but men see things differently from women, don't they? He became impatient with the English very quickly;

couldn't get a handle on them, he said, and he was bored at the opera and things like that." She sighed. "We're never really satisfied, I suppose, with what we've got. I wish it were possible to have all the good things about England here — but then here would be different, wouldn't it? Tamed, perhaps, and I shouldn't want that."

Hetty's company shortened the time of waiting for Otto and the winter was dry and bright, tranquil in Miriam's memory. But in the spring, about a month before Otto returned, she caught rheumatic fever and had no recollection of his homecoming. Convalescence was slow and Miriam spent much of every day in bed. Otto moved out of their bedroom, then, and into what had been the linen room. "I will disturb you less, poor darling, and you will get better more quickly." She was grateful because his meetings and his late work in the study meant he often woke her when he came to bed. But his move seemed to set a seal on the separate directions their lives had developed since Else was born. She mourned it but, in her weakened condition, could not resist. By the time she was well again, it seemed irreversible.

Else's anxious face beside her and the pair of canaries, swinging in their cage on the verandah outside her bedroom, were her chief memories from that time. Otto had bought her the canaries to keep her company during the day and she watched the flash of their bright wings for long, solitary hours. They did not sing because they had each other and were happy.

Else's anxiety worried her: the child was convinced she had failed Otto because Miriam was taken ill before he came home. Otto tried to laugh her responsibility away but it was not so easy to dismiss as it had been to impose.

"I'll tell you what!" he said to cheer her, "When Mummy's better we'll have the most smashing Christmas and I'll get you and Bluey the very best and biggest Christmas tree you ever imagined. And all the children we know can come and help us to decorate it."

Miriam recovered in time for Christmas, though the doctor said the disease might have weakened her heart, and Otto kept his word to Else. He bought the biggest Christmas tree that could be fitted on to the verandah and six dozen candles and as many coloured balls for its decoration. For Miriam, because she had become attached to the canaries, he had an aviary built in the garden and filled it with parrots of every hue. The "proper German Christmas" he organised was a huge success with Else and Eric, and with Miriam's youngest nieces and nephews and the neighbourhood children. When they had all gone home Otto said, "We must do that every year and teach Australian children how to celebrate."

Otto had found his toolmaker, a Swiss, who arrived in Brisbane in March, and Aseptic Australian Implements went into production during 1910. But almost as soon as the first implements were ready for sale, Otto had conceived a new scheme which Miriam first heard of at a dinner party. Klaus Buchbinder, back in Brisbane for a few months, was among the guests, and old Dr Isambert, the agriculturalist. The new German consul, Dr August Birnhaum, whom Miriam had not met before, was there with his wife. Dr Birnbaum was a medical man of about Otto's age who, according to Otto, was very up and coming and had just been appointed a foundation member of the University Senate: a great honour, Otto said, not only for him but for the whole German community. His wife was Australian born, a Britisher, and very well dressed. Miriam felt dowdy beside her.

"I hear you are now an industrialist, Otto!" Klaus said. "What is it you have been up to while I've been away?"

"Oh, I have this little factory in a broom cupboard, so I'm not yet a magnate, whatever you might think! Still, Australia must develop a manufacturing industry if we are not to be dependent on imports forever, so I'm taking a small step in the right direction, perhaps. But, Klaus, I have a proposition for you, since you're sitting on so much money these days: I think you should put some of it into an export business."

"What! You are already talking of exporting and you have yet only a cupboard!"

"I'm talking about agricultural exports. I think we should be finding markets in Asia for our produce. We're so infernally Europe-centred in this country. Here we are, slap in the middle of

Asia, and yet you would think we were an island off the coast of England."

"You are serious, then," remarked Dr Isambert.

"Absolutely! I'm considering going myself to the Philippines to see what markets might be opened up there. I know producers who could supply but they don't have the time or the organisation to arrange the marketing themselves. Shipment, of course, would not be a problem and would be so much cheaper than transporting perishable produce to Europe."

Miriam was shocked that he planned another overseas trip without telling her. As the conversation progressed and Otto became more excited, she could see it would probably be quite soon. She might have been angrier with Otto had she not become protective of him. During the conversation, Dr Birnbaum had not spoken, had seemed bored and, at length, had visibly stifled a yawn.

"You are not interested in trade, Doctor?" Otto asked.

"I know nothing about it, I'm afraid. My interests are rather more academic. But I am entirely with you when you speak about the need to develop this country's resources. In my own case, I am concerned about the intellectual resource which has been so sadly neglected. But there are parallels with your own argument, Mr Gluck. I agree that we behave as though we were part of Europe and we expect that we will continue to get our educated elite from there. So we import people whose education and training are frequently unsuited to our society and the conditions which prevail here."

He began to speak of the need for appropriate curricula in schools and of the importance of the new university. His discourse was too technical to allow much interchange, except with Dr Isambert who shared his concerns, and so he dominated the table for most of the evening. Otto was not accustomed to being out-talked in his own home and Miriam felt indignant. She did not like Dr Birnbaum or his very superior wife.

"You're from Melbourne, I gather, Mrs Birnbaum. Do you find Brisbane pleasant after the colder climate?"

"Oh the weather is preferable, I grant you, for most of the year, at least. But Brisbane is, after all, much like a country town, don't you think? I confess I miss the concerts and the theatre and we have no significant library here yet, though it will come, of course. But in the meantime one does feel rather deprived, don't you think?" She smiled at Miriam and returned her attention to her husband's monologue.

Otto seemed awed rather than irritated by August Birnbaum. "He's a man of tremendous intellect, Miriam, and I admire that. And he is deeply committed to the welfare of the Germans here. His wife is from a prominent Melbourne family, so it's understandable that she finds Brisbane a bit of a backwater."

Miriam privately hoped she would not have to entertain them again. "He's Jewish, of course," she told Hetty later. "I can't think what Otto sees in him."

Later that year, once his manufacturing business was firmly established, Otto set about organising a display of Queensland produce for a trade exhibition in Manila. Since he needed to visit producers on the Darling Downs, he suggested Miriam go with him as far as Marburg and spend a few days with Dr Leclerc. Miriam would not have remembered the occasion particularly except that it seemed to her, much later, that here was the beginning of something more difficult to explain than washing lines and massage machines.

Otto had asked Dr Leclerc about Pastor Ullrich.

"I think he has many difficulties," Dr Leclerc replied. "While you are here you might visit him if you have time. I see him about the town and he visits his parishioners in the hospital, but he no longer calls on me socially. He doesn't approve of my Matron and me, you understand. But there is some sort of trouble in his congregation and poor Gerhardt is obviously crushed by it."

Pastor Ullrich seemed glad of the chance to talk when Otto and Miriam visited him next day. "I thought, when the drought was ended, that our troubles would be over. I should have known better; prosperity has its own dangers for my people and our Lord did not describe the poor as blessed without reason. Now the younger people are abandoning the faith of their fathers. They are taking up with enthusiasm the religions whose liturgies are in English. The Baptists, the Disciples, all are claiming them."

"But what has that to do with prosperity, Pastor? Surely you wouldn't wish them to stay poor?"

"When they were poor they clung to one another and to the Church. Their language, faith and identity were one thing, *Deutschtum*, if you like, and it supported them through their troubles. Now they are well-off; they feel expansive, they wish to cast aside their old clothes, their shabby houses, their poor ways. And they see that very *Deutschtum* as the culture of poverty and of backwardness. It, too, must go.

"It is true their leadership has been divided; we pastors have quarrelled among ourselves and those who have been trained in Germany have sometimes disagreed with those who have been trained here. Theological education here has been poor and has cost us dear. But we did not foresee this turning aside. Now, just recently, we have had a missionary from the American Disciples come here. He has, as they say in their language, been "barnstorming" about the country and he has been telling them what they wish to hear: that prosperity is a mark of God's favour. It is the religion of Calvin, not of Luther, and it affirms their new ways. In its name they cast aside their language and worship in English because it is easier for the young people not to learn German. They lose their identity: it is better to be good Australians, they say. They abandon their community for the new individualism and so they no longer support one another. Truly, they were more blessed when they were poor!"

The theological niceties were beyond Otto. "I am sorry to hear the language is being lost," he said. "Surely there must be ways to encourage the young to learn?"

Pastor Ullrich shook his head. "They are not cultured people, Herr Glück. Once they cease to think of themselves as German they no longer see the need to maintain the language."

The discussion had no importance for Miriam but she could see that it worried Otto and he returned to it again on their way home.

"Language, for me, has always been a pleasure," he mused. "I have not thought of it, before, as part of identity, certainly not of faith. But Pastor Ullrich has a point; for most people it's probably a chore to keep up and they need a practical reason for doing so." He fell into preoccupied silence. Later, though, he took the question up with the consul.

"Dr Birnbaum has encountered other pastors with the same complaint as Ullrich," he reported to Miriam. "When I get home from Manila, he and I will work on a remedy together."

Otto's visit to Manila was his first real contact with Asia and he came home laden with presents: wooden carvings inlaid with pearl-shell, lengths of printed fabric, brass ornaments and cigars. When the artefacts were distributed around the house Miriam was reminded of Maud Pendle's remark about clutter and surreptitiously hid them away before Maud's next visit.

"Manila is such a vital place, Miriam, and the music is extraordinary; everyone plays or sings. I am sure we would benefit enormously here by greater contact with Asia. There is real poverty, of course, and they need trade as we do. But what they want from us now is live cattle. I have been asked to put together a shipment as soon as possible." For a time, because he was occupied with that, there was no more talk of the needs of the Lutheran pastors, but once the cattle were afloat the issue arose again.

Miriam did not know whose idea the German language society was, Otto's or Dr Birnbaum's. She heard both claim it in conversation when, in mid 1911, they decided to establish it. "August thinks it an excellent idea," Otto told her. "He believes the pastors in their parish schools are the front line in the struggle to maintain the language and must be supported in their work. Of course, he knows more of them than I do. He points out that many are physically isolated and, up till now, they have laboured without any reward, so it's not surprising their morale is low. The language society would provide a forum where they could share their ideas and discuss their difficulties.

"Because I travel about a good deal, I have undertaken to visit the pastors wherever I go and enlist them into the society. August thinks he may be able to persuade the German Government to recognise their efforts in upholding German culture. Such recognition, in the form of certificates of accreditation or something of the sort, would give them a great boost, he thinks, and they would double their efforts. Their students, too, would be issued with progress awards, much as the Alliance Francaise students are. August is going to write to the Imperial Government in Germany and sound them out on the idea while I recruit the pastors."

Miriam was uneasy. Perhaps, she thought now, she had been chilled by that shadow flitting over her, whose significance then she did not recognise. At the time she merely resented Otto's involvement with the German community.

"I've always supposed," she complained to Hetty, "that he'd grow away from them when we married and had a family. But he seems more involved with them now than ever. Of course, he has his old friends; I understand that. But this business of a language society seems so unnecessary to me and I'd have thought he had enough work to do without it. He's away from home far too much as it is."

Hetty was sympathetic. "It must be difficult for you. Charles says immigrants never really change from their old ways of doing things. But at least Otto doesn't expect you and the children to learn German and eat cabbage all the time."

"Of course he doesn't!" said Miriam, rather shortly. It had never occurred to her that he might.

Though she could not help discussing her anxieties with Hetty, Miriam was careful not to mention these doings before her family, but Otto felt no such constraint. He always seemed to make a point of letting her brothers know how busy he was, how significant his activities. Miriam understood that his boastfulness was a counter to their dismissive attitude to him, but she was surprised when he announced to them that he was forming a German language society.

"For what purpose?" asked Joshua, genuinely at a loss.

"To help people remember their mother tongue. It's not easy to do when you speak another language every day and have little contact with other German speakers. And the society will help to maintain cultural links with Germany, much as you Britishers do with England through the Victoria League. But we have the added burden of language, which is not a problem for you, of course."

"I shouldn't have thought it was the same thing at all," Joshua said. "This is, after all, a British country and that is the culture we wish to build here. People who come here from other cultures must surely accept that, if they wish to remain, and must learn our language and customs — as you, yourself, have done," he conceded.

"But I have had no difficulty in retaining my other language and no-one would say, I'm sure, that I'm less of a good British subject because of it!"

"Not at all, but you, perhaps, are something of an exception."

"Oh no, we Germans are all good loyal settlers! Did you know that when Leichhardt arrived at Port Essington, he sang "God Save the Queen"? Perhaps we are just greedy and wish to have the best of both worlds, as they say!" Otto laughed and changed the subject, then. But he continued to talk of the language society wherever he went: to pastors and teachers, to friends and associates; and he was anxious to begin. The consul, however, was convinced the project needed the imprimatur of the German Government and the exchange of letters was slow, delaying its inauguration.

Otto was impatient with the delay and frustrated because he had no other new venture to occupy him. He was also, Miriam could see, worn out with the hard work of the last few years. He would soon be forty-four and she worried that he pushed himself with the same urgency now as he had done, fourteen years ago, when they were first married. Apart from their fortnight then at Sandgate, he had never had a proper holiday. The occasional few days at Marburg could hardly be counted as rest, she thought. Yet, despite his fatigue, he was not an irritable man. He seemed to absorb other people's inadequacies as though they were his own and if he could not overcome them he became depressed. In the first months of 1912 Miriam often came upon him sitting with his head in his hands, gazing abstractedly at the floor between his feet. Stimulus, she knew, was what he wanted, but because she had never entered into his plans she had no help to offer, and could only try to engage him in some small domestic project to distract him.

One Sunday in April, after they had returned from church and were drinking tea on the verandah, he suddenly burst out: "I think I shall go to Europe again, Miriam! I've grown very dull, lately, and I could do with a change. A sea voyage always does me good." She acknowledged to herself, sadly, that it was so: he would always need the adventure that she, and a plain life at "Cooloola", could not supply.

"What will you do there, Otto?" she asked, knowing he would need to justify his going.

"I'd like to investigate some new vaccines that are being developed. And I'd like to see what's happening in Germany, as well."

"But isn't there a war somewhere in Europe?" She had seen something about it in the paper.

Otto dismissed it. "Oh, only in the Balkans; it won't make any difference to me."

She did not really know where the Balkans were. Everything in Europe looked small and close on the map, but she accepted his assurance. Another question nagged. "Do you still miss it, Otto? Germany, I mean?" She asked it gently, fearful of his answer, and thought for some moments that he would ignore it.

"I have everything here that I could wish for, Miriam," he said at last, "and yet I seem cursed with *wanderlust*." He gazed out across the garden and his voice was low and uncertain. "You won't understand me, but sometimes I think it is myself I'm looking for. When I am in Germany I find a part, small only, that is answered by the people and the landscape there; a part that is never at ease in this country, never finds kinship here. Yet when I am there, most of me is restless; unchallenged and cramped, and I can't endure that for long. So I am happiest in Australia and I should be content. But still I know that I am always inventing myself here, trying to find the right note, the one this country will recognise and answer."

"Am I not able to answer, Otto?"

"Dearest girl! I'm happiest when I'm with you and the children and for your sakes I wish I could reconcile myself. I sometimes think that's why I have always longed for a kind of world citizenship. Perhaps, if all the people of the world were one, no-one need feel restricted to part of himself only, but could live in his whole being."

Part Three
The Great War

1 Rumours of War

Miriam no longer felt anxious for herself when Otto was away. She had built secure routines for herself which were less perturbed when Otto was overseas. But the children were distressed by his plans. Eric begged to go with him and would not be dissuaded. He took a basket from the pantry and packed his pyjamas and some fruit for the journey. He would not be separated from the basket, and the fruit leaked and mouldered into his pyjamas before Otto left.

On the day he was to leave Otto said to him, "Now look, Bluey, men have got to take care of ladies, haven't they? That's their job. Well, I've got to go away. Who's going to look after Mummy and Else if you come too? You must be the man of the house till I come home, right?"

The little boy put down his basket, lifted his tear-stained face and squared his shoulders. "Good-oh. I'll look after 'em, Dad," he said. Else put her arm round him for comfort but he shook her off, proud now of his lonely role.

Because Else could read, Otto sent the children cheerful picture postcards from every port of call, but he did not write so often to Miriam and his letters were strange, lacking their usual breathless descriptions of what he had seen and done. Miriam thought he had not succeeded in throwing off his depression.

Then, towards the end of his visit, he wrote: *There is a great deal of anti-British feeling abroad here and much militaristic talk. The new Imperial navy is said to be the Kaiser's pride and joy and people boast openly that it will "put the British in their place". I confess it makes me anxious and I can't wait to come home.*

Alfred Borden had called in on the morning the letter arrived and Miriam read it to him. Alfred brayed in derision. "You know Otto, old girl! He gets worked up over things. One bloke might've said something like it and suddenly Otto thinks there's a war on! Take no notice. He'll be home soon and, you'll see, he'll have forgotten all about it."

But Otto had not forgotten and was grave when he returned. "Germany's not at all the place I knew, Miriam, and it worries me. Everyone seems taken up with a single idea, a notion of Empire and German glory."

Miriam laughed. "Otto, they're probably all just like you! I've never known anyone to be so taken up with an idea as you are!"

"You're probably right about me but I fear this isn't a joke!"

"I'm sorry, Otto. But I can't understand why Germany would want a war."

"Germany is a bit like Britain's younger brother. We are all of the same family but Germany admires the older brother and wants to be like him. Then, as he gets older, he wants to compete with him, to show everyone he's as good, if not better, than the one he has admired. But older brothers don't like to have their position in the family challenged, so first you have estrangement and then you have fist-fights. Germany is shaping up now and I think people ought to know."

He contrived an invitation to speak at the Brisbane Club, to a businessmen's dinner, and his speech was reported in the *Brisbane Courier* under the headline "Germany Preparing for War, Local Businessman Says." Their telephone seemed never quiet for the next few days and Otto was asked to give an address on the subject to the annual general meeting of the German Club. Then Dr Birnbaum came to see him and Otto was closeted with him in the study for over an hour.

"I think August is barking up the wrong tree," Otto said when he had gone.

"He says all this talk of war is poppycock and will only frighten people. He wants me to deliver a different speech to the German Club than the one I gave at the businessmen's dinner. I know he's the consul and must give the Imperial Government's official response, but I cannot deny what I have seen and heard in Germany." There was no more talk of the language society,

Miriam noticed, and Otto's relationship with Dr Birnbaum seemed to cool.

Otto needed so much to be liked that he had never before allowed a difference of opinion to interfere with a relationship of importance to him. Miriam understood the depth of his conviction, then, and began to be afraid. She could not imagine war. Despite Otto's frequent travels, Australia seemed far from everywhere else in her mind, almost as though it existed in a different time; an everlasting present where the quarrels of the old world, trapped in the past, could not reach. She had not met any of the men who had fought the Boers in Africa; they, too, were only history. The idea of a war which touched their lives frightened her, not because she could imagine the blood and death of it, but because it relocated her country in a way she could not conceive.

"In any case, Otto," she said to reassure herself, "a war between Britain and Germany couldn't possible involve us, we're too far away."

Otto shook his head. "The world I have always hoped for is small enough for everyone to belong everywhere; to be able to travel and speak in one language and, eventually, to be one people. And gradually it's happening; the world is becoming smaller, closer. But it is now also small enough, if the will is there, for a single war to engulf us all."

Miriam took the children for a walk down to the creek and sat on a rock in the sun while they played along the bank. She watched Else holding Eric's hand as he bent over the edge to dabble his free arm in the slow brown stream; the timeless play of children by water that she and Edward had shared at Lake Cootharaba. She tried to conjure an image of war, of battlefields, horses and guns; of blood and the terrified screaming of men. She tried to imagine how such a war might engulf her place and her children; but the rock struck warmth through her spine and the children's laughter mingled with the cooing of fruit doves. She could not reconcile the image with reality at all.

Otto was late home from his German Club meeting and came into Miriam's bedroom to tell her about it. "There was quite a brawl over my speech," he said, sitting wearily on the bed.

"Some of them take August's view that it's all a fearful exaggeration and a few seem to think a war is overdue if Germany is ever to prove herself a great power. But they've elected me President so I suppose most of them must agree with me."

"You don't seem very pleased to be President," Miriam remarked, surprised.

"I think I shall have a great deal of work to hold them all together in difficult times." He sighed and took her hand, "Dearest girl! I'm so glad I have you and the children!"

Miriam did not see the connection but made room for him in her bed. He slept like a child beside her and sleepily made love to her in the early morning. Miriam knew that their third child, Caroline, sprang from that morning and she later thought it curious that this child, so vigorous in the womb and so animated and different from Else and Eric in infancy, should have been born to Otto only after he had lost his own ebullience. For Otto was changed by his visit to Germany and he never recovered his optimism.

Her doctor advised Miriam to take her pregnancy quietly because of her weakened heart. But Otto seemed more dependent on her now, more vulnerable without his enthusiasm, and since he was president of the German Club she felt obliged to go with him to official functions there. At a luncheon just before Christmas she discovered that Willi Schuler shared Otto's view of Germany's demeanour.

"I read the German papers very regularly, as you know, and I receive the overseas cables. There is an unmistakable rattling of sabres in them. It is the industrialists in Germany who are eager for war. They are pushing the poor silly Kaiser to build ships and buy guns. For them, war would mean undreamt wealth and power."

Otto listened gloomily and said, "It was quite ordinary people and small businessmen who, it seemed to me, were eager for war." But he did not bridle at Willi's opinion as he would have in the past.

Willi was surprised and spoke gently. "I am sure that, for as long as we have here a Labour Government in power, Otto, Australia will not get into a war. It is unthinkable that the working people of all these countries should willingly take up arms against one another. But if the conservative parties win the next election, and if there should be a war between Britain and Germany, I do not think we can be so hopeful that Australia will stand aside. We must try even harder now to build solidarity among the workers of all countries so that there can never again be war."

Again Otto ignored Willi's proselytising. "If there is a war between Britain and Germany, Willi, you and I will have to take sides."

But when Edward voiced the same view, Otto echoed Willi's opinion. "Edward, I didn't say I think there's going to be a war, I said I think Germany is preparing for one. But I'm sure it may yet be averted."

"But if there is, where will you stand?"

"I think it's still possible to be on the side of peace."

" Along with the cowards and the socialists?"

Otto did not answer him.

Miriam was disturbed by this equivocation but to discuss it with Otto was to give credence to an idea she would not accept. Yet most people they knew seemed to be taking up positions, some stridently, some almost imperceptibly. Miriam's father, though he was old now and had retired from Parliament, was no less loud in his opinions.

"The British should thrash the Germans now. They've been throwing their weight around all over the world for far too long. There's no doubt left in anyone's mind what they're up to, after all: world dominion, that's what! We knew that thirty years ago when they took over New Guinea but the British were still being polite. If they don't hit 'em now and hit 'em hard it will be too damn late!" That he said all this in front of Otto was somehow reassuring. Otto was again silent.

The New Year concert and supper at the German Club drew a much larger crowd than usual that year and Otto circulated among the tables greeting people he had not seen for some time. Miriam sat next to Klaus at their usual table while the band, the *liedertafel*, and the string quartet alternated on the stage. Baiba Ryko was to sing after supper and had not yet made her appearance. Miriam was surprised that she and Kurt von Kotze did not join them for supper. "Where are they, I wonder?" she said to Klaus. "I hope they aren't going to desert us altogether." Klaus shrugged and turned his mouth down, as though he might surmise but would not comment.

When the audience was buzzing with talk and laughter after their meal, the two appeared on the stage. Without any announcement they took up their positions and waited for silence. Then they began, and Baiba sang, as she always did, the sentimental songs the audience expected and loved to hear. At the end of the bracket, when the applause was at its height, she held up her hand, commanding silence.

A hush fell and Baiba spoke, her voice rather low and husky. Miriam did not understand what she said but recognised the word Mozart. Then Baiba stepped back to the piano and von Kotze struck a martial chord. There was an immediate and electrifying change of mood. Baiba threw back her head, her eyes flashed and her back was straight and stiff. The piano clashed and rang in a strident military march and a cry of recognition went up from the audience. Around the hall men rose to their feet, standing as if to attention, their backs as straight as Baiba's, their eyes seeming to answer hers. The euphoric atmosphere clutched at Miriam.

"What is it, Klaus?" she asked, grasping his arm, scanning the hall for Otto.

"It's called "I Wish I Were the Kaiser", but it is not the song they are excited about." Klaus's face was grim. "Baiba announced that von Kotze is returning to Germany and this song is in his honour. Through the song they are telling us that he will join the Kaiser's army."

Miriam caught sight of Otto then. He, too, was standing but he was slumped against a pillar and his head was bowed. When the song ended, Baiba seemed exhausted. She leant against the piano, dabbing her eyes with lace, while von Kotze stood to receive the thunderous plaudits of the audience. Miriam, stirred by the rousing music, joined in enthusiastically, but many did not clap and they looked down fixedly, avoiding other eyes. Then the concert broke up, the audience separating into those who went home immediately and those who remained to argue or to shake von Kotze's hand. Their own party did not, as usual, wait to share a glass with Baiba and Kurt. As they left the hall, Miriam thought of Kurt's fine white hands and could not imagine them grasping a gun.

"Von Kotze is a Prussian of rigorous honour," said Otto later. "He has taken a side and he is leaving to join it. That's as it should be. I hope everyone may be as honest."

Otto seemed more distressed by an agitated letter he received in March from Pastor Ullrich.

I am just now in receipt of a circular letter from our consul about the proposed German language society. Because I understand that some of the impetus for this society came from the confidences I placed in you, I am writing to set certain matters straight.

Dr Birnbaum proposes the Kaiser's jubilee in June as an appropriate date on which to inaugurate the society; appropriate, he maintains, because the Kaiser embodies the Fatherland and preserves and enlarges the German Empire. These sentiments, especially when uttered at such a time, are anathema to me.

You, Sir, have entirely misunderstood my own position. Though I wish with all my heart to preserve the language and culture of my people, and though I would have welcomed a society to support this work, it is solely to enhance the faith we have inherited from our fathers that I have done so. My church has no desire to enlarge the German empire. Indeed, it is fundamental to the religion of our founder that Lutherans should maintain allegiance to the state to which they are subject. In our case, we are unswervingly loyal to the King and to Australia which has nurtured us. I cannot endorse a society which has the aims and inaugural ceremonies the consul has proposed and I have written to him and to Vorwärts Australien *dissociating myself and my congregation from anything of the kind.*

Otto was stunned. "It seems I have offended the very man I wished to help," he said. "But I haven't spoken to August about the society since I came home from Germany and I had no idea of these proposals."

He went immediately to see the consul but returned, puzzled and upset. "I feel caught between extremes of opinion, Miriam," he said. "August still holds that the talk of war is nonsense and so there is nothing in his proposals which a loyal British subject should object to. But, even if there were no war talk, I have no desire to celebrate the Kaiser's jubilee and can quite see how, in the present circumstances, that alarms Pastor Ullrich. At the same time, the language society would do much good and I'm sorry Ullrich feels he must abandon it."

"Otto, I wish you would abandon it too! I can't believe in a war, either, and I hope Dr Birnbaum is right, but if there's the slightest chance he's wrong, wouldn't it be better to, well, to be as Australian as possible?"

"An honest man doesn't behave like a thief, Miriam, does he? I've always been as Australian as possible and I'm sure I, personally, have nothing to fear. As far as the German community as a whole is concerned, I believe our best course is to go on with our ordinary lives and avoid extremes. That way our honesty and our loyalty must speak for themselves."

So he convinced himself and lived accordingly, amid all the signs which, Miriam could now see, might have warned him.

The German Language Society was inaugurated, as the consul had proposed, on 15 June 1913, at a church service to commemorate the Kaiser's coronation. It was held at St Andrew's Lutheran Church in Wickham Terrace. The pastor there, a man called Treuz, was a friend of the consul and the only Lutheran clergyman to support the Society. Pastor Ullrich's letter had so upset Otto that he considered not attending the inauguration but, since the Premier and the Governor were to be present, he was persuaded that, as president of the German Club, his absence would be insulting to them. Miriam's advanced pregnancy allowed her to stay at home.

When he returned home, Otto's anxiety seemed relieved. "I was introduced to Sir William MacGregor and we had a good talk. He is a great admirer of German culture and speaks the language very well. The Governor could hardly be accused of disloyalty, could he? So I think Ullrich may be a little hysterical." His relief made him playful. "Would you like to go to dinner at Government House, Mrs Gluck? The Governor's wife is very charming and she enquired about you. I expect an invitation any day!"

"Ah, but in my condition I should have to decline and you could hardly go alone!" she teased.

"Then all my hopes of following your father into Parliament would be in ruins!"

Miriam wondered whether he was entirely joking. "You wouldn't want that, Otto, would you?"

He laughed. "No, I should be utterly bored by it. But I'll tell you a secret: if August retired from the consulate, I would think that a useful job to do."

Though Otto's relationship with Dr Birnbaum had cooled, they continued to work together in the Language Society until early in 1914. Then the German Government changed its law to allow expatriate Germans to take up their German citizenship again. The change, and its publicity by the consul, made Otto uneasy.

"It means one has dual citizenship," Otto explained, "and August is busy promoting the idea because he says it will foster German culture abroad. But it would also make one liable to the Kaiser for military service. I've told him I think it's most inopportune when everyone knows there's a risk of war; it looks too much like recruiting a fifth column. But he still refuses to admit there is any possibility of conflict. He even tried to persuade me to apply! I told him I've never been a German citizen and have no intention of becoming one now. He wasn't very pleased with me and made it clear I won't be on his list of recommendations for an Imperial decoration. He says the president of the German Club has a duty to exemplify German patriotism. Sometimes I wonder if he has any idea what is going on around him!"

Otto quietly withdrew from the work of the Language Society then. But in July, Dr Birnbaum was appointed by the Governor to the upper house of the Queensland Parliament, and so Otto's doubts about his good sense seemed unjustified. The whole German community, on the eve of war, had regarded their consul's elevation as a sign of their secure establishment.

In the meantime, there was a federal election in June 1913, a month before Caroline was born, and the Labour Government was voted out of office. Joseph Cook, a Liberal, became Prime Minister. Otto, a Liberal supporter, was delighted, but Miriam was reminded of Willi's gloomy prediction that a conservative government would welcome a war.

Otto dismissed Willi's remarks as so much socialist propaganda. In any case, he said, Britain would avoid a war and Cook was not a conservative in the terms Willi had meant. His certainty and Caroline's imminent birth drove the possibility of war from Miriam's mind.

Miriam developed toxaemia at the end of her pregnancy. Her legs and hands swelled and her doctor insisted she remain in bed for the last three weeks. It was then that Isobel came. Just for a little while, Kathleen and Otto and Carrie said, having conferred.

Isobel: twenty-nine and unmarried, capable, energetic and cheerful; handsome, perhaps, rather than pretty, with strong dark brows and a swanlike throat. She had worked in her father's office in Gympie and had helped her mother with all the children until they were grown. She would be a comfort to Miriam, and perhaps, they said, she might meet someone suitable in town.

By the time Miriam had recovered from Caroline's birth, Isobel had established her place in the household. From her bed Miriam could hear her in the garden, playing cricket or tennis with the children, urging them in her strong voice to "Come on, have a go!". She could hear Otto talking to her about his day's work as they sat together in the dining room, while Miriam, in bed, ate her dinner from a tray. And after Miriam had fed Caroline at night, Isobel would sing the new baby to sleep. She was like Kathleen when Isobel was born and Miriam felt, as she had then, that Isobel eclipsed her.

Poor Isobel was with her still, having no-one else now except nieces and nephews. She still stood between Miriam and the world; interpreter, nurse and keeper. Though she was nine years Miriam's junior, she, too, was old. But she will see me out, Miriam thought. One way or another she will nurse me to death.

Then, aloud and firmly, she said, "But today I am pursuing my life," and the words made her feel unexpectedly brave. She looked at the marcasite watch pinned to her blouse: it was three o'clock. Isobel would not be home until after six; there was plenty of time. She took up her stick and walked away from the riverbank, up the incline to the road, leaving her jacket where she had discarded it, on the back of the bench.

2 The National Hope

Jacketless, hat askew, Miriam stepped out jauntily along the road that led towards the Victoria Bridge. On the other side of the river lay the city which, so long ago, had cast her out. It glowed now, complacently, in afternoon sun. Courage to retake it fired her heart. She raised her stick in salute to a coster on his cart. War! The word rang in her thoughts like a gong. "Too right, Missus! And we ain't got over the last one yet," the coster said, but the brass band in Miriam's head swept over him. It was war! Impossible not to feel proud when the boys marched down Queen Street, the sun flashing on rifles and burnished leggings. Irrepressible, the heart's soaring to bless their stern young faces. Her feet would not break step with theirs in the overwhelming music.

She and Doreen Telfer had gone to Brisbane shopping together and had seen the first of their troops on parade. A blustery spring wind blew the music down the street to them and they watched with the cheering crowds as the men came into view. Doreen embarrassed her by calling out, "Good on you and God bless you, lads!" But Miriam, too, was caught up by the fervour and for a few yards they both swung along the pavement beside the column. Then, clutching handkerchiefs to their noses, they turned into Rowe's Cafe to collect themselves over a cup of coffee.

It was then, as the two women faced one another, that reality flushed away Miriam's euphoria. When Doreen asked her what was wrong she was unable to name her treachery. She stared dumbly at her friend, remembering Otto's anguished face when, hardly more than a week ago, war had been declared. Now Miriam had seen the soldiers with their guns and she had cheered them on. Doreen would not understand the conflict. There could be no conflict for her, only one clear loyalty which Miriam, having tasted its sharp sweetness, longed to share. But lodged in her heart like a stone was her husband's pain and it alienated her from her friend and her country. She stared at Doreen's creamy skin, her wide mouth and snub nose, as though fixing them in memory against a time when she would never see them again.

Doreen's expression changed, then, from puzzlement to comprehension. She reached out and patted Miriam's hand. "Let's go home," she said. Miriam did not challenge the word but got up and returned, in silence, to the suburb where she lived.

Doreen never pretended to enter Miriam's griefs; she could not have done. She never apologised for her own allegiances, either. She simply allowed no difference in their friendship, even when Miriam, cowering in her house for fear and shame, would have repulsed her. Children, fashion, the races, recipes and shopping trips: these were the simple staples of their friendship and, through them, Doreen's love and comfort flowed unstinted. There was almost no-one else with Doreen's strength. As soon as war was declared everyone else changed. The Pendles, with whom they had shared far more serious things, called on them during a Sunday drive, a few days into the war. They swung into the house with their usual familiarity but, once they were in the drawing-room, there was an unease about them. Maud's nostrils and eyes were tight and rimmed with pink. Geoffrey's manner was loud.

"Of course, we are at war," he said, accepting a cup of tea from Miriam but addressing Otto. "Still, one hopes we can behave like gentlemen to one another."

"But Geoffrey, you and I are not at war!" Otto protested. "I'm a British subject and I've lived in Australia for twenty-nine years!" Maud's tongue clicked impatiently and her cup rattled in its saucer. Geoffrey looked at her, as though for direction, and continued, "Yes I know, Otto, but you're still a German, aren't you, and you must feel. . . Well, there's no need to go on about it, is there? Let's just accept that we're different in this . . ."

"I can't see that the war should make any difference to us," Otto said, putting down his cup with finality. "Come and see my new rose. It's flowered at last."

Miriam was amazed by his mildness. He was sleek with it, like a man swimming under water. Her own hands trembled with something like anger and she hardly knew what to say to Maud when they were left alone.

"It must be difficult for you," Maud began, in a sympathetic tone.

"I suppose that will depend on how other people behave!" Miriam replied, and was surprised by the strength of her own voice.

"Of course." Maud recognised the rebuff. She had been glad to be Caroline's godmother only a matter of months before war broke out; now she could not meet Miriam's eyes.

But Hetty was direct and the clean blow she dealt had amputated a part of Miriam which had never grown back.

It was Miriam's turn to visit Hetty and she went, as usual, in the mid-morning, taking a cab from the station. Hetty met her at the door but her face did not, as usual, light in welcome. They sat in Hetty's small parlour and Hetty rang for tea, but while they waited the usual flow of gossip was dammed. Miriam did not ask what was wrong. She knew it must be the war that had come between them but refused to acknowlege it.

At last, Hetty said, "Miriam, Charles has enlisted." Miriam could immediately see him in uniform: handsome, tanned, fit and tall. Hetty must be proud of him, she thought.

"But he's not young anymore, Hetty. I'm surprised they accepted him!"

"That's not the point, Miriam!" Hetty cried out, jumping to her feet. "He was one of the very first to enlist! Regardless of his age he's willing and proud to fight for his King and country. He's dead keen to get his hands on those filthy Germans. And he's all I've got, Miriam; all I've got, do you hear!"

"Hetty! Dear! I can see you're upset. . ."

"Upset? You listen! Don't you interrupt! You have your children while I have only Charles. And your husband is sitting at home. He won't enlist because he's one of them. He'll be safe and sound while my husband has to go and fight his kind on the other side of the world. I can't bear to see you any more, Miriam, knowing that; I simply can't bear it. Please go away now!" And she ran weeping from the room.

Miriam, shocked beyond thought, gathered her handbag and gloves and went into the hall. She should telephone the station and ask the stationmaster to send her a cab but she wanted to go to the lavatory. She turned into the passage which led to the back of the house. Hetty was standing there, leaning against the wall, her angry breathing growling from her open mouth.

"Get out! Get back to your skulking Hun!"

It was two miles to the station. Miriam began to walk in a stupor. Nothing could have prepared her for this. Nothing worse could ever happen to her. Hun! She had hardly heard the word before. Her best and oldest friend to spit such vile, obscene words in that animal voice! Only her painful bladder wrenched her mind from Hetty. I shall wet myself, here in the street! The humiliation was more than she could bear and she hobbled up the path of the nearest house in tears of shame. The woman who opened the door was kind and telephoned the stationmaster for her while she was in the lavatory. Since there would be no train until late afternoon, Miriam took the cab all the way home, rocking herself back and forth with the motion of the horse to drive away the pain.

Isobel scooped her up, comforting her, while Else and Eric watched their mother's weeping with dismay. She knew they heard her story but she could not control it until they had been sent away. She was dimly aware of their faces, contorted with disbelief: Auntie Hetty making her cry, turning her out with angry words? Miriam told it all but knew she could not tell Otto more than the bare facts.

"Don't tell Daddy, children. Promise me?" It was the first of the silences they were obliged to keep.

But Otto knew. He listened to the bare facts and she could see that he knew.

"I went for a Turkish bath today, Miriam," he said, heavily, when she had finished. "And Tom Welsby turned his back on me. Quite deliberately. Tom Welsby. You don't know him but he is one of the most cultivated men and liberal-minded. We always talk at the baths. He has written books about Moreton Bay: history, Aborigines, that kind of thing. Cultivated." He shook his head and his lip trembled.

"Otto," she almost whispered, "what does Hun mean?"

"*Hunnen*," he said reflectively, as though it were an academic question. "Warlike Asiatics, Miriam. Vandals, destroyers, barbaric despoilers of everything fine and beautiful and good: in short, Germans!" He got up and strode out into the garden where the spring flowers and vegetables flourished in their orderly rows. Miriam could see him in the deepening evening, walking among them, looking intently, as though to find something he might have dropped there.

Miriam nursed the bleeding wound that Hetty had given and knew she would never recover. She was a very private person and not an initiator of friendships. Hetty's companionship had been a solace in those first years in Brisbane, interpreting the town and making it bearable to her. She was an open, lively person, in every way different from her own nervous and retiring self, and they had grown together, accommodating one another, for twenty-seven years. Only with Hetty had Miriam been able to discuss the trials and pleasures of her marriage to a foreigner, knowing that Hetty understood and would never use her confidences against her. Miriam, at forty, would never make another such friend but she could not cauterise the wound with hatred because Hetty was as dear as Otto to her. She could only shrink back from all love, all need, and staunch the bleeding with denial.

Miriam had heard that amputated limbs were sometimes replaced by phantoms which ached and throbbed as their fleshly counterparts had done. The phantom of her love for Hetty hurt her now, as she toiled along the road to the city. She stopped briefly, in hope that the present would banish it, and was assailed by another memory which, since that time, had never again obtruded.

Though they had never been truly religious, churchgoing was

important to Otto, a ritual obeisance to the society in which he lived, and they regularly attended the local Church of England. One Sunday morning (it must have been very close to the beginning of the war and had associated itself in her mind with Hetty's repudiation) they heard a sermon there from a visiting bishop. Miriam thought it was the Bishop of Tasmania who, staying with relatives in the parish, had been invited to preach. His subject was the war, of course; they could not escape it, even in church, and Miriam had detached her mind from it until some word or phrase had seized her attention.

"We like to say, dear friends, that God is on our side." The Bishop's voice boomed like the sea in the little wooden building. "I hear it said every day: 'But God is on *our* side!' as though that were a foregone conclusion. We believe this is a righteous war, a war in which justice is clearly with our cause. But God? My friends, to ask whether or not He is on our side is entirely the wrong question. We should, instead, be asking ourselves whether or not *we* are on *God's* side. Are we, indeed, on God's side?

"Before we can answer that question, brothers and sisters, we must give very serious consideration to the quality of our stewardship, as Australians, of this wonderful land in which He has permitted us to live. Have we treated it with reverence? Have we nurtured it lovingly, concerned for its best good and the needs of the generations that will come after us? Or have we torn from it as much wealth as it would yield, without further regard for God's precious gift? I think we would have to acknowledge that, frequently, we have allowed greed, hunger for money and earthly glory, to deafen us to God's plea that we should care for His creation. Are we on God's side, or are we on the side of Mammon?

"And there is a yet more serious question. How have we responded to God's call to go and preach the Gospel, the good news to the poor, in this land? Oh yes, we have built churches and sung God's praise in them. But what of the original inhabitants of this land; those children of God's whom He entrusted to our care? Have they heard any Good News from us since we drove them from their hunting grounds? Have they had the tender compassion from us that He commanded for His widows and orphans, His poor and oppressed? I cannot answer for Queensland, but I can tell you, dear Christian brethren, that in Tasmania, where I live, those children of our God have been hounded into the sea, murdered, raped and dispossessed by us. And now, even if we should repent of our sins, it is said that there are none of them left — none left! — to hear the Good News of Christ for the poor. Are we then on God's side? Or on the side of the frightful god, Moloch?

"So let us not demand that the God of infinite compassion be on our side in this terrible war, my friends. Rather let us repent and pledge ourselves to be on His."

Miriam was not sure why she wept during that sermon. Perhaps it was the pent-up grief over Hetty; perhaps it was gratitude that not everyone would unquestioningly bless the warmongers; perhaps the sermon had touched something at the heart of her own experience, unstopping long-sealed wells. Otto held her hand for comfort but the angry buzz in the churchyard afterwards reminded them both that the Bishop had not represented the majority view.

"It's early days yet, darling girl," Otto said as they walked home. People would get over their initial shock and hysteria, he thought, and in any case, everyone said the war would soon be over.

They had mustered their dignity and tried to go on as before. But they knew, now, that insults and rejection were likely, and the knowledge infected them. Miriam felt that she approached the world obliquely, like a crab or a beaten dog, looking out of the corner of her eye for a blow. It was harder, physically, to stand up straight, to walk into a room as though she were expected, welcome there. Otto, Miriam noticed, became louder and heartier with everyone, as if to defy or outface any snub. At home, his insistent jocularity was oppressive. The children did not trust it: Else would creep away to her room when she heard his booming voice from the front door and Eric was quickly whipped up into a frenzy of high-pitched, nervous laughter by him. Miriam found herself shut off by his impregnable barrier of jokes, gossip and business talk. Only Isobel coped with him.

"Hello there, Izzy!" he would shout when he came in but, before he could begin on some rigmarole, she would strike a melodramatic pose: "Help! Forsooth, it is my dastardly German uncle come to frighten me!"

The first time she did it Miriam was horrified, indignant for him, but Otto only drew a sharp breath and then smiled wryly, letting the heartiness drop away. "This German is too old for dastardry, if only you knew!"

But, next time, Otto played up to Isobel, twirling his moustache, adopting a heavy accent and a grotesque visage to suit. It filled the children's faces with relief and so became a routine performance, easing with laughter his daily return from the world. Miriam was grateful to Isobel but could not emulate her.

Only Caroline was untroubled. Conceived to an anxious father, born of a sick mother on the eve of a war, and growing in a household torn with fear and uncertainty, Caroline was the strongest, sunniest and liveliest of their children. Otto would sit silently, watching her kick and gurgle in her cradle. "What a bonza baby!" he marvelled. "When I look at her I feel some hope."

And all around, young men were being burdened with the hope of the nation. Josh Wemyss was seventy-five in the first months of the war. Kathleen held a party in his honour, gathering the family together for lunch. Otto and Miriam went: he, armoured in his heartiness and she, trembling with the need to belong. Carrie and Brian had come from Gympie the previous day and it was Carrie who greeted them at the front door.

"Did the children come too?" Miriam asked her.

"Only one!" Carrie said, and her eyes shone as she drew them into the room where the party gathered. "Billie is here. Doesn't he look fine?"

Billie, Carrie's second son, stood in the corner by the windows, clutching a fragile glass in his large red hand. He was wearing khaki.

Isobel, older than Billie by five years, pushed past Miriam and Otto and threw herself on her brother. "Billie, dear! Now what've you gone and done!" She buried her face in his uniform and wept. The young man patted her shoulder awkwardly, not knowing what to say. Otto moved towards him, his hand outstretched as though to congratulate him, but Isobel turned, her face fierce, and the men shook hands in abashed silence.

At that moment Harriet arrived. Her elegance was complete as ever but there was something old and forlorn in her bearing. Kathleen went forward to her but she stepped aside from the doorway revealing Guy, behind her. Although he was fifteen years older than Billie, Guy too was wearing uniform. With one hand on Harriet's arm, Kathleen hugged him, drawing mother and son into the one embrace. "Guy, my love!" she said, and there was the faintest reproach in her voice.

"I couldn't prevent him," murmured Harriet, and laid her forehead on Kathleen's shoulder. The others looked away.

Guy stepped into the room, smiling about him with handsome assurance. Billie, still in his corner, offered the older man a shy salute. Guy returned the gesture and then held out his hand. Pride exhaled itself around the room: here were brave and handsome men who knew how to behave!

Sarah's son, Harry, younger than Guy, older than Billie, and still a civilian, sauntered self-consciously towards them, but Josh Wemyss, a glass in one hand and a decanter of whisky in the other, got there first. Pouring the liquor for them, he said, "You young blokes have given me the best birthday present I could have had, d'you know that? I'm proud of you! James would've been too, if he'd been spared. You are going out there to prove Australia's manhood. You'll show the world we're equal to the best any nation has got to offer! Better, in fact, because this country breeds toughness. And the Wemysses have always been among the toughest. So here's to our lads. Let's drink to 'em!"

Everyone drank, then Josh turned to Harry. "What about you, Harry? When are you joining them, eh?"

"Josh!" Kathleen said, warningly.

"I'll bet he wants to go, Kath! You're not holding him back, I hope, Sarah? After all, he's still single, not like Guy here, with a wife and son as well as his mother. Keen to get into it, are you, Harry?"

"Well, er, yes, Sir." Harry clasped his hands behind his back and squared his shoulders. Miriam could see his knuckles locking; red, white, red again, and she was reminded of Edward. There was something almost lascivious in her father's expression as he laid on these young men his hope of vicarious potency.

"Good fella! But you'd better hurry up or it might all be over before you get the chance." He clapped Harry on the shoulder and moved to talk to Alfred, saying, "What d'you reckon, Alfred? You'd've been sharpening up your bayonet at his age, wouldn't you?" He passed Otto without acknowlegment as he went.

Sarah stood, white-faced, beside the sofa where Carrie was upbraiding Isobel for her tears. "You shouldn't be like that, Izzy, you should be proud of your brother."

"But Ma, I remember him when he was only tiny and his little knees used to knock together when he ran!" She covered her face with her hands.

Kathleen and Harriet joined them, Kathleen sitting by Isobel and putting her arm round her. "There, lovie," she crooned. "It's a terrible thing, war, and all we can do is pray for the boys. You be glad!" she said sharply, turning her face up to Sarah. "You thank the Lord with all your heart if Harry doesn't go, and never mind what your Pa says! And James would agree with me, wouldn't he, Harriet?" Harriet stood with her eyes closed, as though praying. She nodded without speaking, but Carrie protested, "Mother, I'm sure that's wrong. James was a gentleman and he would have been proud of Guy, just as I'm proud of Billie!"

"Aye! And I'm proud of all of them!" retorted Kathleen. "They're brave lads, indeed they are. But I'm not proud of them that caused this war and them that force them to it!" But Sarah's lips were folded in a thin line and Miriam could see she was ashamed for Harry.

Miriam had hoped to find relief in the midst of her family from the alienation she had felt since the day of the soldiers' parade. Instead it became more acute. She sat a little apart, watching their responses to the soldiers whose day it had become. She saw that, though her family feted them for carrying their favours and the national hope into battle, there was no question but that they expected it as their absolute due. Kathleen and Harriet, old women now, could be forgiven their errant opinion. Isobel, not old but single, perhaps forever, could be forgiven her grief. A young wife like Guy's, prostrate at home in her pregnancy, could be forgiven her fears. But young men who would not go, and those who had it still in their power to sacrifice them and refused – they could not be forgiven. Miriam watched the people in the room saying as much with their faces, their shoulders, their hands: Harry, Sarah and Alfred were being subjected to an intense, threatening pressure. Otto and Miriam were of no account because they had no son old enough to sacrifice. Nor had they, Miriam clearly understood, any right to share the nation's hope or offer a blessing to the men who bore it.

3 Faces of Barbarism

"I am thirsty." Miriam said it aloud and was surprised: physical reality had impinged so little on her struggle to redeem the past. There was a shop a few yards further down the street and she turned into it. The sign over the door said Muller's Smallgoods. The shop, cool and dark inside, smelt of ham and cheese. The man behind the counter was young and fair. He wore an apron and poured ginger beer for her from a stone bottle into a glass on the white marble counter. Miriam took up the glass and drank, considering the young man over its rim. "You're German," she said.

"No, Madam," he replied in a steady voice, but his eyes darted to the door, "I was born here."

"So was I," Miriam answered. "Of British stock, and only married to a German. But they need an enemy at home, you see, and so we must be Germans, or how else will they persuade the young men to fight?" She put the drained glass back on the marble. "May I use your bathroom?"

He was shaking his head but he raised the wooden barrier to let her through from the shop and led her into a back room where a woman was feeding a child in a highchair. "This lady wants to use the bathroom, Anna."

When she returned through the room the man and the woman were standing together, whispering. Miriam stopped and looked at the child. "Your children, too, and mine: all Germans for as long as they want." She said it flatly because, though the young people must be warned, there was no point in histrionics. "Thank you for your help. I can find my own way out."

They had not understood her, though, she could see. They

thought she was mad, perhaps, or spying out their loyalty for one Government or another. Well, they might remember when the propaganda began to appear.

She rested on her stick outside for a moment, staring at an advertisement for tea, huge and garish, on the building opposite. She stared, but saw instead another garish poster, filled with blood.

Blood had dripped from the teeth and nails of the frightful, helmeted monster and had fallen in gouts from the dagger upraised in his hand. Blood had fled in rivers, too, from the woman's body sprawled beneath him. She was supposed to represent Europe and her eyes, still open, begged men to avenge her. But she represented nuns and young girls raped, and mothers whose babies had been torn from living wombs. The monstrous face of the Hun was smeared with lust.

Otto had seen the poster first, on the Wilston railway station as he went to work. At every station along the line to Brisbane it had been repeated so that by the end of the journey he could not doubt his eyes. He came home late and in a cab so as not to pass them again that day and he locked himself in his study until the children had gone to bed.

When he told Miriam what had upset him he could only say, "The vilest recruiting poster, Miriam. I cannot find words to describe it." Miriam went herself next day, at a time when there would be no-one else on the station, to see what it was he could not say.

Because of its size and vivid colour, the poster was obvious from a distance. Miriam walked briskly on the crushed quartz of the platform and the crunch of her footsteps was reassuring. It was only a picture, after all, and public morality forbade that it should be so very shocking. But when she reached it she was mesmerised by its obscenity. This was the face of the Hun who violated women and speared and ate little children in his rampage through Europe. Unbelieving, she had read such things in the *Brisbane Courier*. Yet now, seeing the poster authorised by the Government to inspire men to enlist, it seemed it must be so. Why else would the Empire be at war? Miriam could not imagine what Germany was like nor what sort of people could commit such hideous crimes. The other side of the world was such a long way away and there things must be different, steeped in a degeneracy she could have no inkling of.

She had heard no warning footsteps but a woman's voice, shaking and deep with emotion, cut through her attempts to make sense of the poster's dreadful message. "Well might you gaze! Your man and the likes of him is what you're looking at." Miriam turned. The woman was one she might nod to on the way home from the train, not a person to whom she would speak. Miriam stared at her with amazement. "You've got no cause to be hoity-toity!" the woman continued, grasping Miriam's sleeve. "You ought to be ashamed, married to a thing like that!"

With a violent shudder Miriam shook her off and walked unsteadily away. There was no-one else on the platform because no train was due for hours. The woman had come, as Miriam had done, to look at the poster. As she turned to leave the platform Miriam was compelled to look back. The woman was sitting on the railway bench under the Hun. Elbows resting on spread knees, she was sobbing into her handkerchief.

All the way home the Hun's image loomed in Miriam's vision and his face was Otto's. Otto's face, like the Kaiser's, was dressed in a thick, waxed moustache, but it had never, in her memory, been distorted with hate or lust. Yet these were Otto's people. They were not just the enemy, honourable in war: they were barbaric animals whose cruelty went beyond war's horror to the limits of depravity. It could not be explained by distance or location in the old world: England, too, was at the other end of the earth, yet Englishmen were not barbarous. Some evil must be locked away in a race like that, waiting to spring and rend with the ferocious pleasure of a dog at a wallaby. The same dog would lie by the fire later; would roll, grinning, on to its back and beg to be tickled.

When she got home Isobel and the children were out and there was nothing to distract her mind from the image. She set herself to turn out the linen cupboard, a job she liked and reserved for herself. The cool, starched linen, the appliqué and embroidery, slid pleasurably under her fingers as she smoothed and folded. But now its power to soothe was gone and she was scarcely aware of what she did. Such a picture could not have sprung from nothing. No-one who was not himself depraved could have portrayed it, nor dreamt the awful stories she had read in the paper. They derived their force from truth, she knew; something in her own experience twitched in acknowledgment of it. She stared, unseeing, at the counterpane her hands were smoothing and beside those hands, for an instant only, she saw another, black against the creamy cloth. She flung the bundle back into the cupboard and slammed its door, whimpering against this derangement of mind. She heard Pa's voice then, snarling in contempt. "Snivelling fool!" he said, and she remembered his face, ugly and frightening. Terrified, she ran out of the house and across the road, calling for Doreen.

"Miriam, whatever is it?"

"It's the poster, Doreen. I must be going mad. I've begun to see things!"

Doreen held her tight, in silence, while Miriam sobbed desperately on her shoulder. Afterwards, when her panic had subsided, Doreen made some tea and Miriam told her about the poster. "It's so grotesque, Doreen, that if it were not true I'm sure I would have dismissed it, laughed even, or simply been angry at such terrible lies. But I felt it!" She beat with her fist on her breast. "I felt it was true!" But a profound sense of shame prevented her telling of the black hand beside her own.

Doreen, practical and direct, said, "I'm sure such things do happen in war, Miriam. We can't imagine what it must be like. And perhaps the Germans are being very brutal. But Otto isn't like that. He's the kindest and best of men and you must keep it all in that perspective, you know, and not let ignorant, foolish people distress you so."

Miriam knew that Doreen was right but the image of the Hun haunted her, superimposing itself on Otto's every glance and mannerism. She avoided him, ducking from his gaze and busying herself in her own room until at last he took her by the shoulders.

"What is it, Miriam? What have I done?"

"Nothing, Otto. My dear, you have done nothing! But would you . . . I would like you to shave off your moustache."

She had not thought of it until then, as she looked full in his face, and the demand seemed to come of its own accord, shocking her. He did not ask her reason but stared at her, a long, resigned look, and then he dropped his hands from her shoulders and went into the bathroom. When he came out the moustache was gone but, as if shamed by his naked face, he did not meet her eyes again all day.

The advertisement for tea, innocent washing-blue, yellow and white, resolved itself again. A woman bearing a teapot ran as though a life depended on her ministrations. Miriam walked on. The Hun would come later, she thought, as he had before. When the first flush of volunteers for the front had dropped away, he would exploit the building hatred to draw men to his monstrous orgy of blood. For the moment, brass bands and petty patriotisms were sufficient.

When the war was only a month old, one of their maids left. She had been with them for two years and lived locally. It was a good position, Otto made a point of paying all his staff well, and unemployment had risen steeply since the war began.

"Why, Janet?" Miriam asked. The girl looked steadily at the wall behind Miriam's shoulder and said nothing. "Is it the war?"

Janet nodded and then faced her. "I can't work for Germans, Mrs Gluck. Everyone's on at me all the time!" Their other maid was of German parents and so would stay; they would manage. Miriam counted out Janet's wages and fought down envy at this simple termination of engagement.

She did not tell Otto why the maid had left and he did not ask. They no longer described to each other the daily incidents of hostility each encountered. Miriam thought she stoically bore the indignities heaped on her for Otto's sake but she did not, then, wonder whether loyalty to his Australian wife was part of Otto's burden. Only when the children fell victims to the growing hatred did she glimpse the turmoil in Otto's heart.

Isobel was in the habit of taking Caroline for a daily walk in her pram to the park down by Breakfast Creek. Usually, Else and Eric were at their lessons across the road, but measles had laid the Telfer children low and so, on this morning, they had gone with Isobel and the baby. And on this morning Otto had not gone into the office because he was preparing to visit his Lismore branch. He had just got the car out of the shed when Isobel and the children returned early from the park. Miriam heard a commotion at the gate and went out to see Otto kneeling before Eric, holding the boy's face in his hands. Isobel's face was white and Else stood holding her hand, tears coursing down her face from tight-shut eyes. Blood oozed from a graze already purpling on Eric's cheek.

"They called us half-breeds, Dad!" the little boy gasped between convulsive sobs, "and they threw stones at us and one of them landed on Caroline." Else was shaking her head violently, her eyes still screwed up, as though to drive away the nightmare. Caroline, though she was wailing, appeared unhurt.

"Bastards!" spat Isobel and burst into tears.

"Mongrel bums, they said." Eric appealed to Miriam for enlightenment because Otto had turned away. "Auntie Izzy shouted at them to remember their manners and that's when they threw stones at us and we ran home."

Inside, Otto tried to explain the incident away. "They are just silly, rude children whose mummies and daddies don't set a good example to them. They think that because our soldiers are fighting with German soldiers, a long way away, they should fight with people here who come from Germany."

"But we don't come from Germany, Dad," pleaded Else.

"No, Else, you don't, but I do, you know. A long time ago and I'm an Australian, too, now. But those rude children don't understand that. You mustn't take any more notice of them. Perhaps you'd better not go to the park for a while, but when I come home from Lismore, I'll take you for a picnic in the car, instead. How's that?" They trailed away, dissatisfied. Young as they were, they knew that ignorance and bad manners did not explain what they had met that day.

When they had gone, Otto's control collapsed under the weight of his anger. "This is the country I have worked for and loved! This is how I am repaid. They expect me to remain loyal, to support them when my countrymen are reviled and slaughtered, and then to keep silent when they turn on my innocent Australian children. You tell me why I should, Miriam!"

She had no answer for him. It never occurred to her that he had any choice but loyalty. Remembering, Miriam was ashamed that she had actually been angry with him then for using the word loyal. They, she had thought, were the loyal ones: she and the children who stood by him, though he was a German, and suffered insults and blows for his sake. And Isobel who lost her chance of marriage through him.

Isobel had been seeing a widower, a government clerk, before the war but came home red-eyed and grim one evening soon after war was declared. "I've done with him," she announced. "He thinks all Germans should be rounded up behind barbed wire and kept there. Don't you tell Otto, Miriam. He's got quite enough to put up with!"

"Would you rather leave us, Isobel?"

"Of course not! Otto isn't the enemy and anyone who thinks so isn't worth bothering about. Good riddance to him!"

Gratitude, Miriam thought at the time, was what was due to them.

Otto's anger led him to make a public protest. The declaration of war had been followed immediately by a spate of letters to the papers, excoriating the enemy at home. The country was not safe while Germans were at large in it, they said. Germans continued to work and trade, profiting from a war in which our boys were fighting and dying for King and Empire. Women were not safe while their men were away, and Germans roamed freely among them. Though some letterists spoke out against the irrationality and injustice of these views, they were a minority and they were all "loyal Britishers". No Germans had written in in their own defence. Until the children were stoned, Otto had tried to believe the letters would abate along with the first euphoria of the war. Now he was goaded into replying. Miriam was horrified. She wished he would not draw attention to himself and begged him not to mention the children.

"I will not sit here, day by day, and say nothing, while such lies are told and wrongs are done, Miriam. If you insist, I won't mention the stoning, but I cannot be silent any longer."

His letter took up two columns in the *Brisbane Courier*. It was mild and reasonable in tone and detailed the efforts of the Queensland Government, over many years, to encourage German immigrants, because of their acknowleged industry and thrift. It spelled out his own labours for his new country, his good reputation as a citizen and an employer. It proclaimed his continued loyalty to the King and the British Empire. He signed the letter with his own name. Otto was convinced he had said the last word on the subject and that good sense would prevail when the facts were known. He became cheerful and expansive again.

"Let's go out tonight, for a change, Miriam," he said. "I'd like to go to the Club," by which he meant the German Club since the Brisbane Club did not admit women. Miriam wished he would put as much distance as possible between himself and the German Club, but she agreed to go because he looked happy for the first time in the six weeks since the war had begun.

The taproom of the German Club was palled in uneasy quiet. Men talking at the bar did not guffaw, and the little knots of women and men at the tables gave off no aura of enjoyment. There was no sign of Willi and Lili but Heinrich and Jane Rohl, the agents from Ipswich, and Gaspar Bielefeld, seed merchant from west of Toowoomba, were sitting together at a table in a corner.

"Ah!" cried Otto in greeting. "We have an influx of country members!" His incongrously cheerful tone drew every eye in the room. "How are you, my dear Mrs Rohl? Heinrich? Gaspar?"

"We have found nothing to be cheerful about, Otto, since we have met each other," Heinrich replied with an edge of bitterness.

"I know, my friend. Things are very bad." Otto modified his tone. "But they surely cannot get worse and perhaps, as they say, the war will be over by Christmas."

"Pray Gott it is so, or my boy may be killed fighting his brodders!" Gaspar Bielefeld's voice trembled.

"What, Gaspar? Has your son enlisted?"

"Otto, this is not the word. He has been pressed. He has gone for my sake and for Marthe's." He put his head in his hands to cover his distress. Otto did not understand and looked at Heinrich.

"The local men have forced Paul to enlist to protect his parents," Heinrich said through tight lips.

"How have they forced him?" Otto was incredulous.

Gaspar raised his head. "Furst dey threw stones on our roof during the night end den dey frighten my wife when she is out shopping. Den dey say to Paul, 'When you are going to fight der filthy Hun, eh? When you are going to proof you are Australian? Your old men and your old woman are filthy Huns, so you will not fight dem. We will fight your old men end your old woman here instead, eh?'

"Dey comm one night end let my chooks out end send them into my storeroom with all der seeds. Der chooks eat, eat, eat end blow up end die. 'Who is winning der war, Paul?' next day dey say to him. Next night, dey tip der cen of night-soil outside my front door. I hear dem end get out off bed to clean up end dey beat me end push me in der filth. Paul cennot bear it! He hes signed deir bloody piece of paper end he hes gone. Dear Gott forgive me."

"Gaspar, didn't you go to the police?" said Otto, appalled.

"Off course I go to police! Dey laugh. Boys hev der high-spirits, dey tell me! And still der spirits are high because I hev yet another son!" He broke down and sobbed. Otto put his arm around him and stared at Heinrich. Jane Rohl wept silently and held Miriam's hand in a painful grip. Miriam's mouth was dry and she fought an impulse to pull her hand away and run from the room. She knew this horror also was true and wanted no kinship with its victims.

"It's happening everywhere in the country towns, Otto," said Heinrich. "Our business has gone down to nothing and another agent, British born of course, has opened a second branch in Ipswich to capitalise on my unpopularity. Fortunately, we have enough money saved to manage for the time being and we have changed our name to Rule. Our youngest won't go to school any more and Jane is having to teach her at home. I am thinking of moving but I wouldn't be able to sell the business, the way things are."

A steward rang the dinner gong and, as they were moving to the dining room, Willi joined them. "Lili is not well," he explained to Miriam. "She has had a nervous stomach almost every day now, since the war, and cannot eat. So I am often here for my dinner. Not that I have much appetite. The news becomes worse every day."

"What do you make of all these reports of German atrocities, Willi?" Otto asked in a low voice as they drew in their chairs.

"What else does one expect from the capitalist press? It is all lies! No, I am serious, Otto! It all comes from the same source, the Northcliffe press. I told you before the war began that the barons of industry wanted a war, and now they must whip up enough hysteria to keep it going. Does anyone have any idea what this war is all about? Of course not! There is not one sensible explanation of it in any newspaper, only horror stories. Because without a good reason, how else can they keep up the cannon-fodder."

"You also told me before the war that Labour would never agree to join a war, remember?"

"Otto, my wounds over Labour are deep. Don't rub salt into them."

"And then," said Otto mercilessly, "there was the question of sides. Whose side are we on now, Willi, you and I?"

Willi did not answer for a moment, but looked darkly at Otto, and then said, "I will stay where I was then, Otto, despite my wounds."

Miriam was mystified by this exchange until some days later when Klaus visited them. "I am having to go back to Rockhampton for a few months," he told them, "so I have called to say goodbye. But how long I will last, God knows!"

"What do you mean, Klaus?" Miriam was alarmed, thinking he must be ill.

"There is such strong feeling against Germans working in the Public Service, Miriam. We may lose our jobs at any time."

"But you're a British citizen!"

"Do I sound like one? My English gets better, I think, but I am not like Otto who sounds now like an Aussie! They will not take any notice of my citizenship, they will look at my name and listen to my accent. But they are very foolish to do so because there are many, like me, in the Public Service who have valuable knowledge which we do not lose when we get the sack. Some will be happy enough to sell that information if the Government is disloyal to them. Some will give it gladly because they will be very angry and will think themselves better off under a German government when the war is over."

"Have you been approached, Klaus?" Otto asked sharply.

"Oh, yes, my friend! Railways are important to invaders. Someone telephoned me and asked if I would meet him on a very urgent matter. I was not in much doubt as to what, though the telephone exchange would make little of it. But who he was I do not know. I told him I would not meet him and I hung up. But I'm glad I did not have to explain why. Just now I would find that difficult to say." There was a thoughtful silence. "And you, Otto?" Klaus asked.

"I, too," Otto replied.

Klaus did not press him further but hurried on, "If Germans are forced out of the Service I shall go bush and you will wonder where I am. So if you hear nothing from me, don't worry. I will be in touch when the war is over."

"Klaus, I can't believe all this. Surely you're exaggerating!" Miriam expostulated.

"For me, no. But I didn't want to frighten you, Miriam. For Otto, it is different. He is his own man and he is an important personage in Brisbane. Also he is married to an Australian of a well-known family and he has Australian children. These things are all protections. I have no wife and children, no Australian relations. I am a good engineer and perhaps that will protect me for a while. But the workers are saying they will not take orders from a Hun, and so what use is a good engineer, if the men will not build what he designs? We will see." He changed the subject. "That was a good letter of yours to the paper, Otto, but I'm not sure it was wise to draw the fire to yourself like that."

Otto's letter had not been the last word, as he had hoped. Instead it had brought furious howls from the letterists. This man

Gluck, they said, was just the sort of arrogant German the country did not need. Certainly, some of the German peasants were hardworking and innocent, but such a man as Gluck, who set himself up as though he were as good as or better than the British, was a danger to the community in time of war. Who knew what insurrection a man in his position might organise for the German Government? He should be sent back whence he came. No, answered another, for there he would only fuel the Kaiser's war effort. He should, instead, be arrested and imprisoned until the end of the war and then sent back to give his much vaunted talents to the ruined Fatherland. Otto, believer in reason and the ultimate triumph of justice, had despaired.

Miriam agreed with Klaus that Otto had been foolish, but said nothing. Nor did she tell either man that Otto's letter, cut from the paper by an unknown hand, had been pushed into their letterbox covered in excrement.

4 Kites

The War Precautions Act was introduced in October 1914 and proclaimed in February 1915. Its successor, the National Securities Bill, alike in all its powers, was passed by the Parliament on 9 September 1939. Yesterday. Miriam halted in the middle of the pavement. She had reached the intersection of past and present. Here was the nub of this day's turmoil, the impetus of her march to reclaim a life and a belonging.

"'Scuse me, Missus, yer in the way." A man, one of many carrying heavy bags on their shoulders, addressed her. She stared at him, uncomprehending. "We're trying to load this lorry, Missus. Would you step aside, please." Still she stared. He pushed past her, dumped his bag on the tray of the lorry and came back. "You all right, lady?" he asked, peering into her face. Miriam recovered herself. She saw that she had come into the throng of Stanley Street where the wharves reached out to ships and the warehouses disgorged their hoarded wealth. The doors of Wemyss and Sons were only a few steps from her and the lorries, drawn up along the street, were governed in their coming and going by her son, in his office above the awning.

"Quite all right, thank you," she replied and moved away. Eric must not see her now. He would not understand or approve of this foray of hers and would prevent it, if he could, because he had too much at stake here. She had once felt the same.

The War Precautions Act had not at first alarmed her. Though it was hotly debated in the press, it was thought to apply chiefly to those pacifists, socialists and trade unionists who would subvert or impede the war effort. It gave the newly elected Labour

Government the power to censor the newspapers and prohibit or restrict public meetings. It allowed the arrest without warrant of subversives, and their detention without trial for the duration of the war. True, enemy aliens were obliged to report regularly to their local police stations, and their places of residence could be restricted, but they were not the Government's chief concern. Otto, in any case, was not an enemy alien; he was a naturalised British subject. People like Willi and Lili, because they were socialists, had cause for alarm, perhaps, and some parliamentarians and commentators maintained the Act was an unprecedented erosion of democratic rights, but to Miriam its provisions seemed logical, necessary in a state at war, and irrelevant to their own lives. She did not shudder then as she had done yesterday.

And the War Precautions Act did not, at first, impinge on them. Its uncomplicated and uncontroversial forerunner, the Trading with the Enemy Act, was the first to bring Otto low.

At the beginning of November they had the news that Guy and Billie had left, sailing with the first convoy of the Australian Imperial Force. The family were not told their destination and could not have imagined Egypt. In the same week, a charge of trading with the enemy was laid against Otto. Then, on 9 November, the German battle cruiser *Emden* was sunk by the *Sydney*, an escort of the convoy, off the Cocos Islands. When Otto's case came to court, a few days later, he was convicted and fined £100. Otto's was the first conviction for trading with the enemy and it was widely publicised; the *Emden* was the AIF's first triumph of the war. Miriam's life lay across a line which was no longer abstract.

She never really understood how Otto came to be trading with the enemy. He maintained he had promised to supply a quanity of syringes, from Grunebaum and Scheur of Berlin just before the Act was proclaimed, and his only thought had been of how to fulfil the order. He had sent it via Sweden, persuading himself that that would accord with the letter of the law. It was only a small order, less than twenty pounds' worth, he said, but the syringes were urgently needed and he had not had time to find another source of supply. When the summons was delivered to him in his office he had telephoned Miriam, but she did not understand until later in the evening that the cause of his shock and fear went beyond the charge itself: his order to Stockholm had been intercepted by the censor.

"Do you see, Miriam? I have been a loyal British citizen always and yet they have suspected me and censored my mail from the beginning!"

But Miriam was angry with his arrogant assumption of unimpeachability. "I can't understand how you could have done it, Otto. You knew about the law and yet you broke it!"

"I had promised August I would get the syringes for him and I knew they were urgent. It's always been my boast that I've never let a customer down."

"August? They were for Dr Birnbaum?"

"Yes, but that's irrelevant. What's worse, I included in the envelope a letter to Germany from Pastor Treuz. The censor must have found that, too!"

"Otto! What was in the letter?"

"How do I know what was in the letter! Treuz is a Christian pastor and a friend of August's. I didn't ask what was in it."

"Why did Pastor Treuz ask you to send it for him?"

"He didn't. August remarked that he believed his own mail to be censored, and Treuz's also, and he expressed concern for Treuz who needed to send an urgent letter on a personal matter. I volunteered to send it, with my order, via Sweden."

"You knew their mail was censored but you never thought yours would be? Otto, how could you be so foolish! It's bad enough to trade with the enemy, but to have done it on behalf of one German, and to have smuggled a letter past the censor on behalf of another – don't you see how incriminating that is?"

She was weeping with frustration and fright but he seemed to hear only accusation in her tone and he got up abruptly and left the room. She heard him call the telephone exchange and ask for the consul's home. A moment later he spoke again and his voice was loud, but this time he spoke in German. Miriam ran into the hall, gesturing for him to stop. His face was cold and set as he watched her and then, terminating the conversation, he hung up and walked away from her down the hall. She ran after him, pounding between his shoulder blades with her fist. "Otto, there is a war on, don't you understand? Don't talk in German on the telephone again! Don't!"

"I have heard you, Miriam," he said, and went into the study, closing the door behind him. They had seldom quarrelled and neither had ever struck the other before. It seemed to Miriam, alone on the other side of the door, that she had dealt their marriage an irreparable blow.

But Otto had behaved like a German. Since the beginning of the war Miriam had buttressed her sanity and self-respect against daily humiliation with the conviction that he was not really a German. Regardless of what the foolish and ignorant might think, he was neither part of the brutal oppression of Europe nor was he, as true Germans in Australia might be, a legitimate object of suspicion and mistrust. Because of Otto, she and the children were all the objects of misdirected patriotic rage, but they had nothing in common with others of its victims. To admit a kinship of suffering with them was also to admit a common Germanness. Otto was naturalised; he was a member of the Brisbane Club and a Masonic Lodge, he was a prominent and wealthy businessman. He had hardly any accent and, as James had once said, he was more British than the British in his reverence for the customs and institutions of his adopted country. But now he had broken a wartime law and he had attempted to circumvent the censor on behalf of two Germans whom the Government might have good reason to suspect. For Germans, he had jeopardised their position and shattered the fragile rampart she had erected against the jibes and insults of her own people. Anger, hatred even, vied with Miriam's remorse.

There was no-one with whom she could share her festering bitterness. Kathleen would take Otto's part and so would Isobel. Carrie, who might understand, was too far away and Miriam would not trust the telephone. Her father, Sarah, Joshua and Edward would now believe their dislike of Otto had been vindicated. "Don't let her come to me when her card house collapses!" Her father's words, snarling through memory, seemed prophetic. Where once she had had position, friendship and respect, she was now rejected and reviled. What had seemed so secure was now as flimsy as a house of cards. Why hadn't Otto resigned from the German Club at the beginning of the war and cut off all connection with the consul and the German community? If he saw himself as a German, how could he blame others for doing so? How could he blame her when it was he who had emphasised their difference?

The coldness between them did not pass. They went about their lives together with frosty civility, avoiding contact, and exchanged information chiefly through Isobel and the children. When she heard the news of the *Emden*, Miriam secretly rejoiced and was warmed, briefly, by a thrill of independence. She offered Otto no support in preparing for his court case, though she saw that he was more apprehensive about it than she had ever known him to be.

The barrister defending him said, "There's no need for you to appear in court, Mr Gluck, and, frankly, it would be better if you did not." But, when he was convicted, Otto was angry and sure he could have done better if he had spoken for himself. Miriam felt he should accept his conviction with more humility, since he had broken the law, and was unable to express any sympathy with him. Reading the report in the paper next day only fuelled her bitterness and shame. Several local tradespeople now refused to deliver to the house and they were forced to find Germans to supply them. Miriam resented the new butcher's presumption of solidarity with them far more than she did the patriotic rejection of them by the old.

But Christmas was coming, and Otto took up his usual role in organising the festivities at the German Club. Miriam's disapproval was clear, she knew, in every line of her face. Finally, Otto broke down. "For God's sake, Miriam, what do you expect me to do? I have nowhere else to go! On Christmas Day we will visit your family. They will ignore me. I would have been friends with them just as I would with the Pendles or the Curthoys. But now, to all except my own people, I am the enemy. Even my own wife, even you, Miriam, are driving me into the arms of the Germans, because now I have no-one else to whom I may open my heart!"

In his distress his German accent reasserted itself. For an instant, Miriam saw again the young foreigner she had first loved, his face vulnerable with longing and his voice rough with tears. He saw her softening and held out his arms to her. They wept together then, reconciling their sorrows, but there was no joy left in them.

The war was not over by Christmas, as everyone had supposed when it began, and Christmas celebrations were overlaid by solemnity. Few danced at the German Club on Christmas Eve and those who drank more than a glass or two did so with cheerless determination. Baiba's songs were largely sad ones and Otto's speech was short, provoking no laughter. At their table, Willi Schuler railed against the impending censorship of his paper under the War Precautions Act.

"The main intention of the Act is to prevent any reasonable discussion of the war," he said. "And why? Because it will not bear scrutiny. Clear-headed discussion would dissuade the people from supporting it. You will see: they will arrest all the socialists, all the churchmen who are pacifists, all the editors, like me, who would speak out. Democratic freedoms cannot co-exist with war, it seems." Miriam looked at Lili in surprise, but Lili was watching her husband with pride.

"So you want to be arrested, Willi?" Miriam could not keep the sharpness from her voice.

"Of course not! But when they have arrested several thousands of us, perhaps people will begin to ask, 'Why are so many ordinary, peaceful people locked up like criminals?' And then they may realise we are hostages to war and they may demand peace."

But Lili had not missed the hostility in Miriam's question and she leaned across and took her hand. "Miriam," she said, "we have been friends. This war is not of your making nor of ours. We must not let its makers cause also war between us."

The Wemyss Christmas dinner of 1914 was held at Sarah and Alfred's house. It was a subdued affair. Harry, inevitably, had joined up and was in camp. Edith, always more spirited than her brother, was training as a nurse and intended to join the war herself. Just as Sarah was obviously proud of Harry, she was disgusted by Edith's decision and treated the girl with coldness.

Kathleen, oblivious of the servants, took her to task in the kitchen. "God knows, I wouldn't wish the fighting on any of them, Sarah, but you've no call to be angry with Edith. The girl has only taken you at your own word, after all!"

"Nursing is just one step removed from prostitution, Mother, as far as I'm concerned. And no-one, least of all me, has suggested women should go to the war. It's downright degrading for them!"

"It's downright degrading for us all!" retorted Kathleen.

Miriam and Otto were like poor relations that day. They were there and they were fed but they were a source of discomfort to the others who preferred to ignore them. Only Kathleen was warm but she was preoccupied with supporting Edith. Otto and Miriam were seated together at the vast dining table and no conversation was addressed to them. After lunch, as they sat with their coffee in the drawing-room, Alfred came to join them. His face was weary and drawn, his tic more agitated than usual.

"It's a bad business altogether, this war," he said as he sat down. "I was dreadfully sorry to hear you'd got caught by it in that trade business, Otto. Easy enough for anyone to do, I'm sure, but it looks worse for you." Otto nodded silently. Miriam put her hand on Alfred's arm. "Alfred, Harry and Edith. . . You must feel. . ." proud? sad? angry? She did not know what he should feel. Alfred blinked at her.

"You can't imagine what it's been like in this house, lately, Miriam." He blinked again, this time over tears, and stared down into his cup.

As they were leaving, Joshua detained Otto for a moment. "Just a word with you, if you don't mind." He drew him aside, but not out of Miriam's hearing. "Under the circumstances, Otto, we had hoped you might see fit not to come with Miriam and the children today. For the time being, at least, perhaps you will respect the family's need to exclude you from our gatherings. When this rumpus is over, of course, it will be different, but in the meantime. . ." He bowed slightly and turned away leaving Otto speechless in the hall. "Goodbye Miriam," he called from the drawing-room door. "Happy New Year!"

Otto's expression as he joined her reminded Miriam of the

one he had worn on the day he interviewed her father about their marriage; a false cheerfulness covered his pain. "Just a little business matter!" he said, dismissively, and Miriam let it stand.

Two nights later, Miriam, who had gone to bed early, was woken by the telephone. It was most unusual to be rung late at night and she took some moments to recognise what the noise was. As she groped for her dressing-gown in the dark she heard Otto answer it. She went into the hall and lit the acetylene lamp. By its sudden white light, Otto's face was ghastly. He did not speak long and she heard him say, "There's nothing to be done about it now. I'll come tomorrow." He hung up. "Frank Dobbs from Lismore," he told her. "Thugs have smashed and looted all the German businesses, including mine and the picture theatre."

He sat down and dropped his head into his hands. He was proud of the Lismore branch and felt at home in the town. Miriam knew he had shares in the picture theatre which was run by the local barber, a German. She raised him from the hall chair and led him, unresisting, into the kitchen. "Sit down there, dear, and I'll make us some cocoa," she said, gently. In the sticky heat of this summer night, cocoa was absurd, but it was all the comfort she could think of and her own hands were shaking. Five months ago, in August, when Hetty had turned her out of her house, she had believed nothing worse could happen. Now a new year of war gaped before them, black as the pit, and Miriam knew the worst could not be predicted.

At first, 1915 was fairly quiet. Otto went to survey the damage in Lismore and found that Frank Dodds, intimidated by local pressure to eschew German masters, had boarded up the shop and resigned. When he returned he decided to seek Alfred Borden's advice about the branch. "I can't trust my own judgment in this climate of hate, Miriam," he said, and Miriam thought that no admission could so eloquently have proclaimed the depth of his disillusion.

Alfred came to see them, muttering through his twitching moustache that he was "sorry about that Christmas business". After he had examined the books and seen how the war, together with another severe drought, had reduced the volume of trade through Lismore in the past six months, Alfred thought it best to leave the branch closed for the time being. "No sense making yourself a target a second time," he said.

Jack Dakers, in Sydney, reported that, though business had fallen off and pressure was mounting on him, too, he felt he could continue to manage their Sydney branch.

"Redirect as much business as possible to Sydney, Otto," Alfred advised. "You're more likely to keep Dakers on, that way, and you're less obvious there. Keep your head down, that's the style." Otto, hurt and humiliated into compliance with any British advice, agreed.

As he left, Alfred said, "The boys don't mean you any personal harm, you know, Otto. It's just they've got positions to maintain."

"And you, Alfred? You also have a position to maintain."

Alfred neighed in hollow laughter. "Only to stay right side of Sarah, old son!"

Otto and Miriam held hands as they watched Alfred down the path. They were grateful for the friendship of this shambling, twitching man but they knew they had passed over the control of their lives to him and it was powerlessness, now, that their hands conveyed.

Dr Leclerc came to visit them early in February. "I have left Matron in charge and slipped away to see how you are getting along. The telephone is no longer a suitable means of exchange for us, I fear."

Miriam longed to confide in him, to say plainly that they were isolated and stripped of all respect. But Otto had been the doctor's benefactor and could not admit defeat to him.

"Oh, I've had a silly little brush with the Trading Act which you may have seen in the papers," he said airily as he poured beer. "And local feeling is against me at the moment, understandably enough, I suppose. What with that and another drought, business is not good. But we shall come through it. I mean to build up the manufacturing side because there is now such demand for things we have previously bought from Germany. In the long run it will do us good; we'll become less dependent on imports."

Dr Leclerc studied him closely. "It is much worse in Marburg, then. There are great divisions now between people who had always been friends, and the German farmers live in constant fear. And not just the recent immigrants. Only last week a young farmer was arrested and charged with disloyalty. He is a second generation Australian. His grandfather was born in Germany; he and his father were both born here."

"How can that be? He would be a British citizen!"

"Yes, but they arrested an enemy alien who travelled in the district for a German firm. He was spying, apparently, and making lists of people whom he considered loyal to Germany. Young Boetcher's name was among them. I know the lad. He speaks no German and could hardly find the place on a map!"

"Then he will surely be exonerated at his trial," declared Otto, confidently.

"Under the War Precautions Act they will not be obliged to try him and, in any case, a fair trial in times like these would be hard to ensure. But, in the meantime, his wife, who is of Scottish descent, is in the hospital suffering a nervous collapse."

Dr Leclerc stayed only a night and Otto kept the conversation resolutely optimistic. As he was leaving, Dr Leclerc said, "Otto, you idealise British justice but I have lived as a Frenchman in Canada under that same British justice and I have seen too much of it to share your absolute faith. Please, my friend, be careful!"

A few days afterwards the War Precautions Act came into force. They thought they understood it and they believed it did not directly affect them. But the encouragement it gave to informants against suspicious persons increased the flow of anonymous abuse through their letterbox and on the telephone. The general public, apparently, could not tell the difference between naturalised British subjects and enemy aliens. Letters to the editors of the press called for all Germans to be interned. Naturalisation, they said, was worth nothing to the perfidious Hun, who used it as a screen for his certain disloyalty. Still Otto clung to the belief that citizenship would protect him and he dismissed the crescendo of hostility. "It's distressing, Miriam, but we can bear it and more they cannot do."

But the Government built on the Act. Regulation after regulation was added, like steps to a scaffold. For the first time, Miriam met the term "naturalised alien", a new description of naturalised British subjects, and it seemed a contradiction to her. In April these "naturalised aliens" were forbidden to own firearms or ammunition or to travel outside Australia without permission. Aliens were further forbidden to own wireless transmitters, motor-cars or petrol.

"You have no right to that motor-car and we know about your transmitter," said one telephone caller whom the exchange either could not or would not identify.

"Why don't you sell the car, Otto," Miriam begged. "It only inflames people's envy and dislike."

"I'm not going to give in to that sort of pressure, Miriam. I'm not an enemy alien so I've a right to own a car. I am not even a naturalised enemy alien, since I've never been a citizen of Germany." And he wrote, seeking official clarification of his position, to Major Wallace Brown, the commander of the 1st Military District, under whose jurisdiction, according to the Act, all these categories of alien fell.

Miriam found him in the study, rifling through a trunk of papers which had been stored under the day bed there, untouched since they moved into "Cooloola".

"I've been looking for my *Demit*," he explained. "My official discharge, I suppose you would call it in English, from the rights and duties of German citizenship. See, here it is. 'The Imperial Government of Prussia certifies hereby that Otto Gluck was, at his father's request on account of emigration to Australia, released from Prussian citizenship.' So it's quite plain, isn't it? I was too young to be a citizen when I left at seventeen and I was released from the citizenship that would have applied when I turned eighteen! I shall send it with my letter to the Commander and then we'll have no more to worry about." But he had no reply for six weeks. Then his *Demit* was returned to him with a curt acknowlegment: his letter had been "noted".

Perhaps Otto had only drawn attention to himself. A week or so after he had posted his letter, a police officer arrived at their door. Otto was not at home and the maid called Miriam to speak to him.

"Good morning, Ma'am." The man looked uncomfortable. "I have information that certain persons have been flying kites of some sort from this property."

"My children fly their kites in the paddock, Constable."

"May I see those kites, please, Ma'am?"

"Of course, but why?" It was useless to deny him. Under the Act, he had the right to enter and search any premises at all.

The policeman would not answer her until he had inspected the kites, turning them over carefully in his big hands. "It is possible to transmit messages using kites, Mrs Gluck. I must ask you to ensure that no-one flies a kite here again."

Miriam could not believe what she had heard. "Constable, my children are Australian born. My eldest daughter is twelve and my son is seven years old. They aren't able to play in the park any longer because the local children stone them. Surely they should be able to fly their kites in their own paddock?"

"I'm sorry, Ma'am, those are my orders. That's war, I'm afraid!"

As he left he commented on the splendid show of roses in the front garden.

5 Weeping and Waiting

Billie was killed at the Dardanelles. His name appeared on the fourth page of a list published at the end of May. For more than six weeks the lists had appeared, swelling the papers with their tale of dead and wounded. Miriam searched them all for Borden, Curthoys, Warrington, Wemyss. Warrington was the first of the names she had dreaded to find and she saw it before Isobel. Otto had gone to work, Else and Eric, to their lessons across the road. Isobel was tidying her room. She howled when Miriam told her, a raw animal cry unlike any other human utterance, and the image of the little boy whose knees had knocked together when he ran jarred Miriam's mind. She saw him running now and she saw him brought down.

The image was furnished by Harry's letter. Alfred had brought it when he came some weeks earlier, fumbling it from his pocket shyly, needing to share it but hating to inflict it on them.

I'm scared sick, Dad, and so are most of the blokes. The only thing that drives away the fear is the madness of killing. Then there's a sort of red mist comes over you and you run through it, shouting, lunging with your bayonet, tearing into the Turk. You leave the fear behind you for a bit, but afterwards there's the horror, and that's worse. You see men leaping in the air, twisting to the bullet. They fall to the ground and twitch horribly in death. The stink of death, the rotting stink, makes you gag. If only this frightful thing could be a nightmare and we could all wake up we would never want another war.

He had written a different letter to his mother whose honour he was defending and begged his father not to show her this one.

Miriam found relief only in the thought that it was Turks Harry was fighting; that it was not a German who had felled Billie. But Isobel, when she broke off weeping for a while, said, "It doesn't matter who fired the bullet, you know, Miriam. If people had ever really loved their little bodies; if they'd remembered patting their bottoms when they'd got wind or plastering down their hair to go to church, and holding their little hands on the way, they couldn't have sent those boys to war, could they? It's us who killed Billie, really. And all the others; Germans, Turks, English, it doesn't matter. We just never loved them enough!"

Miriam gave Isobel some of the medicine she kept in the bathroom cabinet for headaches and tucked her into bed, sitting with her till the spasms of grief were overtaken by sleep. She thought of her own children, of the soft warm smell of their tender bodies; of Else and Eric's faces, permanently creased and drawn, these days, with anxiety. What could undo the corruption already wrought in them by war, or what protect Caroline, still happily oblivious of the turmoil around her, from the inevitable osmosis of hate? She thought of Otto's body, stocky and energetic; of the black hair, greying now, which lay in damp whorls on his chest when he was exercised by work or love. She saw the delicate tracery of veins throbbing under the white skin of his forearm. In the beauty and vulnerability of these familiar bodies she felt Isobel's truth. Another body jerked, bloodied, into her mind, flung up by the great saw, and her throat, unbidden, gave vent to a low ululation of mourning.

But the keening of women and the bitter wounds of men did not stop the engine of war, could not quell the pink rage of Empire which drove it on. Grief turned, instead, and rent the enemy at home. The tide of arrests and internments under the War Precautions Act swelled, but it did not exhaust the cisterns of hatred. New regulations were added to the Act: use of the German language was forbidden in Lutheran schools and German newspapers. Speaking German in public could lead to a charge of disloyalty. Thuggery was encouraged but was never sated.

A mob smashed the windows of the German Club in an attempt to get at the bust of the Kaiser in the lobby. The Club was a focus of German nationalism, loyal Britishers said, and a hotbed of subversion. On the 14th of May, it was raided and closed by the police. Willi Schuler's prediction came true; Britishers — socialists and pacifists — were interned as well, but there were not many brave enough to stand against the frenzied hunger for revenge.

Nor were the Germans brave. After the German band was charged with a subversive act for playing the German national anthem in public, Baiba Ryko sang no more German songs. Dr Birnbaum resigned all his public offices, including his seats in the University Senate and the Legislative Council. Otto, too, was quiet. He made no further protests, not even in defence of the Club, and wrote no more letters to commanders or editors. He clung blindly to Alfred's advice and kept his head down, publishing no tracts and issuing no advertisements. He was unable to travel abroad and risked few trips to the country. As to the Brisbane Club, after his conviction for trading with the enemy, he had been asked to resign.

Of the Germans Miriam knew, only Willi Schuler spoke out. When Gaspar Bielefeld learnt of his son's death at Anzac Cove, he hanged himself from the beam in his seed store. His wife, coming upon him soon after, did not cut him down but threw herself to the ground under his swinging corpse and prayed to be taken up with him. Willi Schuler told the story in his newspaper, in English now, for all to read. He told, too, of women whose husbands had been interned, leaving them with no income to feed their children; desperate stories of needless anguish.

The Government answered the absolutely destitute with a weekly pittance. Loyal Britishers protested that the German wives should be forced to suffer worse privation than the war widows and orphans because the war was their doing. The German community begged Willi Schuler to be quiet and not to draw any more attention to them. They did not mind that Lili collected alms for the bereft wives and visited them tirelessly, but the daily newspapers published letters calling on the Government to intern the German women also, because their loyalty to their husbands was a danger to the community.

Otto admitted that he admired Willi and Lili for their bravery, but their politics, he said, were foolish and subversive and must surely lead to their arrest. Now that the German Club was closed, he distanced himself from them and Miriam was grateful. Their life together became what she had desired for them when they were first married: they had few visitors and went out very rarely; Otto spent less time at work and no longer travelled; the enthusiasm and conviviality, which she felt had excluded her, were all gone. But in their place was a profound depression which she could do nothing to dislodge.

During that winter, Otto made half-hearted attempts to play Ludo or cribbage by the fire with the children, or he would take Caroline on his knee and begin a story or a song. But he would break off without warning and stare into the fire while the older children waited and watched him, not daring to speak. If Caroline pulled at his face to bring him back he would put her down and go to his study, locking the door.

After Billie's death, Isobel went home to Gympie for a few weeks and "Cooloola" became like a crypt. Otto and Miriam did not raise their eyes as they moved about in it and might have been at constant prayer. But Miriam did not pray and they had given up going to church since the sinking of the *Lusitania* when the priest had preached a militant sermon, reviling all things German. Now they simply waited, like hibernating animals or comatose hens on their eggs, obeying an imperative instinct but unable to discern its end.

Else and Eric spent as much time as possible across the road with the Telfers and they often begged to take Caroline with them. Miriam could sometimes hear their laughter drifting across the garden to her as though from another world. But their lessons there would end with the year because the tutor had taught them as much as he was able. Next year they must go to school and Miriam feared for them and feared, too, the utter barrenness of her life when they were away. She did not know whether Isobel would come back and could hardly blame her if she did not. There was nothing here for her, now; nothing for any of them except the deadly waiting.

But Isobel did return, her grief folded away behind a determined commitment to the living. Miriam, who had wanted her, now found her as irritating as a stranger on a train who insists on talking when you have a headache. Isobel did not understand the pre-eminence of the waiting, the need for animation to be suspended, heartbeat reduced and thought suppressed. But she undertook the things that needed to be done, enrolling Eric for the following year at the Cathedral School and Else at the Church of England School for Girls. They would have to travel daily on the train but they were excited at the prospect of beginning. Envy briefly stirred Miriam's heart: a beginning might never happen to her again.

Outside "Cooloola", spring seeped into the winter and summer's heat eclipsed the warmth of spring, but nothing warmed the blood of their waiting. On Christmas Day, though, Miriam broke out, as a sitting hen in the heat of noon rushes from her nest to forage. She would not have gone to her parents' home for the family dinner, leaving Otto alone at Christmas, had her father not been ill.

"It might be his last Christmas, Miriam," Kathleen said, bluntly.

"But I may not bring Otto, Mother."

"Oh my dear, and that's none of my doing! I shall come and see him myself on Boxing Day. You know I love Otto and I cannot see that the war should make any difference. But the boys and your Pa are determined, and I'm too old to fight them. Come, Miriam, for my sake, do!" So Miriam went and took the children with her but Isobel staunchly refused to go and had her Christmas dinner at home with Otto.

Carrie had expected to see her daughter. When Miriam explained Isobel's absence she said, thoughtfully, "She's as brave as Billie in her own way, isn't she? I'll come with Mother tomorrow and see her then."

But Brian took his stance with their father and brothers and would not come. War to them was brave and love, disloyalty. Despite them, Miriam was aware of a strange, hectic enjoyment of the day. She laughed as she had not done since before the war and tasted her food as though she had been starved of it for a long time. The children romped with their grandmother and their laughter had an hysterical edge. The family drank to

Billie's memory and to Guy and Harry at the front. Kathleen added, "And to Edith in Egypt, God bless her!" There were tears in the silence that followed.

But it was a conversation after lunch which reminded Miriam of the chill lying over her home. Edward was holding forth, self-importantly, about the new Labour Premier. "TJ's very shrewd, a fine mind. If we must have a Labour Government, it's my view we couldn't do better than him at the top. Personable, too; not at all a Labour type."

"Bloody socialists, just the same!" said Josh, "Can't imagine why you waste your time with 'em."

"Be reasonable, Pa," Joshua cut in. "Ryan's the Premier. We can't do away with the fact. And if you want Government business you've damn well got to cultivate him. Fortunately, as Edward says, he's a lawyer, not some upstart from a coalmine."

"And he's a toady to the Huns!" cried Josh, red in the face. "All that codswallop about keeping them on at work when they should be bloodywell incarcerated."

"He's got a pretty sizable number of German voters to look out for in this State, Pa, if he wants to stay in office," Edward pointed out.

"And that's another thing: the absolute stupidity of allowing the enemy to vote in the elections of this country! How many of them have you still got on our payroll, Edward?"

"None, Pa, none," Edward soothed him. "We gave them all notice before the holiday."

Miriam gathered the children together then, and took them home. She did not say goodbye to her father and brothers.

Kathleen and Carrie came, as they had promised, to see Isobel and Otto the following day. He put on a linen jacket to greet them but his face, when he smiled at them, looked like an animal's, kept long in the dark and then exposed to sudden sun.

"Otto, dearest boy, I cannot tell you how it grieves me to come to you like this, with my own sons so full of hate!" Kathleen wept against his lapel but Otto's arms were slack. She took up his hands and chafed them. "God knows, there's nothing in this war to redeem such wickedness, and Billie dead as well!" She was only a little, frail woman now, but Miriam thought she would have drawn them, Carrie and Isobel as well, with all their woes, like chickens under her wings for comfort. Yet, for all her love, she could not reconcile even her own family and so Miriam thought that love was futile.

They did not stay long. The important things between them were too raw for most of the words they knew and small talk was an irritant. "I must be gone, my loves," Kathleen said when they had had tea. "Josh's heart has been troubled by all the food and excitement, these last days, and I would not leave him alone for long."

And soon after they had left, Kathleen's housekeeper telephoned. Josh Wemyss had suffered an attack and had died before his wife's return. Kathleen was to blame herself, always, because she had not been there to shepherd him into eternal life. "Perhaps, if I'd been there, he'd have died a better death," she mourned, for she learned from the housekeeper that he had died cursing in his agony. For her own part, Miriam felt no grief at her father's death, only the hopeless sense of a wrong that could never now be righted.

But her presentiment of an approaching end was deepened by his death and in January, when the crows of government stripped the flesh from their still-living victims, Miriam was beyond shock. The Government decreed that no alien or naturalised alien could continue to hold shares in Australian companies and must, within three months, hand them over to the Public Trustee. The Trustee, at his own discretion, would either hold them until twelve months after the end of the war, or sell them at auction to people of British stock. Otto's business, his land and his shares had all to be handed over. He would be allowed, for the time being, to continue to manage his own business and draw an income from it. The shares which Otto had bought in Miriam's name, and those for the children, had also to be given up. Otto was dazed, like a man, almost unconscious, who seems not to feel the blows which continue to rain down on him. Beyond explaining to her what it would mean to their income, Otto did not discuss it with Miriam. "I must comply," he said. "I have no choice." And he lapsed again into waiting.

The days were hot and no breeze stirred the rank paspalum

grass in the paddock. The hens in the fowlyard stood with their wings outspread and their beaks agape to cool themselves. Heat made phantoms on the road outside their gate; mirages of a still lake, glinting in the sun. Flies hung in the air of the verandah, awaiting their chance to dart inside. Eric and Else fidgeted, counting days until school began, and Caroline was listless. Isobel sat in the shade, knitting socks for soldiers, and Otto turned the pages of the newspaper over and over. At night, in the barely abated heat, the house was restless. Miriam, tossing on her bed, could hear Caroline cry out in her sleep or Otto get up and go to the kitchen. Mornings came wearily, crawling damp and pallid over the garden and slumping heavily into the house.

The police came with such a morning. It was the middle of February and Miriam woke to the sound of hooves and wheels. She got up and went to the window as boots thudded on the verandah steps. A policeman stood at the gate and she glimpsed another, disappearing along the path to the back. The doorbell and the knocker sounded simultaneously, tearing the clammy silence of her house.

"Mrs Gluck?" the short one said, "We have a warrant for the arrest of your husband." It was, in some ways, a relief.

6 A Pillar of Salt

In all the years that followed, Miriam had never acknowledged that moment of relief, but now, reliving that dreadful morning, it would not be denied. Relief from waiting for an unknown nemesis, certainly; perhaps even Otto felt that. But more, and shame was bitter as bile in Miriam's mouth: relief from the stigma of being German. She had been trapped, in that moment, by a fleeting vision of return to the enfolding warmth of belonging and the pride of heritage. It was a phantasm, sterile as salt.

The police came into the hall as Otto, fastening the belt on his dressing-gown, emerged at the other end. His face then had recurred to Miriam often since. His look of tragic reproach was not directed at her but at everything he had believed in and hoped for, everything which, in that moment, had failed him. And Miriam knew, in that moment, that for Otto, to whom everything symbolised something larger than itself, she was the cypher of that hope, perhaps even its sacrament, effecting what she signified; she, who had been relieved when they took him from her.

Remorse, close-palled in the petrified integument she had worn since that day, welled up, threatening to dissolve the carapace. And that was what she had feared: the power of remorse to dissolve identity and overwhelm the self. She had resisted it then, denying its cause, but she embraced it now. It was a small act of courage, too late to redeem the past, but perhaps it marked the end of this day's journey. Perhaps she could now return to the present. The grave of her dream opened before her, waiting.

She was leaning against a wall, trembling with exhaustion,

the salt of her tears drying on her face. A young man, approaching, stopped. He was dressed in naval uniform, an officer, she thought, and he lifted his cap. "Can I help you?" he asked. She did not answer because she was thinking that here was a boy who would very soon fight, and perhaps die, for this country. He was not especially handsome but his face was clear, his eyes gentle and concerned for her. "You seem to be unwell," he persisted.

"No, it's just the war." She looked up into his face and said, urgently, "I wish you would not go! We would need to be a better people to be worthy of your life."

"Let me call you a taxi," he begged. He was uncomfortable with her intimate gaze, her hand on his arm, but he would not give her up.

"No." She was firm. "I think I shall continue, after all. There's more to this than my own restoration. But perhaps I've earned a cup of tea!" She smiled at him and gestured with her stick to a cafe across the road. He guided her through the traffic to the cafe door but his face was anxious as he raised his cap in farewell.

"Don't worry about me!" she said, almost gaily. And then, "This war may make you a hero, as the last one made a scapegoat of me. Wars must have both, you know, and both are equally false. So try not to fall for it. Goodbye, and thank you for helping me." She turned into the cafe and took a table at the back, away from the late afternoon sun which slanted through a grimy window.

The tea, steaming in a thick china cup, now seemed a disproportionately large reward, a glowing amber in her stomach, but she did not linger over it because there was more to do. The Victoria Bridge was a block away. On its further side lay the city she had, until these last few minutes, hoped to reclaim as her own. From the moment of Otto's arrest, like Lot's wife, hungering for Sodom, she had looked back in longing for it, seduced by its power into accepting as justice what she ought to have resisted. The feeble curses of an old woman would not penetrate the din of commerce and of war but, for Otto's sake and for her children, she would go now and fling them at its door; and, she thought, suddenly and with surprise as she paid for her tea, for the sake of that young sailor, so gentle and willing to die. She left the cafe and returned to the war.

William Morris Hughes, the new Prime Minister (a Labour man, Willi, whatever you say,) was vigorous in prosecuting the war. At home, he set himself to "rip out the German cancer" from Australian industry and commerce. So pleased was he with his success that he travelled to England where he exhorted the British to do likewise. (He had torn the German cancer, too, from the homes and hearts of Australian women and children, but he did not mention that.) Otto had been ripped out. There was no charge and there would be no trial. The warrant merely said: "Because of the hostile origin and associations of Otto Gluck and in the interests of public safety and the defence of the Commonwealth, it is expedient that he should be taken into military custody during the continuance of the war". The Minister for Defence, Senator George Pearce, it said, would receive any representations against the order.

Otto, who had never struck even a child and rarely raised his voice in anger, did not resist. He went with a policeman into his bedroom to dress. He was not allowed any breakfast nor permitted to pack so much as a razor and, in his confusion, he did not ask to say goodbye to the children.

"There's a mistake, Miriam," he said. "I'll write immediately to the Minister and it will be cleared up. Don't worry, darling girl." He had not called her that for so long and his eyes suddenly misted.

"Where are you taking me, Officer?"

"Enoggera Military Camp." The man was abrupt, without politeness.

"Tell Alfred, Miriam. He will help." They gave him no time to say more and barely allowed him to kiss her before they hurried him down the steps and out to one of the two waiting carriages. Else and Eric, whom Isobel had apparently confined to the kitchen when she saw the police in the hall, ran out when they heard the carriage drawing away, and called after their father from the gate. The policeman standing there restrained them but their voices were shrill with desperation. Miriam ran and caught them up.

Two of the policemen had gone with Otto; three remained, and were now searching the house, pulling out drawers and emptying cupboards. Isobel was shouting at them in the hall but Miriam could not understand what she was saying. The man in charge said to Miriam, "We have a warrant to search the premises," and went on doing so. Else's eyes were tight shut and Eric ran to the policeman nearest and hit him on the chest with his clenched fist. The man pushed him backwards and reached for the telephone, wrenching it from the wall in one angry movement. The action focused Miriam's mind. "Why have you done that?" she asked, almost calmly.

"Aliens aren't allowed telephones," he replied, brutal in speech and bearing.

Isobel drew the terrified children away but they would not go into the garden and stood watching, as if enchanted by horror, from the kitchen door. Miriam could think of nothing but the problem of telling Alfred, now that the telephone had gone. She sat on the hall chair because her knees would not hold her, and tried to collect her thoughts.

One of the men came back to her. "Where's the key to the cupboard in the study?" he demanded. She went with him to look because she had no key to any cupboard. It was a small locker next to the day bed that concerned the man and Miriam watched as he stood back from it and aimed his boot at its slight door. The timber splintered apart revealing a pipe and a tin of tobacco, locked there since Otto gave up smoking two or three years before. Miriam laughed and the man started, as though she had struck him. He strode out of the room and she sat on the day bed, rocking with uncontrollable laughter.

Isobel came and shook her by the shoulders. "Stop it, Miriam. They've gone!"

Isobel took the children to Doreen Telfer and telephoned Alfred from there, asking him to come as soon as he could. Miriam sat gazing out over Otto's vegetable garden and waited without thought while Isobel tidied away the things the police had violated.

When he came, Alfred was sure Otto was right and a mistake had been made. "I'll go and see him as soon as I may, Miriam. He'll want some help with his deposition, proof that his business has no alien connections and so on, but that will straighten it out. I'll let the boys know immediately and we'll set the thing in train. Don't worry, there's a good girl; we'll have him back in a jiffy."

Of course they would. The Wemysses were important and knew the Premier. Now Pa was dead, the boys would help: Mother would see that they did. There was nothing more for her to worry about or to do. She took some medicine for her head, which ached profoundly, and went to bed.

They had arrested Dr Birnbaum and Willi Schuler that same morning. It was in the papers next day; the consul, the editor of *Vorwärts Australien*, and the president of the German Club, prominent Brisbane businessman Otto Gluck. It was a public act and could not be concealed. All the neighbours had known that day and now the whole of Brisbane knew. On the corner of their road, little knots of sightseers gathered. From time to time, one or two would break away and saunter casually past the house, staring at the curtained windows.

"What does it matter what they know or think?" demanded Isobel.

But Doreen said defiantly, "I'll fix them!" and she walked out of the house and across the road as the next pair approached, staring them down with bold, challenging eyes. They were abashed and hurried to rejoin their neighbours. When she had done that a couple of times the sightseers gave up and went home. Miriam sat behind her curtains and gazed, unseeing, into the empty garden.

Suspected of disloyalty, interned for the safety of the Commonwealth. The children's teachers knew now, as well, but Alfred had thought of that. Else and Eric were too distressed to go to school on that or the next day, but Alfred had organised Joshua to visit Eric's school and Sarah went to Else's, to explain the circumstances and see if the children were still acceptable students. The principals had both been very understanding: the children would still need education, they said. And Edward had undertaken to see about getting the telephone reconnected; Miriam was not an alien, after all, but a Wemyss. Alfred himself had gone to the Enoggera camp to see Otto. They had got everything under control. Miriam fiddled absently with her sewing, accepted the food Isobel put before her, spoke calmly to the children when they came into the room. Between times she gazed at nothing and nodded to herself, thinking, over and over, that the boys would set things to rights.

Perhaps, Miriam thought, if it had been clear from the moment of his arrest that there was no hope of justice, she might have acted differently. Even the memory of an intention to act would have comforted her now. But Otto had clung to his faith in British fair play and Alfred supported him, pursuing the matter through "the proper channels". Together they prepared the representation to Senator Pearce. Alfred reported to her that Otto was well and cheerful enough at Enoggera and, though the conditions were spartan, he was not harshly treated. Miriam, numbed into helplessness, relied on Alfred and did nothing.

But Lili had never fallen for myths and lies. She came to see Miriam one day, soon after the arrests. She, of course, had no relatives in Australia to support her and no loyalty of birth to persuade her that justice would prevail. "We must fight, Miriam!" she declared. "We must get together all the women like us and petition the Prime Minister. We must together write to the newspapers, the trades unions and the churches. We must march to Enoggera in a body and refuse to move until they will charge our husbands and put them to the trial."

Miriam stared at her with amazement. Lili's face was gaunt but her eyes flashed with anger and determination. She moved about constantly, splashing tea from the cup she held between her palms. Her high, harsh voice grated on Miriam's nerves, exhausting them. The idea of forcing a public trial, of dragging their names into the newspapers and exposing them all to further humiliation, appalled her.

"Have you spoken of this to Mrs Birnbaum, Lili?"

"Yes. She says her family will press for her husband's release. They are in Melbourne and so at the seat of Government." There was disgust in Lili's voice.

"And and the other women?"

"The other women . . ." Lili shrugged. "They are all poor, or they have the little children which they cannot leave to march, or they are afraid. But Miriam, it is because they are isolated that they are afraid. And we could take the children with us and make a camp outside Enoggera. What can they do to us? Only they can arrest us and then the children at least would be fed! If they arrest women and children, don't you think the newspapers would protest and the people would cry to the Government to stop? Our husbands have the right to a trial. We would not be asking for anything wrong or subversive. If they have proof that the men have spied or have been traitors to this country, so be it! But otherwise, why are they there and why cannot their crimes be told?"

Miriam thought of Eric, Else and Caroline camping outside the military base; of arrest and gaol, of the contempt and anger of her family that would surely follow. "I'm sorry, Lili. I can't help you, I'm afraid."

Lili was exasperated. "I do not ask you to help me, Miriam! I ask you to help Otto and yourself!"

"I am not a socialist, Lili, and I can't accept your view."

"What I am urging is not socialism, Miriam, only co-operation to get justice. Capitalists also do that!" But Miriam continued to shake her head.

Lili's shoulders collapsed. She put down her cup. "Miriam, you are not even an individualist! You are a victim of the notion of Authority and have given up your own power to it. But I tell you that the authorities in this country will sacrifice even such as you for their own purposes if you will not stand with others for the common good."

Lili went away then and, through the window, Miriam watched her walk towards the station. Her hands were thrust in her pockets and her head was bent in disappointment. She looked like a mad woman now, with her greying hair escaping from under her shabby hat. Miriam hoped she would not come back.

Alfred came to collect Otto's *Demit*. "Otto's going to make a translation of it to send with his deposition so there can be no doubt," he explained. "We have great hopes of Senator Pearce, Miriam. He made a good speech, you know. Said there was no need to harass people of German origin who've lived and worked in this country for years. We'll soon have Otto out. Sarah sends her love and says you must all come and spend the day with us soon." He went away with the *Demit* which, he said, would be posted off with the other documents to Melbourne that week. There was nothing more to be done now but wait for the outcome.

The telephone was reconnected and Else and Eric were back at school, kindly treated by their teachers and unmolested by the other students.

"When can we go and visit Dad?" they asked.

Miriam shrank from the thought of visiting Otto in those circumstances and Joshua had advised against taking the children. "Better to shield them as much as you can," he said.

"Dad will be allowed to come home soon, I'm sure," Miriam told them. "And, in the meantime, we must all be brave and go on as if nothing was wrong." They wanted to believe her, she could see, but their short lives had taught them to mistrust optimism.

Doreen Telfer had Caroline over daily to play with Bubbles and Isobel encouraged Miriam to accept an unexpected invitation from the Pendles. "Life must go on, you know," she admonished, out of her own experience.

It was during those few weeks of waiting on Senator Pearce that Kathleen fell ill and sent for Miriam and the priest to hear her story. Since her husband was now dead, Kathleen was able to be fully restored to the Church and need no longer suffer the aching loneliness of exclusion while others filed to the sanctuary steps for Communion. Though Kathleen's story did not make much impression on her then, Miriam had understood and envied her restoration. For herself, she thought that when Otto was released he would be publicly exonerated. If Senator Pearce accepted his deposition then the Government had been wrong to arrest him and must certainly make a public apology and perhaps some restitution for the wrong. She had not mentioned this hope to Alfred but nurtured it privately. Then the

German stigma would be permanently expunged and they, too, would be restored to their place in the community.

Two days later, Senator Pearce rejected Otto's appeal and committed him to Holdsworthy Concentration Camp in New South Wales for the duration of the war.

The river, turgid and foul-smelling from the city's waste and commerce, wore the yoke of Empire. Other bridges built here had been torn down and dashed in violent flood but this Victoria Bridge stood high on stone pylons. Its steel girders were strong and beautiful, its slender lamp-posts decorated with wrought-iron crowns. Miriam set out across it towards the city; the city in which, on the day after Otto's appeal was rejected, she had sought for three just men. She had found only one and he was insufficient.

7 The City

The lobby of the Queensland National Bank was of marble and cedar and the footsteps of employees sounded clipped and officious as, like sacristans in a church, they crossed and recrossed it. Customers moved more reverently and with less confidence. Miriam, being neither, felt like an outlaw and dreaded that an official would stop her and demand her business there. But she made her way unimpeded to the ornate lift, up through the core of the building and out into the carpeted corridor that led to Joshua's office. Joshua had summoned her, had sent a cab to bring her here, to a family conference. She knocked on the panelled cedar door. Alfred opened it. "Come in, old girl," he muttered, grasping her elbow and grazing her cheek with his moustache. His tone was sympathetic but the pressure on her elbow conveyed a warning.

The men of her family were grouped around Joshua's vast desk. To judge by the crystal ashtray on the broad arm of Edward's chair, they had been meeting for some time. They rose briefly when Miriam came in and Alfred drew up a chair for her. It was he who had telephoned Senator Pearce's verdict to her the previous day and foreshadowed a family conference to consider the future. She had waited, numbly, for Joshua's summons and she waited now for him to begin.

He remained standing, framed by the lofty windows behind him, and he looked out of them as he spoke. "Well, Miriam, now we know the worst, I'm afraid. The Minister has considered Otto's appeal and has turned it down. He doesn't give his reasons, of course. In time of war they have to be very careful, you know." He turned to face her. "But we must believe that his decision is well-founded, Miriam. The Government has a great many means of knowing these things: the censor and so on. And, informally, I've heard that their chief concern is not any one individual so much as a network of influential men who might, in the event of a German victory in Europe, have the means to, shall we say, ease the path of the invader."

Miriam gave a very small sob and stared at the gloved hands grappling each other in her lap. Joshua was undeterred. "I put all this to you quite bluntly because it's best we should understand exactly where we are in this." Miriam nodded but did not look up. "Now, Edward and Alfred and I have been talking this morning and we've agreed to do everything in our power to help you through. Everything. Alfred will go on handling your business affairs but he's making considerable sacrifices to do so. Several firms have threatened to withdraw their accounts from him if he continues to work for someone they now feel justified in believing to be a traitor. I can't stress that to you strongly enough, Miriam. Alfred is to be commended, I think, for his loyalty to the family in this." He bowed slightly towards Alfred who attempted to speak, but Joshua swept on.

"Looking through the record of Otto's business affairs, I realise that his dealings have been very widespread and various. Probably you have not understood a great deal about them?" Miriam nodded. "But we would be grateful if you'd think very carefully if there's anything you do know which might have given the Government reason to suspect Otto's loyalty. It's important we should know if there is." He paused, waiting for her reply.

Miriam's thoughts were wild and would not be corralled. She gazed around at the faces of the men. Edward was staring upwards through a cloud of smoke; Alfred's gaze was fixed on the toe of his shoe; only Joshua looked at her. His mouth wore its usual downward cast, his eyebrow was lifted slightly and his eyes did not flinch from her wretchedness. "Anything at all you can think of," he reiterated, and she saw she must offer him something.

"Only the language society," she bleated, and the blood of shame rushed to her face. "But, Joshua, Edward, I suppose Otto may have been foolish, sometimes. He believed so implicitly in his British citizenship..."

"Oh, very foolish of him!" said Edward, his voice heavy with sarcasm.

Instantly, Miriam remembered James and was emboldened. "But I'm sure, quite sure, that he was never disloyal. James once said he was more British than the British, and it's true!" She sobbed now, unrestrainedly. There was silence in the room and Alfred reached across and patted her knee.

Joshua pulled the bell-cord. "I've let my secretary know we want tea," he said. "Sarah is due in a minute. We thought she should be here to discuss what needs to be done." He took one of Edward's cigarettes and smoked while Miriam's weeping dried up.

Sarah must have been waiting somewhere in the building for she arrived with the woman who brought the tea. Her role was apparently to take charge of the personal matters while the men decided on the future of Otto's business and Miriam's income. Miriam was not required to contribute much more to the discussion.

"Now, Alfred," Joshua continued to lead, but he had sat down behind his desk, "you say they're going to move him from Enoggera?"

"Yes, next month. The place isn't suitable for, er, prisoners, apparently."

"Well, Sarah, I expect it will be necessary for Miriam to see him before he goes, and to take the children? Holdsworthy is a very long way away and I don't imagine she'll be able to visit him there."

Sarah nodded. "It will be hard for the children, Miriam," she said, doubtfully. "To see their father in a prison. But it's only right he should say goodbye to them, of course."

"Otherwise," Joshua went on, "the best course, and I think I speak for us all, Miriam; the very best course is for your life to go on as normally as possible. You should be able to stay in the house for the foreseeable future and there appears to be enough income from the business at present to pay the children's fees. I've spoken to Carrie and she is more than willing for Isobel to stay on. Though that's a matter for the girl, herself, I suppose. Edward, you've spoken to Gluck's Sydney partner: I gather he's happy to manage the whole business?"

"Jack Dakers, yes. So far, so good," affirmed Edward. "He's a Britisher, obviously, and he thinks he may be able to rebuild some of the business that's been lost over the last year if he's given a free hand – under Alfred's direction, of course. The Public Trustee has agreed that Dakers should take over the management for the time being, and they will continue to pay Miriam's allowance out of the profits."

"Good. Well, I think that's all satisfactory, then. Have you anything to add, Sarah?"

"Only to agree with you, Joshua. I think Miriam must make every effort, for her sake, the children's and, of course, for Alfred and the family, to hold her head up, behave as normally as possible. We don't know how long this frightful war will go on, Miriam, and when it's over Otto will be let out and... well, we don't know. But for now you'll need to forget him and so must the children, too. I feel very strongly that it would be better if he were not mentioned again, among us or between you and the children. That way the memory of his disgrace will fade in the community and we will all, in due time, be able to live it down. I don't pretend it will be easy but I think our reputations stand high enough in Brisbane to finally outweigh this terrible thing. Don't you agree, Joshua?"

"Absolutely! We've all suffered by the association in people's minds, and Alfred will continue to do so, I don't doubt. But if, er, that name, is not mentioned again, I'm sure we will come through. I think we need *your* agreement on that, Miriam."

She shook her head, bewildered. They were doing all they could for her and they knew the ways of the world. She had no choices before her. "Yes," she answered, and they breathed relief.

"Good. Then I think that's all we can do for now. I must get back to work." He was fingering a file on his desk.

Miriam was startled. "But what about Otto?" she cried out. "What are you going to do about him?"

"In what respect, Miriam?" Joshua's voice was as level and fine as a plumb-line.

"Well, to get him out; to clear his name!"

"We've just agreed not to mention his name, Miriam. And Alfred has already done everything, in that regard, that could possibly be done. I'm afraid you're going to have to accept that your husband is now beyond our help until the end of the war. And now I really must . . . There will be a cab waiting to take you home."

Miriam had reached the end of the bridge. The Treasury Building stood, massive and forbidding, ahead of her. An image of gold stored up there flitted through her mind: the common wealth it guarded, swelled by Otto, safe from him; the shares they had stripped from him, the land he had been forbidden to own, all taken and added to this common treasure for its protection. Perhaps here was the fortress she should assail. But her mind, she knew, was muddled. Age, and this day's weary journey through her life, had confused her. It was not here she was going, after all: she was going to see Edward. She turned right into George Street and the Houses of Parliament loomed at its end, their copper domes like the foreheads of wise men conferring.

Edward had a suite of rooms at the Bellevue Hotel, opposite the Queensland Club and the Parliament. Though he still lived chiefly at home, he liked to be close to the centre of power. She stared for a moment, bemused, at the cars in the street and then the present reasserted itself: Edward was dead. He had fallen over one night, between the Club and the Bellevue, and struck his head on the kerb, they said. She had never wept for his death but tears slid from her eyes for him now. He drank too much. Miriam thought he had done so ever since that day, which she had confused for a moment with this one, when she visited him at the Bellevue to plead for his help.

On the day of the family conference, as she drove home in the cab, Miriam clutched at Edward's sarcasm amid the whirling confusion of her brain. It had reminded her of James; of his speech on Otto's naturalisation, of his affection for herself and friendship with Otto. And more: it reminded her that, once, Edward, too, had loved her. She knew that if only her brother would, he could use his influence – on the Premier, perhaps, or any one of the important people he knew, to get Otto released. She had not yet told the children of the Minister's decision and would not even think about it until she had exhausted the possibilities for changing it. Edward had not been willing to see her when she telephoned him that afternoon but she told him it was important, she must talk to him in person. Let him think she was about to confide Otto's perfidy, let him think anything, provided he would see her. She dressed as well as she could, knowing Edward regarded such things, and went that night to the Bellevue, marshalling her argument in the cab.

Edward always dressed expensively and his rooms were ornately furnished and lined with books. He was still a handsome man but his skin was puffy, his mouth rather loose and his chin uncertain, now, in the folds of flesh. Miriam studied him closely over the glass of sherry he gave her. She had only one shot to fire and must aim carefully.

"Edward, I've come to ask, to beg you, to help Otto get out of prison. You're an important person. Lots of your friends are in Parliament or work for the Government and, now that James is dead, you're the only one of the family who might help me."

"I'm flattered, Miriam, but I'm afraid it isn't possible."

"It must be possible; he's done nothing wrong!"

"Miriam, we tried to spare you this morning but it seems you haven't understood: we don't believe we would be justified in attempting anything more for your husband now that the Government has made a judgment on his appeal."

"If you won't do it for Otto, please won't you try for my sake? Edward, remember when we were little and you used to look after me?" He turned his head away impatiently. "Only listen to me, Edward! I loved you so much then and you used to love me, too. It's all Pa's fault, Edward, that we aren't friends now. Pa, with his bullying, is to blame. You were never good enough for him and he said you were a cissy because you cared for me, a little girl! And so you gave up caring for me and I was so lonely until I met Otto. That's the truth, Edward. And now the Government's taken Otto away from me, too. Please, Edward, help me get him back!" She saw that his lip trembled and she held her breath. She had never begged for anything in her life before and it had come awkwardly to her.

He got up and went to the sideboard for more whisky but when he turned back his face was ugly. "I warned you, Miriam, didn't I, all those years ago, about marrying a foreigner? But you were desperate for him. No ordinary Australian bloke was good enough for you; you had ideas about yourself. We were a rough lot, as I recall, from slaving away at the mill. But three generations of rough work have made this country what it is: a strong nation we can be proud of and fight for. He, on the other hand, read books, he had fine clothes and polished manners. Oh, and he'd travelled the world, hadn't he? He was nothing but a johnny-come-lately! He wasn't rough because he hadn't contributed a tap to the wealth of this nation and owed not a jot of loyalty to it. He swanned in when the hard work had been done and wanted to marry into a family that could smooth his path, give him position and influence. You, poor silly girl, imagined it was your charm, your allure perhaps, that hooked him, and you were ready like a ripe plum to fall into his grasp! But we saw through him then, Miriam, even if you were blind. And now your fancy foreigner has proved to be a vile, treacherous Hun who's brought disgrace to you, to our name and to everything else I care about. The Government says that – not me, not Joshua! He's as bad as the other bloody Huns who are busy killing ordinary, rough Australian blokes out there in France. Or don't you read the papers? I wouldn't lift a finger to help him, even if the Government was mine to command!" His voice had risen with his anger but he dropped it now. "You're better off without him, Miriam, believe me. Now you can hold your head up like a decent woman again."

Miriam had no recollection of getting home from her interview with Edward that night and remembered only the deathly emptiness within her when she woke next morning. But the children had now to be told and she lay in bed trying to find reasons she could give them for the family edict. The things Edward had said washed to and fro like a tide of effluent through her memory. The look of reproach on Otto's face when she had last seen him was now irrevocably stained by her brother's words. What she had believed was love might have been ambition; hope and faith, mere greed and vanity. Was it for these she had grovelled to Edward, exposing herself to contempt and humiliation? She steeled herself with disgust.

The children were breakfasting on the verandah outside the kitchen. Caroline was in her high-chair, Else and Eric sat at the wicker table and Isobel hovered, buttering toast, pouring milk. The maid was tending the stove in the kitchen. Miriam closed the door on her and leant against the verandah rail.

"I've got bad news for you, I'm afraid," she said. "Dad's not coming home for a while. The Government won't let him. Instead," she would not allow any time for them to take this in, to question or respond. "Instead, they're going to send him away to a place called Holdsworthy, near Sydney, where there are a lot of other men the Government thinks have done something wrong. They will keep him there until the war's over. We don't know how long that will be so we will just have to be very patient and wait. In the meantime," again she overrode their interruptions, "Uncle Joshua, Uncle Edward, Uncle Alfred and Auntie Sarah all think we have to be very careful. They say we mustn't talk about Dad at all, not even in the house." Isobel's face was aghast, her mouth already forming a protest. "They know more about all this than we do, and we need them to help us until Dad comes home, so we must do as they say." Isobel's mouth snapped shut and her eyes narrowed. Miriam avoided them. "We can go and see Dad at Enoggera before he leaves, just to say goodbye. I'm going to arrange that with Uncle Alfred. When we go, we'll only talk to him about happy things; what you've been doing at school, things like that. We don't want to make him unhappy because he will be sad enough about leaving us. You will be able to write to him sometimes at Holdsworthy and we must try and write happy letters to cheer him up." She could not bear the children's faces, the tears that had welled in their eyes, and she could not counter Isobel's anger. She left the verandah quickly.

Else and Eric came to kiss her goodbye before they went to school, but their expressions, by then, had closed firm against the world outside.

It was only two stops up the railway line to Gaythorne station, opposite the Enoggera military camp. "We could have come every day, after school, if we'd realised," Else said quietly to Eric as they got down from the carriage. Miriam bit her lip: this would soon be over and Holdsworthy was nearly a thousand miles away.

Alfred, who had come with them, led the way across the dirt road to the gate of the camp, where soldiers stood guard in the dry, blistering heat. Cicadas shrilled in grating cacophany and the air was full of dust. Alfred spoke to the guard, the gate was opened, and they went through. They were to meet Otto in the mess hall, empty except for guards at the several doors. Alfred waited outside, chatting in the shade of the verandah to an officer who had come up at their approach.

Miriam shepherded the children ahead of her, Caroline trotting between brother and sister, their footsteps hollow on the wooden boards. Otto was seated at one of the tables and he rose as they came in, calling their names, moving towards them. Caroline broke free and ran to him. Else and Eric were more hesitant, though Else, too, after a moment, began to run. Miriam kept her eyes on the children as though, like a good nurse, she must assure herself of their safety and their manners. Otto hugged and kissed the girls and gravely took Eric's proffered hand.

"Bluey, dear! Oh, it's good to see you all!"

"Everyone calls me Eric now I'm at school, Dad."

Otto's face fell for an instant. He quickly rearranged it and said, brightly, "Yes, I'd forgotten how grown up you are, now! And Else, too. Not Daddy's very good girl, any more, I expect, but a real young lady, now you're at school!" Else buried her face in his shirt-front and sobbed. Otto closed his eyes tight and there came from him the very thinnest, high-pitched noise, as of a dog, whimpering.

Miriam went to him, putting her hand on his arm. "Otto, don't!" she whispered. "Please don't. It will be all right. It's only for a short while. The war can't go on forever. Please! The children. . ."

"Of course." He forced control of himself. "We will be together again one day, my dears," he told them. "And perhaps Mummy will bring you all to see me in Sydney. She's never been to Sydney yet, you know, though I promised her I'd take her there one day. So now you must persuade her to bring you all. It's a long way. You'd have to make it into a little holiday; stay in an hotel and have a trip on the Harbour, as well as coming to visit me. Wouldn't that be fun?"

The children tried to enter into the spirit of it but Miriam quailed. She could not tell him or the children that a trip to Holdsworthy was not likely, but Joshua had made that plain. "We are all going to try very hard," she said firmly, "to live a normal life while you're away." To soften the warning, she added, "Then, when you come home, we will be just the same and you'll think you'd never left us!"

But Otto had understood and his eyes were bleak. "Of course you must live a normal life! A good and happy life, if you can. But you won't quite forget me, will you? Please, my dears?" He tousled the children's heads and kissed them all, his tears running with theirs as he pressed them to him. "Take care of Mummy for me, won't you? Give her my love every day. And write to me. I shall write to you as often as I'm allowed."

He kissed Miriam then and held her tightly. For a moment, as she leant against him, her resistance ebbed, but the muffled sobbing of the children recalled it. "Alfred is outside, Otto, and he wants to talk to you, too. We must go. Goodbye, my dear. Take care of yourself."

She hurried the children away to the station where they would wait for Alfred and the train to take them home. If she had doubted the wisdom of Sarah's edict, she saw it now: they would all be far less distressed if they locked their memory of Otto away with their grief, until the war was done.

8 Habitations of the Dead

Miriam stood outside the Bellevue Hotel. Men – Government employees, lawyers, some representatives of the people, perhaps – were gathering there, streaming out of Government offices, pouring across the road from the Parliament buildings, joining with their kind for an evening drink in the bars and lounges of the grand hotel. She could not address them there, it was not a place she could enter alone. Figures, faces, loomed and swam before her, distorted images of power and complacency; men armoured in suits. They did not even see her and their loud opinionated voices, their harsh humourless laughter, pressed her down. She beat upon them in her mind and saw her own frail figure rushing at them, holding out her arms and her voice to push them back across the road to the Parliament, to curse them and their power in that forum where a citizen could be heard.

But it was as useless now as it had been then. She was not like Lili, could not seize men and compel them to listen, or force them to retreat before her flaming eyes. Even Lili had not succeeded, though she might have done if other women had joined with her and shared her courage. Miriam wished for Lili now and wondered where she was in this new war.

Lili had said to her, "If you can do nothing else, Miriam, you can refuse to believe their lies; you can continue to live by the truth and you can shake the dust of their habitations from your feet." That she could have done and did not.

The stuggle to imprison memory and grief had been bitter and near fatal to Miriam. Morphine, brutal friend, had obliterated the connecting tissue of time and left only grotesque vignettes, like nightmares, in her recollection. Isobel's anger seemed like a physical conflict between them; her teeth and nose, her splayed, thrusting fingers, as though reflected in a convex mirror at a fun-parlour: "How can you? How can you abandon him like that, forbidding the children? Cowardly! Shameful!" Lean on the door, the prisoner is seeping around it!

The faces of the children, pitifully twisted by obedience, yearned to shape the forbidden name, the first and easiest syllable they had learnt.

"Dad said to give you his love every day."

"No, Else! Remember what you've been told. We must not speak about him!" Doctor, I've run out of the medicine for my headaches.

Otto's letters came regularly: Concentration Camps, Australia. Prisoner of War Letter. There was no pretending to the postman, no escaping the reality emblazoned on every page. But the censor obliterated the more grotesque truths from the letters themselves and left only the connecting tissue. *I was ――― very soon after I arrived here, by ――― and I am only just on my feet again.* Bashed by a gang of thugs who ran a protection racket, she discovered later, and was grateful the censor had spared her. But Otto did not complain and his letters were mostly about them. *I wonder what you are doing today. I think what should be coming up in the garden and imagine how warm it must be there now the spring has come. How are the children doing at school? Caroline must be lonely without them. Does she still go to Doreen's to play with Bubbles?*

She could see him sitting in front of the writing paper, as she sat before hers, wondering what to say, how to tell the reality of his dreary existence; struggling with the desperate inability to project, beyond the grave of his incarceration, the tremors of a living heart. He told her that the winter had been very cold and wet, the camp a sea of mud. Blankets were inadequate, the huts draughty, the food was very poor and there was nothing to do. She knew that was the worst of it for him, the most unendurable misery: nothing to do. Nothing at all to do.

Otto appeared in opiate dreams and begged, "But Miriam, please – there's nothing for me to do here!"

Her own voice responded, "Otto, please, go away! There's nothing I can do for you!" Back and forth the voices rang, echoing down the well of sleep, speeding to a gabble, slowed to a deathly groan. Nothing.

Isobel was not angry anymore. Her face peered into Miriam's, surging forward, large and worried, then retreating sharply to a tiny point of concern which winked and went out. Alfred, too, was worried and his twitching made her laugh, but secretly, because Alfred was a good man. The boys laughed at him secretly, as well, because he was plodding and without ambition. But Alfred had stuck. It was just like his refusal to go Home for his wedding tour: he had stuck then, and Sarah could not budge him.

"I'll see what I can do for him, Miriam. I'll try. Promise me not to take any more of the medicine? Promise!"

"You've got very run down, Miriam," Isobel said. Nobody spoke the truth. "We must build you up. The children need you to be strong, you know, and for their sakes you must try and have courage." It took all her courage to sit every day on the verandah and watch Otto's canaries flirting with the spring sunshine; courage to open the letter lying in her lap and hear Otto's voice, broken by the censor, come through the writing on the scarred page. *Alfred says you are not well. You must keep well, darling girl. I cannot bear to be away from you when you are ill. I am – – – and with Alfred's help – – –. Meanwhile, be brave.* Alfred interpreted it for her. "'I am appealing once more against this unjust sentence and for clemency because you are ill, and with Alfred's help I may be allowed to come home and look after you.'"

"I suggested to him that he appeal again," Alfred explained, "and I said I would support him with a letter to the Minister telling him of your illness. But he has been refused again. I'm sorry. I promised to try, Miriam, and I wanted you to know that I did. And I'll go on trying, only you must do your bit, too, and hold up, you know."

"Am I ill, Alfred," the words trembled from her, "or is it that I have done wrong?" The question bewildered her, springing unheralded from somewhere behind consciousness. But Alfred seemed unsurprised by it. He took a letter from his pocket and folded it so only a few lines were visible.

"It's from Harry," he said. "From the Somme. Most of it would only distress you, but read this bit."

I wish the Germans would win and win quickly, Dad. I do, and I'm not ashamed of it. Then all of us poor sods could come home. There's no hope of us winning that I can see, the officers are such bloody fools, and this whole war is a madman's nightmare.

"Harry's not bad, Miriam; just a victim, same as you, and any way out seems fair enough." The difference, Miriam saw, lay in Harry's courage to speak the truth.

Despite Alfred's efforts, the proper channels had been exhausted and Miriam knew there was nothing, now, to hope for from them.

"Hold up! Where's your pride? Maintain your dignity, pretend this has nothing to do with you. Forget Gluck, remember you're a Wemyss!" The family crowded into tortured dreams, enjoining, insisting. Opposing voices, Isobel's, Lili's, and now Harry's, entreated, "Resist! Fight! Speak the truth!" The silent faces, ghostly pale, of Otto and the children, waited on her decision. Miriam drove them all away, nightly, with the medicine now hidden under her mattress. Daily, Isobel propped her up, tidied her, fed and protected her so that she and the world of war, beyond her gate, should not meet.

Sarah eventually intervened. "This can't go on, Miriam! You must know you're behaving very badly. Isobel is worn to a shadow with looking after you and the children. Alfred is forced to spend far too much time coming and going out of anxiety about you, and you are being utterly self-indulgent. I never thought to see a member of my family so morally weak as to become a morphinist! Where are you hiding it?" It did not take her long to find it, she had that sort of instinct for rooting out another's weakness, and she carried the two bottles triumphantly to the bathroom.

Miriam, distraught, followed. "Don't, Sarah! Don't tip it out! Haven't you done enough, taking Otto away?"

Sarah turned on her. "I? Take Otto away? You're quite out of your mind with this stuff, Miriam. Otto has been taken away by the lawful authorities. It's got nothing to do with me. But, as responsible citizens, we all have a duty to accept and uphold the law. Where would we be if, every time the law went against us, we all went about in an opiate daze? Pull yourself together, for God's sake! You're only compounding the disgrace your husband has brought down on us all."

But Miriam was beyond the help of exhortation and Sarah called the doctor to her. She could hear them conferring on the border of her consciousness and was aware of Sarah collecting things together near her bed. Isobel came and sat with her, holding one limp hand, until Sarah bustled in again, saying, "We're going to put you in hospital for a little while, Miriam. The cab is here, you need only to put on your dressing-gown and slippers." She pushed and pulled her into the gown, caught at her hair, forced her feet into the slippers and propelled her towards the cab. Isobel kissed and patted her, sad and apologetic, but helpless. Miriam made no protest. She had capitulated and now she knew she would die.

They took her to St Julian's. Matron Bloom was no longer there but they put her in the same private room she had occupied when that first, fortunate child had died. She thought it wry that Otto's gleaming equipment still furnished this sterile antechamber to death. They tumbled her into bed and arranged her neatly, they propped her up and held a cup to her lips, they laid her down and drew the blinds so she would sleep. They woke and washed her, forced a cold steel pan under her, lifted her limp wrist to tell her pulse. Miriam submitted silently to everything. She even ate some of the food they brought her, so as not to give offence. But in the long nights, when the squeak of shoes on linoleum and the groans of other patients limned her isolation, Otto would come and kneel by the bed, his weeping muffled by the counterpane. She would stroke his head, then, and tell him not to mind; the war was nearly over.

The men were emerging from the bars of the Bellevue. It was closing time. Their laughter was looser now, their gestures less curt.

"And I did die!" Miriam cried, and saw her own amazement

reflected in the face of the man she had addressed. "Until this day," she assured him, and turned away into the lobby of the hotel. She found the Ladies Room and went in. She took off her hat and surveyed herself in the mirror. She washed her face and hands, combed and pinned her hair in place, brushed her skirt and looked down at her shoes. They were dusty and she took some toilet paper from the roll in a cubicle and scrubbed them clean.

"There Lili!" she remarked, smiling a little to herself. "Now I may go home."

The light of this spring evening was clean, gilding the windows and chrome of cars in the street. Isobel would now be home. Home. The word insisted on her attention. It was a long way and Isobel would be worried before she got there. Where? Isobel was kind and good. She had steered Miriam through living death for all those years of the war. Eric and the girls were fond and protective and they, too, would worry soon if she did not return to her allotted place. It was not their fault that place was the grave. She had accepted it at Joshua's insistence, at Edward's and Sarah's. But she would not go back to it for Isobel's sake, nor for the children.

Dear Doctor Hugo had rescued her from St Julian's. Isobel, worried then, too, had sent for him and he had come one afternoon. Pushing aside the Matron's protests, he said, "We must get you out of here. Will you come and have a little holiday with my Matron and me? Tomorrow then. I will collect you and we will set off!" He made it sound like an adventure. She did not believe in it but she acceded anyway. No-one could object to it.

Dr Leclerc had a motor car ("It has made such a difference to my rounds") and they drove to Marburg. Miriam was scarcely conscious of the distance, and the farms and orchards slid by like water, soothing and peaceful. Dr Leclerc did not talk very much above the noise of the engine but, as they turned off the main road into the Marburg village, he pointed to a sign: Townshend. She did not understand.

"Marburg is dead; long live Townshend!" he said, bitterly. "Named for Major-General Sir Charles, an Englishman, who is busy fighting the Germans. It is ironic, I think, that men build monuments to the glory they wish for on the grave of a history they have rejected. I have complained and will continue to fight it, not just because it is insulting to the people who live here, but because no people can build a sound future on foundations they have spurned."

Dr Leclerc and his Matron had nursed her back to a semblance of life. They did not talk much about Otto or the war, but about the ordinary doings of their busy lives and these, in time, drew her out. At her request they let her roll clean bandages and sterilise equipment, or arrange the flowers in the study and lobby; small tasks she could do on her own. She wanted nothing to do with the patients and would turn her head away when someone was carried past her on stretcher or bier. She could not endure the sight of suffering and would allow no-one to claim her sympathy.

For the most part she sat alone in the grounds. The dry wind, sweeping across the valley, sealed her wounds, encrusting them, so that their pain was dulled. The craving for morphine, which had caused her to pace her room at night and reduced her to tears of rage and frustration several times a day, gradually ebbed. And when the rage and the pain had gone, Miriam felt nothing. She could look at the hospital Otto had helped to build, she could accept sharp, unbidden thrusts of his memory, without wincing. "You're looking so much better, Miriam, my dear," Matron said, and she accepted that it was so.

The doctor and his Matron invited Isobel and the children to come for Christmas because, by then, they knew Miriam would be strong enough to return with them to the new year. Her hosts bustled about their preparations for the visit with excitement but Miriam felt only apprehension that the visitors would bring with them the sorrow of the real world and cause her wounds to weep again. When they arrived, she saw her children as through a lens, saw their own anxiety at the meeting dissolve into eager laughter and playfulness under the doctor's good humour and the Matron's solicitude; saw it all with relief, protected from them by an invisible shield.

The children went with the doctor on some of his rounds and were encouraged to visit the rooms of convalescent patients.

Isobel joined the Matron's routines, glad to learn from her about the care of the sick. Miriam listened to the children's tales of school and Isobel's gossip about Carrie or Doreen. She was attentive to them all, smiling and nodding, furrowing her brow as appropriate, and Dr Leclerc watched her.

On the eve of their departure for Brisbane, he called her into his study and said, "Once before, Miriam, I lectured you about the need to forgive yourself. Physically, you are recovered, but if your heart is to live again, now too, that forgiveness is necessary for you."

Miriam bowed her head in acknowledgment, but she could no longer distinguish herself from those others, at whose behest she had surrendered her life, and whom she could not forgive.

Part Four
The Nowhere People

1 Homeless

Miriam turned her back on the city as the dying sun fired its lifeless buildings. The streetlamps had not yet come on and the river was dark under the bridge. Stanley Street, to her left, followed the river past Wemyss and Sons and would take her back to Isobel and her safe, dark flat overlooking the city. She was not roofless, because she owned a place to sleep, nor rootless, either, for the ancient bones of her land still anchored her being, but she was homeless, because she had no place among a living people. She stood in the dusk considering that idea. It was not new; she had fought it strenuously since war's end, striving for belonging where none was possible. Now the rictus of conformity relaxed. She felt lightheaded, almost weightless, as she did when, at the end of a long, tight day, she took off her stays. It was curiously pleasurable. A couple of men carrying ports trudged past her, and she set off to follow them across Stanley Street and up the hill beyond, suddenly wanting to experience the difference between herself and the homeward-bound. "The foxes have holes", her mind sang the words, "and the birds of the air have their nests, but the Son of Man has nowhere to lay his head." She had heard them often but had not known their power until now.

Otto must have been so unendurably lonely. Not once had she visited him, in all the four years of his internment. It was hard to credit that, now. But when she returned from Marburg, in the new year of 1917, she had set herself a course which allowed of no diversion: to preserve herself, the children and a skeleton of normality; for Otto's sake, she told herself, so he would have something to build on when he came home. To do it she must crawl under the protection of her family. She had no energy or desire for anything else.

She became a recluse at "Cooloola" and only Doreen Telfer persisted in friendship with her. The word recluse was Otto's.

"Let's go and have lunch in town, Miriam. It's such a nice day!"

"I'd rather not, Doreen, if you don't mind."

"What would you like to do, then? You must get out, you know."

"I really don't like to go out any more."

"Miriam, I don't want to bully you, but I have my instructions from Otto. He wrote particularly and asked me to make sure you did get out. 'Don't let her become a recluse, Doreen,' he said. So there! Now, where will we go?"

Doreen could not avoid knowing of the family's embargo on Otto's name and she rarely mentioned it but was driven to employ it then against Miriam's intractability. They went to the Botanic Gardens and had tea at the kiosk, but Miriam was terrified of meeting people she knew and scanned every path for approaching figures, dragging on Doreen's arm to divert her when anyone appeared. At the kiosk they sat in a corner, Miriam with her back to the room. Otto, despite time and distance, had discerned her state of mind. She, on the other hand, knew nothing of his.

Alfred, of course, came and went, and Sarah occasionally intruded, her eye sharpened by suspicion to prise out any vestige of Miriam's moral weakness. Even German sausage, served at luncheon, was evidence to that eye of an unpatriotic leaning. Edward and Joshua made formal visits, from time to time, to impress her debt upon her and collect their dues in seemly behaviour. She had paid them and never once mentioned her husband or the possibility of travelling to see him. So hens, as if mesmerised, will follow a white line drawn on the ground, believing, perhaps, that it leads to a broken bag from which wheat has trickled.

Kathleen and Carrie visited when Carrie could leave Gympie for a few days but Kathleen, old and infirm now, did not come alone. Otto wrote to them all, Miriam knew; to Kathleen and Carrie especially, but the family ban prevented them from telling her what he said. Only Kathleen occasionally transgressed.

"I had such a terrible story from Otto! About some poor men who were transferred to Holdsworthy from another camp. Torrens, I think it was. And they had been so badly beaten, poor fellows; scarred and bruised all down their backs. Otto said he couldn't believe it could happen in this country but sure and I believe it, after what I've seen!" The censorship must have relaxed — perhaps they had too much to do, now that they had seven thousand people behind barbed wire. (Where was the cry for an end you so confidently predicted, Willi? Was everyone just like me?)

But to Miriam, Otto was his own censor and perhaps that was why she imagined he would emerge from the concentration camp unchanged, like a coat folded away in mothballs for the winter, if she did not disturb the tissue in which his memory was stored. Their letters to one another were now merely signals that each still existed and bore no clues to change or growth. The children, under Isobel's supervision, still wrote weekly, and Isobel herself wrote and received letters from Otto. Miriam did not enquire about their contents and Isobel never offered information. Miriam might have been jealous had she not rigorously suppressed anything that would make her heart beat faster. But it was to Isobel that Otto wrote the mysterious letter which had damned all their hopes.

That was right at the end and Miriam could not think about it yet, but she knew she could not go on blaming Isobel, always loyal to Otto, now she had so clearly seen her own betrayal of him. I will come back soon, Isobel, and tell you so. Only wait a while more.

For the rest of the war, Miriam read the papers only for hints of its end and now remembered little of the contour of those years. She had set her compass through their wasteland by the iron certainties of her family, and only when their monolithic opinion cracked over conscription did she glimpse the wilderness and sense she was astray.

When Prime Minister Hughes (she would not think of him as Billy) appealed to the country for a mandate to conscript men into the forces, Kathleen was vehement in support of Daniel Mannix, Catholic Archbishop of Melbourne and leader of the anti-conscription campaign. Joshua and Sarah detested him as typically Irish, and, since the Easter Uprising, as an anti-British traitor. Edward was perplexed because his friend, Premier Ryan, was also opposed to conscription, and so the powers he courted were at odds. Ryan was a Catholic, too, of course, and Joshua dismissed his views. But Kathleen had letters from Edith which she flourished in support of her opinion. Edith, treating the wounded in France, tended prisoners of war as well.

Sending more soldiers will only drag this business out so I hope the referendum is defeated, she wrote. *Left to themselves, I'm sure the fighting men would end the war tomorrow, since they've no reason to hate each other. Do you know, Gran, that at Christmas time there was a truce? Our lads and the Germans met in no-man's land at the Front and swapped cigarettes and sang Christmas carols together. I thought of Uncle Otto when I heard that, and of the marvellous Christmas parties he used to give for us all. How is he, do you know? I wish you would give him my love. The prisoners of war here suffer just as bad as our blokes do.*

No-man's land: a place where men could cease from war, sharing their smokes and songs around a glowing brazier in that horrendous dark. The image had flared, transforming the wilderness for Miriam into a place of celebration. It was a heresy, of course; quickly suppressed. The boundaries of ownership, the paths of certainty, all surveyed and mapped from a single high perspective; these were the bastions of civilisation. Beyond them was chaos and the void. But now, as lights were lit in houses along the street, she remembered the brief illumination of that image and thought perhaps she had entered into a state of no-one's land, neither man's nor woman's, where her being was unbound. Through a nearby window, she saw a child laying a table for tea. The close, dark warrum encompassed her mind; the no-one's land of childhood, where belonging transcended ownership and a knowledge more fluid than certainty led sure feet among the trees. She reached out her hand to touch a soft papery trunk but it receded and the twilit street lay ahead.

The conscriptionists called for naturalised aliens, and their wives as well, to be stripped of their right to vote in the two referenda. Such people, they said, would be bound to vote No in the interests of a German victory. The Government either did not agree or, more likely, was unable to find a way of disenfranchising them in time. Miriam told herself she no longer cared about the anti-German rhetoric and if they took away her vote, well, she had no son old enough to be affected. But she could not avoid seeing the wounded on the streets whenever she went out; legless or blinded, shattered, she saw if she looked closely enough, somewhere in their deepest being. Were they better off than Guy, killed at Ypres, or Billie left behind in Turkey? Would Harry, shell-shocked in an English hospital, ever be whole again? And Hetty, whose husband died at Fromelle: she would be as shattered as these wounded and must wish herself dead.

Nor could she avoid the posters urging the women of Australia to vote Yes. Women, it seemed, had death in their power, for this time it was they who held the daggers in their hands and their victims were the exhausted boys at the front, desperate for reinforcements. But the song which Isobel sang, defiantly, before the maids – "I didn't raise my son to be a soldier and kill some other mother's darling boy" – that was banned under the War Precautions Act. Miriam could not afford the vulnerability of compassion. She fought the memory of Hetty and avoided the eyes of the wounded, but she voted No to conscription and reminded Sarah, when quizzed by her, that the ballot was still secret. Twice the people voted No and twice a tremor of hope disturbed her heart.

The Armistice was signed in November, a few days after their twentieth wedding anniversary. She had not seen her husband for two years and nine months. Else was overcome with excitement, the effusions of adolescence bursting through the gravity of her wartime childhood. "Now Dad can come home!

Now we will see our Dad again!" And the others had taken it up, finding as many excuses as they could to say the long-forbidden name. Dad this, Dad that; she felt the word like blows about her head and needed to escape to her own room where she said "Otto" to the mirror, over and over, watching her face for signs of reality.

The telephone jangled and Alfred wept in her ear: "Harry will come home, Otto will come home! Thank God, Miriam! Thank God it's over!"

Doreen ran across the road with cakes and a bottle of champagne. Isobel fumbled the cork and hysteria foamed with the bubbles. Miriam wept and trembled, laughed and sobbed. Kathleen came with her maid and sat among them, beaming.

"I wanted to be with you today, if it's the last thing I do," she said.

The exultation lasted a fortnight or more. When? When? The children plagued her with it but she had been given no word. Otto wrote, and his excitement flew off the page, encouraging their own, but he had no idea of when. Everyone else was taken up with the question of when the troops would return and they could get no help with their enquiries for Otto. Then the dull certainty that hope had cheated them crept steadily into "Cooloola" and the children hesitated again to speak of their father.

Alfred said, "It may be soon, Miriam. In the meantime, go on as you are." But his tone was unmistakably doubtful and, at Christmas, no-one, not even Kathleen, mentioned Otto's likely release. The newspapers spoke of the deportation of Germans, already begun, but Otto was a citizen and could not be deported. The burden of patient submission, once lifted, was harder than ever to carry, but surely it could not be for long. She had not noticed, in 1917, the changes made to the denaturalisation provisions, and no-one now alerted her to them.

Otto had been gone three years when, in February 1919, the Government denaturalised him. Alfred brought the news; Otto, he said, could not bear to tell her himself and wanted someone to be with her when she heard.

"It means they will deport him, Miriam." She reeled with the shock. "Sit down, my dear," he urged gently, "there is something else. It means that you, too, are now an alien."

So hard did the news of Otto's denaturalisation strike her that the revelation of her own status simply did not penetrate. Isobel put her to bed and called the doctor, but she needed no medicine to sleep. Utter exhaustion swamped her. The effort of years to maintain their life for Otto's sake had been futile and all her hope was vain. She felt as though her very bones had caved in.

"We will appeal, Miriam. There's to be a Board of Enquiry into the cases of men who don't want to be deported." But Miriam would no longer believe in anything and would live without hope rather than suffer so much again. Once more she thought that nothing worse could happen, but she reckoned without the Treaty of Versailles.

Spanish Influenza swept the country that winter and Kathleen was felled by it. Fighting for breath, she told Miriam, "It's to heaven I hope to be going; to the company of the faithful. And if the dear Lord will have me, I'll pray for you and Otto, lovie. Tell him I never believed their terrible lies."

Kathleen's family were uncomfortable at the Catholic funeral, holding themselves aloof from it and from each other. Edward was not sober and swayed on his feet. Joshua seemed ice-bound, and his wife, Lucy, said to be slightly mad now, was shepherded by her anxious daughters, for she had borne no sons. Harriet, bedridden since Guy's death, was absent, and James's family was represented by Oswald; charming, benign and unmoved by this death. Carrie wept unrestrainedly, in contrast to Sarah's refined grief and Isobel's silent misery. Harry, recently home, stood shivering next to Alfred, but he turned away when the coffin was lowered into the ground. Miriam's heart was clenched like a fist in her chest but she could not weep.

It hurt her now to think of it. All her life, love seemed to have been walled up; never, now, to be released. The communion of saints, to which her mother hoped to belong, might exist – Miriam had no idea – but its demands were surely too great for the small spring of her own love. Even Kathleen, even Otto and the children, had been beyond its meagre power. It was too late, now, either to pity or berate herself but, when she had done wandering, she would turn back to Isobel and the children and tell them what she had learnt on this day's journey. It was all of love she could give them.

Otto, too, caught the influenza. The camp was rife with it, the papers said, and now the war was over they were disposed to be outraged on the prisoners' behalf. German doctors interned there were not allowed to treat the prisoners and were refused the drugs and facilities so desperately needed. The huts were draughty and there were not enough blankets. Men were dying like flies. It was a scandal, they said. Miriam, schooled in cynicism by despair, thought the Government's problems would be solved if the prisoners, like Kathleen, were to choke on the fluid in their lungs. When she caught the 'flu herself she hoped her weakened heart would fail under the strain, but it struggled, perversely, against death and she endured her convalescence with weary resignation.

The Boards of Enquiry, set up to hear the appeals of the denaturalised against their deportation, were to sit during that winter, but Miriam had no word from any authority and Otto did not write during his illness. In August, when the days were warming and Miriam was well enough to sit on the verandah in the sun, Alfred came.

"They have turned down Otto's request to stay," he said. "There's no avenue left to pursue and it's only a matter of time, now, before they deport him."

It was no more than Miriam had expected, but Otto had hoped.

It cannot have been a fair hearing, Miriam, he wrote. *I wasn't allowed a lawyer and could call no witnesses. The Board would not reveal the evidence against me, so I could not challenge their reasons. I could only reiterate what I have already told them a hundred times: that I have been loyal and hard-working for Australia; that I have an Australian wife and children to provide for, and no means of support in a country which has never been my own. I had only just got over the 'flu and was so washed out and weary with it I could muster no enthusiasm to persuade them. So now I am denaturalised and, since I have never been a German national, what remains for me? I am nothing and have no home left on earth.*

He was to be deported from Sydney on the *Valencia* in October.

Miriam could not live any longer without a vestige of hope and so she tried to manufacture some. Otto at last would be free and, with his boundless reservoir of enthusiasm, would build a new life which she and the children could join. There was no time left for appeals or legal challenges but, in some ways, the sooner Otto was deported, his assets restored to him and his life and work begun again, the better.

She had a note from Lili whom she had not seen since the day she refused to join her in protest. *It is over and I return to Germany with Willi. There are signs of hope there for us now, and though you do not share our views, I hope that you will come to Otto and that we may meet again in friendship and happiness.*

Miriam had never left Australia and had no desire to visit any other place; none of them spoke German and the children would have it hard at new, foreign schools. But she would go to him as soon as she could, and they would make a home together again. In the meantime, she would take the children to Sydney to say goodbye to him. They would kiss and hold hands and would speed him on his way with the thought of the future. Perhaps it was not hope she felt, but it was, at least, a relief from despair.

The Treaty of Versailles. When had she finally understood its implications? She could not remember. Otto's departure and the horror of realisation were all ravelled together in that blighted spring. Germany, the Allies demanded, must pay them for the cost of the war. But because that country was broken and could not pay, the Treaty allowed the Allied Governments to seize, as reparation, all the assets of German nationals in their countries. Otto's business, his income and his property, all still in the custody of the Public Trustee, would now be sold and the proceeds taken for reparation. And because Miriam, too, was now a German national, "Cooloola", the house Otto had given her, must also be surrendered.

They went to Sydney on the train. Isobel saw them off with blankets, sandwiches and a Thermos of coffee. It was a long, wearisome journey through the night and when they pulled in to Central Station next day they had had no sleep. They left their bag and blankets at the cloakroom, taking only the gifts they had brought for Otto, and made their way on foot to the cheap, travellers' hotel commandeered by the Government for prisoners in transit.

A soldier guarded the door of the bleak room where they met. It was three paces, not more, from the door to the chair where he sat, where he rose, uncertain; smiling, blinking. Three paces by four years stretched the distance into infinity. The man who held out his hands was flaccid and shabby, awkward in their presence; a man without hope or self-esteem. The children stared at him with unbelieving eyes, and when he took them in his arms they looked to Miriam for support.

She went to him, stroked his head, his cheek, and held his trembling hand. "We would come with you if we could, my dear," she said, "but now we haven't got the money." The threadbare room resonated with despair.

The workers were gone now from the street, each into a lighted house from where voices welcomed and the smell of food briefly drifted. Miriam could go no further. Ahead, between fine houses and poor, lay the dusk of Musgrave Park and, in it, the deeper dark cast by great fig trees. Miriam, like a wounded animal, sought out the darkest place and sank, desolate, on to a bench.

2 Stateless

The gentle susurrus of sea caressed, disturbing her stupor. Phosphoresence surged along the crests of waves, an illusion of shining skin over the chaos of the deep. Yet this was not that insubstantial floor of sea and lay, not below her, but above, in the leaves of dusk. A breeze she could not feel moved in the fig tree and the sound was a dry whisper like skin on skin, stroking, soothing. The polished upper surfaces of the leaves focused the diffuse light of early stars. Miriam sighed. The dark was never deep enough to quell the treacherous light of hope, nor the silence of despair sufficient to muffle whispering comfort. So it had been, those years ago, when the trackless wilderness of sea had lain before her, shimmering like a mirage of endless space, or thrown up in wild hills and valleys of an unnamed country; so then she had been seduced. She had allowed the sea to wear away the sharp edges of her bewilderment and pain, had submitted to its lullaby of belonging, its assurance that the universe was unconfined; the trammel-nets of men, their surveys and their title deeds, as inconsequential to it as the petty regimen in the fragile ship on which she sailed. But the sea had been harnessed, for all its power; had become a highway, transporting her to a hard and narrow place.

The leaves, rustling in the warm dark, were brittle and destined to fall in a season but, fleetingly, they caught the light of eternity, transmitting it a little space. In some parts of the world gallstones, gravel from kidneys and balls of hair wound tight in the gut are as precious as the pearl contrived by the oyster around painful grit. They need only to be torn out, expelled from the dark caves of the body, handled and polished, and they, too, refract that glow. Hope, Miriam saw, lay not in the stays of conformity, the anaesthetic of morphine, nor the blandishments of an anonymous ocean, but in bringing forth hard, bright, pain-wrought jewels to share the ancient light which bathes the universe.

Otto had gone, cast on the ocean in search of a home. Miriam, at the mercy of the Public Trustee, continued to live at "Cooloola". Because she no longer owned her house, she could not sell it, and she was unable to save enough money from her allowance to pay their passage to Germany. Alfred said, "Hang on, old thing! Either Otto is a German, in which case he's entitled to compensation from the German Government for his losses here, or he's not a German, and so the Australian Government's got no business seizing his property. It's only a matter of time before we get it sorted out. But we need that damned *Demit* thing to prove the point and it's never been sent back to Otto or me. It wasn't sent here, by any chance?"

Miriam knew that it was not; that it remained with Senator Pearce who had rejected all the appeals Otto had founded on it. But she searched wearily through the desk for Alfred's sake. When he was convinced, he went away to write another letter to the Senator's office.

The *Brisbane Courier* carried regular lists of shares, previously owned by enemy aliens, which were to be sold at auction by the Public Trustee, and it was there she saw, advertised for sale, her own and the children's holdings, bought by Otto in their names. When, on the following Sunday, Geoffrey and Maud Pendle called in, as they sometimes did now that Otto was gone, Geoffrey said, "Oh, by the way: I saw a parcel of shares advertised which had belonged to you. I thought, since Maud is Caroline's godmother, it would be nice to buy them for her. Sentimental value really, I suppose, but I got them at a good price and we'll hold them for her, don't you worry, until she's eighteen." And he helped himself from the last bottle of Otto's port.

Maud, whether from spite or shame, added hurriedly, "They aren't worth a thing, of course, at the moment. There's such a glut of them on the market for restitutions. But we hope they will be worth a bit by the time Caroline's old enough to look after them herself." Miriam maintained a dignified bearing then, but afterwards she needed comfort from Isobel.

"They were always an envious pair and I never did like them. One of these days you'll have the last laugh. Otto will come home, you'll see, and then you can both cut them dead!" But there were so few friends left to Miriam and the hope of Otto's return seemed to exist only in his own heart. His letters still dwelt upon his efforts to convince the Government that he should not have been deported and, for as long as Otto persisted, Isobel maintained her faith in him. "There never was such a man for achieving things!" she said, but she had not seen him in the Sydney hotel, trembling and blinking for shame, and Miriam could not erase that image from her mind. She could not describe it for Isobel and nor could she confess that it did not invoke pity in her so much as fear and disgust.

Yet, while he wrote of his determination to clear his name and be returned to Australia, Otto also spoke of the warmth and kindness of the people who had received him among them.

They have suffered so much during the war, you can have no idea. So many lives have been lost from this small place and so many wounded. And yet they have welcomed me and made me at home here. I have a cosy little room in a cottage not far from my sister's house and though my landlady is a fine cook I am seldom allowed to eat at home, having invitations from a dozen relatives and friends to join their family meals. Of course, I am not here much of the time, since I must travel about quite a bit in search of occupation for myself. I have a promising appointment in Koblenz tomorrow, with a company manufacturing pharmaceuticals, so I shall put on my best bib and tucker and take myself off on the early train. I am sure it will not be long, my dear, before I find something suitable, and then I shall soon be able to send you the money to join me. We could have a good life here and the children will benefit from a wider experience of the world. Meanwhile, do all that your brothers advise in your efforts to free "Cooloola" from the Public Trustee. They will know the best course of action, I'm sure, and if you are able to sell it we can be together all the sooner.

Her brothers, in consultation with Sarah, did advise. At another smoke-shrouded conference in Joshua's office, Alfred told her of the disposal of Otto's business. It had been maintained during the war under the management of Jack Dakers, but now it was in danger of running down and the Public Trustee had advised Alfred of his decision to sell it.

"I can't prevent it, Miriam," Alfred said, "and I know the grief it will cause Otto. But Jack Dakers is willing to buy it and the PT will sell it to him for very little. Jack has promised, if Otto comes back, that he'll immediately offer him a directorship in the firm. That will provide Otto with a better start than a broken-down business would have done." Joshua and Edward showed little interest in the matter. Miriam was simply glad it was not up to her to tell Otto that, after all, his loyal manager had bought him out.

"That's settled, then!" said Sarah, smiling as though some happy decision had been made. "But Joshua, is there no way the Public Trustee can be persuaded to give Miriam the proceeds of the sale?" She recited the question as though she had learnt it beforehand.

"I'm afraid not, since the business belonged to her husband. But, as a matter of fact, there is a way she could get her own property back." Joshua seemed surprised by sudden insight. "There's a clause in the Nationality Act which allows wives of aliens to apply for denaturalisation. If Miriam were denaturalised she would be able claim the return of the house, since it's in her name."

"But I've already been denaturalised, along with Otto! What difference would it make to apply to them for something they've already done?"

Joshua turned away, sighing at her obtusity. Edward and Sarah jostled each other to make the point clear.

"Wives take the nationality of their husbands, Miriam," Sarah said primly, but Edward could not be misunderstood: "You're a German because you're still nominally married to that Hun. Apply for denaturalisation and you'll be again what you were born: an Australian and a Wemyss."

"But that's effectively a divorce!"

"No, Miriam. It would allow you to be restored to your former status without the public ignominy or the delay of a divorce." Joshua's voice was now heavy with patience. "And we advise it because, as things stand under the Treaty, we frankly cannot see any other way for you to reclaim your own property. And your marriage is only a formality, surely. You've been separated now for — what is it? — nearly five years? And your husband is clearly unable to provide for you and the children."

Miriam bowed her head and asked in a low voice, "And what about the children?" They thought she would agree and sat back in their chairs.

Joshua's answer was brisk. "They will automatically be Australians if they remain in Australia until they are sixteen. But if they leave the country permanently before then, of course they take their father's nationality."

She rose to leave then, thanking them for their advice, and only Alfred, who had remained silent and watched her, knew that she had stuck and would not slough off her husband so easily.

Alfred telephoned her that afternoon from his office. "I can see you're fed up with our advice, Miriam, and I don't like it much myself, to tell the truth. But couldn't you and Otto see it as a way out of this mess? The boys and Sarah don't see it like that, of course, but what does it matter what anyone else thinks, if it will give you your independence?" Miriam was silent. "Are you still there? Look, to be blunt, I don't think the boys will be prepared to do anything more for you if you reject their approach. In all fairness to you I think you should know that before you make a decision."

"And you, Alfred? Will you give us up, too?"

His sigh blew in her ear. "You know me, old girl! I'll do what I can for you, but it doesn't seem to be much good, does it?"

"You've been a loyal friend, Alfred; we've all been grateful for that. And I can't betray Otto now, any more than you would. For the children's sake, I want our name cleared and Otto back in Australia, nothing less. I'll be glad of anything you can do to help us."

For the children's sake she had found this shred of resistance.

She alone remembered Otto's face when they had been born; the tender joy in it then, and the exuberant delight he had taken in their growing. But she could have turned aside, even from that. It was the desperate yearning for laughter in Else's eyes and the anxious search for approval in Eric that stiffened her against this easy resolution. Only Otto, only the possibility of reunion with him, she thought, could lift the unhappiness from Else and Eric and allow them to grow whole again. Renouncing him, she thought, would betray them and fix them forever in their crippled state. If they had all been as young as Caroline when Otto was taken away, perhaps it would not have mattered. Caroline was still a sunny child, quick to learn and slow to take offence or hurt. Of them all, only Caroline, who hardly knew him, could mention Otto without hesitation or embarrassment. But she had inherited her father's temperament and that, Miriam knew, was not easily broken.

Over morning tea next day, Miriam told Doreen and Isobel of her family's proposal. "They say it's the only way to get my money back, but I can't bring myself to do it."

"Of all the wicked hypocrisy!" Doreen, who disapproved of the Wemysses but had always been careful not to criticise them before Miriam, now almost dropped her cup into its saucer. "They'd be the first to go on about family values if you'd wanted an ordinary divorce and yet, when it comes to money, they'd cheerfully destroy..."

Miriam caught the look from Isobel which stopped Doreen and knew that her own face had frozen. Isobel's tone was full of warning, "They're our family, Doreen, and Miriam's had to rely on them all these years."

Miriam understood what she was saying and she was ashamed, knowing it was true. "They are probably right," she said, coldly, "but I'm not strong enough to do it and that's all there is about it." She poured more tea and Isobel asked Doreen about Bubbles's recent visit to the dentist but, while they talked, Miriam looked at them anew.

Isobel, at thirty-seven, seemed older than her years. The strenuous energies of her youth had turned to fussiness. Her brows were heavier and her long white throat had developed a fold of skin which she plucked, nervously, whenever her hands were unoccupied. Over all, there lay an artificial brightness, a determined cheer, which jarred on Miriam and, she thought, generated a growing mistrust in her. Doreen had become more common with age. Untidy and blowzy now, the creamy skin of her face was marred by a tracery of broken veins and the lines of her laughter cut deeply between the pouches of flesh. She was a friend, no doubt, and had always been loyal, but Miriam could understand Sarah's distaste. All very well for Isobel to criticise the Pendles and Doreen to castigate her family, but what sort of society did these two women afford, and how was she to spend the rest of her days with them? She closed her eyes and tried to imagine Germany, but the villages, cosy cottages and family dinners of Otto's letter would not take a recognisable form in her mind and appeared only as woodcuts from a children's book.

"If you'll excuse me," she said, "I must go and write a letter."

Miriam did not know whether a little reservoir of courage had welled behind the pebble of resistance to her family, or whether the letter she wrote that day to the Attorney-General was inspired by fear of an alien future, but she was glad, now, to remember something to her credit.

Dear Sir, I write to enquire your reasons for deporting my husband to Germany where he has never been a citizen and forbidding him to return to his home and family. I would like to point out to you that he has always been a loyal and hard-working citizen, husband and father and that he has already suffered great hardship in the camp where you sent him. At present he is unable to support his family as he should and as he would like. His Australian children need him and I hope you will see fit to change your mind now and let him come home. Yours faithfully, Miriam Gluck (née Wemyss).

When she had done it she read it to Alfred on the telephone. He sighed. "I suppose it can do no harm, Miriam," he said. She looked at it again but she could not bring herself to beg, and sent it as it was.

It was some weeks before she received a reply but, in the meantime, to have acted at all seemed to imbue her with new energy and she set herself to take stock of her household. Since their assets were seized, the Government had repaid her a monthly allowance for herself, the children and the upkeep of the house. Else and Eric had been granted bursaries by their schools and Isobel had effected the myriad necessary economies, among them a cut in her own wage. "It doesn't seem fair to her, Miriam," Alfred had said, "but I've had a talk to her and she insists she will stay as long as you need her." The maids and the gardener had had to go and most of the housework now fell to Isobel. I will try to take more responsibility, Miriam thought.

By the time the thick, crested envelope from the Office of the Attorney-General was delivered, her health and strength had improved. Nevertheless, she sat down to open the letter.

I am directed to inform you that the decisions in your husband's case are due to the evidence which the Government possesses as to Mr Gluck's disloyalty during the war. I am further directed to advise you that the Government sees no reason at this time to reverse its decision to bar your husband from entering Australia.

Miriam felt her first real anger in years. It was a hot, clean feeling and, spurred by it, she snatched up pen and paper to write an immediate reply.

You say your Government's decisions are based on evidence in your possession of my husband's disloyalty yet at no stage have you ever produced any or been prepared to try him publicly. I now ask you to furnish me with any details, documents or letters which make up the evidence the Government allege they possess.

Lili, she thought, wryly, when she read it over, might have been looking over my shoulder. But, despite her newfound courage, she half hoped the Attorney-General would not reply; it was one thing to demand and another to receive their evidence. This time, she did not tell Alfred what she had done.

She did not mention this correspondence to Otto, either, but wrote:

We are getting along quite well despite our difficulties. Though old Mr Franks still does an hour or two a week in return for some produce, Eric has taken over most of the gardening — you would be proud of him — and so we still have our supplies of fresh vegetables, fruit and flowers. Else is a tremendous help with Caroline and has turned into a very clever dressmaker. Caroline is as chirpy as ever and is doing well at the new local school. So you mustn't worry about us, my dear, but keep cheerful yourself until we meet again.

Though his letters to her were always cheerful enough, Miriam knew that Otto had not settled to life in Germany as well as he should. He had remained in his home village of Grenzhausen, a place so small it was not marked in the atlas. Otto had sent her a map of the region, near the Rhine, on which he had marked its approximate position in ink. It was not likely, she thought, that he would find work there. Though he spoke of travelling to various towns in search of opportunities, nothing had come of it. He had, however, applied to the German Government for compensation for his losses in Australia, and seemed to have pinned his hopes on regaining sufficient capital to start a business of his own. Miriam did not approve of this application; it looked to her like an admission that he was, after all, a German.

Otto was not Miriam's only source of information. He corresponded regularly with Dr Leclerc who, in turn, reported to Miriam on the telephone. "He does seem low," Dr Leclerc admitted, "but he's been through a devastating experience and it's bound to take time to readjust. Even for a younger man it would be difficult, but to start again with nothing at Otto's age! That takes a great deal of courage."

"But you did it, Dr Hugo, when you came to Australia!"

"I had surveyed my life and decided, of my own accord, to make a change. No-one seized me and forced me to leave; no-one destroyed my life's work before my eyes, wrested me from a wife and children or stole my property to make me destitute. For me it was an adventure; for Otto it is a sentence and one for which he can find neither remedy nor explanation. Try and go to him, Miriam, as soon as you can. Perhaps I could lend you some of the fare."

"I am still trying to have him exonerated and returned to us," she said.

It seemed ironic to Miriam that support should come from the German Government, but when Otto's application for compensation was refused, Miriam thought her objective was in sight. The Germans, Otto wrote, had examined their records and found that he had never been a German citizen. Miriam and Alfred danced together in their delight when Otto's letter came.

"Now we have something to fight them with, old girl! They'd no damned business taking his property and now they'll have to give it back!"

When Alfred had gone, Miriam sat down to write again to the Attorney-General.

I have had as yet no reply to my request for the evidence you claim to have of the disloyalty of my husband. You should be aware, however, that, since my letter, the German Government has positively stated that my husband was never a citizen of that country and therefore confiscation of his property for war reparations by your Government was illegal. My attorney is taking that matter up with the Public Trustee. My purpose in writing to you is to point out that, if he was never a German national, your basis for deporting him to Germany was false. I therefore ask you again to undo the wrong you have done and return him to his proper home.

She did not dare to say, but desperately hoped, that whatever evidence they had against Otto might now lose its force.

It was not long before Alfred's efforts bore fruit. "The Public Trustee has at last found Otto's *Demit*, Miriam, and he is graciously conceding that the legality of taking reparations from Otto is doubtful. I wonder whether they'd have found the wretched thing if Otto had been drowned at sea and never applied to the Germans! Anyhow, we're making headway, so keep your chin up!"

His optimism ran like a charge through the telephone wires and, when she had hung up, Miriam embraced Isobel, an effusion so rare as to make her niece blush. "Izzy, Izzy, imagine! They're admitting they were wrong!"

When the deeds of her house were returned to her, and the remainder of Otto's property was made over to him, Alfred said, "Now we'll seek compensation for the shares and the loss of the business, Miriam. We've got an excellent case, I'd say. In the meantime, you can sell "Cooloola" and go to Germany!"

"No, Alfred," she said firmly, "I'm determined to get Otto home." And now she showed him her correspondence with the Attorney-General. Exoneration, recompense, restoration of their place in society; these were the things she longed for: to be whole and to belong again. Her being was keyed to that hope, which now took the substance of expectation, and all her plans, all her routines were informed by it. Fortunately, the Attorney-General did not delay much longer.

I am directed to advise you of the following: Though the Government may have been mistaken as to your husband's nationality it does not accept any responsibility for losses incurred by you or your husband during the period before which the Public Trustee was satisfied that your properties were not subject to the charge created by Treaty of Peace Regulation 20;

Though your husband may not at the time of his arrest, internment and deportation, have been a German National, the evidence of disloyalty against him was and remains sufficient for the Commonwealth Government to maintain its bar on his return to Australia.

I am not at liberty to supply you with all the documentation relating to your husband's disloyalty. However, I am directed to provide you with the attached censored extracts from a letter, sent by your husband to Miss Isobel Warrington in January, 1917, as evidence of his attitude.

Miriam could hardly bear to turn the page. The extract was a typescript, studded with the censor's dots, representing the lost context of Otto's thought.

Xmas here in Camp – – – we all prayed extra hard for an early German victory on all fronts, wished damnation to war – – – if only half the curses which I heap on those flaming Australian idiots who are responsible for my internment hit their mark they will roast in hell for all eternity – – – Am taking every possible care of myself so as to be fit as a fiddle when the fight for Germany's commercial and economic victory comes to be fought.

And that was all. Such sentiments Miriam had read in letters from the Front; had heard magnified by Harry since his return from the war; sentiments expressed, not before Otto's arrest, which might have justified that outrage, but after a year of his incarceration; sentiments taken out of the context even of the letter in which they were expressed. But Otto had never written in such a way to Miriam during that time. What was it in his correspondence with Isobel, in his relationship with Isobel, that could have prompted him to say such damning things?

In the fury of dashed hope, Miriam ran from the room in search of Isobel. "You!" she raged when she found her, "You are responsible for this! What did you write to him that encouraged him to say such things as are here in this letter? Do you realise, you parasite, that it is because of you he is not allowed to come home?" Even as she lashed Isobel with the flail of her despair she remembered Hetty.

Isobel left them then, of course; how could she have stayed? She had been with them since Caroline's birth. For eight years she had nursed, cared for and supported all of them, bearing her own griefs quietly for their sakes, only to be called a parasite. In the memory of Hetty's contorted face Miriam had seen the enormity of her cruelty to Isobel and had fallen to her knees in apology, but both women knew that was not enough. They had lived with the undercurrent of Miriam's jealousy always, and it was something of a relief to them both that it had surfaced at last. Isobel was loved and loving; Miriam, she knew, was not. Isobel was strong and her strength had allowed Otto the freedom to confide his feelings to her. Miriam was frail and unable to bear Otto's need.

"I know you are desperately disappointed, Miriam, and you exaggerated because of that. I've never seen that letter, you know, because of the censor, so I didn't understand what you were going on about. But in some ways perhaps I am a parasite. I've lived on second-hand emotions and I should, after all, try to build a life of my own. So I'll go, anyway."

And, weeping, she went home to Carrie for a spell. She had found a place, then, as companion to another woman, widowed and older than Miriam, and she stayed there until her mother's final illness. Only after Carrie's death did she return to Miriam. Each needed the other now, and their rift had never again been mentioned, but it floated like a succubus in every room of their lives.

Her going was another wound for the children who loved and trusted Isobel, but only Caroline grieved openly. Else and Eric understood, without explanation, that there had been conflict and they closed silently about their mother. Their distress was palpable to her and it was that which finally decided her to go to Germany; or so she told herself and Alfred at the time.

"Otto says if I sell "Cooloola" he can buy quite a big house for us in Grenzhausen. He's seen one he thinks we'd like which will come on to the market early next year. He wants me to cable a decision so he can put a deposit on it."

Alfred missed the doubt in her voice. "You'd get a good price for "Cooloola" now. We could put it up this week and I reckon it'll sell quite quickly. You could easily be in Germany by March, old girl!"

"I'm still not sure, Alfred. Grenzhausen is such a small place and Otto has found no work there. It seems foolishness to buy a house until he's settled in his occupation. And, till then, we'll need an income. Perhaps I should rent "Cooloola" until we see which way the wind blows."

"I don't know how much longer the property market will hold up, though, Miriam. We did quite well out of the Lismore shop and the remaining land, but when prices are high everyone wants to cash in and there could soon be a glut. Otto might have enough money out of those sales to set up a business of his own now. But, you know, to my mind what he wants is incentive. If he buys a house, he'll have a base and, when you get there, he'll have a reason for getting on with it. Give it a go, there's a girl!"

"I'll have to think carefully, Alfred. There's a lot at stake."

Next day she voiced her doubts to Doreen and Cedric Telfer. Doreen was enthusiastic. "I'm a betting woman, as you know, Miriam, and I reckon you don't get much joy out of life if you don't take risks. I'd chance it if I were you. And Otto's a brilliant businessman once he gets started."

But the usually docile Cedric demurred. "Gambling's all very well, Doreen, but you've got to have reasonable odds. Germany's got a massive war debt of her own, plus reparations. It's a difficult place to be setting up in business from scratch, even if you are brilliant."

"I think I'd better consult the boys," Miriam said.

She had known, of course, what they would say; that they would oppose her going to Germany at all. She wrote to Otto.

I know how much store you always set by my brothers' advice and so I have asked their opinion about investing in a house in Germany. They, I'm afraid, are quite set against our coming at all, given the financial and political climate over there. Of course, I shall oppose them because nothing could be worse than this divided life we lead at present. But I think it would be better if, for the time being, we saw it as an experiment, a trial period of a couple of years, and in that case it would be premature to invest in a house, don't you think? We will be perfectly comfortable in a rented house, my dear, and you mustn't worry so much about our creature comforts! I will rent "Cooloola" out and the income will make us all a little bit more secure.

She eased her mind with the thought that the total embargo the Government had placed, since the war, on Germans entering Australia was due to be lifted in 1925, and perhaps then Otto would be allowed to return. Four years was not so very long and, in the meantime, they would visit him.

She applied for passports, booked passages to bring them to Europe in the spring, and arranged for the storage of their furniture. When it was done she felt worn to transparency, light and brittle as the dragonflies that darted above the mangroves by the creek. She went to sit by the creek then and watched them, thinking of the strength she had once sought to draw from this place, of the roots she had determined to put down here. It was impossible to imagine that other land while this one shimmered in its summer heat before her; unthinkable the energy necessary to transplant herself. She longed, in that moment, to evaporate and to drift, formless, in the haze above the land that was her home.

"Mum!" Else stood at the top of the rise with an envelope in her hand. "I think the passports have come."

"Bring them here then!"

Else scrambled down the track to the bank, excitement rank like sweat about her. Miriam took the envelope. There was only one passport - Else's - and a folded paper. Miriam spread it out on her knee: *Permit to Leave Australia, issued to Miriam Gluck, born in Queensland, married to Otto Gluck* . . . There followed a brief summary of Otto's naturalisation, denaturalisation and deportation; a story, a humiliation, she must carry for every petty official across the world to see. There were the names of the two children who were not old enough for passports of their own and then permission was given for them all to return to Australia. Her description followed: *Nationality*, it said, *German*.

Else watched her read the document, watched her stand and turn her back on the creek. Reflected in her daughter's expression were the bitter lines of Miriam's own face.

"I think, after all, Else, I shall be glad to leave this cruel, wicked country!" Miriam said. Else burst into tears.

3 Weary Sailors

There were those (and Otto was one) who revelled in shipboard life, who rode high on the excitement of departure: the champagne with well-wishers in cabins, the streamers, thrown from deck and dock, and the tears as the ship pulled slowly away, snapping the coloured paper; freeing the passengers from their ties for six weeks of voyaging. Miriam, Otto had teased, did not share his joy in adventure and, waiting on the wharf to embark for Germany, she quailed at what lay ahead.

Dr Leclerc had travelled from Marburg to see them off and held her hand in both of his. Doreen had fashioned a spray of flowers and pinned it to her lapel. Isobel was there, waiting to kiss the children, and Sarah was advising importantly about salt tablets in the tropics and the proper tips for stewards. "You must give the cabin-boy three shillings now, to ensure good service," she said, "and another three at the end, if he looks after you well." Alfred winked at Miriam across his wife's shoulder.

The air was heavy with the smell of tar and hemp, of salt, coaldust and engine oil. It intoxicated Caroline who darted among the knots of passengers and demanded, at ever shorter intervals, when they would board. Miriam watched her anxiously, afraid that this child, who had least reason to leave her home, would slip over the edge of the wharf, would disappear in the churning chasm that lay between present and future. Else and Eric stood side by side, bonded together in wordless sympathy, amid the chatter of their friends. Miriam could almost hear the hum of their suppressed excitement. The ship loomed, vast, above the wharf, her iron plates vibrating with the throb of impatient engines. The gangway seemed immensely high and it shuddered under the feet of embarking passengers. Miriam did not want her friends to come aboard with her; wanted nothing of her country to pass the purser who waited, white as a guardian angel, at the top of the gangway. Even the flowers that pulsated on her breast unsettled her with the smell of her garden. A blast from the ship's siren cut across the final, trivial conversation. Miriam kissed them all hurriedly and, herding the children across the fragile gangway, looked neither back nor down.

The purser took her travel permit and read it. Miriam trembled but met his eye when he looked up.

"Welcome aboard, Mrs Gluck," he said deliberately, as though sensing her humiliation, "I hope you will do me the honour of dining at my table." And he summoned a Lascar steward, blue-black in his starched, mattress-ticking suit, to show them to their cabins.

Eric was to share a double berth with an elderly Finn. Miriam, Else and Caroline had a four berth cabin to themselves. The girls were delighted with the mahogany panelling, the commode and washbasin which opened from the bulkhead, the porthole which wound outwards to catch the breeze; they were impatient to explore the rest of the ship, but Miriam insisted they all go back on deck. They would wave goodbye, would watch their country recede, and then she would set herself to wait, to hibernate, until life opened again on to a new continent.

The voyage was a release for Else and Eric. In a one-class ship everything was open to them. They made friends among the passengers and crew, were shown the bridge, the baggage hold and the engine room, played deck quoits and tennis and took their beef tea on the deck in the afternoons quite independently of Miriam. Eric seemed enraptured by the ship itself, unselfconscious with any sailor who would uncover its mysteries to him. Else threw off the awkward remnants of adolescence and emerged, at the supper dances, a shy young woman, easily delighted by music and gaiety. Miriam felt she had been right to come and gave herself up to the assuaging rhythms of the sea.

She regretted going ashore at Durban. Its self-assured white settlers, its wide streets lined with feathery jacarandas and vibrant coral trees, all reminded her of home, tugging her heart backwards. The throngs of brightly clad blacks, jostling to sell their wares at the docks, were alien, disturbing both the dark ghosts of memory and the woodcut dreams of a foreign future. She would not leave the ship again and, making Caroline her excuse, sent Else and Eric off in the care of other passengers. Hamburg was her goal and, though she leant on the rail of the ship watching continents advance and retreat, breathing in their deep, exotic smells, the world would not divert her. Only when England gleamed on their port bow did she waver but, by then, Hamburg was near and she kept to her resolve.

"So, Mrs Gluck, you're going to live in the Westerwald, Eric tells me," said the purser, on the eve of their arrival. "You're fortunate; it's a splendidly romantic region. I'm sure you'll enjoy it and I wish you the very best of luck. We'll be in the Elbe at dawn. Ask your steward to give you an early call and you'll have your first sight of Germany as we sail upriver."

They rose in the dark and dragged on the clothes they had laid ready, fumbling laces and buttons in their excitement. The ship's engines were subdued and the motion of the sea was left behind. There were few passengers aboard now, and most gathered on the forward deck to watch the flat, twilit landscape glide by. Miriam waited, breathless in the sharp air, for the unveiling of the land. The sail of a Cervantes windmill caught the sun's first beam and soon the river lay like a shining path before them. On either hand, fishing smacks bobbed at anchor before villages clustered on the banks; green pastures rolled away behind. In the distance, copper spires and domes lay like jades against a blue silk sky.

The port of Hamburg was already busy with the day. Smoke from a dozen steamers churned, turgid, into the still air and groaning derricks swung their loads over wharves and holds. Their ship hung back, feigning reluctance to the tugs which came to draw her in.

"Gosh, Mum, I wish they'd hurry up. I'll bust with excitement soon! Do you think that's where we're going?" Else pointed to an imposing stone building, roofed in copper and fronted by a wide quay, on the port bank. A small crowd stood there and the ship began to sidle coyly up to them. Else flung herself at the rail, yelling, "Dad, Dad!"

"Where, Else, where?" shrieked Caroline. But Eric took Miriam's arm as they approached the rail and Miriam felt a tremor run through it, whether his or hers she could not tell.

Otto was jumping up and down, waving his hat to attract their attention. He blew them kisses when they saw him and hugged the man standing next to him in excitement. Miriam sighed with relief. Here was not the sagging form, blurred at the edges by incarceration and defeat, she had farewelled three years ago in Sydney: Otto had regained his definition, his energy, the blue fire of his eyes. As the gangway was wheeled up she watched him push through the crowd and then charge up to the deck. Else and Caroline were first into his arms but she was close behind them.

Otto could endure no delay in introducing them to Hamburg. Inside the terminus he talked loudly in German to the customs and immigration officials, beaming as he waved his arm over his family, explaining, no doubt, how long he had waited for this time. Soon he had shepherded them through and had engaged a porter to bring their luggage on.

"I have booked us into a fine hotel in the Rathausplatz. It's an extravagance, I know, but this once I wanted to treat you all. It's not far; would you like to walk? Dry land is strange after the ship, isn't it, but there is so much for you to see. And we will have some coffee along the way. The best coffee in all the world is in Germany. And cakes! You wait! Oh my dears . . .! See now, Hamburg is a city of canals . . . And it's a very modern city; all these grand buildings are built in the last twenty years. It was so prosperous before the war, but now . . . ah, well, perhaps it won't be long before it is so again." He was like a flustered tour guide, anxious to show everything at once to honoured foreign guests.

Miriam, whose feet had not touched land since Durban, felt the world was reeling. She slipped on the polished blue-stone cobbles and clutched at Otto for support but she insisted she would walk, as he had planned. She had saved herself, all she had of curiosity and wonder, for this new land, and she would admire everything: the tall brick buildings, the spring flowers in boxes on every windowsill, the pretty canals and the fresh, aromatic coffee which they drank at a table in the sun. She admired the man who, in his good woollen overcoat, sat opposite her, beaming expansively; the husband whose English, once again, bore the cast of German.

"It's lovely, Otto; very nice indeed. And everthing's so clean!"

"Ach, Germans are nothing if they're not clean. And orderly. You will find that everything here has its proper time and place. Nothing is allowed to take its chance, to happen along, as things go in Australia." A sudden gloom fell over him and he stared for a moment at nothing. "But we will not talk of Australia now you are all here." He jumped up from the table. "We'll go to our hotel and there we will have our midday food and then I will take you to see all the sights. Tomorrow, we must go on the train very early to Grenzhausen so we'll make the most of today!"

Perhaps, if they had had a little longer in Hamburg, a few days of holiday, of honeymoon . . . At the hotel their three rooms overlooked a huge square, beyond which were gardens and a lake. The beds were covered in eiderdowns as heaped, as white and soft as cumulus cloud. Miriam thought, after lunch, that they might rest for a while; Caroline would be weary. But Otto would not hear of it. "I will carry her, it will be my delight!" he said.

"Otto, she's eight! You can't possibly!" Miriam laughed.

"Then we'll sit down often."

So, after they had eaten ("You must eat fish in Hamburg, it's wonderful!"), they traipsed around after him, gazing in bewilderment at churches, statues, the art gallery and the theatre. They saw ancient buildings, like illustrations from a book of Robert Browning's poems, which delighted the children, but it was the grandeur and modernity she saw which surprised and reassured Miriam. Otto pointed out the poverty, too; the wounded men begging, the shops boarded up for want of goods to sell.

"They lost 40,000 men from Hamburg alone in the war," he

said bitterly, "and now those who remain must pay." But Miriam would not notice whatever did not augur happiness.

Despite her relief and pleasure in the day, despite her utter weariness, Miriam longed for the evening. All day there had been between her and Otto a distance, a foreignness, which she had expected and dreaded, but it had awakened an unexpected desire in her. Not the sharp cutaneous shocks of desire she had known when first they courted, but something closer to the need for food or warmth; a longing to cling and hold, to encircle and to be subsumed. The day and the need gave her confidence, when they were alone, to approach and embrace him, to kiss his averted cheek and slide her arms under his jacket. He trembled and wrapped his arms around her neck, rocking them both from side to side as if for comfort. In a little while she freed herself and switched off the light to undress. But in bed, though he pressed her to him and though she stroked his skin and kissed his face, the trembling did not abate and tears seeped from his closed eyes, salting her lips. She cradled him in her arms until the weeping stopped, but then he was asleep. She was entirely ignorant of these things and thought perhaps he had become habituated to celibacy. Her face burned with shame at her own timid advances and his rejection of them, however sorrowful. The eiderdown, at first so light, was now oppressively hot, the central heating stuffy and the night sleepless.

There was no time in the morning for repair. Their train left very early and Otto woke with the urgency of marshalling them all to the station. Their faces were grey in the smoky light filtering through the huge glazed roof. Miriam's head rang painfully with the engine's hooted warnings, the clamour of porters and Otto's need for excitement.

"Who wants to see the engine? Come on then, we've still got time!"

Miriam watched them run down the platform, dashing between passengers and luggage. She sank into the plush seat and closed her eyes, thankful to be rid of them. Yesterday she had liked Hamburg and been ready to love her husband again. Today she was flat and exhausted, wanting only to go home. But home, now, was unimaginable and waited at the end of this train journey. Whatever it was like, she would, at least, be able to take her clothes out of the suitcase and hang them in a cupboard; she would be able to kick off her shoes and put her feet on a chair, drink tea instead of coffee, and know the journey was done.

Otto and the children came back with pink faces and a basket of sweet rolls and coffee. "Caroline was hungry again," Otto said. He would indulge the child and she would adore him.

"What do we do with the basket and cups, Dad?" The train was pulling away as they ate and Eric was anxious, as always, to know the right procedures.

"We give them to a porter at the next station. Now look, here comes Germany! We travel across about half of it today." He was determined to teach his children, to encourage and inspire, as though the six years of his absence from them must be redressed as quickly as possible. He pointed, explained and translated into German, making them repeat words and phrases.

"Come along, Mother! You must learn, too," he cajoled, but Miriam had no ear, and when she bungled pronunciations the children laughed. She resisted, then, and gazed out at the passing countryside, letting them get on together without her.

The landscape was flat and the train travelled through it very fast. Miriam liked the open country, its gentle blues and greens, the clusters of farm buildings in deep coppery brick. ("See how big the farmhouses are? The farmers store their hay under the roofs and the animals spend the winter in the barns under the houses. That way everyone keeps warm during the winter.") She liked the luminous emerald of the beech forests in new leaf and the villages of half-timbered houses along narrow cleanswept streets. But in the dark of a steeply sloping pine forest, snow glimmered among black rocks beside the tracks.

"Snow? Whoopee! Will there be snow at Grenzhausen, too, Dad?" They had never seen it before and longed to touch.

"No, Caroline, not now. It will probably be raining." It was warm in the carriage. The gloomy pine forest with its vestige of winter lay, harmless as a woodcut illustration, on the other side of double-glazing.

As they ate their lunch in the elegant dining car, Otto said,

"Soon we will be at Düsseldorf where we will meet the Rhine. Then we follow the river through Köln, that is Cologne, and on to Koblenz, where the Rhine joins with the Mosel. That's called the Deutsches Eck, the German Corner. There's a great monument to German unity built there, but we'll visit that another day."

At Düsseldorf the Rhine was wide, slow and brilliant in the sun. When they had passed through Cologne, Otto exclaimed, "Now this is the best part of the trip!" He smiled to himself as he gazed out at the vineyards striating the hillsides and Miriam realised with a shock that his tone, his smile, were proprietory. She looked more closely now, to see what his country was like.

The river ran beside them, so close they could see the cargoes of gravel or coal, the boxes and bales, in the great barges sailing on it. It was narrower and faster now, faceted deep-green and silver. Steep hillsides, rocky or vine-decked, rose on either side. A village on the far bank, prettier than Miriam had ever imagined, seemed to admire its own reflection in the water.

"Look, Mum! There's a castle up there!" A ruined medieval tower reared above a turn in the river, guarding the waterway and the frivolous village against intruders.

"That's the Burg Hammerstein. There are lots of castles further up the river, where it is narrower," said Otto. "One day we'll go and visit some. Would you like that?"

The children were eager but, as their train followed the bend, the sun slipped behind the hill, casting the farther side of the valley into shadow and, against the failing light, the castle seemed full of menace to Miriam.

"Is the river dangerous, Dad?" Eric asked.

"It sometimes floods very badly in the autumn. I was in Neuwied (we'll see that soon — it's on the other side of the river) when it flooded last. The water rose three feet in the first floor of the house where I was staying. We were marooned for two days and the damage to furniture and goods in warehouses was terrific. We had a high old time of it cleaning up, I can tell you!"

"Can you sail on it, though?" Eric had begun a love affair with boats.

"People do. Would you like to try? We'll hire a boat in

Koblenz and do it together. But we'll have to beware of the Lorelei!"

"What's the Lorelei?"

"Ah! Some famous, cruel rocks, upstream from Koblenz. Sirens with beautiful voices live there. They sing to weary sailors coming home, and lure them to their deaths." Otto said it so lugubriously that Caroline was alarmed. "True, Dad?"

Otto laughed. "So it says in the old legends! But not for us poor weary travellers, little treasure! Soon we will be in Koblenz, where we change trains, and then it's only a short journey before we are at home, safe and sound, in time for tea!"

It was dark when they reached Koblenz; too dark to see the German Corner and the monument to national unity. And it was darker still as their next train climbed through the forest, drawing them steadily higher, into the night.

4 Occupations

Miriam was swamped and drowning in darkness. Night had flowed down the Brisbane Valley and flooded Musgrave Park, lapping jealously at the phosphorescent leaves. Darkness had rolled in a torrent down the Rhine Valley to join, at the German Corner, with this night. The tumult of darkness swelled and rose, overwhelming her consciousness. But the drowning also dream.

The purser, clad in shining white, stood above the raging chasm, beckoning to her. "Do me the honour," he said, and threw out an arc of light. Miriam laboured to climb its slippery glow, but where the ship had stood now loomed a castle, all of black stone, gleaming in the rainy night.

"Welcome to Grenzhausen," Otto said, for it was he who had beckoned. "This is an important border-post," he lectured, "and it guards the soul of Germany." He pushed her through a narrow gap in the sentinel stone, into a room where women sat, in a spelled circle of warmth and light. "Take your proper place beside the stove," Otto said.

The women sighed, *"Ah-so!"* And nodded, *"Ja-ja!"* Then they spoke to her, all at once, questioning, accusing. She did not understand and, though she smiled and smiled at them, the pitch of their voices climbed and the babble rained like angry blows about her ears. Suddenly, Miriam understood: she was not wearing an apron, such as the women wore, of crisp white linen, ruffled and tucked. The women rose as one and seized her, pushing her out again into the roaring dark. As it rushed towards her, Miriam heard a great cry which carried in it all the desolation of her life and, before it, the tide of dark fell back. Only the glimmering flotsam of leaves remained.

Miriam breathed deeply, trying to steady her wild heart. Her cry still rang in her head.

"Yes, it was like that," she said, aloud, to exorcise it. "But that is not the whole." In hindsight, all the elements of conflict in Miriam's life seemed gathered in Grenzhausen, distilled to their essence there.

Grenzhausen stood on a hill, its church in pride of place. The streets winding round it were narrow, grey-cobbled, walled by houses of grey stucco, or half-timbered daub and wattle on stone rubble foundations. The steep-pitched slate roofs were were silver as fish scales in the fine rain. Scattered among the houses, tall brick chimneys of potteries proclaimed the firing of kilns. The pottery of the region, cold blue-grey clay, patterned in brilliant cobalt, was salt-glazed, and the damp air was acrid with wood-smoke and the smell of burning salt. But the name of the village had nothing to do with pottery: the village had once marked the boundary of a duchy and the word *grenzhausen* meant border-post. It was a place where customs duties had been collected and the permits of travellers inspected.

The village was born in the Reformation, when Protestant converts from the Catholic village of Höhr, in the valley below, had moved up the hill to build their church and establish their own severe traditions, free of papist indulgence. The village of Höhr had a graceful Gothic church, surrounded by gardens and terraces; Grenzhausen's church was austere, square-towered and onion-domed. The village huddled protectively about it. Now, since the war, both villages were in an occupied zone, their separate jurisdictions overriden by the Allied conquerors.

In December 1919 American artillery had been lined up to block Grenzhausen's streets, leaving the populace in no doubt about the power of the new dispensation, nor the penalties of disbelief. After a year, the guns were removed, but the shadow of their long, deadly muzzles still lay across the ways of thought. (It was, said Otto, a blessing, since outside the occupied zones of the Rhine and the Ruhr, political violence and chaos reigned.) Whereas, for centuries, it had been necessary to obtain permission from the local authorities to travel to or from this village, now the Americans were responsible for deciding who could come and go. The Americans also demanded that the names of all the occupants, permanent and temporary, should be displayed on the doors of their dwellings. Miriam's name was duly posted outside this new home. The deceitful ocean had delivered her up to a place where constraints bit deeper than any she had known.

Miriam had chosen to come to Germany for the children's sake and, perhaps, for Otto's. Of her own feelings she was, even now, by no means sure. But if she had wanted to join Otto among his people in Grenzhausen, she had not wanted the woman who opened the door to them on the rainy night of their arrival. In that brief moment she had taken her for the maid, because she wore an apron, and had been distant, perhaps condescending to her, always. Yet this was Hedwig (Frau Steuler, for the village was excessively formal), Otto's niece, a woman widowed and orphaned by the war and left with one daughter, a year younger than Caroline. Hedwig spoke no English but was kind at first and seemed anxious for friendship, glad to have her home filled up by a family; her own family. Had it not been for the relationship, Miriam might have been more unbending, she thought now, but she had a family and a home; she wanted no more and no other.

"Since the boys were unwilling for us to buy a house, Miriam," Otto had explained on the train, "I have looked for one to rent, but the costs are high and we would need to employ a servant, as well. My family wouldn't hear of it. They all insist that Hedwig will be glad to have us. She needs the money, too, and is happy to do the cooking and housekeeping. It seemed the best arrangement." But in his letters he had been determined they should not have to live in rooms. Miriam knew resentment was unjustified (it was she, after all, who had insured against commitment by refusing to invest in a house) but she could not suppress it. She had turned it against Hedwig, poor lonely struggling woman, and had repulsed her. She had not understood the nature of the village, the close ties among the major families, which would preclude her from any friendship once she had offended one of their number.

Miriam thought the house itself was not unsuitable. It was a large brick building on the main street, and the tramcar ran past its gate. It had a cellar, two floors and an attic. A conservatory or winter garden opened from its drawing-room, overlooking grounds which were pretty with trees in burgeoning leaf and spring flowers, neatly ranked. Beyond them, the fields and orchards of the village ran down to a valley and from there the forest marched away to the horizon. The house was centrally heated except for the attic where, it was decided, Otto and Eric would sleep. On the floor below, Miriam, Else and Caroline had a large bedroom. One of the formal rooms on the ground floor, facing the street, was given over to them, and they were to eat their meals in the dining room with Hedwig and her daughter.

There were several grander houses in the village, belonging to the foremost families. Otto, in his boastfulness, had given Miriam the impression that his family were of considerable importance and she had presumed there would be society to welcome her, a guaranteed position among them. Now she learnt that, in the hierarchy of potters, the Glücks and their pottery ranked low among the owners of the larger factories. Below them were the artisan potters who worked for themselves and below them, again, were the potters who laboured for the pottery owners. Otto's sisters had married above them; Otto and two of his three brothers had left Grenzhausen to make their way elsewhere in the world. The third brother, Peter, carried on the family business but, since his mother died, it had declined. There was no automatic admission for Miriam to the ruling society.

The women of the village were a powerful force, especially since the war had decimated the male population. Their decision-making was done behind lace curtains and around the huge, tiled stoves at the heart of their houses. Over ritual coffee, wine and cakes, they discussed with equal vigour the future of their industry and the manners of their sisters. Miriam, a curiosity, was invited to these gatherings; was, perhaps, given the chance to make her own place among them. But she could not speak to them and lacked the animation necessary to communicate in any other way. Besides, her heart was soured by disillusion.

When it came to returning invitations, she was at a loss. She was not in her own home and was obliged to rely on Hedwig, her labour in the kitchen and her meagre resources of flour, coffee, sugar, to provide for them. Though Otto had explained that everyone here was poor, Miriam had not, at first, understood or believed him. She had seen the poverty of the peasants; had seen a child ploughing a field with his dog in the harness, but Hedwig's house was well furnished; Turkey rugs and inlaid furniture, crystal and silver, all belied poverty. Miriam thought Hedwig grasping to take in family as boarders; thought the meagre, meatless dinners, the endless apples and potatoes, a sign of her parsimony. Hedwig owned land: an orchard and fields beyond the village where peasants grew apples and pears, potatoes and rye. An acre of beech forest was hers as well, and Miriam knew that timber was valuable, could be sold here in the village where beech was used to fire the kilns. Yet Hedwig meted out the coffee as though it were gold-dust and Miriam gave up attempting to return hospitality.

"How can Hedwig be so poor, Otto?" Miriam asked, as they stood together under apple trees borne down with rich blossom.

"The Treaty of Versailles has made everyone here poor," he replied, "except the black-marketeers and those whose income is in sterling, like us. In that, at least, we're fortunate." The Allies, he explained, had insisted their reparations must be paid in gold, but a shortage of gold reserves, the loss of an empire and the unwillingness of the Allies to trade or invest, had caused economic inflation. "Only last month have the Allies finally set the guilt repayments at 132 billion gold marks, to be paid over sixty-six years until 1988," Otto told her. "So far, we have paid a mere 8 billion. If this goes on, the workers will starve and businesses will collapse because they cannot afford new plant. In the meantime, the value of Hedwig's money is being reduced. She must sell as much of her produce as she can to earn the money for other necessities. So coffee is a luxury she can't afford. Our rent is essential to her. And it's not so bad here, is it, Miriam?" There was a note of appeal in his voice but Miriam did not answer.

They were walking in the late afternoon through the sweet spring pastures beyond the village. Cows, wending their way to the dairies for the evening milking, lowed gently in the still air. The village, no longer drab, wore glowing tones of apricot and peach in the long light. Two girls carrying baskets of vegetables home from the gardens passed them. *"Guten Abend! Guten Abend!"* each said as they went by and their voices were musical as a peal of handbells. A soft mist rose steadily from the valley below and soon would mingle with the smoke from stoves, swaddling the village against the night.

Otto took her arm and guided her on to the cart-track that led back to Hedwig's house. "Our tea will be ready," he said.

In the dining room, the children were already at table. They had been out all day in the woods and fields and their faces were flushed with the sun. Hedwig, carrying in a silver, covered dish, quizzed them about their day and, between them, they cobbled together an answer in German, laughing with her at their mistakes. Otto joined in, teasing and teaching together. Hedwig sat down and heads were bowed for grace. This reunion with their father in a safe, peaceful place, this laughter and family flowering, was what Miriam had wanted for her children but, looking about her then, she felt as though her life had been stopped by a photograph, frozen forever in a picture postcard. She was suddenly stifled by its prettiness, knew herself to be utterly alien in it and yet completely trapped.

When he lifted his head, Otto beamed around him and said, *"So! sehr gemütlich, ja?"* And it *was* cosy in the postcard. To Miriam, he said, "Don't the children look wonderful? This simple village life is so healthy for them." Otto had retreated into an idyll.

After the meal, when they were alone in their parlour, Miriam said, "Otto, my dear, I can't see how you're going to find any suitable work if we stay in Grenzhausen. Surely there'd be a better chance for you in a city?"

But he shrugged, as if to say his own concerns must be set aside. "Grenzhausen is better for you and the children, Miriam, believe me. Here you have the opportunity to experience the true, undisturbed values of German life. Perhaps there's more work in the cities, but they are all now expensive and dangerous. Every day, in the papers, I read of murders, bombings and riots." He sat back in his chair, preparing to expand on his subject. Miriam recognised the signs; he would divert her from her object.

"But, Otto, those are political issues. They wouldn't affect us much, and if you need to work . . ."

"To my mind it's much more than political, Miriam; it's a war for the soul of Germany and it affects everything. I have visited the cities and I know. You cannot go into a cafe or a public place without being confronted by the rallying cries of so-called modernity and socialism; imported values, determined to oppose and destroy the ancient roots of German culture, the traditions and beliefs which have made Germany great and prosperous. These things are fragmenting us, tearing us apart. Germany has yearned to be whole, to be one nation, so her greatness could flower. It breaks my heart, Miriam, to see what has happened to that unity."

Miriam was irked by his self-important filibustering and remarked, waspishly, "Yes. It led to the war that broke your heart, at any rate."

"The competition for empire led to war, Miriam, not the union of Germany itself. Britain and Germany are kindred souls, they should never have fought each other. Now that Germany is defeated she must look again to the values, the beliefs and traditions, that bind her people together. We must return to our poets and philosophers, to our history. The modernity, the licentiousness, the socialism which people are chasing, run clean counter to the values you see here in Grenzhausen, of honour in men and modesty in women. They deny the value of hard work and they demand allegiance to foreign ideas instead of to Germany herself. They cannot possibly unify us and that is why the battle is so fierce in the cities: the people know in their hearts that the very soul of Germany is at stake."

He was agitated, breathless with the intensity of his feeling. He had spoken as though of himself, of his own conflict, and not simply of a political crisis. Miriam did not attempt to argue with him and soon she went to bed, but his high-flown talk, so personally felt, seemed dangerously remote from the real problems confronting him and she lay awake in anxiety for him. That Grenzhausen enjoyed advantages — fresh air, safe streets and beautiful countryside — Miriam acknowledged, but, when Otto spoke of a German soul which could be identified and fought over, she could attach no meaning to his words. No-one would speak of the soul of Australia, its traditions, its icons, its high priests of art or philosophy, as Otto now spoke of Germany's. For that matter, no-one Miriam knew (except, perhaps, the warmongers of recent times) would characterise her country as "she". Otto himself had never adopted such language about Australia. There, he had eulogised the future, the opportunities for progress, the challenge and excitement of developing a new nation. Even in this he had often sounded absurdly fulsome to his acquaintance. Talk of nationhood was embarrassing to most people; Australia was merely their country. To some, who thought nationhood belonged to Britain, it was close to heresy. To speak of the nation's soul would be in bad taste, almost indecent.

The flat Bradford accents of her grandfather came back to her then. She remembered the fervour with which he said "this land of promise", the rigid code which, alone, he believed could bring that promise to fruition. Matthew Wemyss would not have used the word "soul" of his country; only men have immortal souls, in constant jeopardy of hell. Matthew Wemyss would not have looked to poets and philosophers; there was, for him, only the Word, and that was flawed in incarnation. Yet her grandfather would have approved the hardworking, Godfearing people of Grenzhausen and the values Otto had espoused. Miriam herself approved them. But when she thought of the soul of her own country, she smelt the damp intimate warmth of the warrum along the shores of Lake Cootharaba and heard the seething of leaves in the wind.

"Are you all right, Mum?" Else whispered from her bed. Miriam blew her nose and claimed a slight sniffle. Else, happy enough in Grenzhausen, would probably be anxious all her life and Miriam would not confess homesickness to her. She turned over again in the too-soft bed and tried to think about the real issue.

Beneath all Otto's reasons for staying in the village lay his fear. For Otto's eyes had not regained their fire; they had burned, briefly, with the excitement of reunion but now they were overlaid by a defensive film and they seldom met Miriam's own. He talked and laughed with the children, showed them off to his relatives and boasted about them, but he avoided serious discussion about their future. He had determined that, as soon as they were familiar with the language, Eric should go to the Keramikschule and learn the art of potting; Else should learn shorthand and typing at the local business college and Caroline should attend the local school. Behind these decisions stood assumptions which he gave Miriam no room to challenge. They were seldom alone now, having little privacy in the house, and Otto avoided opportunity elsewhere. Miriam could not see a future for Eric in the potteries and doubted the value to Else of learning shorthand German. Otto seemed to have forgotten that they had come to Germany as an experiment which would one day have to be assessed. Now she feared the deep well of Otto's despair which mocked brave plans with hopeless echo, and her sleep, when it came, was racked with foreboding.

When Otto first arrived among them, the women of the village had taken him up out of kindness and family feeling. They had passed him from house to house for meals and outings and found a comfortable room for him, supplying his wants from their own kitchens and linen stores. He, perhaps, had entertained them, as he had entertained Kathleen so long ago, with his traveller's tales and urbane good humour. Perhaps, too, he had boasted about his family and painted pictures for them of his good and charming wife, her patience under suffering, and the relief and pleasure she would feel in Grenzhausen. But in a small community where everyone worked so hard, his idleness, his long, brooding walks in the forest, his opinions manufactured in solitude, must soon have exhausted the charity of his friends. They, after all, had enough difficulties of their own. Almost every family had men returned from the war who suffered dreadful injuries or derangements beside which Otto's seemed small.

He had, in time, found some work: three days a week he had done the book-keeping for a pharmaceutical firm in Koblenz. Otto's acquaintance must have expected that, once his family arrived, his problems would be resolved. But he had given up his job to go and meet them in Hamburg.

"It was very menial work, Miriam; no room for me to influence the direction of the business. But it kept me out of mischief, I suppose, and took my mind off my troubles. Now, however, I am a free man for a while. I knew you and the children would need me at first; to show you around, introduce you and interpret for you until you settle in." After that, he planned to begin a mail-order business from Hedwig's house. "I know a bit about the pharmaceutical suppliers and the needs of the district now, and I can see opportunity here for me. I won't have to go away from home very much, so it will be convenient for us all."

Else and Caroline settled in quite quickly, picking up the language in their eagerness to make friends and discover the district. Eric was slower, shyer, and had inherited Miriam's poor ear. As well, he was more resistant to Otto, retreating from his boisterous attempts at affection or humour into adolescent awkwardness and silence. Miriam, for her part, made no friends. At first, when she was invited to visit in the village, she had attempted a few words in German and had listened, nodding and smiling, to catch the drift of conversation, to appear a participant. But the effort left her exhausted and something in her rejected the language, almost as if acquiring it would mean the sacrifice of identity. At social gatherings now the talk washed around her and she no longer made any effort to understand, from look or gesture, what was being discussed. It was not surprising to Miriam that she and Otto were no longer very welcome guests.

As the summer progressed, the children became competent in basic German and were enrolled at their various schools for the start of the academic year in the autumn. But Otto seldom mentioned the mail-order business and Miriam could see no sign of industry, no application to his plan. Instead, he would set off for his walks, intending, he said, to think things over, and he would return, hours later, sometimes full of exuberant hope for the future of Germany but, often, utterly cast down with melancholy.

Miriam, at first, accompanied him on these walks and tried to steer his thought towards practical goals but, with the coming of autumn, rain and sleet set in and the ground was slippery with wet fallen leaves. The cold and damp seeped into Miriam's joints and lungs and she no longer went out. The children, at school in the mornings, cheerfully spent their afternoons helping with the autumn harvests, carting hay up into attics, digging beets or picking apples and pears, helping to store the produce in the cellars or crush the fruit for juice and wine. Otto tramped the dank woods alone and Miriam sat, by the hour, in the parlour overlooking the street, watching the faces of the passers-by. She told herself that she neither wanted nor needed to be part of them. Otto must be persuaded to find work in a larger centre where he would make friends and where they could be independent of family.

But Otto evaded her. It was not until the winter, when the night air cracked with frost, and months were filled with the smell and flurry of snow; when the children joined in the harvest of coal, fallen from wagons on to railway lines, and peasants stuffed thin boots with straw for warmth; not until her bones ached with desperate chill that Miriam perceived how far Otto had slipped from her grasp.

"For God's sake, Miriam, leave me! Leave me! I am only half a man. We will move from here, if you like, but I know, now, wherever I go it will be the same. When I lived in Australia, I tried to be truly Australian: to think and behave as though the future was entirely open; as though history and tradition did not lay down immutable rules, and anything was possible for the enterprising. I fooled myself, thinking I could be free of my heritage. Now I am supposed to be a German and forget the visions I had. But Germany today is shattered, at war with herself. I, too, am shattered, Miriam, and sometimes I think there is wholeness only in death."

5 Returning Shadows

Miriam prevailed over Otto. In 1923, when the winter was past, they moved to Neuwied. There, by the Rhine, her heart, at least, was eased; the river's fluid identity spoke to her own. The Wemysses had been millers, of one sort or another, for as long as there were records, and so had always lived by water. Miriam thought it strange that the need for it should be so deeply ingrained in her, so insistent, as much a part of her inheritance as the colour of her eyes. The rippling or roaring of water, the glancing light from its skin, the smell of a river's depths or the sharp salt tang of the sea were primal as pulse to her.

Perhaps Otto, too, was briefly cheered. Neuwied was provincial but gracious; its wide streets, laid out on the square, were fringed with plane trees, bare still, but throbbing with the promise of spring. They had, at last, a bedroom, a house to themselves; a tall well-furnished house fronting a street, where cafe owners were repainting their outdoor furniture in readiness for the time when the light under the trees would be the colour of crème de menthe.

Eric found work as a storeman and book-keeper for a manufacturing firm and Otto bought him a bicycle to take him there. Caroline, a keener student than either of the others, was happy at the Zinzendörfer school for girls, two blocks away. Else remained at home to keep Miriam company and, with the help of a maid, they managed their household together. Else's anxiety seemed to ebb in this new relationship of shared responsibility. Otto joined a club frequented by American officers and so, for the first time, they had some English-speaking company, the warm, easy accents dissolving Miriam's isolation. Miriam scoured the shops for dinner-party fare but suspected the soldiers had better in their mess. Sometimes she hoped Else might form an attachment to one of those free, charming men, and caught herself imagining what life might be like for her daughter, away from their dark history in Brisbane or the Rhineland. But time for that was short: the Americans were soon to go home and their role would be assumed by the French. Even Miriam had heard enough of them to be apprehensive.

The vainglorious French, whose own soil had soaked up the blood of millions, whose agriculture and industry had been devastated by the war, and whose honour was not satisfied by armistice or treaty; the French humiliated the Germans over whom, in Saarland, and the Wiesbaden district of the Rhineland, they had jurisdiction. Because Germany had fallen behind in payment of reparations, the French took their own estimate of them in coal, railing it past angry Germans into France; coal which might have fired German industry and warmed German homes. They controlled the press and banned films and books. They banned, as well, the black, red and gold flag of the Republic. They forbade Germans entry into cafes and railway carriages reserved for themselves and whipped any, regardless of age or sex, who would not give way to them in the streets.

When, the previous December, the French had marched into the Ruhr to take over the factories and force the pace of reparations, Germany had begun a campaign of passive resistance to them, dragging the economy down even further, sending the chronic inflation into a dizzying spiral which the Government countered by printing money. There were shortages of everything and the black market thrived. Something had to be bought as soon as money was changed because the Mark's value dropped between the bank and the shop.

Miriam and Else would queue, separately, for food while Otto changed their sterling. The bank weighed out the notes, too numerous to count, and wrapped them in huge, cumbersome paper parcels. Otto would run to the queues, hoping that the money would still be enough to cover their purchases. Any change from the shopping was worthless. They tried to make it all into a game but could not ignore the tragic faces of the obviously poor or the plight of the well-dressed, who trundled out their valuables in handcarts to sell or barter for food.

They were living on the income from Australian investments and the rent from "Cooloola". German railway fares and rents were fixed and now amounted to nothing; their income was worth more daily, as inflation favoured sterling. Otto still had no work but seemed bolder, and willing to travel further in search of it. Whether he actually tried for it or merely indulged his old love for travel, Miriam did not know, but even a return of wanderlust was a healthy sign.

"Some of the industrialists are getting fabulously rich from all this inflation," Otto told her, on his return from a visit to Berlin. "They borrow money to buy factories and, within a month, their debts are chicken-feed. They are growing fat on the starvation of the people!"

Miriam smiled. She was reminded of Willi and Lili and wondered whether they were active in the growing conflict. She had never answered Lili's farewell note and had no idea where they might be. Some of the old political sparring might have been good for Otto. When she remarked as much, Otto's face grew dark.

"That was all very well then, in Australia, but they will be among those Communists and socialists who see this instability as opportunity. They are probably separatists, as well, given Willi's views on culture. I wouldn't want anything to do with them. Germany needs order and stability. She's not ready yet, even for democracy." Miriam was sorry to have mentioned them.

But she was reminded of Lili again when she saw a knot of ragged people abusing a black-marketeer. *"Schieber!"* they shouted, *"Jude! Jude!"* Lili would have taken up the cause of the poor, Miriam knew, but she was Jewish, too, and perhaps the issues would not be so clear for her now.

The Americans left. "Sure has been good meeting you, Ma'am," said one they had entertained. "Y'ever happen to come Stateside you know just where to come; don't you forget that, now!" Miriam knew she would never come Stateside, but the sadness she felt seemed disproportionate.

Neuwied turned out to send the Americans off. They had been as popular as occupying forces could be, and the Rhinelanders feared the French. They would encourage the separatists, Otto said, because they weakened Germany. France would prefer a separate state on the left bank of the Rhine. Otto spoke quite good French and, in other times, had entertained Brisbane ladies with his glowing descriptions of Paris, a city he claimed to love. Miriam was surprised at his bitterness against them now; his deep identification with the local hatred. But he had travelled to the French zone of occupied Germany and said that war corrupted the most civilised of men.

Miriam and Else were returning one afternoon from a walk along the river. It was late August and although the morning had been very warm, the tall, flat-faced buildings now cast cold blue shadows across the streets, and a thin mist was rising from the Rhine. The street was busy with people going home and children chasing hoops or playing hopscotch in the last hour before evening. Suddenly, a rowdy group of men with banners, proclaiming support for a Rhineland state, marched around the corner. A man on a bicycle shouted abuse and one of the marchers attacked him, dragging him from the saddle and throwing him to the ground. Soon a brawl was raging. A policeman, armed with a truncheon, ran into the fray, vainly trying to restore order. Two mounted French cavalry officers sat calmly, watching from their height, while the policeman was kicked to death. The mob ran off, leaving his body on the pavement. The French officers, casually elegant on their sinuous horses, moved slowly across the street and seized the only man remaining: the cyclist who sat, bleeding, in the gutter. When Miriam stirred from her horrified trance and turned to Else, the girl's hands were over her ears, her eyes were tight shut and her face was screwed into its childhood bud of resistance.

Neither of them would have mentioned the incident to Otto but the maid, who had heard the disturbance and looked along the street from an upstairs window, saw that they had witnessed it. When they returned, white-faced, to the house, she fussed over them, hissing through her teeth that the French were swine, an expression which even Miriam could understand.

"Tell her not to mention it to your father," Miriam said, but as Else was doing so, Otto came home. The need to keep him in ignorance of what they had seen would have sustained their strength but, once he had heard, they broke down. Miriam trembled violently and was unable to speak and Else sobbed in long, deep spasms.

Otto sat silent, his head bowed, his hands limp between his knees. Then he got up. "You cannot, you cannot stay here!" he said, and went out into the street. Gladness, relief, surged uncontrollably in Miriam. She had not known until he spoke how much she detested this place or how keen was her longing for home. But he would not mean it; he would not surrender them and she refused to dwell on his words.

Next day, the censored newspaper reported that the cyclist had been responsible for a disturbance in which a policeman had been killed. The cyclist had later died of his wounds, it said. But it was the leading item which held Otto's attention and broke his gloomy silence.

"Stresemann has been made Chancellor!" he exclaimed. "He is a monarchist and he understands small business. Perhaps, under him, we will make progress." He said nothing more about their going.

Since Eric had begun work, Miriam was aware of a growing tension in the boy, a stubborn unwillingness to talk in Otto's presence. It was Otto's habit, out of concern for Eric's future, he said, to quiz him about his work over their evening meal. "Is business good? How many orders did you process this week?"

Eric's answers were always monosyllabic but Otto was undeterred. One night he said, "I noticed an advertisement for your company today. Look, here it is; I cut it out." He read the advertisement aloud. "It's not very imaginative, is it? You could do better than that. There's not enough meat in it. They should be convincing people you can supply better than your competitors. Why don't you have a talk to the manager? Take this with you and explain how it could be improved. I'll help you with the German, we'll do it after tea."

"No thanks, Dad."

"Why not? I don't mind helping you. You're too modest, Eric!

You'll never get on if you don't push your ideas. The manager will be delighted if you show some initiative."

"Leave me alone, Dad!" Eric's voice cracked: it was a plea and not defiance. When he got up from the table, Miriam could see tears in his eyes.

Otto was stunned, his face pale, and he held his peace until Eric left the room. "He's too sensitive, Miriam," he said, at once defensive and reproachful of her.

"I think he probably just wants something of his own, Otto. Boys of his age don't like their parents interfering in their lives."

"You mean, I think, that it's too late now for me to be a father to him." And there was truth in that. More, Eric was lonely, homesick and unwilling to risk his affection again, either for this rediscovered father or his father's country. His reserve and his pride were like Miriam's own and she knew that he held Otto responsible for this dislocation of his love and his questing roots; that he blamed Otto bitterly, but would never be able to tell him so.

In November, a shadow sped fleetingly over the early snow.

"The National Socialist Party has made a putsch in Munich," Otto read to her. "More killings, more unrest. Adolf Hitler and General von Ludendorff have been arrested but they have a great deal of support in Bavaria. What's to become of us, God only knows!" Miriam, standing by the window, shivered. Outside in the street, a group of Moroccan soldiers stood, disconsolate, shivering too in this alien cold. They spoke no European language and the Germans hated them. They were black and they served the French; they raped the fair German women, it was said, and they symbolised the ultimate humiliation of Germany. Miriam watched them stamp their feet from cold and wipe their dripping noses with the backs of thin black hands; saw their eyes dart about them in fear and bewilderment. Her own body stiffened and vibrated with their suffering. It was not compassion Miriam felt, but a convulsion of kinship.

That winter was bitter, the coldest for years. Coal was desperately short and the house grew damp. Miriam contracted bronchitis and burned with fever, falling from time to time into delirium. There, Sandgate shimmered, blue and gold. The sand was hot to her feet, the sun burned the back of her neck and the smell of eucalyptus filled her nostrils and lungs. The shrilling of cicadas rang joyously in her head. When the cold grey room returned to her, she was clammy with despair. Perhaps, in her incoherent ramblings, Otto heard her longing.

Christmas was the saddest time, pierced through with silent pleading and farewell. Otto took his children into the forest to find a little fir tree. Miriam could hear them in the hall below her when they brought it home, stamping the snow from their boots, summoning enthusiasm with their noise. Otto had bought tinsel and coloured balls to deck the tree and a gramophone record of carols.

He carried her downstairs on Christmas Eve. The room was lit with candles. From the fir tree, brittle shafts of ruby and emerald pricked the gloom, and the gramophone wheezed, *"O Tannenbaum"*. Otto plied them all with wine and dried fruit, with chocolate and marzipan but, when he had carried Miriam back to bed, he laid his head on her heaving breast and wept.

"You must go home, Miriam," he said at last. "There is no future here. You must make a place for our children among your own people, where they will be safe and happy."

6　A Sign of Peace

Miriam returned to the Australian autumn of 1924. In their last weeks together they had nurtured between them the specious myth that Otto would come back to them in 1926, after the Government had lifted its embargo on German immigration.

"But I will not depend on it," Otto assured them. "In the meantime, I will see whether New Zealand or South Africa will have me. Perhaps, who knows, I shall do so well in one or the other that you'll all be able to join me and then we can thumb our noses at the Australian Government! In any case it won't be long before we are together again."

He had fussed about their cabins and stowed their baggage for them. He had tested their bunks to see they were comfortable and spoken to the purser and the steward to ensure their well-being. There was nothing more he could do for them. He kissed them, clung to them, mingled his tears with theirs.

"Pray for me, my dears; be sure to do that," he begged, and then he was gone.

He would not wait on the wharf and they remained below until the ship had left the port. Miriam went up, then, and watched the verdant fields of Germany slip past; watched until they reached the open sea and evening turned the world to slate. Caroline crept into her reverie, sliding her hand into Miriam's.

"Will we ever see our Dad again, Mum?" she whispered and Miriam, looking into the child's swollen face, denied her own heart's certainty.

They rented a place at Sandgate; a weatherboard cottage with a verandah. It had jalousies at the windows and coarse buffalo grass in the sandy garden. A lemon-scented gum grew behind it, filling dewy mornings with its perfume. Miriam bought a pair of canaries and hung their cage on the verandah outside her bedroom window. They did not sing but she knew they were contented.

She had not wanted to return to "Cooloola" and Alfred sold it for her. She did not go to the auction of either the house or her furniture, but Doreen told her that Sarah had bought the Meissen dinner service.

Doreen was really the only visitor she wanted and she came when she could. "I wish you were closer, Miriam," she said. "Do you think of living in Brisbane at all?"

"What should I do in Brisbane, Doreen? You and Dr Hugo are the only friends I have left. In Brisbane I should be obliged to see, daily, those people who reviled me and turned their backs on me in the street. I'd have to pretend the war had never happened and be polite to them. I'd have to endure their pretence of friendship, their sickening hypocrisy!"

"The war is over, Miriam," Doreen said, gently. "Perhaps those people are ashamed of the way they've behaved. You can't stay here for the rest of your life, brooding on the past. You must try to forgive and forget!"

"How can I forgive, Doreen, when no-one has ever asked my forgiveness; when not one has ever apologised! As to forgetting, I've a better chance of doing that here, where I'm not confronted with those people."

Sandgate was now the only place she had shared with Otto which was untainted by the bitter memories of war. Otto could, perhaps, think of her there with pleasure. It was a distance for the children to travel, Caroline to her school and Eric to his job in Brisbane, but the train service was good and the young people were glad of the beach at the weekends. Else had found work close by, in a bank at Sandgate, and Eric had been taken into Wemyss and Sons. Edward and Oswald still ran the firm, though Edward's contribution was apparently small, these days. Oswald was glad to have Eric, he said, and would train him with his own youngest son, James. The boy reminded Miriam of the grandfather for whom he was named and she was glad when Eric brought him home for a weekend.

The two cousins sailed together, hiring a boat from the little harbour, around the headland, where Otto had once painted a child's picture. When they came home after a day on the water, their faces burnt and their hair stiff with salt, Miriam thought that, here, Eric was rescuing a fragment of childhood. She wished such a reclamation were possible for Else, too, and sometimes urged her to look for work in Brisbane, where there would be dances and theatre, opportunity for the few things that lifted the veil of anxiety from her eyes. But Else still bore the burden of responsibility for Miriam that Otto had carelessly laid on her so many years before and she would not go, she said, until Otto returned to take care of her.

Miriam did not really need Else. Perhaps she no longer needed Otto. She had abandoned all hope of reconciling the past with her present and she felt a kind of freedom she had never experienced before. It was not happiness; that had always eluded her. But when she walked where the waves trailed their arcs of wedding lace across the sand, or sat up against a sun-hot rock and heard the whipbirds in the coastal scrub split the air with their jubilations, she knew uncomplicated pleasure. Even in winter, when the surf and sea gales pounded the shore, it was as though they relieved Miriam of her anger and left her at rest. For Otto, she wished only that he too could find such a haven, a place where she could think of him without disturbance of her ease.

If she had abandoned him it was only according to his instructions. To make a safe, secure place for her children among her own people, as he had wished, he must be put aside; he knew it himself.

I have approached the New Zealand Embassy for permission to settle there, and if they accept me, I think it would be best to give up all thoughts of returning to Australia. My presence, particularly in Brisbane, would disadvantage the children. They are better off, now, without me.

When she read the letter to Eric he did not demur. Though he had never considered changing his name, as Miriam had once thought he might, Eric had worked, in all the ensuing years, to live it down. Nowadays he never spoke of the past, of his father or their life in Germany and, in this new war, Miriam knew that Eric would enlist if he could. His acceptance into the Forces would be the badge of his restoration. The girls, Caroline especially, were different; their grief and their loyalty more open. They had joined the *Goethe Bund* in recent years and resigned from it only when Nazi excesses had repelled them.

"But, even so, I can't think of myself as an Australian, Mum," Else said.

"Bugger Australia and Germany! Dad was a citizen of the world and that's what I intend to be!" Caroline proclaimed. This war would test the safety and security of their place among her own people.

Miriam sighed deeply and shifted on the bench to ease the pain in her leg which, with the present, had impinged again on her consciousness. The urgency which, this morning, had driven her to disinter the past, was gone. The grave she had dug for herself among the respectable people of Brisbane would never again receive her. She had lain there these past thirteen years, since leaving Sandgate: forgiving and forgetting, Doreen said; belonging again, she had told herself. But she did not belong and could not forgive what had never been revoked. She felt now only a great weariness and a dry, hopeless anticipation of the shadow which might yet swoop down upon them all. Her children now had children of their own, a second generation; too young to fight or to spy but not too young to suffer that stigma which had been borne, in the last conflict, even by the third generation. For this day's struggle she had only a frail skeleton of truth to show, but this much she knew: she would never again connive in its burial.

The Australian Government, in 1924, had neither forgiven nor forgotten Otto Gluck's supposed crimes, and advised the New Zealand Government not to accept him as a resident in that country. But Otto was by then desperate to leave Germany.

Though conditions here are more stable and, with the Treaty of Locarno, we may look forward to peace, I know now that I can never be happy here. I am beset with feelings of worthlessness and the dark promptings of death. Your letters fill me with nostalgia for life in a British country, the climate and freedom where optimism can flourish. So now I'm determined to try South Africa and plan to kill off the despised "Gluck" and adopt my mother's name for the purposes of gaining entry. It will be a completely new start for me but I think I still have the energy to make a go of it.

The South African Government issued a residency permit to the new Otto Klein in mid 1925 and he determined to leave Germany before Christmas. Miriam, as usual, took Otto's letter with her to the headland and sat there, above the sea, to read it. His handwriting, this time, seemed small and crabbed, shrunken with his name, and his enthusiasm for a new life was tempered with self-doubt. He did not yet know, he said, where in South Africa he would settle or what business would best suit him. But Miriam's glimpse of Durban persuaded her she could think happily of him in that country. She dismissed his faltering courage as a temporary thing.

The sea, grey now with winter, stretched out below her, rippling small muscles in lazy calm; a connecting tissue, nerved by impulses from every continent. Miriam breathed deep the heavy winter air and wished her husband peace. Then she went home and made a pot of tea, sitting in the pale sunlight on the verandah and watching her canaries while she drank it.

And Otto soon seemed renewed in South Africa. He settled in Cape Town and his letters were filled with anecdotes illustrating the warmth and generosity of the people who had helped him in setting up a home and a business. "Klein's Aseptic Instruments" would soon be a going concern, he assured them, and then they could all come and join him. Eric, he acknowledged, might prefer to stay where he was, since he had settled well at Wemyss and Sons, but the girls would have plenty of opportunity for work and enjoyment, and Miriam would find the climate healthy and the society congenial.

Then, *By the way,* he added casually, *I have posted off to Alfred the necessary details for my application to return to Australia, when the embargo is lifted next year.*

A warning sounded, momentarily, in Miriam's mind. But of course Otto wanted to clear his name; it was a point of honour rather than an expression of desire or need to return. As for going to South Africa, she need not think of it yet. It would be some time, years perhaps, before Otto could support them there. She gave herself up to the pleasure of the day, the small routines she had collected, like coloured baubles, around her bower. But in April 1926:

A letter to hand this morning advises me the Australian Government will not allow me to return. This is a savage blow to me, especially since I hear from Alfred that August Birnbaum has been readmitted. I am quite laid out by it and feel I can never forgive the treatment I've received. But damn them all! It's clear my presence in Brisbane, even if it were permitted, would always be a scandal to the good people there, our friends and associates of days gone by! You would all suffer from it; Eric, I think, especially. Thank God, I have established myself here and can confidently offer you a good life. Now the issue is finally decided there need be no more hesitation. Make your plans as soon as you can and let me know. I will begin house-hunting immediately, since my flat is too small for us, and if you will send me the necessary cash, as soon as you can free it up, I will have a place for you to come to in no time. How I long for us all to be a family with a future again.

"No!" said Miriam, aloud to the sea, "No!" to the kestrels climbing the blue steeps of air. She walked back to her cottage. She stood on the verandah and clung to the rail, as if the cold rage inside her would sweep her away. "No! I will never leave again."

She had no love left to dissipate that rage, but it was Else who was cast adrift and swept away by it; Else who was bruised and wounded on that other shore.

"If you won't go, Mum, then I will! Dad must have someone."

Perhaps Else had come to understand that, now, Miriam needed no-one and wanted only to float, weightless, here; to evaporate into the blue-gold air. But Else's anxiety was integral to her nature and would never leave her; she simply transferred it from mother to father. "I'll go and look after him for you until you decide to come." Her voice was pleading. "I'm sure you will, Mum, once you know how happy we can be."

Miriam agreed to pay her passage but she would give no

money to Otto. Her own needs were small but she would sacrifice nothing that might risk the safe secure place she had found for herself.

The darkness was absolute, now, in Musgrave Park. Miriam felt the cold weight of that resolution still in her chest. She could not judge whether she had done right or wrong but knew her reason was not love. It had not even been love of the self, which she had willed out of being, translated into the salt-hazed blue of Sandgate. Else had gone to her father and Miriam had been relieved, both of her hovering presence and of responsibility for Otto. She had not allowed considerations of right or wrong, of love or its lack, any longer to disturb her.

Caroline was eager to follow Else. "Lucky thing! I'd love to go to Africa!" Daily she wondered how long it would be before they had news. "She'll be arriving in Durban tomorrow. How long does it take to get from Durban to Cape Town? Wouldn't it be fun if Dad met her in Durban? He might have booked on the ship, mightn't he, as a surprise, so they could arrive in Cape Town together. That would be just like him, wouldn't it? I'm sure she'll send us a postcard from Durban, anyway."

They were sitting, next day, at the kitchen table, in a pool of September sun, when the telegram-boy arrived. The back door was open and he came to the top step. He was faceless, his back to the light, and his shadow fell across them. Miriam put out her hand for the envelope, the boy retreated, the sunlight glared back from the slip of yellow paper. *Have been advised by friend here Dad passed away in Cape Town yesterday. Details by air mail. Else.*

Miriam's shimmering mirage shuddered and fell away like scales. Now there was only the darkness.

"Jesus Christ!" A man's startled voice ruptured memory's horror. Miriam's stick clattered on to the cement plinth beneath the bench. The man had tripped over it. Miriam saw him now, a dark shape against the night.

"Christ Almighty, it's a bloody white bitch!" The shape swayed above her.

"You git home, Wes Walker, before the coppers git yer!" said a woman's voice behind him. The shape stumbled away, muttering.

"You all right, Missus? Wes's drunk but he don't mean any harm." The woman was black and she carried a parcel under her arm. Her tone was defensive, almost hostile.

"Yes, I think so, thank you. It was my fault. He tripped over my stick." Miriam reached under the seat to find it.

"I'll git it." The woman squatted and retrieved the stick. She looked up at Miriam. "You don't look too good. What're you doing here, anyhow?" Her voice was puzzled now.

"I'm just very tired. I've been walking all day."

"Where'd yer come from, then?"

"Not far away." Miriam groped for a way to make sense of what she had been doing in the sixty years since this morning. "But I've been walking through my life." The woman sat down on the seat next to her and tried, Miriam could see, to look at her more closely, out of corner of her eye. Miriam smiled, "It was a long walk!" The woman nodded her head slowly and was silent.

"Was that your husband?" Miriam asked, out of politeness, since her companion made no move to go.

"No, my husband's dead." She said it dispassionately. "The grog killed him." But then she added, fiercely, as though seizing an opportunity for truth, "There's no life left for us blackfellas now; nothing fer the blokes to do 'cept drink and forget."

"No," said Miriam, because she knew about forgetting, and the silence around them was bled of anger. Miriam could smell the strong warm odour of fish and chips rising from the newspaper parcel on the woman's lap. She swallowed the rush of saliva to her mouth.

"You got a husband?"

"Mine's dead, too. Like yours."

"What happened to him?"

Miriam struggled to brush away the thick cobweb of euphemism she had aways employed. This morning she had felt impelled to seize a stranger, to impose on man or woman the burden of her story. Now the words she had never actually spoken halted into the willing night.

"My husband was a foreigner. The Government had him arrested for something he didn't do. They sent him away from us, to another country. He was very lonely, very lost. In the end, . . ." and the words had, each, to be dragged out now, "in the end, he took a revolver and put it in his mouth and blew out his brains. But it was my country that killed him."

It had cost her all her breath to say it. She stared in silence at her own hands, lying still and white in her lap. She wanted to tell more to this woman, so silent and warm at her side, but she could not find words to explain that she, Miriam Gluck, was a part of her country.

The woman said, "Yer hungry, aren't you, eh." It was a companionable tone, a question without upward inflection.

"Yes. I haven't eaten all day, that I can remember. How did you know?"

"I kin hear yer belly rattlin'." She giggled, one fluid hand fluttering to her mouth, and the sound, the sight, made Miriam laugh as well.

The woman unwrapped her parcel. "Here, have some of this."

The smell, the rich goodness of it, brought tears to Miriam's eyes. She put out her shaking hand and broke off a piece of fish. The woman took some. Black hand and white dipped together into the paper.

"Good, eh."

"Very good." And they wiped their greasy mouths on the backs of their hands and smiled with their eyes at each other. Miriam felt restored, her mind and limbs suffused with extraordinary well-being.

Suddenly, they heard a sound behind them, of footsteps on brittle leaves. They turned and stared into the beam of a torch. The black woman gasped, "Coppers!"

They had come, then. Now was the moment this day had presaged. Miriam greeted it almost with gladness: this time she had found courage and would do differently.

"Mrs Gluck? Is that you?"

"Yes, Officer, it is." The woman beside her made to get up but Miriam put a hand on her arm.

"We've been looking for you everywhere, Ma'am. Is this woman troubling you?"

Miriam stood. "This woman is my friend," she said, and, turning, "Thank you." The woman's smile flickered in the darkness and then she disappeared.

"Now, Officer, do you have a warrant?"

The policeman looked puzzled. "I've come to take you home, Mrs Gluck! We found your jacket by the river, and Miss Warrington's been very worried about you."

For a moment, Miriam's understanding faltered, and then she laughed. "Oh, I see! Home. Well, in that case, Officer, I'm most grateful to you!" And, following the thin wavering beam of the policeman's torch, she accompanied him out of the park.

Afterword

As I finish *Struggle of Memory*, Australia is celebrating the 75th anniversary of the 1st AIF's landing at Gallipoli in 1915; an event which, according to the overwhelmingly masculine mythology of this nation, symbolises Australia's coming of age. Whatever significance such a bloody initiation may have for the national psyche, another contemporaneous and related purging of innocence has been almost completely repressed. In society, as in the individual, repressed events may shape the future as surely as those we recall and celebrate; perhaps to more sinister ends.

In 1916 Prime Minister W.M. Hughes boasted of "tearing out the German cancer" from Australian commerce. That tearing out was not restricted to commerce but occurred at all levels of Australian life. During the First World War, 6890 people were interned in concentration camps. Of these, 4500 male civilians had been arrested and detained without trial on mere suspicion of disloyalty. These civilians were all residents of Australia, most were of German origin, and among them were 700 Australian citizens. The suffering of their wives and children was commensurate with theirs. Many in Australia today still feel the injustice done to their families, still cannot wipe from their names the smear of shame. For them there has been neither apology nor redress. None of this should be irrelevant to a putatively multicultural society.

I think it is important to know that the bone structure of this novel is fact: the life and fate of Otto Gluck is based on the story of Brisbane merchant Carl Zoeller. But I have written a novel, not a biography, and through the devices of fiction I have tried to explore the nature of the society which gave rise to such a story. Though I have pinned the narrative to historical protagonists, I have imagined their personalities and their responses, their families and relationships, so that none of my characters should be taken as representing any person, living or dead.

The historical facts of Carl Zoeller's life are documented in a book called *Internee 1/5126*, written and published by Robert Paterson in 1983. I am in debt to Dr Paterson for allowing me to read supplementary material in his possession.

For my imaginings I have drawn heavily on the memories of those who lived through the First World War, both in Australia and in Germany; most particularly on the recollections of Lisette Macneill, whose vivid letters to me provided fascinating detail. Liselotte Wickenhagen, Edith Berlin and Mabel Bassett also remembered their experiences for my benefit.

I am grateful to Anne Macneill who made available to me her unpublished thesis, *The Enemy in Our Midst*, and her research material. It was among her newspaper clippings that I found, reported in the *Argus* (4 January 1915), a sermon given in Hobart by the Anglican Bishop Stephen. It forms the basis of the sermon in this book. Rosslyn Read helped me to understand something of the religious background of German immigrants and Tony and Dorothea Powell threw light for me on life in Germany during the Weimar Republic.

I was greatly helped in Germany by Erika Blum, Brunnhilde and Johannes Menningen, Else and Käthe Zoeller, and especially Uschi and Detlev Wickenhagen who made my stay in Grenzhausen possible.

Perhaps I owe my greatest debt to my husband, Richard Zoeller, whose initial research in the Australian Archives was my inspiration and whose patience and advice sustained me throughout this particular struggle.

Joan Dugdale, 1990

Also by
Joan Dugdale
The Gripping Beast

"Joan Dugdale has a bold and exuberant sense of history as it bears down on the present offering redemption. She is an important and urgent new voice in Australian writing."

Helen Daniel

Ursula Kenning succumbs to an irresistible urge to kick the orderly ants' nest of her responsible bureaucratic life. Alienated from her colleagues, she embarks on an impassioned quest back through her father's life and her own heritage. With her novelist friend Celeste as companion, she travels to Norway, then to Orkney, her accidental birthplace, and on to Cumbria, home of her ancestors.

Her Anglo-Norse heritage, like the gripping beast of Viking art, proves to have a tenacious vitality for Ursula as she explores the mythic landscapes and sacred sites of the old gods. Restored by the energies of the past and her quickening interest in Robert Applethwaite, she finds life opening to her again among the fells and valleys of the Cumbrian Lake District.

Joan Dugdale's first novel, *Struggle of Memory*, won the Foundation for Australian Literary Studies Best Australian Book of the Year Award for 1991, and received high praise:

"An important and profoundly moving book ... In the age of multiculturalism, this book has a lot to offer. Measured and non-judgmental, it shows us how we were and possibly how we still are."

Mollie Missen, *Age*

"The narrative skilfully interweaves history and fiction ... [and] leads us to examine our own cultural conditioning. This challenging novel spurs us to reflection about our Anglo-Saxon heritage and what people call 'traditional values'."

Rob Johnson, *Adelaide Advertiser*

ISBN 0 7022 2577 0